The Unrecovered
Smiling Flu Book 1

Len M. Ruth

Ruthless Press

Many thanks to Slappy Jack, whose early encouragement gave me the fuel I needed to keep going. Without him, this book wouldn't exist.

Big thanks to my sensitivity reader, Rob Peters, for helping ensure I treated my Native American characters with the respect they deserve.

A heap of gratitude goes to Devora Gray—my writing partner, friend, and confessor. Thanks for keeping me going, Dev.

And, of course, a truckload of love to my editor and life partner, Emory Davis. Without them, this book wouldn't be readable.

Author's Note

If you've picked up this book, you're here for horror. That means grief, fear, violence, and trauma—sometimes seen, sometimes only felt.
I don't offer a traditional trigger warning, because horror works best when it unfolds. But if you're carrying fresh wounds, please read with care. The human monsters in this book are just as real as the viral ones.
Here there be dragons.
—Len M. Ruth

Chapter 1

Jamie

August 21, Destination, Idaho

Jamie strained for a glimpse of the approaching fires in the dusty orange sky to the west. The forest on the other side of the cornfields wasn't visible through the kitchen window, but she could smell fire on the breeze that rustled the curtains.

Ed's footsteps creaked down the stairs.

She swept aside a few of the coupons littering the kitchen table, set her coffee down, and sat gazing at them with a mix of disdain and resignation.

"Sky's a funny color," she said as Ed shuffled past her.

"Smoke from the fires," he mumbled.

She watched him take the Laetanol bottle down from atop the fridge and tap one into his calloused hand. He filled a red jelly glass from the tap, swallowed the pill, then stared out the window just as Jamie had moments before.

"Do you think those are working?" She clipped a coupon for cornflakes from the circular and laid it on the growing pile.

"Do you?"

"I suppose," she paused, looking at his muscular arms and back silhouetted against the orange sky. "You don't seem as sad."

"Yeah," he said, "I don't feel as sad."

"So that's it. You gonna do it?" she asked, changing the subject. His depression was a rabbit hole she'd rather not go down this morning.

"Yeah." Ed turned from the window and leaned against the counter. "Harvester's fueled."

"It's a lot of money to lose," she said, returning her attention to her coupons.

"We talked about this." Ed sighed. "I can still sell the early corn. We'll lose about ten percent on that acreage. Better that than lose it to the fire. Forest Service says it'll make a good fire break. After harvest, they'll come burn the stalks. Ted's doing the same with his fields."

"How long will you be?"

"Midnight, I figure." He picked up the thermos and lunch bag she'd prepared for him.

Jamie rose and stopped him at the door. "I love you." She put her arms around his sunburned neck and felt the hard muscle of his shoulders under her slender fingers. She did love him. Didn't she? Or was it the idea of him? The ghost of Ed, the one she'd married, was bright and full of promise. A young college student on the rise like herself. And she'd been swept away by their love like a solar wind. Swept years later to his parents' farm in Destination, Idaho, clipping coupons and putting up with his drinking.

"I love you too." He put his arms around her. The lunch bag and thermos pressed against her back.

"It's going to be alright, Jamie." He kissed her.

Jamie accepted the kiss, tasting the familiar tang of vodka. She wondered as she kissed him back if he meant the crops, the farm, the fire, their marriage? So many things weren't right.

"Ew," came a small, playful voice, "can I go outside?" Aella stood in the dining room doorway.

As Aella ran the back of her hand across her nose, her fingers brushed the tips of long brown ringlets that framed her face and set them jiggling.

"Go blow your nose. You're twelve years old. You shouldn't have to be told," Jamie said. "You're not getting sick, are you?"

"No." Aella went off in search of a tissue.

"Probably all the smoke in the air," Ed said.

"I hope that's all. I don't want her sick for the big trip tomorrow." Jamie rested her head on Ed's chest and slipped her hands into the back pockets of his jeans. "I wish I could go with her."

"She'll be in good hands," Ed said. "She's got who? Cheryl Thompson, plus three other chaperones from her troop. She sold a lot of cookies to get there. Can't keep her home now."

"I know. I just wish I could share the wonder with her. I always wanted to see the Smithsonian and the Lincoln Memorial."

"I wish I could earn enough money so you didn't have to wait tables. Take us on a real vacation. Speaking of money, I've got to get that harvester rolling before we lose everything."

"Okay," Jamie said. She kissed his cheek. Her eyes followed him down the steps and around the side of the house.

"Can I go out now?" Aella tossed a tissue into the trash.

"You sure you feel okay?" Jamie asked, looking her over.

"I'm sure." Aella gave her mother a sweet smile.

Jamie let out a breath. "If you're all packed?"

"Yup."

"Stay around the yard. Don't wander off. That fire's too close."

"It won't come here. Dad said. Isn't that where he went? To harvest near the woods?"

"Yes, yes. Okay, go on, and don't get your new sneakers muddy before the trip."

"Okay." Aella crossed the kitchen. The screen door made a "graaanngg" sound as she opened it.

"And don't let the—" CLACK "—screen door slam." Jamie shook her head and went back to her coupons.

"Mom, the eclipse is happening!" Aella's voice floated in through the screen door a few minutes later.

Jamie went to the window. "I totally forgot about it. Don't stare at it."

"I know."

"I'll bring out those special glasses."

Jamie fetched the cardboard-framed plastic lenses and joined Aella in the yard. After making sure Aella put them on, Jamie put on her own. Then stared up at the cosmic spectacle.

Smoke wafted low out of the cornfields and swirled around them. It barely registered through their dark glasses, just a faint gray shadow, but from the corner of her eye, Jamie could see its faint pink color. The swirling vapor vanished as quickly as it came, leaving a chemical taste on her tongue. Strange smoke. What the hell burned to make that shit? She shrugged it off and turned her attention back to the eclipse. The moon slid perfectly across the sun, creating the fiery halo of totality.

Chapter 2

Carl

August 21, Bethesda, Maryland, Beachwood Assisted Living Center

"Enjoying your dinner, Mr. S?" Carl asked from the doorway.

Dr. Anthony Silva looked up from the polished dinner service on the lustrous wooden tray. The beam of sunlight through the window gave his smile a sinister quality. "Technically, it's Dr. S., but I suppose it doesn't matter anymore." He touched the knot of his tie to make sure it was straight.

"Really, Mr. S.? I've been taking care of you for three years now. Two years ago, you told me it was Okay for me to drop the 'doctor.' Still, we go through this absurd verbal dance every time."

"Oh, Dr. Parks, I didn't see that it was you. Where are my glasses?"

"You could see the TV just fine." As he entered the suite of rooms full of luminous wood furnishings, Carl wondered how much of his fortune Silva spent making these rooms look like the inside of an old English manor house.

"Aren't you afraid I'm going to tell the administration of this facility how disrespectful you are, and they will fire you?"

"What? And miss the pleasure of collecting your stool samples? You'd be doing me a favor."

"This is exactly what I'm talking about." Silva looked over the tray. "Care to join me, Carl?"

"What's in it for me?"

"You can have my meds." Silva smiled.

"No deal. Those are just placebos; everyone knows you hide the meds in your cheek and spit them out when we're not looking. We've been mixing them into your food for months."

"I don't believe you. This is the best facility on the East Coast. Senators reside here. It's not some cut-rate nursing home for indigents. They're not mixing meds into my foie gras." Silva prodded his food suspiciously with a silver fork.

"Suit yourself, and that's chicken, not foie gras," Carl said, taking a seat on the bed. "Are you going to eat your brownie?"

"How on Earth do you stay fit eating all my desserts, and presumably the desserts of the other residents?" Silva held out the brownie.

Carl took it with a dark, delicate hand. "Well," he began as he broke off a piece of brownie and popped it into his mouth, "it used to be that between this job and working at the clinic, I was always on the go, but since I quit the clinic, I guess it's just vigorous sex with my boyfriend keeping the unwanted pounds at bay." He swallowed and popped another chunk of brownie into his mouth.

"I'm trying to eat here, Carl, don't be vulgar. Is that your modus operandi—putting the old man off his dinner so you can pilfer my food?" Silva cut his chicken into meticulous squares that were precisely the same size.

"Actually, Mr. S., I have something to tell you."

Silva stopped cutting and looked up at him. "Oh?"

Carl sighed. He had been dreading this conversation. Silva wasn't like the other residents of Beachwood; he was sharp and a doctor, like Carl himself. "I put in my two weeks' notice today," he said. "I'm starting at A. L. Memorial, at the trauma center."

Silva set his cutlery down on the tray. "Well." He cleared his throat. "Good for you. That is an excellent facility, excellent staff. I have no doubt you'll do well."

"I'll come see you when I can."

"Don't lie to an old man, Carl. It isn't nice. You will be working long shifts. In your off time, you are going to be fighting to maintain any relationships you have outside of the hospital. It was a long time ago, but I remember how hard it was."

"I'm still coming." Carl put the last of the brownie in his mouth.

"You are a good man, Carl, but your naiveté concerns me." Silva ate his chicken in the awkward silence, occasionally flipping the channel on the muted TV.

When Carl sensed that the old man had nothing more to say, he rose to go. "I'll still be around for you to torment for a couple more weeks."

"It's not very English, you know, talking about one's feelings," Silva said, "but I will miss you, Carl." He paused, looking up at Carl. His eyes grew soft with emotion for a moment, then hardened. "Now get the hell out. I'm trying to watch the bloody tele."

Carl smiled. He took a step, paused, then turned back. "You know, for a stodgy old bastard, you really are very sweet." He placed his brown hand over the older man's white, liver-spotted one.

Silva looked up at him with an odd expression. He looked sad and tired.

The sunlight waned a few degrees.

Silva set his fork down. "In your life as a doctor, you will, from time to time, find yourself in a situation where you have to choose between the rules and your heart. Between helping patients or helping yourself." He held Carl's eye. "In those moments, stay as close to the rules as you can, but follow your heart. Don't wind up like me: old and too full of worry and regret to die."

Carl frowned. "Why are you talking like this?"

"Because I wish someone had said that to me."

The light coming in through the window dimmed further.

"Okay," Carl said. He squeezed the old man's hand. "I'll be back after my rounds."

"See if you can't lay hands on another one of those brownies. That looked good, and I regret letting you talk me out of it," Silva called after him.

Minutes later, Carl was down the hall with another patient when he heard Silva's voice.

"I don't need a goddamn nurse; I need an outside line. Now!"

As Carl stepped into the hall, he saw Jody, the nurse, rush into Silva's room.

"Jody, I'm not senile. I just need an outside line!" Silva shouted.

"Why are you yelling like that? You are disturbing the other residents." Jody's stern voice drifted down the hall.

"I need to place a call. It's a matter of life and death! Am I not speaking the Queen's English?"

"Don't worry, Dr.. Silva, everything will be alright. You are here at home in Beachwood. I'm just going to give you a little something to help you relax," Jody said.

"Don't patronize me, Jody, and don't you come near me with that needle! I'm not losing my mind. I'm just trying to make a call!"

"Of course," Jody said. "Just lower your voice and have a seat, then we'll make a call." Jody's voice was softer now.

"I said it's a matter of life and death! Are you listening to me, Jody?"

Carl ran into the room. "What's going on here?"

"Carl, will you tell this patronizing—HEY!" Silva jerked back too late. Jody used the distraction to jam the needle into Silva's arm and push the plunger down.

"Carl, Carl, will you tell Jod... Jo... Judas that I need to speak to... to... someone at the..."

Carl rushed in and caught Silva just as he crumpled and, with Jody's help, eased him onto the bed.

The sunlight grew faint.

Silva wasn't giving up consciousness without a fight. He grabbed Carl's arm and looked at him, wide-eyed, "Carl, please, Carl... the call." Then Silva slumped back, eyes closed, mumbling.

"Why did you dose him?" Carl asked, his face tight and drawn, his nostrils wide enough to vent steam from a locomotive.

"He was screaming, hysterical."

"You didn't even try to calm him down."

"I did, actually, but he wasn't lucid. He wasn't rational."

"Oh, bullshit." Carl looked down at Silva. Even with his eyes closed, the man looked worried. Carl thought about what Silva said about being 'too worried to die.' Silva's hands were still clenched. Livid brown spots stood out against the pallid skin.

"Your friendship skews your judgment," she said.

The room grew darker still.

"Yours is skewed by your lack of compassion. Why are you even working here?"

"Twenty bucks an hour plus an amazing benefits package," she said. Then she picked up the needle, and left.

Carl uncurled the old man's fists. He went to the cabinet, withdrew a soft blanket, and covered Silva. The sunlight coming in through the window all but vanished, leaving the once warm wood tones of the room's furnishings cold and dark. "Anthony," he whispered after he pulled the blanket up. "I don't know what this is all about, but I'm going to help you."

The sun went out completely.

"The Pentagon..." Silva murmured.

Chapter 3

Erica

August 21, Washington, DC, offices of The Washington Voice

Erica sat with her elbows on her dented metal behemoth of a desk, head in her hands. Auburn curls spilled out between her short, chubby fingers. A cacophony of ringing phones, conversations, and clicking keyboards surrounded her.

Mary Washington sat down at the desk, facing Erica. "You missed the eclipse. A bunch of us went up on the roof."

Erica raised her head, gave Mary a withering look, then lowered it again. A cell phone buzzed and vibrated on her desk. She ignored it.

"Bad meeting?" Mary asked.

Erica didn't look up. "They're all bad meetings." Her cell phone buzzed again.

"You gonna get that?"

"Does it look like I am?"

"So, what happened? More dog and pony stories?" Mary asked sympathetically.

"I got a piece on the flu."

"That's great! A real story!"

"No."

"What? Why not?"

Erica raised her head. "Because I've shoveled shit at this paper for five years doing, as you put it, 'dog and pony stories,' trying to prove that a woman can break into the boy's club. And now that I got one, I need to call in a favor from a man. And not just any man, a man who might not even talk to me."

Mary leaned in closer, resting her elbows on the desk. "Who? What man?"

"Tom."

"Your ex?" Mary pressed.

"Yes."

"The one who left you for the CDC job?"

"Yes, that's the one. God, for a reporter you're really insensitive."

"For a reporter you've got thin skin."

Erica's landline rang.

"You gonna get that?" Mary asked.

Erica flashed her a chainsaw look.

Mary picked up the phone. "Mary Washington, Washington Voice, Washington desk, Washington, DC... Did you say, Karl Marx... Okay then, I'll see if she's available." She stabbed the hold button. "There's some smart-ass named Carl Parks on the line for you," she said, balancing the handset on the tip of her outstretched index finger.

"Thanks, Mary," Erica said, taking the receiver. She reached across to Mary's desk and tapped the hold button with the end of her pen. "Hi, Carl. Long time. How are you?"

"I'm well, Erica. How are you doing?"

"Slogging away at the boy's club, same as always." Erica paused, waiting for Carl to get to the point. He didn't. "Is this a social call? I don't mean to be rude. I've got something I need to be working on. Maybe we can get together for a drink soon?"

"No, Erica, not a social call exactly, although I'd love to take you up on that drink."

"What's up, Carl?"

"I had something happen today, and I can't really explain it on the phone." Carl paused again.

Erica waited. As a reporter, she'd learned that the best way to get to the good stuff, sometimes, was to shut up and listen. Wait out the silences.

"Um, I think it might be important. I can't explain why. Might be a story in it for you."

"Oh, reluctance, mystery, and a gut feeling? Color me intrigued. I can meet you for a drink at the 21st Amendment tonight, say, eleven o'clock?"

"Okay, it's a little late for me, though."

"That's the life of a reporter." The editor's secretary put a small pile of papers on Erica's desk. Erica smiled at her, waved a hand in thanks, then set the papers aside.

"Okay then. The thing involves a man named Dr. Anthony Silva, so anything you can find out about him might help shed some light on it."

"Okay, Carl, I'll poke around a little." She wrote the name on a sticky note and added it to the collection on the bottom of her monitor. "See you at eleven."

"Thanks Erica, see you then."

Erica hung up and let out a breath. The papers the editor's secretary had just brought over were a bulletin from the CDC about this year's flu season.

"Who's Karl Marx?" Mary asked.

"Um, communist, wrote a manifesto," Erica said without looking up.

"Your call, you know, meeting for drinks tonight?"

"Oh, Carl. He's a friend." Erica said, frowning at the memo.

"A special friend?"

"Try to get a grip on your hormones, Mary. He's gay."

"Someone has to be in touch with their hormones around here. You certainly aren't. Have you even been on a date since Tom? That was what, two years ago?"

"If you want to make me feel like an emotional cripple, could we do that later? I have to jump on this flu story." Erica said.

"What is it? What's got you so engrossed?"

"CDC press release. It's dry as toast, normal for the CDC, I guess, but it suggests the sky might be about to fall. No, suggests isn't right. It *implies* that the sky *could* fall. Listen to this: The H20N13 flu virus is both very mild and very contagious. The virus has a long incubation period. It survives outside the body on surfaces for up to two months. The virus is so mild that many infected may believe they have a common cold. Many of the infected will choose to continue normal activity. Given these factors, it is estimated that infection rates will be the highest on record. The CDC urges frequent hand washing, good hygiene, and fastidious housekeeping. Do not touch your face while out in public and wash your hands immediately when you arrive home. The CDC also urges people feeling ill to stay at home and avoid contact with others."

Erica shifted her eyes to Mary. "What do you make of that?"

Mary shrugged. "Sounds like the bulletins we get from the CDC every year, except this flu doesn't sound so bad."

"Yeah, but the high infection rate and urging people to stay home doesn't seem to match up to a really mild virus."

"You gonna call Tom?"

"Yeah, I'm going to need a drink first."

"Don't put it off, Erica. If your spider sense is tingling, make the call. Drink after. Besides, if you're half in the bag, will he even talk to you?"

"Yeah," Erica said, "I guess." The call went straight to voicemail. Erica left a message asking Tom to call about an important matter. While she waited for her phone to ring, Erica started looking into Dr. Anthony Silva.

The Twenty-First Amendment wasn't particularly dark, smoky, or loud, which made it one of Erica's favorite places to meet people she wanted to lube with booze to get them talking. She scanned the oak and brass-adorned room and spotted Carl at a two-top table against the wall, drinking wine by himself. He rose as she approached, standing head and shoulders above Erica. As he hugged her, she felt her hair catch in his five o'clock shadow.

"It's so good to see you," she said into his chest. He was a little thinner than she remembered, which made her feel self-conscious about the extra twenty pounds she wore. Her gaze lifted to his dark, perfect face. "You look great!"

"So do you," Carl said, "If I was straight, I'd—"

"Yeah, yeah, spare me, Carl. I look like crap. I'm going to get a white zin.

Carl motioned to the glasses of wine on the table. "I took the liberty."

"You remember." She smiled. She really did miss him.

"Do you know how many empty bottles of white zinfandel I had to lug to the curb when you stayed with Brian and me? How could I forget?"

"You make me sound like a lush."

"If the shoe fits..." He grinned.

"Shut up, Carl. I'm sorry I haven't kept in touch. I don't want to be the friend that only calls when she needs something."

He waved her away. No. Besides, I called you. I need something from you this time. Maybe. I guess I'm that friend.

She frowned. "What do you mean 'maybe?'"

"I've been having second thoughts about involving you. It's probably nothing."

"Uh-uh, Mr., I put a bunch of time in on this. I've got the start of a decent dossier on Silva already, so spill. There must be something to it. Otherwise, you wouldn't meet me in the middle of the night. Let's have it."

Carl sighed, sipped his wine, and began. He told Erica about his relationship with Silva. "So today I told him I was quitting. I'm going to work at the trauma center at Abraham Lincoln Memorial—"

"Hey, congratulations!"

"Thanks. Anyway, when I told Silva, he starts giving me this weird speech about following my heart in medicine more than the rules."

"Sounds like good advice."

"Yeah. But he ended it with this line about being too old and full of regret to die. It was weird."

"Okay?" What the hell was he getting at?

"I know that doesn't sound like anything, but then a few minutes later, he's screaming hysterically for someone to 'get him an outside line.' You have to understand this is a very sharp, very sedate Englishman. Anyway, he's so hysterical that a nurse came in and gave him a shot."

"How is he?"

"He's fine, probably still out cold from the sedative. Anyway, right before he passed out, he said something about the Pentagon."

"What was he doing when all this started?"

"Just watching TV."

"And there was no one in the room talking to him?"

"I don't think so."

"Then something on TV probably set him off."

"That makes sense," Carl admitted.

"Is he a Fox or CNN kind of guy?"

"He's a doctor from England."

"Okay," Erica smiled, "CNN then. Let's see what CNN was showing today." Erica poked and swiped at her phone for a minute. "Okay, here's what CNN has for top stories: there's a push for legal pot in Texas—"

"Won't pass," Carl said.

"No shit. They have the CDC bulletin about the flu—"

"What CDC bulletin?"

"Later. Focus. Let's see... healthcare is dead on The Hill again, wildfire threatening Fort Johnson, a dead sports star, and the eclipse..." she trailed off.

"What? The sports star?"

Erica went digging through her shoulder bag and came out with a notepad. "That fire thing might tie into something I found. Let's see, there was a picture with Dr. Silva published in Stars and Stripes..." she flipped pages. "Yes, taken at Fort Johnson. The caption read, "Dr. Silva works to help soldiers in Vietnam, Fort Johnson, Idaho." She looked at Carl. "Got any idea what he did at Fort Johnson? He ever talks about it?"

"No, not a word. Never heard of Fort Johnson."

"The article attached to the picture ran in Stars and Stripes in '73. That's the last year we were in Vietnam, isn't it?"

"I've never been to Vietnam." Carl smiled.

"Don't be an ass, Carl, you know what I mean." She looked at her notepad. "The article is no help, really. It just says he was working on a special project, but it does connect him with Fort Johnson, which is burning to the ground as we speak." Erica sipped her wine. "Question is: why did Silva flip out when he saw the Fort Johnson story?"

"No idea." Carl sipped his wine. "What else did you find out about him?"

"I didn't do an exhaustive background check, mind you. I just looked around for news stories. The only other thing I found was a story from 2002. Silva was the leader of a team at World Drug that developed Laetanol, a revolutionary anti-depressant." She didn't mention that she took Laetanol.

"Do you think there is a connection?"

"I doubt it. They are thirty years apart, military versus civilian." She took a big swallow of wine. "I think your instincts were right. Might be a story here. I need to talk to Silva."

"I'll talk to him as soon as I can. I'll see if he is ready or willing to talk to you."

"Tell him no one at the Pentagon is going to talk to him. A retired doctor that worked for them forty years ago? They're just not. His best bet, and this is the truth, is to let me help him bring whatever it is to light."

"I guess," Carl said, but he didn't sound so sure.

"Trust me. I do this for a living. You have my word that I'll leave his name out of it if that's what he wants."

"Okay," Carl said, though his expression left the impression he wasn't convinced.

"Carl," she took his hand across the table, "I'm not so ambitious that I would screw over a friend for a story, especially not you."

"Okay, Erica, I'll talk to him as soon as he's up to it."

"I'll poke around some more, see if I can find anything else."

"Thank you, Erica. It really is good to see you."

"Cheers," she said. They clinked wine glasses, then drained them.

Chapter 4

Sarah

August 22, Bitter Butte, Montana

Sarah Sampson grunted and pushed her lithe middle-aged body through another series of jumps, tumbles, kicks, and punches. She paused to towel her face, then grabbed a practice sword from its holder on the wall of her dining room turned dojo. She went through her routine, swinging the sword in controlled arcs. Sarah practiced alone. No one else in Bitter Butte practiced the art of Wushu, or what most people (especially denizens of Bitter Butte) called Kung Fu.

Sarah finished with the sword and toweled again. When the towel came away from her eyes, Laura leaned on the practice room archway.

"Where'd you learn all that karate stuff?" Laura asked, tucking her corn-colored hair behind her ear.

"When did you come in?" Sarah asked, annoyed at the intrusion.

"Couple minutes ago."

"Koontz! Dickens!" At this command, Koontz, her German Shepherd watchdog, and Dickens, Sarah's black lab, appeared in the archway next to Laura. "You two are fired! Who else will you let in without barking? Fired! Now go on!"

They went.

"So, where'd you learn it?" Laura asked.

"Long story."

"You always say that about everything. It looks cool. I'd like to try."

"I used to go into Billings on the weekends." Sarah replaced the towel in its holder. "A friend of a friend had a dojo there."

"Oh, maybe you could teach me?"

"I'm not a teacher."

"You're a great teacher!" Laura spread her hands. "Look at all the stuff you've taught me around here!"

"We'll see. How was your trip to Idaho?"

"Boring, except for stopping to see the eclipse. That was cool. Last trip as a family before I graduate, then I'm out of here." Laura motioned with her thumb.

"I want you to go to college. Though, a selfish part of me wants you to stay and work for me. Speaking of work, did you get the proposal submitted?"

"Yes, your grant proposal is on its way. It should do well. There's lots of money out there for no-kill shelters. I also got all the new arrivals posted on the adoption page of the website. I was going to go out to clean the bird barn. Unless you've got something else?"

"No. Thanks for doing the paperwork. You know how much I hate that stuff."

"Yeah," Laura grinned, "you're crappy at it too. I mean, really, how did you stay in business before you hired me?"

"Hey!" Sarah tried to put on a hurt face, but she couldn't help smiling. The girl was right. They both knew it. "Okay, head out to the bird barn. I'll come to help you in a few minutes."

"Teach me karate!"

"This again?" Sarah turned and mopped her face without taking the towel from the rack.

"I'm not letting you off the hook with 'we'll see,'" Laura said.

"First of all, it's Wushu, and second, just because I can do it doesn't mean I can teach it. I might not be any good."

"You must be pretty good. You broke Mr. Sterling's arm."

Sarah's finger shot out. "That guy is a dick—"

"His first name is Dick," Laura giggled.

"Second, how do you know about that?"

"Everyone knows. The whole town is talking about it."

"Terrific. Look, Laura, that was a stupid mistake. I shouldn't have done that. I lost my temper, and that's a big no-no in any martial art, and it's exactly why I have no business teaching you."

Laura gave her an appraising look she wasn't at all comfortable with. "How come you dye your hair black and cut it so short? I bet you have beautiful blond hair."

"Okay, this is getting awfully personal. Why are you asking?"

Laura looked down. "My mom says you are a lesbian. She says she doesn't want me to work here anymore."

"I don't know what to say. I would really miss you around here. You do an amazing job, and I don't know how I would ever replace you. Do you still want to work here?"

"Yes, of course."

"Are you uncomfortable working with me?"

"No."

"Then tell your mama it's none of her business."

"She'll say, 'As long as I'm under her roof—'"

"Ah, an oldie, but a goodie. I heard that a lot when I was your age. Let's sit down and talk." Sarah got a beer for herself and a coke for Laura. In the living room, she handed Laura a coke over the second-hand store coffee table with buckled veneer. The beat-up easy chair with seventies avocado green upholstery creaked as Sarah sat. She sipped her beer, stalling. Handling people was not her forte. Nor was talking about herself. Or talking at all, really. This was why she worked with animals and lived on an isolated ranch in East Nowhere, Montana.

Laura sat bolt upright; her unopened coke sweated a ring of condensation into the collection of similar rings on the coffee table.

Sarah wiped her brow, still sweating from her workout and the summer heat trapped by the old farmhouse. "Well..." She wasn't sure how she was going to do this. "I guess I should start by saying I'm not a lesbian. There's nothing wrong with being a lesbian. I'm just not one. As for my hair, I cut it and dye it because I want people to look at me and think, 'I'll just leave that one alone.'"

"So, if you're not a lesbian, what's your deal? I've never seen you with a boyfriend."

"My deal?"

Dickens, sensing her stress, put his soft black head on the thigh of her jeans. King, Sarah's hundred-pound pit bull, heard the note in Sarah's voice, entered the room, and sat staring at Laura. Koontz followed him and sat with his tan and black flank touching the side of Sarah's leg.

"Yeah, your deal," Laura replied, "Straight, bi, transgender—"

"Whoa-whoa-whoa Laura, this is very personal stuff. You're charging around like a bull at a rodeo. This might be how you talk about it with your friends, but it isn't the way you should talk to anyone else. Since you ask, though, and I consider you a friend, I'll tell you. I don't really have a deal. I've got no use for romance."

"Okay. I'm sorry if I was rude. It's just that I've never met anyone who is different like you."

Sarah sipped her beer and petted Dickens. "No, I suppose you haven't," she said, smiling despite her awkwardness.

"So, you never met anyone you wanted to fool around with?"

"Jesus, Laura..."

"Sorry. I just can't imagine getting old and being alone—" Laura stopped.

The kid—though she was seventeen, Sarah thought of her as a kid—was so cute in her embarrassment Sarah couldn't help but soften. "Old? *Old!*"

"Sorry." Laura cringed.

"Let me tell you something, kid: fifty is the new thirty."

"Which is still old."

Sarah shot the girl a look of mock anger. "As for alone: I have three of the best friends a girl could ask for." She scratched Dickens between the ears.

"Four," Laura said, cracking open her coke and raising it to Sarah.

"Four of the best friends." Sarah agreed and raised her beer to the girl.

"So, I'm your only human friend?"

"I said best friends, not only friends; I have Sheriff MacFarlane and Nancy."

"Yeah, but they are like your mom and dad, so it doesn't count."

"Yeah, but they're not, so it does."

"You need to get out more. Maybe you'll even meet a someone you like."

"I'm just fine."

"Animal friends aren't as good as human friends."

"No, Laura, they're better. People will always let you down. No matter what they say or how hard they try, they always do."

"Wow, that's dark. People are good. They help each other when times are hard. They take care of each other."

"Yeah, when it's convenient. Take your philosophy and try to get a starving man to share a sandwich. Everyone thinks they are the good guy. Let me ask you this: if any animals here could talk, would they say about people? Parrots that live to be one hundred get dumped here because 'my new apartment doesn't allow pets,' or dogs who have bonded with the children in a family, dumped here because they keep getting into the trash. What about the ones we take because other shelters are going to kill them? What do you think they'd say about people?"

"I bet they'd say: 'I'm glad there are people like Sarah and Laura to take care of us and help us find new homes.'" Laura took a victory sip of her coke.

Sarah snorted.

"Why are you so down on people, anyway? Did your mom drop you on your head when you were a baby or something?"

"My mom was amazing. When my dad died in Vietnam, her heart broke. She broke." Sarah hadn't thought about it in a long time. Hadn't let herself think about it. The awkward subject of her ambiguous sexuality and now talk about her parents soured Sarah's post-work-out endorphin rush. Long-suppressed emotion strained against her hard veneer.

"See, she didn't let you down."

"Yes, she did."

"How?"

"She died."

Laura looked away.

The words tumbled out. Sarah couldn't stop herself; somehow, this girl got to her. "I won't tell you what happens to a pretty blond girl in the foster care system in the Florida swamps, but I will tell you it makes you not want to be pretty and blond... ever. I will tell you it makes you change the way you think about people." Sarah looked at the urn of her mother's ashes with her father's dog tags draped over it. She could see it through the doorway to the hall. Its brass surface shone in the sunlight coming through the screen door.

Laura shifted awkwardly on the couch.

"I've been thinking about taking a trip to see my father's name on the Vietnam wall." Sarah realized she was talking more to herself than Laura. Time to wrap this up. "So," she spoke so suddenly that Laura jerked to attention, "Did you get your answers? Figure out what to tell your mom?" Sarah's voice came out a little harder than she meant it to. She tried to smile warmly at Laura. This was the longest conversation she'd had with a person in years—and it wasn't about animals. Sarah wasn't sure she'd ever shared all this. And as much as she hated to admit it, it felt good.

"I guess I'll say you're not a lesbian. Just someone who's had a hard life and wants to be left alone."

"Sounds good," Sarah smiled.

Laura looked down.

"Laura, look at me. It's okay. You're my friend."

"I won't let you down," Laura said.

"Don't worry about me. Just don't let them down." Sarah pointed to the animal barns. "Now, let's forget all this and go clean some bird shit." Sarah gulped the rest of her beer and set it down hard on the coffee table. Dickens jumped to his feet, tail wagging.

Laura sneezed.

"Are you getting sick?" Sarah asked.

"I've got a scratchy throat. I might be getting a cold."

"Terrific," Sarah said.

Chapter 5

Jamie

August 22, Destination, Idaho

Jamie Hargrave sat behind the wheel of the family's old blue Chevy pickup with a lump in her throat. She glanced at Aella, and wished she was going on the trip, too. Aella's runny nose and sneezing seemed a little worse today. Not good. Jamie felt the telltale tickle in her throat. She was *not* getting sick. The family just couldn't afford for her to miss a shift waiting tables at the truck stop.

Aella sneezed and lifted her arm to wipe her nose on her sleeve.

"Use a tissue! For goodness' sake, Aella, we stuffed every one of your pockets with them."

"Okay, Mom, sorry." Aella pulled a crumpled tissue from the pocket of her sweatshirt and blew her nose.

Jamie pulled the pickup into the church parking lot and stopped near the fifteen-passenger van. She hauled Aella's suitcase from the truck, then bent down to say goodbye. "You be good. Do everything Mrs. Thompson and the other chaperones tell you. Remember to say please and thank you, and remember to use your tissues."

"I will, Mom." Aella squeezed her mother.

"Have a lot of fun," Jamie said as the lump in her throat reasserted its presence.

"I will."

"And remember, I love you very much."

"I love you too, Mom."

Jamie walked over to the troop leader. The two women talked about the itinerary: once they landed in Washington and checked into the hotel, the girls would call their parents, then tomorrow, a White House tour and a bus tour around the city. Next day: Lincoln Memorial and so on. Jamie told Mrs. Thompson that Aella had the sniffles. Probably from all the wild fire smoke in the air.

Afterward, Jamie called Aella over from where she was playing tag with the other girls and hugged her one last time before she got in her truck. She both felt the urge to cry and felt silly about it. Lots of mothers spent a lot less time with their kids than she did, and they were good parents, weren't they? Aella was only going for a week. The entire train of thought was ridiculous. Jamie turned on the radio to lose herself in the music, but the radio gods conspired against her. First, the Dixie Chicks sang about a girl leaving home in *Wide Open Spaces*, then, of course, they just had to play "In My Daughter's Eyes." The bastards. Then the waterworks started. The tears lasted until she changed the station to classic rock. She felt better by the time she reached her driveway. Better still when she saw Joe Collins pulling off the dirt track with two fully loaded trailers of corn. Joe threw her a wave, and she returned it, dumbstruck. When she pulled up to the house, Ed was sitting on the porch drinking coffee and smiling a big old confident smile she hadn't seen in years, the one she fell in love with.

"What was Joe Collins haulin'?" She asked as she walked up to the porch.

"Corn." Ed grinned, just a bit too wide. Jamie could tell it wasn't just coffee in his cup.

She put a hand on her hip and tilted her head. "No shit, Ed."

Ed's grin broadened a bit. "He was haulin' last night's harvest."

"Last night's harvest?" She walked over to him.

"Bobby called this morning. He heard we were harvesting early because of the fire. He had a rush order from some gourmet restaurant chain. We agreed on a price, then Bobby came over and loaded up."

"And the price?"

"Top dollar," Ed said, his grin rounding the corner from wide and progressing to shit-eating. "But that's not the best news."

She waited. Ed was deliberately waiting for her to ask, partly to draw out the suspense, partly just to irritate her. She knew the game well. If she played her part, she would get what she wanted. "What?"

"I got up early and walked out to the edge of the forest. The buffer zone held. Forest Service was out there putting out a few hotspots. They said to leave the irrigation on for a day or two, but the danger's over."

"Yes!" She placed her hand over his on the coffee cup and guided it to the table. Then she straddled him. As they kissed, long-dormant things stirred—warm, wet, remembered.

"You know," she murmured, "I've got an hour before work. If the farm's saved, the corn's sold, and the house is empty..." She smiled, voice dipping into a mock-pleading drawl, "but you were up late, and up early... probably too tired."

"The hell I am!" he barked, nearly tossing her from his lap as he jumped up. "Last one up-stairs makes lunch!" he called, already halfway to the stairs. His shirt was over his head before the screen door slammed behind him.

Ed left a trail of clothes going up. Jamie followed, peeling off layers—until a sudden sneeze caught her mid-shirt.

Aella

The day started cool, but warmed considerably. Aella took off her sweatshirt, tissues bulging from its pockets, and draped it over her suit-case in the back of the van. As she ran with her friends in the parking lot, so did her nose. She alternated between snuffing the mucus back in and wiping her nose on her hand. Once in the van, Aella sneezed, sending an invisible cloud drifting around the vehicle in the air condition-ing current.

At the airport, the girls sprinted back and forth on the moving walkways, running their hands along the black rubber handrails. They played musical chairs at the gate. As they boarded the plane, Aella tapped the armrest of each seat on either side as she followed Mrs. Thompson down the aisle. For the first part of the flight, the girls talked and laughed. Each, including Aella, used the restroom. Eventually,

Aella, worn out from the excitement and the day's early start, fell asleep. Mucus dripped from her nose into the seat-back.

She woke as the plane landed in Washington. Aella sneezed, then rooted around in the pocket of her sweatshirt for a tissue. She blew her nose and stuck the dirty tissue back into her pocket. As the plane taxied to the jetway, she looked out the window, wide-eyed. Mrs. Thompson and the other chaperones had difficulty controlling the rambunctious girls once they were free from the aircraft. Aella ran up and down the escalators, her germy hands sliding along the handrails. Another sneeze on the shuttle to the hotel, sending another invisible cloud floating among the international travelers. She touched the push bar on the hotel's revolving door, which the girls played in, laughing and yelling, until Mrs. Thompson scolded them and made them sit in the overstuffed lobby chairs. Aella couldn't stop smiling. This was the best day ever.

Jamie

Jamie Hargrave woke from her brief post-sex nap. She eased out of bed carefully so as not to wake Ed. She wanted him to get extra rest after the stress of the last twenty-four hours. The only sounds were the rustling of her uniform and the old farmhouse creaking. She worked her long brown hair into a dowdy bun and put on a touch of makeup. Just enough to hide the faint lines at the corners of her eyes, but not enough, she hoped, to encourage the horny truckers she served.

As she left, she leaned over and kissed Ed's cheek. "I love you, Ed. Things will get better. I just know it."

Ed stirred, said, "I love you too," then rolled over onto his stomach and fell back to sleep.

Jamie admired his sleeping body for a moment. His lightly haired, muscled legs ended in an ass that Jamie thought was pretty good for a middle-aged guy. He didn't have the paunch that so many men gained at his age. His back dipped in at the waist and broadened out into muscled shoulders. He had a farmer's tan, which started in the middle of his biceps and extended down to cover his large, powerful hands. She smiled. For all his faults, Ed was a good man. A handsome man. And he was hers.

She drove the eight miles to the interstate truck stop. During her shift, a sneezing fit came so suddenly Jamie barely had time to turn her head and sequester them into her shoulder. She was pretty sure she had missed the plates of food lined up on the stainless-steel counter.

The rest of Jamie's shift was a losing battle with an increasingly runny nose. Jamie did her best to keep clean. She washed her hands every time she blew her nose, leaving them dry, raw, and red. More than one hundred interstate travelers ate from the plates she served during her shift.

Chapter 6

Erica

August 23, Bethesda, Maryland

Erica's impatience got the better of her. Instead of waiting for Carl to tell her Dr. Silva agreed to see her, she drove to the Beachwood Assisted Living Center. The old Toyota Camry's air conditioning strained to keep her cool as she worked on the CDC story in the parking lot and waited for the phone to ring. She needed Tom to call back soon, or the article would fall flat.

One thing that intrigued her about the Silva story was that he developed Laetanol, the drug she took for depression. After her breakup with Tom, she had nowhere to go and slept on Carl's couch. The self-esteem crushing one-two punches sent her to the therapist who prescribed the drug. It helped a lot. Laetanol gave her the strength to keep going, so she kept taking it. Now she wanted to dig up the dark bones its creator buried somewhere in Idaho.

The phone rang. Tom's old picture lit up the screen, opening a fresh wound in Erica's scarred heart. She hit the 'accept' button.

"Hi, Tom."

"Hi Erica," he said, then after an uncomfortable pause, "I'm... returning your call."

"Right," she said, shelving her feelings and slipping into reporter mode. She racked her brain. How to even begin this conversation? Nothing.

"Are you okay?" he asked.

"Not really, Tom." She decided that honesty, and maybe Tom's sympathy, would be her best bet. "Things aren't going so well at the paper. I honestly haven't been able to get a decent assignment."

"I'm sorry to hear that." Then another awkward pause. "How's Jinx?"

"I had to put her to sleep six months ago; feline leukemia."

"I'm sorry, Erica, really." Then another long pause, "I'm sure you didn't call specifically to depress me, so..."

Jesus Christ, he always made it about himself. She did her best to ignore his last statement, at least outwardly, and dug in. "Tom, I was hoping you could shed some light on this CDC bulletin about the flu."

"What specifically about it, don't you understand? It's pretty self-explanatory."

Oh my god, you condescending, effete, jackass! "Well, the bulletin said the virus has a long incubation period and low virulence. That's a good thing, right?"

"Well, actually, the incubation period can be up to two weeks. It can also be as short as two days. However, a long incubation period is less desirable. Infected people can carry and spread the virus for a long time without knowing it. The host organism—people—are most contagious the day before symptoms manifest. When you combine that with low virulence, you have a recipe for a massive global pandemic."

"I see. The low virulence means people won't get that sick, right?"

"Well," Tom said, "it means that people won't feel very ill, but it also means that they won't stay home. Instead, they will most likely continue their normal routines, exposing a much larger number of people to the virus."

"But if it's not that bad, what's the big deal?" Erica did her best to skirt the fine line between playing dumb to get his ego to explain and having him realize she was manipulating him.

"The big deal," he said as if he were talking to a child, "is the more infections there are, the greater the chance the virus will mutate into something worse. Flu viruses aren't static or stable things; they change all the time."

"The release had a bit of an alarmist tone. Are there other concerns?"

"Are we on the record?"

Damn. She knew he would ask, eventually. "Tom, I really need this story."

"You didn't answer my question, Erica."

"Yes, we are on the record," she sighed.

"I am done talking about this."

"Come on, Tom, I won't use your name."

"I could lose my job if someone connects us."

"Tom, the public has a right to know. You'd be saving lives."

"Don't give me that 'for the public good' crap, Erica. When the CDC feels it's time to release further information, it'll do so. That's our job. We're here to save lives."

"I'm not trying to play you, Tom. I'm trying to get a story."

"Those two things are the same. You are playing me like an old record. That's a crappy thing to do with love, Erica."

"I hoped we could still be friends. I called a friend because I need a little help."

"Friends don't throw love away, Erica. They don't estrange themselves for years, then call out of the blue for a favor. You called because you know I still carry a torch for you, and you wanted to use that to advance your career."

"I... Tom, I didn't know that. I thought you'd moved on. You never called after you left. How would I know?"

"I didn't call because you broke my heart," he said, almost in a whisper.

Another call beeped in on Erica's phone. She ignored it. "I'm sorry. When you left, I still loved you. But long distance relationships don't work. And my career is just as important as yours. I didn't want to follow yours around the country."

"How's that working out for you?"

The irony of her having to call Tom for help with her stalled career brought Erica close to tears. Tom's biting sarcasm crushed that sentiment. "If I say a source inside the CDC, will you speak on the record?" Erica asked, in one last attempt to make the call worth more than an à la mode helping of heartbreak revisited.

"No."

"An unnamed source?"

"Okay, fine, but no CDC."

Erica sighed. An unnamed source with no credentials wouldn't cut it. She'd need someone official to comment on what Tom had told her.

"Okay, what's different about this year's flu—besides incubation time and mild symptoms? What's got the CDC spooked?"

"The CDC isn't spooked. The CDC is concerned. This strain hasn't shown up in over forty years. So anyone under forty has no antibodies. People over forty who had it back then might have some protection—but this version's slightly different. Even those with antibodies to the old strain could be at risk."

"The bigger concern," he continued, "is that this virus mutates more easily than typical flu strains. One genetic shift, and we're talking global pandemic. It could make 1918 Spanish flu look like a chickenpox party."

"Obviously, there are a lot of ifs and unanswerable questions. That's why the CDC hasn't released more information. We don't want a global panic. Erica, I want you to think very carefully about what you print. Even if you can find a source that will confirm it. Seriously, you could be responsible for starting a panic that will cost a lot of lives."

Or for saving a lot of lives. "Okay, one last question. You said the virus hadn't been around for over forty years. When exactly?"

"Nineteen seventy-three," Tom said. "I have to get back to work."

"Thank you so much, Tom. I really appreciate it."

"One more thing, Erica."

"Yes?"

"Wash your hands a lot and don't touch your face."

"Okay, Tom." The way he said it sent a shiver up her spine. His tone suggested that he was giving advice to a death row inmate, yet there was a loving quality to his words too. Despite the contentious nature of the call, she remembered all the reasons she loved and missed him. "We should have a drink with you if you are ever in DC."

"I'm never in DC." He hung up.

Erica sat for several minutes, trying to get the genie of her emotions back in its bottle. When the lump in her throat was gone, she remembered the call that had beeped in while she got her heart knocked around. There was a voicemail from Carl: Silva agreed to speak to her. She thought about calling, but the old Camry's air conditioning was losing the battle with the DC heatwave. Best to just show up and hope for the best. She gathered her things into her shoulder bag and headed across the parking lot to Beachwood. Her shoes clicked on the hot blacktop, and her wide-legged slacks swished, creating a breeze on her legs. A blast of cool air hit Erica as she pushed open the many-windowed double doors and stepped up to the reception desk. "Erica Goldman to see Dr. Silva," she said before the receptionist could speak.

"Are you expected?" The woman checked something on the computer.

"I believe so," Erica said through her most pleasant smile.

The receptionist plucked her glasses from a chain of black beads around her neck and forced the ends through the tight bun above her ears. "Please have a seat, Miss Goldman," she said, motioning with her now magnified gray eyes toward the little waiting area to Erica's left.

"Sure," Erica said. She sat on the elegant and comfortable sofa. This was a nice place. No smell of stale flowery perfume, mothballs, or antiseptic; the only thing Erica smelled was money. The table in front of her was solid wood, not laminate. The burgundy carpet was plush and free of stains.

After a minute or two, Carl rounded the corner. "Miss Goldman," he said with a wink.

"Yes," she said, following his cue not to betray that they knew each other.

"Right this way." He led her down the hall to the right of the reception desk. The carpet gave way to polished hardwood floors, not the linoleum one would expect. There were widely spaced doors on either side of the hall, all heavy wood, all immaculate. Carl knocked on the third door to the right. A muffled "come in," filtered through the oak.

Carl entered, then held the door for Erica.

She hesitated. The old man sat on the edge of the bed, well, but hastily dressed. His expensive dress shirt was misbuttoned by one hole, and the waist of the likewise posh suit pants was twisted far to the right, causing the leg creases to veer hard to starboard. The man noticed her hesitation at the door and said, "come in, please, Miss — is it Miss or Mrs.?" He had a cultured British accent Erica found instantly charming.

"Miss," she said.

"Close the door, Miss Goldman, if you would be so kind, and have a seat." He indicated the chair by the bed that faced the TV. "Can I offer you a beverage? I'm afraid it will have to be something benign, like water or iced tea. They won't let me keep anything stronger in here, I'm afraid."

"I'm fine," she said, though she was dying for some water.

"Come, come, Miss Goldman, it's a hot day, and you look a bit flushed. I believe I could use a drink myself, so it's no trouble."

"If it's no trouble, I would love a water."

Silva smiled. "No trouble at all." As he rose slowly off the bed, he said, "Carl, I'd like you to stay too if you can arrange it."

"Of course, Dr. Silva."

"I see," he said to Carl, smiling, "that it takes the presence of a lovely lady caller to get you to show me the proper respect."

Carl smiled back. "Don't start,"

"Now that's the Carl I'm more familiar with."

Silva shuffled slowly to a heavy wooden wall unit filled with bookshelves, a built-in desk, and

several cabinets. He opened one of these to re-
veal a half-sized refrigerator filled with bottles
of water, tea, and ginger ale. He plucked a tea
and water from the fridge, shuffled back, and
handed Erica the bottle.

Erica wished she had offered to get the drinks
as she watched the man slowly ease himself
back into a sitting position on the bed.

The sentiment must have shown on her face.

Silva frowned. "Now, now, my dear, none of
that. Use it or lose it, or the use of it, at any
rate. That's what Dr. Parks tells me. Of course,
I know that, but sometimes one must be reminded of what one already knows in order for
it to sink in."

"Are you sure you are up to this, Dr. Silva?"
Erica asked. "I understand you had a... difficult
day yesterday."

"Well, normally, I would deny it, but since we
both know better, let me reassure you I'm fine.

"There," Silva said once they were all seated. "Now that we are all comfortable and re-
freshed, down to business." He smiled. "How
shall we do this, Miss Goldman? Shall I tell you
a tale, or shall we work by Socratic method?"

"How about a little of both, Doctor? If you
wouldn't mind answering a few burning questions, then I'd like to hear your story."

"Splendid, Miss Goldman."

"Please call me Erica."

"Very well, Erica, one last bit of housekeeping. Everything I am about to say is off the
record. If at a later time we decide there is a
story, I will decide what to say on the record."
His affable demeanor diminished. "I hope you
understand that much of what we talk about,
and all of what we don't, is, uh, shall we say,
sensitive information."

"Of course, Doctor Silva," Erica said, trying to
hide her disappointment.

"Please call me Anthony."

"Anthony, then. I'm not on a story. I'm here because Carl suggested that we talk, and after doing a little homework, I became intrigued by this..."

"Affair?" Silva smiled.

"Affair will do, I guess, considering I don't know what we are talking about yet." Erica opened her water and sipped.

"Alright then, what are your burning questions?"

"Well, first, I want to ask you what has changed since yesterday? Yesterday, you were upset to the point of having to be sedated. Today you seem totally relaxed."

"Very astute, Miss, uh, Erica. However, I'd like to point out that I didn't need to be sedated. Nurse Ratched has an itchy trigger finger, to use an American expression."

Carl laughed.

Silva smiled appreciatively at Carl, then continued. "Three things have changed, or happened at any rate, since yesterday. The first is: whatever was going to happen either has happened or is now happening, and there's nothing I can do about that. The second thing is: Carl has convinced me, quite rightly, that no one at the Pentagon is going to take the call of an old doctor with a Chicken Little story."

"Is the sky falling, Doctor?"

"Probably not, but that remains to be seen."

"And the third thing?"

"A visit from a beautiful young woman," he smiled.

Erica blushed and sipped her water. "What did you see on TV yesterday that got you so upset? Did it have something to do with the fire at Fort Johnson?"

"That is an impressive supposition. Carl tells me you made the connection between myself and Fort Johnson. I imagine it was quite an obscure find, that old photograph. It caused quite an uproar in its time. Though the accompanying article in Stars and Stripes was vague, the work at Fort Johnson and my part in it were supposed to be quite secret. It was a terrible mistake on the part of the editor of Stars and Stripes. I imagine he is still cleaning latrines in Antarctica."

"What was the nature of your work at Fort Johnson, Dr. Silva?" Erica asked. Though he asked her to call him Anthony, something about the conversation made her feel that using his title was more appropriate, and he wasn't protesting her use of the honorific.

"We have arrived at the crux of the problem. I wanted to speak to someone at the Pentagon because, strictly speaking, my work there was, and I have no reason to doubt, still is, classified. So let me lead you on a little narrative journey. We'll see in the end if I have supplied you with the information you need to go forward."

"One question first, Dr. Silva?"

"Yes, my dear?"

"If what you feared has already happened, and calling the Pentagon won't help, why are we doing this?"

"Simple, really. If this forty-year-old chicken comes home to roost, and even if it doesn't, someone needs to know and take steps accordingly. I tried to get the Army to do the right thing forty years ago. They wouldn't listen."

"But if we aren't on the record, what good will telling us do anyone?"

"Because, my dear, if something happens to me, and the unthinkable occurs, you will know the truth. Maybe you can stop it."

Erica thought about this. Silva was making her some kind of crypt keeper, responsible for guarding or releasing a crusty old military mistake. She didn't like being dragooned into this, but she smelled a story. If the old man gave her one, maybe she could publish it. "Okay, go ahead, Doctor."

"As a young man in England, I saw a great deal of misery. Not the abject misery written about in Dickens, mind you, but the everyday kind—the sort that leads to alcoholism, drug use, and other escapist behaviors. So I wondered how people could find happiness in whatever situation they found themselves. This, of course, led to the question: what is happiness?

"I will skip all the boring details and get down to it. I ended up doing research at university on the chemical process of happiness in the brain. The research was slow going. This was the sixties, you understand. The tools we had were blunt at best. The university decided to terminate the project in favor of curing some disease or another—after all, people can't be happy if they're dead. It was inarguable.

"It was at that time I got an offer to continue my work in America, so I crossed the pond, as they say, and continued at an independent research institute. There, I isolated a particular protein responsible for pleasure at the cellular level. It was a significant triumph, well-publicized." Silva paused for a sip of tea. "That publicity brought me to the attention of the US Army. You must be clear on that point. "What brought me to the Army's attention—do you understand?—what they were interested in... that is the key here. I dare not say more. They made me a very attractive offer, so naturally, I went to work for them." Silva paused, sipped his tea, and then paused again. "Where were we?"

"The Army," Erica said.

"Yessss..." Silva seemed to flounder, "uh, Miss, uh, Erica, things with the Army didn't go as planned. There were certain... problems. Problems with a hefty cost, a cost I am still paying, I'm afraid. I can't elaborate, of course, but I'm trusting you to put enough of the pieces together to get at least a murky picture."

Erica frowned. Murky was an understatement. "I hope I won't disappoint you."

"I hope so too, but my dear." He raised a finger. "I have faith in your intellect, and Carl's. Carl was smart enough to take me seriously and to bring you and I together. You were smart enough to make the Fort Johnson connection," he smiled. "I, um, I'm afraid I've lost my train of thought."

Erica sighed. "You were avoiding elaborating on the costs of your work with the military."

"Yes," Silva pushed his glasses up on his nose with his index finger. "I'm afraid there is more than one kind of cost, and I continue to pay more than one kind of cost.

"I had some fundamental differences of opinion with the Army after problems arose with the work. It became rather contentious, and they showed me the door. I then took a job with World Drug, and with an excellent team, I developed Laetanol. Unfortunately, I had to retire before it came to market, but it was still quite lucrative. Most important-ly, Laetanol was the culmination of my life's work: making people happy. The working poor I wanted to help as a boy now have a chance at happiness. It's not a cure for misery, but I am satisfied with my contribution to happiness."

Erica rubbed her temple. "I'm not sure I have enough pieces of the puzzle to solve it."

"Perhaps not. Let me try to get you a little closer. The most important things to remember are these: I have worked toward the same goal all my life, and I'm still paying the cost."

"I still can't see what use your work would be to the military."

Silva's thin lips twitched into a condescending smile. "Let me ask you a question: how does one win a war?"

"Superior arms, numbers, and tactics?" Carl postulated.

"That's how you win a battle. So how do you win a war?"

"I really don't know." Erica sighed. This wasn't her area at all. "By killing the enemy?"

"My dear, you are smarter than that. History almost always proves that answer wrong."

"I'm stumped," Erica said.

"Find out, my dear. It will lead you down the right path. Please understand once again why I can't just tell you. It's treason, but in my mind, it's also a crime not to tell the world. There is one thing more, this thing I fear I must divulge. It may cross the line into treason, though I don't think so. The problem is that I don't think the puzzle is solvable without it. I must trust your discretion in this matter. Be very careful as you search for it, or *him*. Perhaps you might consider a cover story: someone coming to you for help in finding him, that would be best."

"Finding who?" Erica asked, pen poised.

"Sergeant Mike Sampson."

"Can you tell me anything else about him? Or why I'm looking for him?"

"I'm afraid not. All I dare to say is that he's important to this tale."

Ugh. This guy. Circles and obfuscations. "Earlier, you said that a thing at Fort Johnson was either happening or *had* happened. But during our conversation, you implied that a bad thing could *still* happen. Is there a timeline? A moment when the danger will pass?"

"I have no idea."

Chapter 7

Mrs. Thompson

August 24, Washington, DC

Mrs. Thompson woke Aella and the other girls at 7 AM. They bounced around the hotel room talking about all the cool things they would do that day, especially the White House tour. Mrs. Thompson was a little concerned about the sluggish way Aella acted. She had to keep telling the girl to keep going. "Hurry up and get dressed," she said, "and blow your nose."

Certain Aella had a cold, Mrs. Thompson kept an extra eye on the child as Aella made waffles for all the other girls, fascinated by the machine at the breakfast bar. The girl moved through her morning as if in a pleasant molasses dream, then Aella fell asleep on the way to the White House, forehead pressed against the bus window.

When they arrived, Mrs. Thompson had a hard time waking Aella. The child acted drunk, which she knew was impossible. Just the same, she stayed close as they went on their tour. The girls met the Press Secretary, the lady from TV. They all shook her hand and stood on a stool behind the podium in the press room to have their pictures taken.

Between the Whitehouse and the Lincoln Memorial, Aella fell asleep again. When Mrs. Thompson went to rouse the girl, she saw a line of mucus dripping down from Aella's nose across her strangely grinning lips. "For goodness' sake, Aella, blow your nose," she said.

Aella gave no sign that she heard.

"Aella!" Aella made no response.

She directed the other chaperones to take the girls off the bus and continue the tour, then sat down next to Aella and wiped the girl's nose and mouth. "Aella, can you hear me?"

The girl did not respond.

She took the child's hand and squeezed hard. "Aella!!"

Nothing.

After a few more minutes of poking and squeezing and verbally trying to get Aella to respond, she called 911.

The 911 operator gave Mrs. Thompson instructions on how to rouse Aella, but nothing worked.

A few short minutes later, the paramedics entered the bus.

"Right here." Mrs. Thompson waved a hand. Then she got up to make room for the Emergency Medical Technicians. She relayed all she had done and told the EMT about Aella's sluggishness that morning.

"What's her name?" The EMT asked.

"Aella," Mrs. Thompson responded.

"And how old is she?"

"She's twelve."

The EMT sat down next to Aella. "Aella, my name is Joe. Can you tell me how you are feeling?" Joe got no response. He held her wrist and felt for a pulse.

"Does she have any medical issues?"

"None that I know of. I'm just the field trip chaperone. Her parents are in Idaho."

"What did you have for breakfast, Aella?" Joe asked as he dug into his bag.

"She had waffles," Mrs. Thompson said a little too quickly. She needed the paramedics to know this wasn't her fault. Was it? She'd taken good care of the children. Hadn't she?

"You're just going to feel a little poke to make sure you ate all your waffles."

"She did," Mrs. Thompson said.

The EMT looked up at Mrs. Thompson. "I'm just checking her blood sugar." He looked at the girl's face as he poked her with the needle. He got no reaction at all. The medic looked at the numbers. "One hundred ten," he said to his partner. He checked her pupils with his light. "Unresponsive," he said. He listened to her chest with his stethoscope. "Bilateral breathing sounds, some congestion." He turned to Mrs. Thompson. "Is she taking any medication?"

"No," Mrs. Thompson said.

Joe tried a few more things to rouse the girl, but nothing worked. "Transport," he said to his partner.

"Copy," the other man said. "You got her?"

"Yeah, here." Joe handed the thin man his medical bag. Mrs. Thompson watched helplessly as the EMT scooped up Aella as quickly and efficiently as if she were a baby. He walked slowly down the aisle with the child raised over the level of the seats, Mrs. Thompson right on his heels. He gingerly turned the corner down the stairs, then carried the limp girl off the bus and onto the waiting stretcher.

A crow sitting on a nearby wire cawed and took wing. Its shadow passed over the girl's weirdly grinning mouth, first diminishing it, then revealing it again, macabre in the sunlight.

Joe and his partner strapped the girl down. The thin EMT set the medical bag on the end of the stretcher at Aella's feet, fished out a wire with a clip on the end, and attached it to Aella's finger.

Mrs. Thompson looked on with growing alarm. "I assure you she ate a good breakfast. It's not as if I'm starving her."

"Her blood sugar is fine, ma'am," Joe said. He and his partner pushed the stretcher toward the ambulance.

"Is it really necessary to take her to the hospital? What's wrong with her?"

Joe's partner stopped and stepped to the end of the stretcher. "She's catatonic, ma'am, and since you say she has no medical issues, we're assuming she's not normally catatonic, so we are taking her to the hospital to find out why." The man's face was red and angry. Joe stepped over and whispered in the other EMT's ear. The man reddened further, scowled, and helped Joe put the stretcher into the ambulance.

"Can I ride with her?" Mrs. Thompson asked.

In response, Joe extended a hand and helped her into the ambulance. His partner closed the rear doors, then got behind the wheel. Joe took a radio from its holder on the wall and spoke into it: "WMT seventeen code two to Potomac Pediatric, how copy, over?"

"Potomac Pediatric, we have you loud and clear. WMT seventeen, go ahead," the radio crackled back.

"We are inbound your facility with a twelve-year-old female, no medical history. BP one ten over sixty, heart rate ninety-five, pulse ninety-nine. On two liters O2 via nasal cannula. Blood sugar one-ten. Patient is conscious but unresponsive. ETA ten minutes, if no questions or orders, see you in ten." Joe put the radio back in its holder.

Mrs. Thompson saw yellow-white bubbles of mucus forming where the breathing tubes went into the girl's nose. She was going to say something to the EMT, but saw him looking, too. He opened a compartment above the girl on the wall, removed a package, tore it open, then carefully removed the breathing tubes from the girl's nose, catching the thin ropes of mucus in the gauze. After fitting a mask on the end of the tube, he placed it on Aella's face.

Mrs. Thompson looked on, her mouth drawn into a thin line, her hands kneading the hem of her skirt. She shifted her gaze from the girl to Joe. "What did you whisper to your partner back there?"

Joe smiled and leaned in toward Mrs. Thompson conspiratorially. "I said he should either start smoking again or kill himself."

Mrs. Thompson gave a thin smile.

At the hospital, Mrs. Thompson followed the two EMTs. They wheeled the stretcher into the ER. "WMT seventeen," the thin EMT said to the woman behind the counter.

"Bed four," she said.

They pushed Aella into the second curtained area on the right and parked the stretcher alongside the bed. As Joe and his partner transferred Aella to the bed, a tiny Asian woman in light blue scrubs walked over. "What do we have?" She asked, transferring the oxygen from the portable bottle to the hospital's supply from the wall outlet.

A tall brown woman in a white coat entered, then stood bedside.

"Patient was on a sightseeing tour and became catatonic," Joe's partner said, rattling off the girl's vitals.

"Anyding eltze?" the woman in the white coat asked in a thick Indian accent.

"She has a cold and nasal congestion."

The woman looked at the chart in her hand. "Dhat's why you changed out the nasal cannula?"

"Yes," Joe said. "Any questions?"

"No, tank you," the woman said.

"Are you the modda?" the woman in the lab coat asked Mrs. Thompson.

It took Mrs. Thompson a moment to parse the words through the doctor's accent. She was born and raised in Destination, Idaho, and was unaccustomed to such things. "No, I'm her chaperone. We are on a trip from Idaho with our scout troop."

"I'm Dr. Patel," the woman said, leaning in to examine the girl, "this is nurse Chen," she waved absently at the woman in blue scrubs. "We will need do speak do her parents as soon as possible. Has she been wid you all day?"

"Yes," Mrs. Thompson said, sitting bolt upright, hands wringing the hem of her skirt again.

"Did she eat or drink anyting unusual?"

"No."

"Okay." Dr. Patel turned to nurse Chen, "Let's get a line TKO, two hundred milliliders an hour, full neuro workup, tox screen, and CAT scan. Cath her and get a urine sample. Led's also strip her down and look for trauma and insect bites. And, get psych in here."

As Dr. Patel spoke, nurse Chen entered the orders into the computer in the corner. Dr. Patel spent another minute or two examining the girl and talking soothingly to Aella in her thick Indian accent. Then she looked at Mrs.

Thompson. "We need to speak do her parents as soon as possible. Can you contact dhem?"

"Yes, I'll call right now." She hesitated, though, looking at the sign on the wall which read "No Cell Phones."

Dr. Patel followed her gaze. "It's all right. Please make dhe call."

Mrs. Thompson called Jamie's cell phone; it rang then went to voicemail. She hadn't thought of what she'd say in advance, so she stumbled a bit. She didn't want Jamie to panic and assume the worst, but she also needed Jamie to understand it was urgent. The words "emergency room" would send any parent climbing the walls. The tone came before she fully gathered her thoughts. "Jamie, this is Cheryl Thompson, Aella is... sick, and we are at the hospital. Call me or call Potomac Pediatric Hospital right away." She was about to hang up, then added, "She is stable and not in any... she's stable." Then she clicked off the call.

Next, she called the Hargrave farm. The phone there rang endlessly.

Chapter 8

Erica

August 24, Washington, DC

Erica stood in the editor's doorway, dreading the conversation to come. The CDC story was her first real story, and she couldn't find a source to go on record and confirm the information Tom gave her. She had to admit she was spending valuable time working on the Dr. Silva story instead of the CDC piece. Though calling the Silva thing a story was generous. It was more like a puzzle with no news value—yet. Still, she couldn't help feeling like something big lurked behind the curtain of obscurity Silva drew across the affair.

"Ah," the editor said from under his black seventies mustache, "Miss Goldman, the CDC story is good—"

Erica's pulse quickened. He never called anything she wrote "good."

"—good tone, well written, but the unnamed source won't fly. Strip it down, summarize the

CDC release for tomorrow's edition and get another source, then we'll run the rest."

"Okay," she said, "will do."

It didn't take long for Erica to strip down the CDC story and turn it in. She placed a few calls looking for a source and left a few messages. All the while, she turned the Silva puzzle over in her mind. When she finished her calls, Erica looked over her notes from her meeting with Silva. The whole thing boiled down to three questions. One: how do you win a war, and what does it have to do with happiness? Two: what did Silva mean by 'still paying the costs?' He said there was more than one kind he still paid. She wondered if one kind was literal. And three, who was Mike Sampson?

Well, might as well go in order. She searched 'how to win a war' and found a multitude of answers. Nothing seemed to fall neatly into the puzzle. There was a lot of talk about logistics, the concentration of forces, and morale. Maybe that one had legs—morale. Was Silva working on a way to keep soldiers happy? Silva was a drug guy, though. Was it feasible to dose an entire army? Erica didn't think so. Okay, put a pin in that one.

Paying the costs. Still paying the costs, Silva said. So what kind of costs were there? Financial, obviously, physical, emotional, some sort of cost to his career? Family?

How do you get into someone's financial information legally? She didn't know. She did know that Silva had to shell out a pretty penny to stay at Beachwood. That place was posh. Maybe Carl could tell her something about Silva's finances from that angle. Doubtful it would mean anything, but it was worth a shot. As far as physical costs, Erica didn't think the guy had any. Besides just being old. Emotional costs weren't concrete and almost impossible to quantify. Especially if you were a stranger to the person in question. That meant Silva wanted her to find out about his finances. Her only way into that was Beachwood. But what did Beachwood have to do with the Army or Fort Johnson? Okay, put a pin in that too.

That left only Mike Sampson. An internet and social media search turned up a virtual ocean of Mike Sampsons. She sifted through a couple dozen different profiles on social media before giving it up as futile.

The CDC source problem nagged at her, but the Silva puzzle was irresistible. She sat behind her shitty metal desk and exhaled. Maybe it was unsolvable. Maybe she just needed to march down to Beachwood and confront the old man. Appeal to his sense of duty to the public. Although, when Erica tried that tactic on Tom, he'd seen right through her. Silva was probably too smart to expose himself to treason charges on the strength of her 'duty' argument. Maybe she'd never gotten a decent story at the paper because she just wasn't good at this, and everyone, especially the editor, knew it.

Erica shook off the useless yoke of self-doubt and kept going. What else was there to do? Quit? She dug into her shoulder bag, took out the bottle of Laetanol, shook one into her hand, and swallowed it dry. Silva invented Laetanol. His whole life, he had worked on one thing: happiness. The question came around again: what did the Army want with happiness? You couldn't put the entire army on a Laetanol regimen. If they knew, some would refuse. And if they didn't know, they soon would. It would leak. No way to keep something that big a secret, so...

Erica picked up the phone and called Carl. The call went to voicemail. She started to leave a message. As she did, Carl's return call beeped in. She hit the 'end and accept' button. "Hi Carl, got a minute?"

"I do now," he said, panting.

"Did I call at a bad time?" she asked.

"You are a real cock-blocker. You always were," Brian said in the background.

"I'll take that as a yes. You didn't have to call back right now, you know."

"That's what I told him," Brian said.

"Am I on speaker?" Erica asked.

"Yes," Carl said brusquely, "state your business."

"Fine, I—what are you two doing screwing in the middle of the day? Don't you have jobs?"

"Haven't you ever heard of a nooner?" Brian asked.

"Carl, you drove home from Bethesda in beltway traffic to screw around on your lunch break?"

"What are they going to do, fire me? I've only got two weeks left. I already gave notice. Now, if we're quite done talking about my sex life, and believe me, we are, I say again, state your business."

"I'm not sure I want to get into it now."

"Erica, the damage is done, so we might as well."

"Okay," she told him about the myriad of answers she had found about winning a war. She told him about the truckload of Mike Sampsons she found on the internet. And she told him about the dead-end where it came to Silva's finances.

"Let's try a little free association to loosen the mental logjam here. I want to figure out what the Army wanted with Sampson's work. You can play too, Brian."

"Oh, goodie," came the sarcastic reply.

Erica ignored it. "I say a word, and you say the first thing that comes into your mind. Ready?"

"Yes," Carl said.

"Army," she said.

"Assholes," Brian said.

"Uniform," Carl said.

"War," she said.

"Weapons," Brian said.

"Gulf," Carl said.

"I'm with Brian. I thought of weapons too," she paused.

"So?" Carl said.

"So maybe the Army didn't want Silva's work for our army's morale. Maybe they wanted it for some kind of weapon."

"A happiness weapon?" Carl asked.

"Sounds pretty ridiculous," Brian added.

"Yeah," Erica said, "I guess it does. We're grasping at straws here."

"Yeah," Carl said, "I appreciate you working so hard on this, but I'm going to hang up and grasp something else."

"That's what I'm talkin' 'bout," Brian said.

"Okay, didn't need to hear that. I think I'm going to go pay Silva a visit."

About an hour later, Erica walked into the lobby of the Beachwood Assisted Living Center. She had just spent twenty minutes sitting in the parking lot on the phone with some low-level schmuck at the National Institute of Health, getting him to corroborate everything Tom told her about the CDC bulletin. She knew she really should rewrite the CDC story, but couldn't resist the allure of a puzzle. That she couldn't crack any of the clues Silva gave her only drew her in deeper. Like a moth to a flame—well, hopefully not *exactly* like that. She didn't want to get burned.

The receptionist recognized her. "Are you here to see Dr. Silva?"

"Yes."

"He has a visitor at the moment. I'll see if he'd like you to join them. Please have a seat." The receptionist waved a hand at the waiting area the same way she did on Erica's last visit.

Erica wondered how many times a day she made that same gesture. The plush sofa in the well-appointed waiting area cushioned her delightfully as she sat down and pulled out the puzzles page of the paper. She had the edge—she knew the puzzle contributor. But Erica didn't need an edge. When you dealt with words as your stock-in- trade, you could do pretty well with word puzzles if you had the knack.

Presently, the receptionist returned. "Dr. Silva invited you to join him and his guest. Do you know your way back?"

"Yes. Thank you." Erica walked down the hallway and knocked on the lustrous wooden door.

"Come in," came Silva's muffled voice.

Erica opened the door.

"Hello." Silva smiled. "This must be my lucky day! Visited by two lovely ladies at the same time."

"Hello, Dr. Silva." Erica gave a brief wave.

A woman sat by his bed. She barely fit into the chair. Its thick wooden arms squeezed her thick fleshy waist. Though it was comfortably cool in the room, the woman's short gray hair clung to moist, sweaty temples. The woman looked almost as old as Silva.

"I'm Molly, Tony's niece," the woman said.

"Erica," she extended a hand to the seated woman.

"Good to meet you," Molly shook it.

"Of course. You two have never met. Excuse my manners." Silva looked from one woman to the other.

An awkward silence followed. Erica didn't want to lay bare Silva's secrets in front of his niece. She had no idea what secret Molly kept, but keep it she did. Erica stood awkwardly by the door as the uncomfortable silence stretched.

"Well, Uncle Tony, I guess I'll be going now. Do you mind if I take a water for the road?"

"Of course not. Help yourself." Silva waved a hand at the fridge.

Molly hoisted her bulk from the chair's confining arms and shouldered a floral canvas tote bag big enough to hide the Lindbergh baby. She opened the little fridge in the wood-paneled cabinet and removed a water bottle. She also surreptitiously secreted a small package in her shoulder bag while attempting to hide her actions by blocking Erica's view with her ample body. Erica wondered if she was stealing from the old man.

Molly closed the fridge, walked over to Silva, and gave him an awkward hug.

Erica stifled a laugh.

The hug was awkward. Silva was lying down, and Molly was trying to bend over to embrace him without crushing him. It was also awkward because Molly's tote bag was over the shoulder she leaned in with, and it landed on Silva's belly.

"Ooooffff," he grunted.

The reason the hug was awkward, at least from Erica's point of view, was that it was *emotionally* awkward. Almost as if Silva hadn't ever hugged her before and hadn't expected one now. He reached up with the arm not pinned to the bed by the Lindbergh handbag and the woman's girth and patted her twice on the shoulder with it; the universal 'that's enough' signal of reluctant huggers everywhere. There didn't seem to be any affection on either part.

Molly straightened and settled the straps of her handbag further onto her shoulder. She turned to Erica. "Nice to meet you." To Silva, she said, "Goodbye, Uncle Tony, enjoy the pie. See you on Wednesday."

"Goodbye, dear!"

Molly closed the door.

"Please, Miss Goldman, be seated," Silva said. The motor of Silva's mechanical bed hummed until he sat upright. "I'm sorry if that encounter was awkward for you, Miss Goldman. I confess, I invited you in specifically to chase that boorish goldbricking niece of mine away. Can you forgive me?"

"Of course," Erica smiled. He was lying about something. The last line was rehearsed, a good cover story, but he rushed the delivery.

"Now, what can I do for you?"

"It's Erica, remember? I'm having trouble with our... my—little research project."

"Oh?"

"You asked me to find Mike Sampson. I found a lot of Mike Sampsons, and without more information, I have no way to narrow it down."

"I see. That is a dilemma, indeed. I'm afraid I don't know much about Sampson besides his name."

Once again, Erica had the sense that the old man was lying. He'd been frank and forthcoming the other day. Today, he seemed to be telling more lies than truths. "Too bad," she said. "You told me a clue to what you were doing at Fort Johnson could answer the question: how do you win a war? I found a dozen answers, but none have any obvious connection to your quest to bring happiness to the masses."

Silva looked far away, eyes unfocused. When he turned back, the set of his face showed a great hidden sadness. "Well," he began, "You win a war by getting the enemy to stop fighting. So the question becomes, how do you accomplish that?"

Now Erica had the distinct feeling that Silva was toying with her. "I don't know," she said.

"You must destroy the enemy's will to fight. Conventionally, you decimate their troops and means to make war until they give up. Can you think of no way my work would accomplish this?"

"Make them so happy they don't want to fight?" she asked tentatively.

Silva smiled broadly and said nothing.

Erica was sure now. The old man was fucking with her. She felt her goodwill toward him slipping away. Yet there was a story here, and she wanted it. If she had to play mind games with Silva to get it, she would. So she decided she'd no longer take the old man at face value.

"Is there anything else, dear? I'm feeling rather tired."

"No, thank you, Dr. Silva."

"It was nice to see you again."

Erica rose, slung her bag over her shoulder, and said, "Goodbye, Doctor."

"Erica," Carl called as she closed the door behind her.

She turned to see him walking down the hall towards her. "Hi Carl, you look radiant. There's a certain glow about you. Going home for lunch seems to agree with you," she grinned.

"Oh, shut up," he said. "Let me walk you to your car." Carl opened the heavy front door for her, and they stepped out into the heat. "Did you learn anything?"

"I'm not sure. Silva is fucking with me, I think. Seems like this whole thing is a game to him."

"Well," Carl said, "I've always found him a sweet old man. A little vain perhaps, but harmless. I admit, he is a little eccentric. I always chalked it up to his IQ and the meds that he is on."

"Oh?"

"Well, I'm not supposed to discuss the residents' medical business, but he's on a few things, including Laetanol."

"He's on Laetanol?" Erica raised an eyebrow.

"Yeah, ironic, isn't it? He invented it."

Erica stood by her car. "That's interesting. I'm not sure why yet—but it is. Carl, is there any way you could get a look at his financials? Look at the billing, anything like that? I can't think of any other way to decipher his clue about paying the cost. I'll try to pull his credit. Otherwise, I'm stymied."

"I don't know. I can try. If I get fired, it's no big deal. Next week is my last, after all."

"You're the best." She hugged him. "Call me if you find anything."

Chapter 9

Jamie

August 24, Destination, Idaho

Jamie Hargrave woke to the landline ringing. It seemed a million miles away. Really, it was just on the other side of the bed. She reached out. It was like swimming through maple syrup. Finally, with a supreme effort, she rolled over and extended an arm. The ringing stopped.

She checked her cell. Right next to where it said 'No Service,' it said 9:08 AM. Time to get up anyway.

Despite a runny nose and foggy head, she smiled, luxuriating in the sun filtering through the dusty glass, bathing her in its glow. Aella was on a trip, probably having the time of her young life.

Ed was in the fields, his muscular arms and back working to bring life from the soil.

It was going to be a good day.

Extra strong coffee, she decided, would provide an antidote to the fog of her oncoming cold. She struggled into her server's uniform and brushed her hair and teeth with a sluggishness she'd never felt from a cold. The coffee in the pot Ed brewed when he got up smelled strong and surprisingly not burnt.

Jamie chose the tallest mug in the dish drainer to take her coffee in the truck. She poured and drank half of it standing next to the pot. The lipstick refused to obey her clumsy fingers, giving her reflection a clown-like countenance. Giving up, she wiped it off.

The screen door clacked shut behind her, sending a crow perched on the truck's rearview mirror flapping into the sky, black on blue, cawing in complaint. She stumbled, walking on the uneven but familiar track of dirt and patchy grass between the house and the truck.

The drive to the truck stop featured one thing: corn. The two-lane blacktop ran straight and true for ten miles before the first turn. On this stretch of road, Jamie was rush hour. Her brain fog grew thicker. She reached for her coffee only to realize she hadn't brought it. Silly.

She should pull over, but she felt so good, so happy. She didn't want to stop, just drive and drive and drive.

The right wheels of the truck left the pavement, dropping to the dirt. Jamie didn't notice. She didn't feel the truck jerk hard and bounce into the ditch. Nor did she notice the truck jump into the corn. The bumps knocked Jamie's foot off the pedal. The truck rolled to a stop, its momentum checked by the head-high late August stalks.

Mrs. Thompson

Bethesda, Maryland

Mrs. Thompson sat in the Emergency Room next to Aella, worrying. About the girl, of course, but also that this was somehow her fault. The events of the past twenty-four hours turned over in her mind. She should have kept a tighter rein over the girls at the airport, the hotel, everywhere. What had Aella gotten into when she wasn't looking?

Dr. Patel walked in, checked the girl, then turned to Mrs. Thompson. "We have some of her test resulds back and—"

"Do you know what's wrong with her?" Mrs. Thompson sat bolt upright.

"As I was saying, we have some of her test results back. We really need to speak with her parents. Have you been able do reach them?"

"No," Mrs. Thompson glanced at her phone.

"Do you have any other way to contact them?"

"I could call Sheriff Clay. Maybe he could find them."

"You should do that right away."

"Can you tell me anything about what is wrong with her?" Mrs. Thompson was worried about Aella, no denying that, but she really wanted a diagnosis that absolved her of guilt.

"Her CT scan resulds are consistent with someone who has consumed a large amount of methamphetamine or heroin, but her tox screen returned negative for illicit drugs. I must speak to her parents right away."

Chapter 10

Dr. Silva

August 24, Bethesda, Maryland

Silva looked over his notebook, nodded, put on his bathrobe, slipped the notebook in the pocket, and grabbed his cane. He retrieved a heavy hardbound volume from the bedside table, stooped his shoulders, and drew his face down into a mask of senility. Then, squeezing the heavy book to his body, he opened the door and shuffled down the hall. After passing two dozen rooms, he came to a set of double doors. Silva stabbed the saucer-sized stainless-steel button on the wall with the rubber feet of his cane.

The doors opened into a continuation of the same hallway, but the corridor on the other side was different. Gone were the deep satin browns of the wood-covered walls and floors. In their place were institutional tile and vinyl. Hospital walls. A posh hospital, to be sure, with its etched glass light fixtures and custom-carved nameplates on the doors, but a hospital, nonetheless. The staff called this "the vegetable patch" when they thought none of the residents could hear them.

A nurse behind a bank of monitors said, "Going to do some reading, Dr. Silva?"

"Yes. Dickens today. Sam was quite a Dickens fan in his time." He smiled at the nurse.

She smiled back.

He tottered onward, and the nurse returned to the book she wasn't supposed to be reading. He knew when this particular nurse was on duty and timed his visits accordingly. She was sometimes late for her hourly rounds, if the book was good, and it would take a nuclear attack or a medical alarm to get her out of her seat.

The door he wanted lay at the end on the left. Two metal nameplates stood out from the white vinyl wall at eye level. The topmost read 'Malcolm Cobb,' and the lower plate read 'Sam Sipkomen.' The door was open, as always. Inside, two men sat in special chairs, one across from the other. They had IVs, catheters, heart monitors, and a myriad of wires and electrodes protruding from every orifice.

The man on the left was about ten years younger than Silva, but with no liver spots, freckles, or sun-damaged skin. A porcelain doll with a weird smile affixed to his waxen features. His open eyes blinked occasionally but saw nothing. Two days of gray whiskers bristled on his face and neck. What sent Silva's blood bubbling out of the kettle, though, was the sheet draped haphazardly, exposing the man's genitals to anyone walking down the hall. "Don't worry, old friend," Silva said, adjusting the bedclothes, "I'll be having some words with the weasel who runs this place."

Silva sat in the chair next to the catatonic man and checked his watch. Twenty past the hour. Give it another five minutes to ensure the nurse wasn't rushing to make up the last hour's rounds. He leaned back in the chair so he could survey a large slice of the hallway. Then, satisfied that he was unobserved, Silva spoke. "I hope you like this one, Sam. It's my favorite: *A Tale of Two Cities* by Charles Dickens."

Silva continued talking, but instead of looking at the book, he reached into the pocket of his robe, unzipped a leather case, and manipulated its contents.

"*Book the First. Recalled to Life. Chapter One: The period. It was the best of times, it was the worst of times...*"

Silva continued to work with the items in the case, occasionally casting his eye into the hallway.

"*... it was the age of wisdom, it was the age of foolishness, it was the epoch of belief, it was the epoch of incredulity...*"

Silva set the case down on the little table next to the book. He recited the words to fool the nurse, but in a deeper part of his mind, the parallels between the story he recited and the story he enacted became clearer as he spoke.

"*... it was the season of light, it was the season of darkness...*"

Silva approached the man in the chair with a needle full of clear liquid.

"*... it was the spring of hope...*"

He positioned the needle at the base of the patient's skull and aimed it carefully at a spot in the man's brain he could see only in his mind's eye.

"*... it was the winter of despair...*"

The needle plunged deep into the gray matter.

"... we had everything before us..."

Silva depressed the plunger on the syringe slowly so as not to jiggle it, his hands as steady as a young surgeon's. He stopped speaking as he did this, so not even the movement of his lips could influence his deft fingers.

Exactly half of the fluid squirted into the man's brain. Silva withdrew the needle and began speaking again.

"... we had nothing before us."

He repositioned the needle.

"...we were all going direct to Heaven..."

Then, as he stabbed the sharp steel into the hypothalamus, Silva stopped speaking again.

"... we were all going direct the other way."

Deed done, he wiped his brow with the sleeve of his bathrobe and glanced into the hallway.

Silva continued reciting the memorized text of the book as he stored the needle back in its case and held tissues against the patient's head, staunching the blood from the tiny punctures. Satisfied at last that the bleeding had stopped and that the wounds were all but undetectable, Silva put the soiled tissues in his bathrobe pocket. Then he placed the leather case on top of them. He sat heavily in the chair, staring intently at the motionless figure as he spoke.

The patient sat with his permanent smile and gave no indication he heard Silva. He gave no indication that Silva had done anything to him. He gave no indication of anything at all. He sat as he had for forty years.

Silva reached the end of the passages he had memorized. Opening the book, he began to read, continuing from where his memory faltered, glancing up often, checking for signs of movement, just as he had many times before.

In Chapter Three of the beloved book, he stopped. It was all too real. Too close to the bone. Silva imagined himself a modern-day Jarvis Lorry. Instead of sitting in a coach, he was sitting in a nursing home, but his situation and his thoughts were so close to those of the fictional Lorry that gooseflesh stippled his wrinkled arms under his warm robe. He read—

Now, although several faces appeared in front of him in the night, he couldn't determine which was the face of the buried person. All the faces belonged to a forty-five-year-old man, but they all differed in the expression they wore, and how worn-out they looked. One facial expression followed another: pride, contempt, defiance, stubbornness, submission, and lamentation. Some had sunken cheeks, sickly pale skin, hands, and bodies that had wasted away. But it was almost always the same face, and every head of hair had gone prematurely white. In his dream, Mr. Lorry asked the ghostly figure a hundred times:

"How long had you been buried?"

The answer was always the same: "Almost eighteen years."

"Had you given up hope of being dug up?"

"Yes, a long time ago."

"Do you know that you've been brought back to life?"

"That's what they tell me."

"You want to live, don't you?"

"I don't know."

Silva stared at the man and whispered, "You want to live, don't you? I've been trying so hard that I've stopped asking myself if I'm doing right by you. Yet, letting you waste away forever without trying, or ending your life, are equally unbearable to me. Are you still in there? Do you still have any hope of being dug out?

You have been buried alive twice as long as the doctor in this book, and I'm the doctor responsible. Still, here we are, struggling near the end of our lives. There is still hope. I think this time I have solved the problem. I believe it will work with every cell in my body and every synapse in my brain. You are recalled to life!" Silva's voice had risen above a whisper in his excitement. Realizing this, he glanced into the hallway and then at the clock. Almost the top of the hour.

He rose and leaned in to whisper in the man's ear, "You are recalled to life, do you hear? You are recalled to life—" he almost whispered the man's name aloud. But after so many years of hiding it, he dared not, not to the man, and most of all, not to himself.

Silva picked up the book and cane, then resumed his hunched, aged persona. He checked one more time for some sign that the treatment was having an effect, and, seeing none, shuffled down the hall. The nurse behind the desk guarding the "vegetable patch" entrance gave no sign she noticed him shuffling by. She certainly gave no evidence that she had any intention of getting up to complete her appointed rounds. Silva shook his head and caned the button that opened the doors. He went to his room briefly to drop off his book, then headed for the reception area and the adjacent administrative offices.

Carl

At the far end of the hall, Carl was loading a cart from the supply closet. He noticed Silva heading into the administrative offices. It was an unusual enough event that Carl followed Silva to see if he could learn anything that would unravel the mystery surrounding the aged doctor. He pushed the cart into the closet, locked the door, then walked toward the reception area. Judy, the receptionist, looked toward the admin area with a wry smile.

Carl stopped at the desk, leaned an elbow on the counter, and followed her gaze.

There was a commotion behind the door. "Director Harmon is busy. You can't just—" a woman's voice drifted through the wood.

Silva's voice interrupted her. "Now see here, Gwyneth. I pay a king's ransom to be here, and when I'm not getting my money's worth, I will see Harmon whether or not he is busy."

"Silva's at it again," Judy said. "Harmon will call to have him removed from his office in a minute."

Carl smiled, "thirty seconds," he said.

"I'll time it," Judy said.

"Hey, what the — Silva, you can't just barge in here!" Harmon barked.

"Stop jabbering and listen to me, you bloody-minded bureaucrat!" Silva shouted.

"Gwen, get someone in here to remove this man!" Harmon bellowed.

"I'll go," Carl said. "I want to find out what's going on."

"Twelve seconds," Judy said.

"Told ya." Carl pushed open the door.

Gwen held her desk phone. She looked up, saw Carl, and said, "Never mind, Dr. Parks is here." She hung up and waved a hand, indicating Carl should go into the administrator's office.

Carl hesitated. He wanted to hear what Silva was saying, so he stood in the doorway, listening.

Silva stood in front of the administrator's desk, waving his cane at the man. "I just came from Sipkomen's room. I found him with two days' growth on his face. His genitals were exposed to the world—"

Harmon leaned slightly to one side to look at Carl around Silva. "Dr. Parks, thank God, would you please remove Mr. Silva?"

"It's *Doctor* Silva, and you will listen to me speak my piece." Silva's voice dropped an octave, and his words dripped with menace. "And you know why, don't you, Dr. Harmon?"

Harmon deflated like the bellows in a breathing machine. The air of authority left him with that long exhale, leaving only a pudgy, used car salesman in a decent suit. He gripped the edge of his desk, the last symbol he had any power at all. "I'm sorry, Dr. Parks," he said. "Would you wait outside for Dr. Silva and close the door?"

"Okay." Carl closed the door.

The receptionist gave him a weak, sympathetic smile.

He sat in a chair right outside the office door, hoping to catch the conversation within. Gwen frowned at him. She was loyal to Harmon, he supposed, and didn't appreciate Carl eavesdropping on her boss. As long as she didn't stop him, Carl didn't really care. He couldn't hear what was said for a few minutes. Then Silva started shouting.

"When I bought this place, and you—" Silva hollered.

Son of a bitch! Silva *owned* Beachwood? Why would someone like Silva buy a place like this? Why wouldn't he just use the money to get care at home?

"Now, George, shape the bloody hell up." The handle turned. Silva stood in the doorway.

"Dr. Parks, would you be so kind as to help me? I'm suddenly very tired."

"Sure, Dr. Silva," Carl took Silva's arm opposite the one that held the cane. Together, they made their slow way back to Silva's room.

Carl helped the old man into the chair by the bed. Then he hustled to the closet where he stashed his supply cart. He unlocked the door, stepped into it, and closed it behind him. Then he called Erica.

"Hey Carl, what's up?"

"I've got some big news on the Silva thing."

"Great! Shoot."

"Well, Silva just marched into the administrator's office, complaining about the treatment of a chronic catatonic patient. I didn't get much because they closed the door. Silva acted like he was the administrator's boss, and so did the administrator. It was weird. Then at one point, I heard Silva shout, 'When I bought this place.'"

"Silva owns Beachwood?"

"Apparently."

"That is big news. I wonder if that fits into the clue about 'paying the cost?' Buying an assisted living center is a pretty significant cost, especially Beachwood. Why, if you had the money to buy an assisted living center, would you live there? Why wouldn't you live in a nice big house somewhere and hire a private nurse?"

"I know, right? Silva must be loaded from inventing Laetanol. Why live in a couple of rooms, no matter how fancy they are?"

"Did you get the name of the catatonic patient?"

"Sipkomen. Silva goes back there sometimes. Reads to the guy."

"Sipkomen? What kind of name is that?"

"Beats me," Carl said.

"Hang on a sec. Let me search the name." After a pause, she said, "I can't find anything. It sounds fake. What's the guy's first name, do you know?"

"Sam, I think. I don't work in that ward."

"Sam Sipkomen?"

"Yeah, I think so."

Another pause. "Looks weirder on paper than it sounds aloud," she said. Then there was silence again. "Of course! Right under our fucking noses!"

"What?"

"It's an anagram, and not a very good one."

"For what?"

"I think we just found Mike Sampson."

Chapter 11

Erica

August 25, Bethesda, Maryland

Erica steered her beat-up Toyota into the lot at Beachwood Assisted Living Center under the shade of an overhanging pine. She parked in the far corner because she didn't want anyone to see her in her expensive silk pantsuit getting out of that piece of shit. The car's air conditioning wasn't keeping up, forcing Erica to adjust her outfit, picking the pants out of her ass and the blouse out of her cleavage. Silk on a hot day? Idiot. Inhaling the pine-scented air focused her mind. She let the breath go and slung her shoulder bag into place. Centered now, she walked across the parking lot accompanied by the "pop, pop, pop" her high heels made on the pavement.

When Erica entered the lobby, the receptionist smiled at her.

"I'll tell him you are here." She picked up the phone and, after a brief conversation, said, "go on back."

"Thanks."

The door stood open. Silva, dressed in slacks, shirt, and tie, sat reading in his chair. Though the tie was loose, a thin flap of neck skin still overhung the red double Windsor.

"Hi, Dr. Silva, you look great. Got a hot date?" Erica asked from the doorway.

Silva set the book down on the table and rose to his feet. "Hello, my dear. Thank you. Sometimes just getting up and dressed can dispel the melancholy. You smell divine, and I love your suit. Please come in and take a seat."

Erica sat in the offered chair, shoulder bag on her lap. "Thank you, Doctor." She smiled.

Silva sank slowly onto the bed, sitting with his feet over the edge. "To what do I owe the pleasure?"

"Well, I've solved your three clues. I think I have all the puzzle pieces—except one."

"Oh?"

"Let me take you through it."

"Go ahead."

"You developed something for the Army that takes away a soldier's will to fight by making them happy. Unfortunately, it didn't work correctly. It put Mike Sampson into a permanent coma. You, of course, feel terrible and somehow managed to get him out of the Army and into your care, and you've taken care of him all these years."

Silva's face was gray. He nodded solemnly.

"Why did the destruction of Fort Johnson upset you so much?"

"Forget it," he said.

"What!?"

"I'm asking you to forget this whole thing."

"Are you kidding me? You led me on this goose chase like some kind of Scooby-Doo mystery. And now, when I've brought back every stick you've thrown, you want me to give up on the golden egg?"

"Would you please settle on one metaphor, Miss Goldman? I'm having a hard time keeping up."

"Don't play the doddering old fool with me anymore, Dr. Silva. There's a story here, maybe a big one. You can either let me in on the whole thing, and I'll find a way to keep you out of it, or I finish the story without you, and you can go down with your ship."

"I see. This is once again my fault, I suppose. I was too reactionary. Too scared when I saw the news out of Fort Johnson. Now I'm to pay the cost for my past mistakes one more time before I die."

"However you want to look at it, Doc. You used up all my empathy. I'm not letting you off the hook."

"Very well." Silva sighed. "You have it right. I created a monster at Fort Johnson. More accurately, a monster drug. It behaved perfectly until Sergeant Sampson failed to recover from it. It took years to figure out why. When the Army gave up and kicked me out, they didn't want to destroy the remaining chemical, choosing instead to keep that monster chained up in the basement, so to speak. Stupid. Under the right circumstances, it could be disastrous."

"To whom?" Erica asked.

"To everyone. In any case, when I saw that Fort Johnson was going to burn, I was afraid the monster could get out. However, it has been a few days of quiet in the news. Most likely, everything is fine. That is why I would like you to forget it, at least until I'm dead. Then you can write your story, though I suggest a book."

"You think you merit a book?"

"Oh, I know I merit a book, my dear. The question is, will you be the one to write it?"

"Why is your army weapon such a monster? Is Mike Sampson its only victim?"

"I think before we go any further, we need to reevaluate our relationship."

"In what way?"

"I'll tell you everything. You can have your story if you can keep me out of it. In addition, you agree to hold certain facts from any other living soul, including Carl. No one must know. No matter how repugnant you find me, or the details of my story, you agree to keep them secret until I die. Or you can leave now. And before you think of publishing anyway, realize that I had you fetching sticks, as you say, because my work with the military is classified. We would both be charged with treason if we exposed it."

"I'll find a way to get around you on this story."

"If you don't mind telling me, Miss Goldman, how did you figure it out?"

"Carl heard you arguing with the administrator about Sipkomen. He heard you own Beachwood. Also, Sam Sipkomen is a terrible anagram for Mike Sampson. Why do that? Why not just give him a new name?"

"Ah," Silva smiled sadly, "vanity is my only vice. I guess I'm like the killer in a crime novel, sending notes to the police. On some level, he wants to be caught. He wants someone to know it's him."

"Are you a killer, Doctor?"

"Heavens no. Sampson is my only victim. I have been working hard to correct my mistake."

"You have been working hard on it since the seventies?"

Silva looked away, "Sadly, no. He was under the Army's care, if you could call it that, for many years. It was only relatively recently, after the triumph of Laetanol, that I found him and worked on helping him."

"So he is your regret. You went off and delivered Laetanol to the world while Mike Sampson lay like a turnip in some VA facility with rats gnawing on his toes. Now that you have achieved your goal, you've come back to fix Sampson so that you can ease your conscience. It's all about you, isn't it? It really has nothing to do with Sampson, does it?"

"Don't rush too quickly to judgment Miss Goldman. Mr. Sampson lied twice on the day he took part in the test. First, he was sick and therefore not eligible to participate. That sickness reacted with the drug and left him as he is today. To be sure, the responsibility rests with me, but I had tested the drug extensively. I could not have known that his reaction to it was even possible."

"I'm sorry, Dr. Silva. My remarks were uncalled for."

"Perhaps this would be a good time to visit Mr. Sipkomen."

"Yes," Erica agreed, "I think we should."

Silva took his cane and walked down the hall with Erica. Neither of them spoke.

Beyond the double doors, the nurse said: "I'm sorry, Miss, only family and pre-approved guests are allowed in this area."

Silva waved a hand. "It's alright. She is a cousin to Mr. Sipkomen. You can call administrator Harmon. He'll confirm it."

"That won't be necessary," the nurse said.

Erica followed Silva to Sipkomen's room. Sipkomen was wearing a johnny, his face shaved, hair combed. Erica caught Silva nodding to himself about something.

"Miss Goldman, this is Sergeant Mike Sampson, US Army, Retired."

Unaware of his surroundings, the man in the chair held his lips pressed into an eerie smile. As Erica watched, it faded. His eyes roamed under their lids as if they sought some mechanism to pry up the thin skin shroud. His right index finger twitched out a telegram on the arm of his chair. The silence in the room stretched out.

Dr. Silva gaped.

"What is it?" Erica asked.

"He hasn't moved on his own in forty years," Silva whispered, never taking his eyes off Sampson.

"Shouldn't we get someone?"

Silva ignored Erica or didn't hear her. He just stood, staring. Finally, after several seconds, Silva walked over, put a hand on the man's shoulder, and said, "Mike?"

Sampson's eyes snapped open. Pale ice water pupils searched for something... but didn't find it. The pace of the man's finger tapping on the arm of his chair increased to an urgent S. O.S. A horrible noise exploded from Sampson's unused voice box, rising in pitch and volume, "Uuuuuuuuuuuuuuuuu!"

"It's Okay, Mike. You are Okay!" Silva shouted over the din of Sampson's scream.

Sampson did not respond. His eyes darted around the room, unseeing. His scream grew louder still. "Uuuuuuuoooooooooooaaaaaaaaaaaaaaa," and a breath, "UUUUUAAAAAAAAAAAAAAAA!"

The inhuman shrieks turned Erica's bowels to soup. Her jangling nerves threatened to dump her on the floor. The hair on the back of her neck stood up. Her skin crawled. She shrunk

away. The unholy cacophony backed her into
the corner.

The duty nurse came charging in. "What the
hell is going on in here?" She looked at Silva.
"What did you do?"

"Nothing," Silva shouted.

"Get the hell out of here." The nurse hit a
button on the wall. "Room thirteen-oh-nine,
Code Yellow."

The nurse's command broke the ice in Erica's fear frozen mind. She rushed down the
hall and through the double doors. Sampson's voice did not diminish as she got further
away, as if that malevolent screaming came
from inside her. Her skin crawled across her
bones with renewed vigor as the pace of her
footfalls increased. The heels of her shoes
beat a rapid staccato, and still, the shriek
rattled her brain.

Staff members rushed past her toward
Sampson's room. Erica didn't understand how
they could move voluntarily toward that awful
sound. Sampson's mouth was the gate to hell,
unleashing demons of sound into this world.

Erica passed Silva's room without slowing
down. She had to get the fuck away from
the screaming. As she crossed the lobby, the
timbre of the screams changed. She imagined a hellish beast crawling from Sampson's
mouth and the staff killing it with sharp knives
gleaming under the fluorescent lights.

She burst through the double doors and ran
as best she could in her heels across the hot
pavement to her car. The keys in her hand
jangled like Marley's chains as she unlocked
the door. Goosebumps stood out on her arms
despite the ferocious heat. She turned on the
engine, hand on the shift lever, ready to continue her flight from the hell of Mike Sampson's unnatural howling. Instead, she rested

her forehead heavily on the steering wheel and cried.

The air conditioning in the old Toyota eventually caught up with the heat. As she cooled and calmed down, Erica concentrated on her breathing. When she was calm enough that her hands were no longer shaking, she reached into her bag, pulled out her pill bottle of Laetanol, and took one, swallowing it dry. She pulled some tissues from the big bag and wiped her face.

Sirens approached. Two ambulances pulled up in front of Beachwood in rapid succession.

Erica pulled out her makeup bag and touched up her face as two teams of EMTs rushed into the building. She applied a mask of foundation, constructing it into a psychological facade. Each stroke of eyeliner, eyeshadow, and lipstick became a layer between her authentic self and the world, mortared into place with the skill of an expert makeup mason.

A gurney bumped across the building's threshold. Erica knew it was Sampson on the stretcher only because that horrible hellish noise was still coming from his throat. Goosebumps broke out on Erica's arms all over again, and the scream, which had finally subsided in her head moments before, started anew. The EMTs loaded Sampson into the ambulance and raced out of the parking lot, sirens screaming and lights flashing. A second team of EMTs emerged from the building. The man on the stretcher waved a red book. As the lobby doors closed, they bumped the man's hand.

The book fell.

The paramedics loaded the stretcher into the truck and slammed the doors.

Bang.

Bang.

The ambulance sped away, sirens wailing.

Erica wanted to go back inside to find Carl. The thought sent Sampson's terrifying screams echoing through her head. Finally, she decided she would go home to regroup. As she pulled out of the parking lot, she turned on the radio to distract herself.

She heard this: "... the girl scouts and their chaperones are visiting Washington from Destination, Idaho with the proceeds from their cookie sales. The first girl fell ill yesterday on a bus tour of the capital. Today, two more girls and a chaperone have been admitted to the hospital. Tests indicate a massive overdose of the antidepressant Laetanol. DC police are asking anyone with information to contact them immediately. Police have refused to speculate on how the group could have been exposed to such high quantities of the drug. When asked if they thought the group had been deliberately poisoned, a police spokesperson said it was too early in the investigation to speculate. The names of the victims and their locations are not being released. The remainder of the Girl Scout troop and their chaperones have been placed in protective custody."

Erica didn't hear the rest of the news. Her mind turned this new information over and over. Fort Johnson was right outside Destination, Idaho. She remembered that from her research on Silva. If Silva was right and the Army saved his happiness weapon, and if it somehow got out, this Girl Scout story could be part of it.

When Erica got home, she called the sheriff's office in Destination. She asked if there were more of these antidepressant overdose cases. The woman she spoke with wouldn't give her any information. The silence on the line told Erica the woman was fighting to couch her words, AND she never denied that there were more cases. She *did* say that the sheriff was looking into the situation, and was far too busy to talk to her.

One thing was for sure: this story was wrapped up in Idaho, and she needed to be there. If she could get there first. Be the first reporter on the ground, she might have an exclusive story for a day, maybe two. So she called her editor, and he agreed to let her run with the story, for now. Next, she called the airline and booked herself on the next flight out. While on the phone, she packed.

The silk suit wouldn't do in rural Idaho. So instead, she went with jeans, sneakers, and a Northeastern sweatshirt. In the cab on the way to the airport, she called Carl.

"Hi Erica, how are you doing?" he asked.

"I'm pretty shaken up."

"Yeah, I heard you were there when Sipkomen, I mean Sampson, started screaming. Must have been freaky. I got there right after you guys left. Did you hear about Silva?"

"No. The way that guy was screaming... it was like the sound...happened inside my head. I had to get the hell out of there. Ran right out the door. There were two ambulances, though. Did that have something to do with Silva?"

"Yes, he had a massive stroke. Last I heard, he was still alive. But the prognosis is usually pretty bad for these things."

"I'm sorry to hear that. I had a fascinating conversation with him before we went to see Sampson. Silva wanted me to forget the whole thing. He said nothing was happening related to Fort Johnson, and that he was wrong about it."

"And what did you say?"

"In a word: no. Then he told me the entire story." Erica filled Carl in on the forty years Sampson spent in a persistent vegetative state, waiting for Silva to finish his life's work. And now that Silva was done, he was experimenting with treatments for Sampson.

"Seems like one of them worked."

"Yeah, now he's a very angry vegetable. I think Silva might be wrong about Fort Johnson. Something is happening." Erica told him about the news story involving the Girl Scouts from Destination, Idaho. "I'm on my way to the airport to hop a flight right now. Can you keep an eye on Silva and Sampson? They are important to this story, and I don't think their part is over."

"I was thinking of stopping by the hospital. I'll text you any info."

"You are the best, Carl. I'll share my Pulitzer with you!"

Chapter 12

Sarah

August 25, Bitter Butte, Montana

Sarah's truck crunched down the gravel road to her ranch turned animal shelter and pulled up next to Laura's Jeep. A few rescue horses stood lined up along the corral fence, stamping their hooves expectantly. Hungry. Laura should have fed them hours ago.

"Where the hell is that girl?" Sarah surveyed the ranch, trying to catch a glimpse of Laura working at her chores.

King, Koontz, and Dickens did not run to greet Sarah. Instead, they sat looking from her to the dog barn. Dickens yelped plaintively.

Sarah walked over to where the dogs sat, just outside the fence. Dickens panted nervously. He stood when she approached, tail between his legs. Instead of jumping up to hug and lick her, he yelped again.

In answer, the dogs inside the barn whipped themselves into a frenzy of barks and whines.

Dickens licked her hand and then paced back and forth.

"What is it, buddy?"

King and Koontz looked at her, then shifted their gaze into the barn. Sarah followed their eyes. She could just make out Laura sitting on the ground at the far end. The little red wagon they used to carry the dog food to the various crates stood beside her. Laura's shadowy form wasn't moving.

Sarah entered the enclosure and latched the chain-link fence behind her. The dogs barked from the crates that lined the walls. Their barks grew more urgent as she approached. A little white poodle licked Laura's face.

"That little guy is available for adoption," Sarah began. "You can bring him home and play with him on your own time. The horses haven't been watered and fed. And it doesn't look like you have even started in here." Sarah's anger rose with each step. "Come on, Laura, hop to it."

Laura didn't move.

"Laura?"

The teen sat cross-legged, leaning against a wooden post, her head bowed, while the little white dog licked her face ceaselessly.

"Laura!"

Thin strings of mucus and dog spit ran between Laura's face and the dog's mouth. Sarah squatted and shooed the little dog away.

"Laura?"

No response.

Sarah put a hand on Laura's chin and lifted her head. Slobber and snot made the skin slippery. Laura's eyes stared dully at nothing. A strange smile drew the girl's lips thin across her teeth. Sarah shivered. Something about the grin made her want to run. She slapped the girl lightly on the cheek several times, calling her name. Laura's chest rose and fell. Sarah felt Laura's wrist for a pulse. None. She tried again and finally found one only after her pulse rose like a rocket.

Sarah took her phone out of her pocket and called 911. The operator gave her things to do while waiting for the ambulance. She checked for trauma on Laura's body while talking to her, trying to get her to answer. The minutes ticked by, with Sarah growing more frantic at each failed attempt to rouse Laura.

Finally, she realized she was going to have to leave Laura to get her dogs locked up in the house before the EMTs got there. She heard Koontz and Dickens start barking, and she hurried to the gate. She left it open for the EMTs.

Sarah waved the ambulance down the track that led to the dog barn. Dickens trotted back and forth, barking fiercely. "All right, Dickens, that's enough. DOGS, COME," she commanded. She led King, Koontz, and Dickens into the house, shut the dog door, and then hurried back to the ambulance.

"She's in there," Sarah said, pointing into the dog barn.

The EMTs looked at each other but didn't enter. It took Sarah a moment to understand why. She automatically tuned out the noise of the dog barn, but all the commotion of fifty dogs barking crescendoed as the paramedics pulled the stretcher from the ambulance.

"It's okay. The dogs are in their crates."

The medics exchanged a dubious look, then began wheeling the stretcher through the gate.

Sarah followed them in.

The paramedics tried talking to Laura, asking her questions while they worked. They also asked Sarah whether Laura was on medication and her medical history. She didn't know. Sarah checked the teen's pockets for a cell phone and found one, but she could not unlock it to see Laura's parents' number.

"I'll drive to her parent's house to let them know," she said.

The medic nodded.

They lifted Laura onto the stretcher, wheeled it out of the barn, and loaded it into the ambulance.

Sarah watched it drive away, lights flashing. She let the dogs out, then sat on the porch bench, resting her back against the aged clapboards, fighting the urge to cry. Worry gnawed at her. Laura's smile chilled Sarah's blood. It was the sort of smile bad guys had in movies right before they killed the hero.

Sarah contemplated the trip to Laura's house. She had to tell the same people who accused her of being a dangerous lesbian that their daughter was in the hospital. To make matters worse, it had happened on her ranch. She would probably lose Laura as an employee and friend after this unless the girl had more rebellion in her than Sarah suspected.

After a few minutes of mental hemming and hawing, she stood. "Don't be a chickenshit," she said aloud, "just do what needs doing. Laura should have her family around her."

Dickens stood at her side, wagging his tail expectantly. "It would be nice to have friends along. Wanna go for a ride?"

Dickens yipped in affirmation. He ran toward the truck, then ran back to Sarah, then ran to the truck again, his black tail whipping the air so hard it made his hind end shake. Koontz appeared from around the corner of the house, his tongue hanging from his tan face, panting excitedly. He took up a position between the porch and the truck and stared at Sarah, wagging his tail. King lay on the floor of the porch.

He stood, stretched, and walked unhurriedly to her side, looking up at her with large orange eyes framed in white fur.

"Okay, gang, let's go." As Sarah walked to the truck, King sensed her nervousness and kept pace right at her side. Sarah petted his head as she strode, feeling better knowing her protection detail was with her.

Each dog had a job. Dickens, the black lab, was intelligent and excitable. He helped Sarah decipher people, an emotional barometer of sorts. Koontz, the German Shepherd, was an expertly trained watchdog. He announced the presence of humans, coyotes, other dogs, and, much to Sarah's chagrin, rabbits, cats, birds, and so on. If he sensed the approaching creature had hostile intentions (all cats were considered hostile), he did so with extreme prejudice, barking, growling, and baring his teeth. But he wasn't trained to attack, King was. King's huge hundred-pound body was a pain dispensing machine. Sarah rescued the pit bull from a dogfighting ring. It took her two years to train him, with expert help, to become a silent agent of terror. At her command, King would pounce, bite, and tear at an arm carrying anything from an assault rifle to a banana. The other important facet of King's training was that he was completely silent when working. Koontz drew the attention, and King went quietly for the kill, waiting to pounce until he heard the ex-President's middle initial, the command, "Dub-ya."

Sarah dropped the tailgate. Koontz and King leaped into their accustomed positions. There were two crates in the truck bed for rescue animals, but Koontz and King didn't require cages. They were accustomed to riding free. Sarah shut the tailgate behind them. She opened the driver's door, and Dickens brushed her aside in his rush to leap into the truck. "Excuse you, dude, you act like you haven't been on a ride in months."

It was a twenty-minute drive to Laura's house. The day was perfect, sunny, and mild, but Sarah didn't enjoy it. She slowed when she got to Laura's street, looking for the faded red plastic mailbox among the trees on the heavily wooded roadside. Her truck climbed the driveway's steep incline slowly so that the crates in back wouldn't slide and squash Koontz and King. The house was nice enough, if suburbia was your thing. The split-level ranch was white with green shutters and some railroad ties holding the grassy hill from spilling into the driveway.

When Sarah got out of the truck, Dickens came with. As soon as he was on the pavement, he started whining. "What is it, buddy? What's the matter?"

Dickens paced back and forth next to the truck, his tail pointing at the ground. "Stay," she said to Koontz and King. She walked across the slate paving stones and ascended the concrete stairs to the front door. Dickens whined behind her, refusing to come up the steps.

She pushed the sickly yellow light of the doorbell and heard the faint chime inside. No response. She waited, then pushed it again. No sound inside apart from the bell.

Dickens whined more insistently, crisscrossing the gray stones, turning and doing it again.

Giving up on the doorbell, Sarah rapped her knuckles on the door until they hurt. She'd parked behind two drivable cars. Somebody had to be home.

"Mr. and Mrs. Baker, please open up. Laura is sick!"

Still no response from inside. The stink of burning food reached her nose. She stood on the steps for a minute, waiting for a response. None came. She banged on the door again. The burning scent grew too strong for Sarah to ignore. She walked to the back of the house. The stench became more intense. Wisps of smoke escaped out of the window by the back door. She banged on the white metal frame of the screen door. The smoke thickened. Sarah wanted to go in and make sure everything was okay. But she didn't want to get shot, which was a likely scenario in this part of the world. "Hey, it's Sarah Sampson, Laura's boss. Something is burning! I'm going to come in!"

Sarah opened the door.

Dickens didn't like this turn of events. He barked at her from the safety of the lawn. Koontz and King trotted into view and up the back steps, drawn by Dickens's urgent barking.

Sarah felt as naked as a newborn, but letting her protection detail into the house might worsen a bad situation. She pushed the little metal tab on the screen door piston into place, blocking it open. "Stay," she said.

The dogs sat on the porch.

Inside, black smoke curled from the edges of the oven door. An old woman sat at a table pushed up against the wall just feet from the smoking oven. Between her fingers, a cigarette burned down to the wrinkled papery skin. Ashes fell onto the print of her floral house dress. The woman slowly lifted her head. She wore the same eerie smile Laura had in the barn.

"Hi," the word escaped the woman's lips as if drawn reluctantly from a drunk—slow, slurred.

"Your dinner is burning," Sarah said.

The woman turned her head slowly. "The... smoke is... pretty," she said, as if from a dream. Then she looked down at the cigarette between her fingers. She laughed. "It... doesn't... burn."

Sarah followed the woman's gaze. The glowing cherry smoldered between index and middle fingers. As she leaned over, she heard the woman's flesh sizzle. "Let's put this out," Sarah said. There was no way to grab the stub of the filterless cigarette without burning herself, so Sarah grabbed the ashtray from the scarred wooden tabletop and held it underneath. Sarah spread the woman's hand so the butt would drop into the tray. It stuck to the woman's finger, still burning.

"Jesus!" She grabbed the exposed sliver of unburned tobacco and pulled it down. The butt came away from the woman's flesh and fell into the ashtray. But the cherry of burning tobacco clung to the inside of the woman's skin.

"What the fuck!" Sarah's stomach turned. She flicked the burning lump with her fingernail, dislodging it and sending it down wide of the ashtray to smolder on the lap of the old woman's house dress. There, it burned its way through the fabric and into the woman's thigh. The old woman just smiled that weird smile and said nothing, unflinching.

"Oh, come ON!" Sarah yelled. She grabbed a mug half full of coffee from the table and poured it on the burning fabric. The dress turned brown around the black spot of the extinguished tobacco. Coffee ran in brown rivulets down the housecoat, her along the pale, spotted shin, and formed tan pools on the white linoleum.

"I'm sorry," Sarah said, though she wasn't, really. "Is there someone else home with you?"

It took several seconds for the woman to answer. "Why... yes."

"Who is home? Where are they?"

The woman just continued to smile, then said, "You're pretty."

"Okay," Sarah said, "Let's just turn off the stove." She did, then looked into the next room. A man and woman who looked like they climbed out of the American Gothic painting sat watching TV.

"Hello!" Sarah called.

They did not move.

"Hey! Laura is sick! Dinner is burning! The woman in the kitchen has third-degree burns!"

No response.

Unwilling to approach the couple without backup, Sarah called the dogs. King and Koontz were on her heels in an instant.

She walked across the worn carpet and stood in front of the couple. The same macabre smiles painted their faces. Mucus ran down from their noses, across their lips, and dripped from their chins.

"HEY!" she shouted.

Neither gave any sign they were aware of Sarah. She thought about slapping them the way she had with Laura, but was loath to touch them.

Back in the kitchen, Sarah took a cigarette from the old woman's pack on the table and lit it. Then she called 911.

After the call, Sarah waited outside and smoked another filched cigarette. She hadn't smoked in ten years, but this day was so unbelievably weird, she needed the calm.

Three ambulances came. When the first arrived, she loaded Koontz and King into the back of her truck so they wouldn't scare the EMTs. Sarah answered a few questions from the paramedics, and Laura's family were loaded into the ambulances. Through the reflections of overhanging trees scrolling across the rear glass, Sarah could see the face of the old woman, covered with an oxygen mask. Then

the ambulance turned, and was swallowed by
the trees.

She crushed her cigarette out on the pavement.

A police car pulled into the driveway.

Chapter 13

Carl

August 26, Washington, DC

Carl entered the room at Abraham Lincoln Memorial Hospital to find that Dr. Silva and Mike Sampson shared it. Each man sat propped on an inclined bed. Each was wired to machines. Heart monitors beeped into the otherwise heavy silence. An astringent smell with just a twinge of the ubiquitous, musky, old man stink assaulted his nose.

Sipkomen wore restraints, his wrists and ankles fastened to the bed rails with leather cuffs. He looked at Silva and repeated an unintelligible phrase over and over: "Umma geeoo." When Carl entered, Sampson eyed him, grunted, then turned back to Silva and continued his chant. "umma geeoo."

Carl wasn't sure how to address the man. Whether to use Sampson or Sipkomen. He decided on Sipkomen for the moment since Sampson couldn't yet speak for himself, and his identity remained a secret except for Erica, himself, and, of course, Silva. "Mr. Sipkomen, I wasn't on your ward much, but I helped care for you once in a while. I just want you to know that I'm glad to see you awake and talking."

"Umma giwim," Sampson said.

"Fantastic," Carl said. "It has been a long time since you spoke. You are coming along fast. My advice is don't rush it. Don't get frustrated. It will come."

"Umma giwim," Sampson said again, jerking on his restraints. He had no real muscle mass to speak of. The electrostatic treatments he received at Beachwood did little more than keep his muscles from atrophying completely. In Carl's estimation, Sampson lacked the strength to lift so much as a glass of water. When he pulled on the restraints, he could barely draw tight the strap that held his wrists to the bed rail. Carl questioned whether the bonds were even necessary, but he supposed the staff didn't want Sampson trying to get up and falling out of bed. It was difficult to gauge the man's mental capacity, but Carl could swear there was rage in Sampson's eyes. The way he looked at Silva gave Carl the creeps. Could Sampson possibly know or remember who Silva was?

Carl drew the curtain between the beds so he didn't have to contend with Sampson's disquieting stare. Then he took the chair next to Silva. "I saw your chart outside the door. That was a nasty stroke. Can you speak?"

"Mmmmppphhh," Silva said.

"Can you understand me? Can you nod?"

Silva tilted his head slightly to the right, not quite a nod.

"Was that a nod? Can you do it again?"

After a moment, Silva did it again.

"Very good, Dr. Silva," Carl said. "It's going to take some time, but I'm betting you'll recover nicely."

Silence.

Carl didn't know what else to say. He wanted to tell Silva that Erica had told him everything. He wanted to say that he found Silva's experiments on Sampson not only highly unethical but morally reprehensible. Silva's arrogance had cost Sampson forty years of his life. In Carl's mind, Silva was a modern-day Dr. Mengele. Whether or not Silva was a monster, he dared not say so for fear of causing the old man another stroke. The next stroke would most likely finish him off. More probably, Silva wouldn't understand him. There was no way to tell Silva's level of cognitive function. Carl guessed after a stroke like that, Silva wouldn't be reading Plato.

Still, Silva was alive and working to communicate. If Erica was right and something was going on, there might be a need for the secrets locked away in Silva's head. Carl hoped that head wasn't too damaged to get the secrets out again.

Carl talked about the weather. He talked about starting his internship at this very hospital next week. After he exhausted all the small talk he could muster, Carl said goodbye and put a hand on the curtain between Silva's bed and Sipkomen's.

"mmmm-mmmm" Silva grunted emphatically.

"You want me to leave this closed?"

Silva tried to nod.

"Okay." Carl couldn't blame him. Sipkomen/Sampson gave him the willies. Carl poked his head around the curtain that masked Sampson from view. "Goodbye, Mr. Sipkomen. See you soon."

Sampson didn't look at Carl. Instead, he stared daggers at the curtain. "Ummma gi-wim," he said, tugging on his restraints.

Carl went home to an empty apartment. Brian was in Greece. He got a glass of wine and sat down to watch a little TV. The telephone interrupted his channel surfing. Carl muted the TV and answered. "Hi, babe!"

"Hi, chocolate bar," Brian answered.

"How's Greece?"

"Shitty. I'm coming down with a cold or something. Hell, the entire crew was coming down with something. I'm not sure they're going to let us fly tomorrow."

"I'm sorry, babe, that sucks." Carl sang quietly, "I want you here with me, not way over in the land of Greece."

"Were you just ripping off a Cake song?"

"Yeah, not only do I love that you get me, but I love that you know what songs I'm doing. I miss you."

"I wish you were stuck in Greece with me!"

"Me too!"

There was a long pause, then Brian said, "I feel exhausted and out of it. I think I'm going to sleep for a while."

"Okay," Carl said, "get some rest and feel better. I love you!"

"Love you too!"

Carl was about to put his phone down when he remembered he was supposed to text Erica about his visit to the hospital, so he did. A few minutes later, she texted back: "checking into a fleabag motel. Will start poking around tomorrow. Thanks for the update. Interesting. Keep me posted. TTYL." Carl finished his wine, turned off the TV without watching anything, and went to bed early.

Carl had no trouble falling asleep, but Sampson's screams haunted his dreams. Sampson's eyes turned blood red in the dream, and his screaming mouth featured rows of jagged, pointed teeth. He spoke in some strange language that sounded like the nightmare tongue of hell itself. "Uuuummmaaa ggggiiiiwwweeeuuuu!"He chased Carl down the dark halls of an abandoned hospital. Occasional flickering lights lit filthy, buckled floor tiles and moldy walls. Sampson caught him with a strong, clawed hand and spun him around. Nose to nose with the screaming nightmare Sampson, he gagged on the nightmare's dead-bird breath. "Ummmmma gggi-iiwwwwweeeeuuuuu!" Then, Sampson stood there. "Dr. My Eyes" by Jackson Browne played from Sampson's open mouth.

Carl opened his eyes and realized that the song came from his phone. The ringtone for work-related calls was "Dr. My Eyes." He accepted the call.

"Hello?" he said, his voice thick with sleep and residual terror.

"Is this Dr. Parks?"

"Yes," he said. He rubbed a hand over his face.

"Are you alright?" The woman on the phone asked.

"Just watching a horror movie," he said.

"No, I mean, are you physically alright? Are you feeling ill at all?"

"Yes, I mean no. I mean, I'm fine. Who is this?"

"Oh, sorry, it's Jane Lawson from A.L. Memorial Hospital. We need you to come in. You're sure you're well?"

"Yes, I'm fine."

"No one in your household is ill?"

Carl thought about Brian, but Brian was fine when he left yesterday or today. Carl realized he had no idea what time it was. "No."

"Good. Come in right away. Make sure you have your ID. Don't take public transportation or make contact with anyone."

"I don't have an ID. I don't start until next week."

"Tell security when you get here. We'll get you fixed up."

"Why are you calling me in a week early, in the middle of the night?"

"They're calling it smiling flu. Get here as soon as you can."

"What? Is it localized to DC? What is the infection rate? Mortality?"

"I have a lot of calls to make. Turn on a radio or TV while you get dressed." The line went dead.

When Carl hung up, he checked the time—3:30 AM. Carl went around the apartment, throwing things into a backpack, toothbrush, toothpaste, deodorant, hair pick, a few pairs of boxers, and a few other things. He rarely wore scrubs at Beachwood, but he had a tan pair lying around waiting to be returned, so he threw those on.

On the way to the hospital, Carl turned on the radio. This is what he heard. "... along with the Vice President and several members of the Cabinet. The West Wing has been 'crashed' or locked down since ten PM when the President fell ill. The President and several members of the West Wing staff were moved to the National Military Medical Center.

"The disease is being called the smiling flu and, as of this hour, is being reported in several countries worldwide. At this time, here's what we know: the smiling flu seems to have a rapid onset of symptoms. It presents as a mild case of the flu, then in twenty-four to forty-eight hours, the patient becomes catatonic, and this is the strange part. The patients all seem to smile. In a few moments, I'll be joined in the studio by NPR's medical correspondent Doctor..." Carl turned the radio down as he tried to find a parking space in the staff lot.

The masked and gloved security guard shooed him away. Carl argued...and lost. No credentials. No parking. He got the last space in the patient lot, way out at the far end.

At the entrance, security stopped him again. It took Carl several minutes to get *this* masked and gloved security guard to call someone to verify that Carl was supposed to be there. He was issued a temporary ID and finally allowed to enter.

A few steps down the hall, an orderly stopped him and had him put his personal effects in a sealed plastic bag. Then he was made to scrub in and don Level 3 protective gear: gown, booties, surgical mask, face shield, and two pairs of gloves which the orderly taped to the sleeves of Carl's gown. Afterward, the orderly told him to go through the double doors and report for his shift. A crooked sign taped to the door read: STOP! LEVEL 3 PPE REQUIRED BEYOND THIS POINT!

Past the doors—barely controlled pandemonium. Patients sat in wheelchairs lining the halls, some coughing and sneezing into surgical masks, some smiling strangely, with mucus running down their faces. Hospital staff, dressed out as he was, bustled about.

A nurse yelled at a crowd of shouting people. "Patients only! Everyone else please leave the hospital for your own health and safety!"

The waiting room chairs stood stacked in the corner. In their place were more rows of wheelchairs and a few gurneys, all with patients either grinning or wearing masks. Some had IVs. Most didn't.

"Hey, what are you doing standing around?" A haggard-looking nurse asked. Her straight black hair was sticking up at crazy angles, and her eyes were streaked with red.

"I, uh, I just walked in."

"Is this your first day or something?"

"First minute, actually."

"How are you at placing IVs?"

"Okay, I guess."

"Good. Come on. Oh, and welcome aboard; now it's time to dig in."

Chapter 14

Erica

August 26-27, Idaho

Erica landed in Boise and, while in line at the car rental place, checked her phone. A text from Carl about visiting Silva and Sampson appeared. She responded, sending her thanks and a request for updates. The key she got at the desk fit a little red sub-compact. Erica sat in the lot and entered directions to Destination on her phone. On the outskirts of town, she pulled into a truck stop with a little diner to satisfy her rumbling stomach.

The dawn's pink light made even the cracked parking lot beautiful, outlining the long shadow Erica cast as she walked toward the diner. Erica hugged her thin maroon sweater to her bosom in the chill morning air.

Two servers tried and failed to service the whole place. Erica waited. At last, a waitress in a fifties-style pink uniform came over.

"I'm sorry about the wait," the server said. "We have a few servers out."

Erica pondered the vagueness of that statement. She suspected the waitress had stopped herself from finishing the sentence with "sick."

Erica ordered eggs, toast, and coffee. While she waited for her food, she planned her next moves. There was a hotel across the highway. A little family-owned place, by the look of it. It was called the Sleep Titan Motel and featured a large gray mythic-looking statue of, presumably a titan, standing arms and legs akimbo, staring down at the freeway. According to the maps app, it was the only place to stay in this little country crossroads town. Erica figured she'd check in, find a café, or ask her hotel clerk where people gathered. After that, she'd try Ft. Johnson to see what was what. Erica's meal was passable but, unfortunately, free of gossip, since the servers were so busy.

After breakfast, she drove to the Sleep Titan, entering the parking lot by driving through the splayed, paint-peeled legs of the enormous gray statue. In the office, an elderly woman leaned over the counter, reading the paper. The woman smiled and drew a pen from her tightly drawn gray hair bun. She pushed the paper aside and slid a clipboard to the center of the counter. "Good morning," the woman said through a set of yellowed dentures. "Would you like a room?"

"Yes, please," Erica said, smiling back.

They went over the price. Erica signed the guest sheet on the clipboard, slightly uncomfortable knowing that the pen had been stuck in the old woman's hair. Erica wasn't a germaphobe, but the story was making her question everything. Who'd touched the pen? The clipboard? The door handle?

"So, what brings you to the sleepy little town of Destination?" The woman asked as she peered at the ledger through a pair of thick black-framed reading glasses she plucked from the beaded chain on her chest.

"Well, I'm a reporter here on a story."

"Oh? A reporter? Here in Destination? Things are getting stranger and stranger. Are you a TV reporter?"

"No, newspaper, the Washington Voice."

"Oh, I've heard of that one. They made a couple of movies about that paper. I liked the one with Robert Redford. He's a hunk. What story are you working on? Can you tell me, or is it a secret?"

Erica smiled. The woman seemed bored, lonely, and chatty—perfect. Maybe she wouldn't need to chase gossip in town after all. "I'm working on a story about some sick Girl Scouts that came from Destination, poor things." Erica's addition of "poor things" was deliberate. She didn't want to come off like a vulture circling someone else's tragedy.

"Yes, it's awful. I feel so bad for the families."

"What's your name? I'm Erica."

The woman smiled. "I know. You just signed the register. I'm Marlene. I used to wear a name tag, but it poked holes in all my blouses."

"Do you know the families?" Erica asked. She hoped her bluntness wouldn't cause the woman to clam up.

"Yes, a couple. In fact, I used to babysit the father of one of the sick girls. It's so sad. First, his daughter got sick with that thing while she was visiting Washington, then his wife got it. Poor Ed."

"His wife too? That's awful."

"Yes, she worked right at that truck stop over there. Then last night Emily came down with it right in the middle of a prayer vigil."

"Emily?"

"She's the hostess over there at the truck stop."

Erica's stomach churned. She'd just eaten there. Eggs with a side of virus? "Oh, my goodness! Are there a lot of people getting sick?"

"No, just the Girls Scouts, Jamie, and Emily."

"Jamie?"

"Yes, Jamie Hargrave, she's Ed's wife, the one I told you about."

"That's terrible."

"Yes, it must be awful for him."

"Do you think he'd talk to me?"

"I don't know. He's in a bad way right now, I'm sure."

"I'd like to try," Erica said.

Marlene leaned on the counter with both elbows, cradled her chin, and tapped idly at the side of her nose with her pinky finger. "I hope you have thick skin. He probably won't talk to you. He can be pretty prickly." Marlene lifted one elbow and made a drinking motion with her hand.

Erica nodded. "I can handle it. Can you tell me how to get in touch with him?"

"Well, I'd like to help, but there's kind of a hitch. I don't want my neighbors bothered too much, and I definitely don't want them to know I sent a reporter after them. I've got to make a living in this town. Business is bad enough. Maybe a mention of my fine establishment in your newspaper story could help." Marlene smiled and winked.

Erica was used to this kind of ask. She found it refreshing that Marlene had come out with it directly instead of wasting time beating around the bush. She gave her stock response. "I promise to write a complimentary mention of the Sleep Titan in my story, but there is no guarantee the editor will leave it in."

"I suppose that would be good enough," Marlene said. "You promise not to tell Ed how you found him?"

"I always protect my sources," Erica said. "If I didn't, no one would talk to me. That's the kiss of death to a reporter."

"Alright then. I'll draw you a map to the Hargrave place."

"Terrific."

Marlene drew a map on the back of a blank ledger sheet she pulled from the back of the stack on the clipboard.

Erica thanked Marlene, took her key and map, and went to her room to freshen up. As she showered, dressed, and put on her makeup, Erica thought about what to do first. Her impulse was to see Ed Hargrave, but she wondered if that impulse wasn't just a hangover from doing human interest stories for so long.

She decided to go to Fort Johnson first, since it was closer than the Hargrave place. As she drove, she tried to clarify her thinking regarding what she expected to get out of visiting the burned-out military base. She doubted there was some discoverable relic of Dr. Silva's work. Still, she had to see for herself.

From miles away, Erica saw the large, irregular black patch of burnt forest on the hills that met the farmland on the east side of town. She turned onto the access road to Fort Johnson and found herself in a landscape that looked like hell itself. Tall black sticks that were once trees rose from the soot-stained earth in all directions. Flames had burned away the branches, leaving behind jagged nubs like the stumps of amputated limbs. Nothing moved. No birds, no animals, just death. Erica's hope of finding anything useful sank into the blackened ground.

Two miles from the main road, Erica came to a gate and gatehouse, both new and unmarked by fire. Behind the gatehouse, two big army trucks squatted in the dirt next to a large camouflage tent. Affixed to the gate, a sign read: *MOPP Gear Required Beyond This Point.*

As Erica approached, a soldier in camouflage fatigues stepped out of the guard shack and held up a hand. She stopped the car and rolled down the window.

"Ma'am," the soldier said, "this is a restricted area. Turn your vehicle around and leave immediately."

"Why? What's going on?" Erica asked.

"All inquiries should be addressed to the public affairs officer." The woman took a card from the pocket of her fatigues and handed it to Erica.

"I'm a member of the press," Erica said, reaching for her shoulder bag. "I've got my credentials right here."

"Put your hands back on the wheel right now!"

Erica turned. The soldier had her hand on the butt of her gun.

"Jesus!" Erica put her hands back on the steering wheel.

"Ma'am, I say again, turn your vehicle around and leave the area."

"Okay, okay—shit!" She did a three-point turn in front of the gate and drove until the guard house disappeared in the rearview mirror. Then she turned the car again, so it faced the direction of the gate and pulled onto the crunchy, blackened shoulder.

Once Erica got her breathing and heart rate under control, she assessed what she'd seen. The new gate. The large tent. If everything had burned, why bother with tents and gates?

Then the sign: *MOPP gear required.*

Erica had no idea what the hell MOPP gear was. She took out her phone to look it up. No service. Strange, since she was only two miles from the main road.

Was someone jamming the signal...?

Paranoid much?

Engine sounds coming from the direction of the gate interrupted her thoughts. Erica rolled down her window and held up her phone. The sound grew very loud. It must be an enormous truck. She held down the picture button as the giant truck passed, snapping frame after frame. The men driving the truck were wearing gas masks and hoods. The truck pulled a long trailer. Something the size of a brontosaurus lurked under an olive drab tarp. A Humvee followed the truck. Its driver, masked and hooded, turned towards her. Erica put the phone down and jammed the shifter to *Drive*. No sense in waiting to see if the convoy radioed the guard house about her.

Once the trucks were out of sight, she turned the car around and went back the way she came. She drove slowly, rummaging in her shoulder bag for the map Marlene had drawn her. Her phone chimed when she entered the approximate address (Marlene had not included a street number), and Erica's jaw dropped when the map came up. The car rumbled, the right tire thumping on the blackened dirt shoulder. Erica corrected her trajectory. Son of a bitch. The address was right outside Fort Johnson, across a wide stretch of farmland.

The pieces snapped into place. It started with the out-of-control fire. Rather than spend enormous resources to save a base that was closing anyway, the Army accelerated the closure. Then, something happened at the base that would make the Hargrave's sick and necessitate the use of MOPP gear, whatever the hell that was; probably the hoods and gas masks she had seen the truck drivers wearing.

The thing she wasn't sure of, the thing that didn't fit—the smiling flu was biological. Yet Silva worked strictly in chemistry. But Silva knew this could happen. He had been so upset by the Fort Johnson fire he had to be sedated. So...the reason he knew it could happen was because it had already happened. It happened to Mike Sampson.

For a moment, Sampson's screams echoed in her head. Her flesh crawled, and the hairs on the back of her neck prickled. She shook herself. Sampson was coming around. Why now? After all these years? Silva must have found the key to the Sampson problem.

Could Silva's posited antidote also be the key to this outbreak? Was the smiling flu related to Fort Johnson? If not, it was a pretty fucking big coincidence.

But there was a good possibility that whatever was happening with the Girl Scouts and the women at the diner could easily be something completely unrelated to Dr. Anthony Silva and Mike Sampson. If Silva's monster was still locked away on that base, who knows what else they might have kept up there—what else might have gotten out?

Erica turned the car onto the gravel track that led to the Hargrave farm. Half a mile down, the old farmhouse and barn came into view. A man, probably Ed, sat on the porch. He sipped from a mug.

She pulled up next to the battered blue pickup. As she opened her door, the man on the porch called out.

"This is private property, lady. Go away!"

"Mr. Hargrave, I'm Erica Goldman from the Washington Voice. Can I have a moment of your time?"

"Unless you've got a plane ticket to DC in your pocket, I'm not interested."

"Sir, I have some information about your wife and daughter. Give me two minutes. I will tell you what I know and won't ask any questions. After that, if you still want me to leave, I will."

"First, you wanted a minute of my time. Now you're asking for two." He sighed and took a sip from the mug, and judging from his demeanor, Erica doubted it was coffee. "Alright, speak your piece."

She walked to the plank steps leading to the old whitewashed porch, stood in the dirt, and delivered a rushed monologue about Silva, the base, and Sampson.

Ed went quiet, then threw his mug across the porch. Both silence and ceramic shattered on the old plank floor. "Those sons of bitches!" His face screwed up, and he covered it with his hands, head bent, elbows on knees.

Erica shifted her weight and found something else to look at.

The strap from her heavy bag bit into her shoulder.

"Why not me?" he asked after a minute. "It makes no sense. Why am I not sick? I'd rather be sick instead of sitting here in purgatory, unable to see them, hold them, or even know what's wrong with them."

"Mr. Hargrave, I need to call the Army. See what they have to say. And I have a contact who can update us on Sampson and Silva."

"I don't give a shit about them."

"I know that might not mean much to you. But if Silva gave Sampson something that brought him around, maybe it can help your family, too."

"Okay then," he lifted his head to look at her, "you'll need to use the house phone. Your cell won't work out here."

Erica followed him into the house.

He offered her a cup of coffee, which she accepted. She sat down at the kitchen table and dialed Dr. Carl Parks. The call went straight to voicemail.

Chapter 15

Carl

August 27, Washington, DC

The phone vibrated in Carl's pocket. There was nothing he could do about it. His cell was buried under layers of protective clothing. The suit was supposed to be breathable, but Carl was sweating like a fat man on a treadmill. He wheeled a patient to the front doors of the hospital. A red line of tape crossed the floor just before the doors. Outside, an orderly sprayed the patient with sharp-scented disinfectant from a tank on his back. The patient, the wheelchair, tires, and all, were doused with the stuff. Carl watched from behind the sliding glass double doors as another orderly wheeled the patient down the walkway and into the closest of two massive military tents that now stood in the hospital parking lot. One tent for those infected with the smiling flu, and the other for quarantine.

"Dr. Parks," said a muffled voice behind.

"Yes," he said, turning around.

A short man with dark eyes and dark-rimmed glasses behind his face shield frowned at Carl. The sharpie scrawled across the chest of his level three biohazard suit read *Dr. G. Parez*

"How long have you been geared up?"

"I don't have any idea, Dr. Parez. What time is it?"

Parez looked at the clock. "A little after one PM."

"Of course. Sorry. It's my first day. I don't know where all the clocks are. But, um, I've been geared up for five hours this time."

"That was the last patient on this floor. The decontamination team is already halfway through the ER. Anyway, you are well above the maximum recommended time in a level three area. Gear down and take a couple of hours off. Your time starts when you finish doffing the suit."

"Thank you, Dr. Parez," Carl said.

At the loading dock, he stood behind a line of red tape at the door. On the other side, a queen-size white pad bed lay on the concrete. It was divided into four numbered squares by wavy black marker lines.

A masked and gowned woman stood by the pad. She wore a sprayer on her back and held the wand at the ready. "Have you been through the doffing process yet?"

"Second time," Carl said.

"Good. Follow my instructions. Lift your left foot and hold it up. When I tell you, place it in the first square."

Carl did what the woman said. She sprayed down his left boot.

"Place your left foot in the first square."

Carl did. Now he stood straddling the threshold awkwardly.

"Lift your right foot," the woman said.

Carl lifted his right foot, wobbling dangerously. The sweat, the gear, and the fatigue piled up on him, pulling him down.

"Place your right foot in the first square." Once his feet were both in the first square, the woman knelt down, unzipped his booties, and held them in place. "Carefully step into the second square," she said. As Carl lifted his feet and set them in the second square, the woman held his booties so that they stayed in the first square. Carl stood still while she pulled the tape securing his outermost layer of gloves. Then she removed the gloves and dropped them into a red biohazard garbage can behind her. "Now lift the flaps of your hood, touching only the inside by pinching them between your thumb and forefinger. Do not remove your hood yet." Carl did as instructed. The woman unzipped his suit and peeled it down his body.

It took about twenty minutes for Carl to go through the whole doffing process. By the time he stepped off of the fourth square in sweat-drenched scrubs, all he could think about was how badly he needed to urinate. And how thirsty he was. "Thank you very much," Carl said.

"You're welcome, Doctor. There are fresh scrubs and a restroom in the receiving area straight ahead."

Carl went into the receiving area and immediately noticed the doors to the rest of the hospital were sealed with plastic and red biohazard tape. Piles of scrubs sat on the table, arranged by size. Carl grabbed a pair and went into the restroom. After using the toilet, he stripped and gave himself a sponge bath with damp paper towels before dressing.

Outside in the area where trucks usually backed up to the dock, a folding table held drinks and snacks. Carl downed two sports drinks and grabbed a third to sip. Doctors, nurses, and other personnel rested in plastic lawn chairs. Carl didn't know any of them. He found an empty chair and collapsed into it.

It was several minutes before Carl remembered his phone had been buzzing in his pocket earlier. There were three messages. The first was from Beachwood Assisted Living Center, probably wondering where the hell he was. He skipped that message without listening to it. The second was from Brian. If Brian was calling, that meant he wasn't allowed to fly today. He listened to it. Brian was sick. He'd be sequestered at his hotel in Greece until he felt better.

Carl's stomach churned. Brian might have the smiling flu. How had this thing had spread so fast? Carl tried to call Brian back. The call went to voicemail.

Carl left a message. He told Brian how much he loved him. And that he had started at the hospital and would call back when he could. He would have said more, but as he spoke his message, he looked up and saw a sign taped to a concrete pillar that read:

To avoid public panic, NO social media posts, NO communications regarding the smiling flu or urging evacuation or self-quarantine. THESE ACTIONS WILL COST LIVES.

After he left Brian the voicemail, he looked at the third message. It was from Erica. She wanted an update on Sampson and Silva. Carl pinched the bridge of his nose. He was too tired to give much of a crap about Sampson and Silva. Still, he owed Erica a call. He was the one who brought her into all of this.

"Hi, Carl," Erica said, answering the call. "How are you?"

"I'm exhausted. I started at the hospital last night. I'm on a break. What's up?"

"I thought you weren't supposed to start until next week?"

"They called me in at three AM. I'm not allowed to talk about it."

"Does it relate to my story?"

"Yes."

"You have to tell me!"

"When was the last time you turned on the news?"

"Not since I left DC."

"Holy shit, Erica, how can you be a reporter and not turn on the fucking news?"

"I'm on a hot story. I don't care about what else is going on. I called because I was looking for an update on Sampson and Silva. I wanted to tell you that I'm with Ed Hargrave. His daughter was the first of the Girl Scouts to get sick. His wife has also been hospitalized for the same sickness here in Idaho."

"Where are you?"

"At his house, why?"

"Are you fucking crazy?" Carl shouted at the phone. Several of the resting staff looked his way. He turned so they couldn't see his mouth and walked to the most isolated corner of the loading dock. "Erica, this thing is airborne, it can live on surfaces for weeks, and it has transmission rates that make Ebola look like an ice cream social. You are walking around in a petri dish full of flu virus right now. Get the fuck out of there! Then wash thoroughly. Then do it again. Call me tonight and let me know you're Okay."

"What about Silva and Sampson?" Erica asked.

"Will you forget about that for now? Get safe and turn on the fucking news, okay?"

"Okay, Carl."

Her voice had a condescending tone that made Carl think she wasn't taking him seriously. "I'm not fucking with you, Erica. This is serious. Get out of there."

"I will, I promise."

"Good. Call me later and leave me a message that you're okay."

"Will do, Carl. Bye."

"Bye." Carl slipped the phone back in his pocket. He had no idea what was on the news, but he was sure that the army tents in the parking lot must feature prominently.

Carl tried to call Brian again, and again he got Brian's voicemail. He left another message. He took a sip of his sports drink, sat in an uncomfortable plastic lawn chair, leaned his head on the concrete wall behind him, and fell asleep.

Chapter 16

Erica

August 27, Destination, Idaho

Erica told Ed the gist of her conversation with Carl. They went into Ed's living room and turned on the TV. The screen showed helicopter footage of army tents in a parking lot. The banner at the bottom of the screen said: *Abraham Lincoln Memorial Hospital, Washington, DC, smiling flu, now at 500 cases worldwide, with 106 reported in the US.*

"Holy shit!" Erica said.

A siren sounded outside the house.

"What the hell?" Ed walked to the window. "This is not good."

"What is it?" Erica joined him, peeking out through the curtains. A Humvee and an ambulance stopped in the driveway. Two soldiers exited and stood outside the truck in baggy suits with hoods and gas masks, just like the soldiers she saw at Fort Johnson. "Shit."

Ed stepped onto the porch. Erica followed him. The sun glared off the soldiers' gas masks, obscuring their faces. Two people in white suits with face shields emerged from the ambulance. They had blue gloves taped to the ends of their sleeves, making them look vaguely alien.

One figure in white stepped forward. "I'm Fred James. I'm a contact tracer for the CDC. Are you Ed Hargrave?"

"That's right."

"Who is that with you?"

"You just drove up onto my farm, blasted your siren in my driveway, and now you are giving my guest and me the third degree? What do you want here?"

"I'm Erica Goldman for the Washington Voice," Erica called out.

Ed glared at her.

She shrugged. "It might help."

The white-suited figures looked at each other. The one who identified himself as Fred James spoke again. "Is this your first contact with Mr. Hargrave, Miss Goldman?"

"Ye—" her voice caught in her throat. "Yes, it is."

"I'm afraid you have both been exposed to a dangerous and highly contagious pathogen. You need to come with us."

"Why?" Ed asked.

"You have been exposed—"

"You already said that. So, you want to quarantine us, is that right?" Erica asked.

"That's correct, Miss Goldman."

"How long is the quarantine?"

"Two weeks," James said.

"There is no way we can be in quarantine for that amount of time. I have deadlines, and Mr. Hargrave must attend to his crops."

"I'm sorry, I really am," James said, his words muffled by his protective suit, "but you don't have a choice."

"I'm not going," Ed said. "I'm going to Washington to see my daughter."

"Actually, you do have a choice," the soldier yelled through his gas mask. "You can take a moment to gather a few personal items and come with us, or we are going to dart you with a tranquilizer gun and throw you into the ambulance. Either way, I can tell you this: I'm about done standing in the scorching sun in this gear."

"Okay," Ed said. His shoulders slumped.

"No choice?" Erica said.

"Not really," James said.

"Okay."

"I'm going to grab a couple of things," Ed said. "I'll be right out."

"Be quick," the soldier said.

Ed disappeared into the house.

"Miss Goldman, if you'll come with us," James said.

"I need to get my bag," Erica said. She went into the house to retrieve it. When she came back out, everyone stood in silence, waiting for Ed. He emerged from the house after a few minutes with a small backpack.

"Okay," the Army man said. "Each of you step off the porch, take ten paces, place your bags on the ground, then step back to the edge of the porch."

"Why?" Erica asked.

"So we can ensure neither of you is bringing weapons or illicit materials into quarantine."

"That's an illegal search," Erica said.

"Lady, this is the procedure. Please stop messing us around and comply. It is for everyone's safety," the soldier said. "All we are looking for is weapons. If you want to bring in a pound of heroin, that's fine by me. But I have to confiscate the needles. Now, can we get this over with? It is hot, and I'm done talking."

Erica and Ed did as instructed.

The soldier who hadn't spoken walked over to the bags, inspecting each one. Then he rose and nodded to the other soldier.

"You may pick up your bags. Go to the ambulance," the first soldier said.

Erica and Ed picked up their bags.

The first soldier took a spray can and sprayed the gloves of the soldier who had checked their bags.

"Can I ask one question?" Erica said to the soldier.

"What?"

"That stuff you are wearing, is it MOPP gear?"

"Yes."

"What does it stand for?"

"That's two questions. It stands for Mission Oriented Protective Posture."

"Thank you," she said.

The soldier just looked at her through his gas mask. "Get in the ambulance, lady," he said.

Erica got into the ambulance, and Ed followed. James got in behind them and closed the doors.

"Mr. James, what is a contact tracer?" Erica asked.

James looked up from his clipboard. "It is a very literal title. I trace the chain of contact from person to person. For instance, from Mr. Hargrave's wife to her coworkers at the truck stop and so on. I need to ask you some questions now," he said. James grilled them for the entire ride to the quarantine facility. He asked who they had contact with, and when. Did they feel ill? Had they been in contact with anyone who was? Question after question.

When the ambulance came to a stop, the driver got out. He opened the rear doors and motioned Erica and Ed forward.

Erica stepped into a world she never expected to see except in movies. The whole hospital parking lot was cordoned off with barriers that looked like bicycle racks. Inside the perimeter, there were three huge army tents. Each could hold hundreds of people. Soldiers with machine guns patrolled the perimeter. Two white-suited figures, the same suits that James and the ambulance driver wore, stood at a table outside the nearest tent.

"Go see the folks at the table. They will check you in," James said from inside the ambulance, then added, "good luck."

"You—" Erica began, but the doors slammed shut before she could finish. "—too."

"Name?" the woman at the table asked, her voice muffled behind a faceplate.

"Erica Goldman."

"Got ID?"

Erica dug around in her shoulder bag and then handed her driver's license to the woman.

"Any medical issues or special needs?"

"No."

"Medications?"

"Laetanol," she said, slightly embarrassed.

The other attendant reached under the table and pulled out a wristband with Erica's information on it. "Wrist, please."

Erica held out her left wrist, and the man put the bracelet on it.

"Step to the side and wait for the nurse."

Once Ed had his wristband, another white-suited figure emerged from the army tent behind the table. She held out a pair of white surgical face masks. "Hi, I'm Nurse Ahern. Please put these masks on and leave them on at all times." She waited while Erica and

Ed put their masks on. "Good. Thank you. The smiling flu differs from other influenza strains in that the incubation period varies widely, from as little as forty-eight hours to about ten days. We don't know a lot about this new strain yet. So our quarantine period is two weeks. If you test negative for the smiling flu in two weeks, you are free to go."

Erica could tell from her tone she'd given the speech too many times. The woman's green eyes dart from her to Ed and back behind her face shield.

"We will enter the quarantine tent in a moment. I will assign you a bed. Around your bed is red tape on the floor. Do not cross the red tape except to use the lavatory. If you need to use the lavatory, wait until the center aisle is clear, then follow the yellow tape line on the floor. Keep ten feet between yourself and everyone else at all times. Do not touch anything outside of your red tape area. I can't stress that enough. Please refrain from posting on social media or the internet. Meals are at eight AM, twelve PM, and five PM. Lights out at ten PM and lights on at seven AM. Questions?"

"What about showers?" Erica asked. She couldn't see the woman's mouth behind her surgical mask, but she saw the woman's cheeks rise in a smile.

"We're working on it, hopefully, tomorrow."

"This is just getting better and better," Erica said.

"I need information about my wife and daughter. They are both infected. I want them to hear my voice. I thought that might help," Ed said.

"Oh my goodness, are you the Mr. Hargrave? I'll do my best to help you with that."

"What do you mean the Mr. Hargrave?" Ed asked.

"You're Jamie Hargrave's husband, Aella's father, right?"

"Yes," Ed looked puzzled.

"I'm sorry. Please follow me," Nurse Ahern said.

Ed folded his arms across his chest. "Not until you explain what you meant by the Mr. Hargrave,"

"I'm sorry," Nurse Ahern said again, "it's just that you have the unfortunate distinction of being both the father of patient zero and the husband of Patient One."

Ed nodded, and Erica could see tears in his eyes.

Nurse Ahern led them inside the large green tent. It smelled of antiseptic, old fabric, and body odor. Probably because there were no showers. Fifty beds lined each side of the tent, each with a red tape box around it about the size of a prison cell. People of every description sat or lay on the first several beds.

Erica passed a dark-skinned pregnant woman, crying, elbows on her knees, face in her hands. On the other side, an elderly woman with fine clothes and lots of costume jewelry sat reading the Bible. A Latino man in a suit and tie paced back and forth in the next bed area, muttering under his breath.

"Okay, Miss Goldman, this is you, number seventeen, and you are right next door, Mr. Hargrave, number nineteen. A nurse will be along to bring you some water and comfort items in a few minutes. She will also draw some blood. Okay?"

Erica looked down at the rows of empty beds beyond hers. "Why is it so empty?" she asked.

"Well," Ahern said, "the tents were erected last night. The CDC contact tracers have only been on the ground for a few hours. So I'm pretty sure we will be full up by nightfall."

Ahern turned and walked back the way she came.

Erica sat on the scratchy green-blanketed cot. "Well, this sucks." The best thing to do, she decided, was to focus on her job.

She dug out her laptop, stealing glimpses of Ed's crying face down on his cot, then turned away, giving him what little privacy she could.

The number on the card she'd been given at Fort Johnson had a Washington area code. Erica took out her phone and dialed. The person who answered, rattled off some jargon she couldn't quite make out, then said: "How can I help you?"

"I'm Erica Goldman with the Washington Voice. I want to know what is going on at Fort Johnson."

There was a pause. Then the voice said: "We are doing some cleanup at Fort Johnson after the fire."

"If you are doing routine cleanup, why have you expanded the perimeter of the base, erected a new gate, and require MOPP gear inside that perimeter? Was there an accident involving a hazardous substance?"

"I'll have to get back to you."

"You've got half an hour to comment. After that, I'm filing my story online."

"Will do. Goodbye."

"Hey!" she yelled into the phone.

"Yes?"

"If you are going to call me back, don't you want my number?"

"Yes, of course, Miss Goldman."

She gave the guy her number and then hung up. Next, she called her editor and filled him in on the events of the day.

His reply was terse, as always. "You still need the connection between Silva's work, the military, and the smiling flu. I can't run with hazmat suits at the base and the Hargrave family's illnesses. This thing is global now."

"Yes, but the Hargraves are patient zero and patient one. That's got to count for something?"

"It does, but we don't have it cold. With a story this big, with the implications it carries, we need ice-cold facts, not circumstance and supposition."

"I have this. I know the truth," Erica said with more confidence than she felt.

"You don't have it, and you know it. It doesn't matter what is true, it only matters what we can print, and right now, we can't print this story. Get the connection confirmed. In the meantime, use your time in quarantine with the father of patient zero to get an exclusive. Then write that story."

"Okay," Erica said. She exhaled, and her shoulders sagged.

"And Miss Goldman?"

"Yes?"

"Stay well, then get the hell out of there, okay?"

"Okay, Boss," she hung up.

Chapter 17

Sarah

August 28, Bitter Butte, Montana

Sarah woke before dawn. She lay in bed with her eyes open, wishing for sleep but knowing it wouldn't come. After a while, she gave up and fumbled a pot of coffee together. The clock above the kitchen table ticked into the silence as she sipped. Dickens lay on the floor next to her, his dark fur lost in the predawn shadows.

Laura's awful smile grinned at her out of the darkness. She kept returning to that old woman, the cigarette singeing her flesh away as she laughed. The stink of scorched food and burning fingers filled her nose. The horrid grinning faces of Laura's parents looked at her from the couch in her mind's eye. Mucus dripped from their gin-blossomed noses, past rotten teeth and cracked lips, collecting in their chin wrinkles before dripping onto soiled clothes.

Koontz barked in the living room. Dickens perked up his ears and gave a half-hearted "woof."

"What is it, guys?" Sarah asked, glad for the distraction. Then Koontz started barking like a junkyard dog. That could mean only one thing: company. Sarah looked at the clock. "Who the hell is coming down our road before five in the morning?"

Koontz ran outside. King was right behind him. Sarah smiled as the oversized pit bull wiggled his girth through the dog door.

She took her coffee with her and stepped out onto the porch. Might as well join the party.

The sheriff's truck and an ambulance were racing up the dirt track to her house. Both had their flashing lights on. Just what she needed to start her day.

King slipped into the tall grass by the side of the road. Koontz stood in the middle of the driveway. Dickens stayed by her side, his flank pressing against her knee.

The floodlights came on as the sheriff's truck stopped a respectful distance from Koontz. The sheriff got out and stood behind the door. He wore a white cloth face mask and rubber gloves. Not good. Koontz continued to sound the alarm vehemently, barking himself raw.

"Hello, Sarah," the sheriff called.

"Isn't it a little early for an unannounced visit?"

"Oh," the sheriff said. "Is there ever a good time for an unannounced visit. What time would that be, exactly?"

"State your business, Sheriff. I have a long day ahead of me."

The sheriff sighed. "You and me both. What say we try to make this next part as pleasant as possible?"

"What. Do. You. want?"

"You keep talking to me that way, and I'm liable to get the impression you don't like me."

"Seriously, what do you want, Ralph?"

"I'm here to take you to quarantine."

Sarah crossed her arms. "I'm not going."

"I'm not asking you if you're going. I'm telling you. You're going. Sarah, you were exposed to one of the nastiest flu bugs anyone has seen in a long time. What's more, you were exposed four times in one day. Go to quarantine for your own sake and everyone else's. We can't risk you getting anyone else sick."

"I feel fine, thanks."

The sheriff pinched the bridge of his nose. "This is serious. There are about a hundred confirmed cases across the US. That number is climbing fast. No one knows exactly what we are dealing with yet. In the meantime, we have to isolate anyone who has come into contact with the infected, and we have to do it *now*."

Sarah frowned. "It doesn't get more isolated than this ranch. I'm fine here."

"Why do you have to make everything so difficult?"

"Stop talking to me like I'm a kid, Ralph."

"I'd appreciate it if you'd call me Sheriff when I'm working."

Sarah opened her mouth to respond, but closed it when two figures emerged from the ambulance. They wore what looked like space suits. Sarah couldn't make out their faces through the darkness of their hoods. The figures each carried white hard plastic cases.

"What the hell are they all about, *Sheriff*?"

"They are here to take some samples. Also to provide any care you might need... and take you to quarantine."

Sarah put a hand on her hip. "No way."

"This isn't a choice," the sheriff said. "We have to stop the spread of this thing."

The white-suited figures started moving towards Sarah. Their white boots kicked up small puffs of driveway dust into the glare of the floodlights. Koontz started barking again, and Dickens joined in.

"That's far enough, gentlemen," Sarah said.

Their heads tilted down slightly to look at Koontz. They didn't stop, though, which surprised Sarah. Koontz looked scary, like only an angry, growling German Shepherd can. Everyone stopped, always, until these two. "It would be a shame if my dogs tore a hole in one of those nice white suits, and you fellas got cooties."

The suited figures halted, then turned toward the sheriff.

"Don't look at the sheriff, guys." Sarah was enjoying this a little too much. "He doesn't know the command to call off my dogs."

"Miss Sampson," the sheriff began, "I'm authorized to use any means I deem necessary to get you into quarantine and get the samples we need. To tell you the truth, I'd like it if I only had to use my voice for that. But don't think for a second that I won't use force just because we are... friends."

"Dogs, quiet!" She needed to think. The tough girl act only went so far. The guys in the white suits scared the shit out of her. It wasn't the suits themselves but their necessity that made the danger real and drove the icy spike of fear through her heart. "Who's going to care for the animals? How long would I be in quarantine?"

"Up to two weeks," came a muffled voice from one of the suited figures. Sarah couldn't tell which.

"Uh-uh, no way. Lots of these animals have special needs. And now that Laura is sick, I'm the only one who can do it."

"Miss Sampson be reasonable—" the sheriff began.

"No. You be reasonable. All these animals need to be cared for. In two weeks without care would kill them." She paused, considering. "What about a voluntary home quarantine?"

The sheriff looked at the white-suited figures. A muffled conversation followed. Sarah was too far away to make it out.

"Are those the only motor vehicles on the ranch?" The sheriff asked, indicating the pickup and the jeep with a sweep of his hand.

"Yeah, just the truck, actually. The jeep is Laura's."

"I'm going to disable them for the duration of your quarantine. These folks are going to take some samples. You will do as they say and give them your full cooperation. If you need anything from the grocery store or the feed store, you call me personally. There will be police tape and quarantine signs at the end of your driveway. You understand why we're doing this, right? If you leave here, it is possible you could infect the whole town. Do you understand? We are talking life and death here."

"I got it." She leaned against the corner post of the porch and folded her arms across a faded AC/DC t-shirt. One denim-clad leg crossed the other. The toe of her unlaced boot stuck in the dirt, a flagpole of defiance. The leaning and the crossing hid trembling hands and shaking legs.

One of the white-suited figures approached her. The glaring floodlights obscured the face, but a muffled feminine voice said, "Let's go inside so that you can be comfortable while I draw some blood."

Sarah sighed. Resigned. Maybe this would help Laura. "Okay." She turned toward the house, then stopped. She should call off her pit bull before the dog decided the guy in the white suit was a threat after all.

The sheriff, still behind the door of his truck, stood talking to the other white-suited figure.

"King, come!" Sarah called.

The big dog bloomed out of the tall grass like a man-eating flower. He'd been hiding in the weeds only a few feet from the talking men.

The sheriff's hand dropped to the butt of his gun.

White suit turned to see what the sheriff was looking at. When he saw King, he stepped back and bumped into the sheriff.

Sarah chuckled as King trotted to her side. She held the door for the woman, then took a seat in the kitchen. The woman set her white case on the worn wood table and opened it.

"Sarah, I'm Dr. Jane Willis. I'm with the CDC."

"Hi," Sarah said, "normally I'd offer you a drink or something, but..."

Through the faceplate, the woman's dark hair clung to the sides of her face. Beads of sweat stood out on her brow and trickled down the washboard of crow's feet to the terminus of her pointed chin.

Dr. Willis chuckled, "No thanks, Sarah, but it is kind of you to offer." She paused, appeared to listen to something, and hit a button on a little box at her waist. "Stand by," she said. "My colleague, Dr. Clark, would like to know if it's safe to enter the barn closest to the house to take some samples."

"Yes," Sarah said. "All the animals are in their crates."

Dr. Willis relayed the information into her headset. "Okay, Sarah, I need to draw some blood. I'm also going to swab the inside of your nose and ask you for a saliva sample.

"Okay," Sarah said. She gripped the knees of her jeans with white knuckles. "How bad is this thing, Doctor? Is it an epidemic? What is the mortality rate?"

Dr. Willis spoke to Sarah as she took her samples. "There are over one hundred cases in the US right now, mostly concentrated in Idaho, Montana, and Washington, DC. All we know is that this is a new strain of flu. The first case was reported four days ago. The good news is, at this point, the mortality rate is zero as long as the patient is hospitalized within the first twenty-four hours. The bad news is that all reported cases are in a persistent vegetative state and show no signs of recovery."

Dr. Willis paused, then hit the button on her belt pack. "I'm almost done with her. She'll be out in a minute." She finished drawing blood and put a small gauze pad on Sarah's arm. Next, she removed the cap from a small bottle. It had a swab attached to the lid. With no warning, Dr. Willis jammed the swab up Sarah's nose. Willis sawed the damned thing back and forth like she was trying to get at the other nostril the hard way. The moist scratchy intruder stank of astringent and stung like a swarm of bees.

"Ow, damn it!" Sarah rubbed her nose when Willis removed the stick.

"Sorry, I know that's uncomfortable." She gave Sarah an apologetic half-smile, but her eyes showed something else.

"Are you scared?" Sarah asked.

Willis hesitated. "The thing is—"

"Don't lie to me. Tell me. Are you scared?"

Dr. Willis busied herself with something inside the case that Sarah couldn't see. "We train for these kinds of events all the time," she said without looking up. "You focus on the task in front of you. You rely on your training—"

"Are. You. Scared?"

Willis continued working in the case.

"Look at me!"

The doctor met Sarah's eyes.

"Are you scared?"

Willis sighed. "Yes." A thin film of fog inside her faceplate obscured her features for a moment.

"Thank you." Sarah said, "What are you scared of?"

"I'm scared that the virus could be everywhere, anywhere. I'm scared we won't be able to stop it. I'm scared that I won't be there for my family."

A tear rolled down the woman's face and dripped onto her faceplate. "Shit, I'm sorry. We're not supposed to talk to patients like this," Willis said. She bumped her helmet with a green-gloved hand before realizing there was no way to wipe the tears. "Shit," she said again.

"So only a hundred cases and the CDC is out quarantining people? Doesn't sound so bad." Sarah said it under the pretext of calming the doctor, but really, she was trying to reassure herself.

The doctor locked eyes with Sarah, her face ashen. "The genie is out of the bottle. This flu has an incubation period of two to ten days. An infected person is contagious before they show the first symptom. Patient zero flew to Washington. Everyone on that flight was exposed. What did patient zero touch at either airport? Did she go to the gift shop? Take a shuttle bus? Eat at a restaurant? The flu virus can live on some surfaces for weeks. Everyone on her flight, everyone who touched the same things she did, at the airports could incubate billions and billions of virus particles. And then they spread the virus... all this before the first sneeze.

"The hundred cases we have now are mostly the weak and immunocompromised. Next week there could be ten thousand cases. And then a million. But really, we are just guessing. We are talking about it like it was a regular flu, which it isn't. You've seen it. This isn't the regular flu." Dr. Willis stopped talking. She closed her case and rolled her shoulders. "I'm sorry for sounding off on you like that. This is very stressful for all of us. I'd appreciate it if you didn't say anything about this conversation to anyone."

Sarah swallowed. "Yeah."

"Did the Baker girl work here every day?"

"Yes."

"And did she have a cold or flu symptoms before the day you found her?"

"Yes." Sarah's denim-clad knee stitched the air.

"How long before? Do you remember?"

"I don't know, a few days maybe."

"Chances are, if you were going to come down with it, you'd feel it by now. Are you having any symptoms?"

"No."

"Then you'll probably be fine." The doctor's eyes betrayed the lie.

"What happened to honesty?"

Willis ignored the question, but her hands shook as she closed the case. "Okay, I have the samples I need from you. I'd like to take some samples from your home: doorknobs, light switches, faucets. Things like that. Okay?"

"I guess," Sarah shrugged.

"Would you mind showing Dr. Clark where you found Miss Baker?"

Everything Dr. Willis said swam around in Sarah's head. Phrases like "persistent vegetative state" and "incubation time" moved back and forth across her consciousness like a reciprocating saw, cutting into the last of her calm. Her internal panic rose a notch when she stepped onto the porch. The hood of her truck and the hood of Laura's Jeep were up. Dickens brushed against her thigh, and she patted him absently.

"Miss Sampson!" the sheriff called from behind his car door. It was hard for her to hear him. The dogs in the barn were barking themselves into a frenzy. "I'm sorry, but I took the distributor wires from both vehicles. We just can't risk you leaving the ranch. I hope you understand."

Sarah looked at him for a long moment, trying to decide whether she was angry that he'd disabled her truck, or grateful he'd agreed to let her stay. Let it go for now. Business. Help the CDC people help Laura. "Is the other guy in the barn?"

"Yes," Sheriff MacFarlane said, "he's waiting for you."

Sarah walked to the open gate. She frowned, stepped through, and closed it. Inside, she found the other doctor swabbing the handles on the slop sink. "Hey, Dr. Whatsis."

"Clark," came the muffled reply.

"Right, Dr. Clark. I found Laura over here." Sarah went to the post Laura had been sitting against... was it only yesterday? Jesus. Yesterday when she woke up, everything was normal. Today, the world was going to shit.

"What was she doing when you found her?" The man asked.

"Drooling," she said. His brusque manner brought out Sarah's defensive side, a side she was much more comfortable with than her scared shitless side.

Clark fixed her with a dry look she couldn't miss even through his faceplate. He said nothing, then squatted down and took his samples.

Sarah pictured Laura slumped against the post, a little white dog licking her face. She didn't remember putting the dog in a crate afterward. In fact, she had no recollection of the dog at all after finding Laura. "Shit."

"What?" Dr. Clark asked.

"She had a dog with her when I found her. A little white poodle. I don't know what happened to it."

"What do you mean, you don't know?"

"With all the confusion... the 911 call... the EMTs... I don't know what happened to it."

"Miss Sampson, it's urgent that you find that dog and quarantine it."

"I understand."

"I want to make sure you do," Clark said. He put the last sample in the case and snapped it shut. "That dog probably won't get sick. The virus likely won't affect canines, but it most certainly has the virus all over it."

In her mind's eye, Sarah saw the dog licking strings of mucus from Laura's face. "I understand. I'll find him."

"If it comes into contact with an uninfected person—"

"I said I'll find him." Sarah was embarrassed and ashamed that she'd let the dog get away. It was unprofessional. Still, finding Laura like that, one of the few other people on earth she actually gave a shit about, really messed with her head. All the confusion, fear, and worry led to one little dog getting out. She could be forgiven for that lapse, couldn't she?

She led Dr. Clark out of the barn and shut the barn door, muffling the barking dogs.

Dr. Willis stood in the driveway waiting for them.

"Miss Sampson, I left my card on the table," Willis said. "I'd like you to check in three times a day. Please contact me if you show even the slightest cold or flu symptoms."

"Okay," Sarah said. Dickens nuzzled her thigh again. And again she stroked his head. He always knew how she was feeling, and she was grateful.

"Sheriff," Clark said, his voice muffled through his faceplate, "the Baker girl was found with a white poodle. The animal escaped amid the activity associated with the EMTs removing the girl. We have to find it."

"You want me to put out an APB... on a poodle?"

"A small white poodle," Dr. Clark clarified, as if that made it less ridiculous. Then, to Willis, he said, "Let's get these samples loaded up."

Dr.s Willis and Clark stepped onto the grass, giving the sheriff a wide berth. The suits flashed dazzling white as they passed in front of the cruiser's headlights. The knee-high grass made soft shushing sounds under their vinyl-booted feet.

A high-pitched bark erupted in the darkness. A small white shape launched from the field and latched onto Dr. Clark's leg.

"WHAT THE FUCK!" Clark yelled. "It's biting through my suit!" He swung the sample case at the dog and missed. "God damn it!" He kicked, shaking the animal loose.

BANG!

The dog dropped.

Blood gushed from its head.

It didn't move again.

"NO!" Sarah screamed.

The sheriff stood unmoving, his smoking pistol trained on the animal.

"It ripped my suit!" Clark yelled.

"I'll get the Betadine." Dr. Willis said. She was already moving toward the back of the ambulance.

"You shot him! You... you just shot him!" Sarah's voice was shrill. King, Koontz, and Dickens were at her side.

"Yes, I did," the sheriff said. He still had his pistol trained on the dog.

"Why did you have to shoot it?" Sarah yelled.

"A potentially highly infectious dog was attacking a health official. It had to be done."

Rushed toward Clark carrying a quart-sized bottle and a packet of something. She handed it to Clark and then held out her hands. Clark poured the dark liquid over Dr. Willis's gloved hands, and she worked the stuff in, turning her gloves almost black in the predawn dimness. Then she began smearing the liquid all around the tear in Clark's suit. She tore open a packet, doused the gauze she pulled from it with the liquid, and rubbed it all over Dr. Clark's leg.

"That was some shot, Sheriff," Clark began, "right in the hea — OW!"

"Sorry," Dr. Willis said as she worked the disinfectant into his leg.

"Lucky shot," the sheriff said. "I was aiming for center mass—the chest." He finally lowered his gun.

"Doesn't look bad," Dr. Willis said. "Let's get you in the truck so I can patch you up."

"What about the dog?" The sheriff said.

"We'll bag it up and take it with us. I want to see how this bug affects pets, check its viral load, etc.," Dr. Willis said.

Willis and Clark turned. Before walking away, Clark kicked the dead dog, hard. Its body jiggled with the force of the blow.

"Hey!" Sarah cried.

"YOU!" Clark shouted. "Your negligence may have cost me my life. My life! And you're pissed because I kicked the dead dog that probably just killed me? Screw you, lady!"

"C'mon," Dr. Willis said, grabbing Clark by the arm. "Let's get you in the truck." Together, they walked to the back of the ambulance.

"I'm sorry about the dog, Sarah," Sheriff MacFarlane said. "I really am." He holstered his pistol. "I had to."

Sarah sat down heavily in the middle of the driveway, tears running down her cheeks. "What the fuck is going on? Why is this happening to me?"

Dickens licked the salty drops from her cheek. King sat between Sarah and the sheriff.

"I'm sorry," Ralph said again. "I hate to see you like this. You're like a daughter to me. But this is happening to all of us. You're not alone."

"The fuck I'm not. You can't come near me. You're over there hiding behind a surgical mask and a car door. The CDC people have to wear space suits. Laura's gone. Feels pretty fuckin' alone. The thing is, alone was Okay. I wouldn't have found Laura or her parents if I'd been alone. This would all be some shit I saw on the news. It was better when I was alone." She buried her face in her hands. There was a good chance she was a dead woman.

"I'm sorry, Sarah," the sheriff said a third time.

"Yeah, well, me too." She said from behind her hands. Dickens rested his head on her shoulder and whined softly. Koontz stood so close to her side that his flank touched her arm.

Dr. Willis appeared from behind the ambulance with a black bag. She rolled the dead dog into it. Its crimson blood was dark on its white fur. She closed the bag. "I'm sorry about all this, Miss Sampson. I truly am."

"I—" Ralph started. Then, "I'll check on you later."

The ambulance and sheriff's truck backed down the driveway. Then Sarah was alone with her dogs. She sat in the middle of the driveway as twilight crept across the plains. When she moved her hands away from her face to wipe her tears, her eyes came to rest on the dark patch of gore in the grass and the bloody gauze next to it. Sarah didn't rise from the dusty track until the sun crested the distant horizon.

Chapter 18

Carl

August 31, Washington, DC

Carl woke disoriented. He stared up at the ceiling tiles with the little black holes in them. The on-call room. The bed shook as someone climbed into the lower bunk. Carl eased himself down and shuffled off in search of coffee. He rubbed the sleep from his eyes as he shambled down the hall. The windowless hall's analog clock gave no indication whether it was day or night.

"STOP!" someone shouted from behind him.

Carl froze and turned toward the voice.

A nurse stood just outside one of the patient rooms, looking at him. "Watch where you're going," she said. "That's a yellow zone now. That hallway is contaminated. Someone tripped, carrying a tray of samples. They're cleaning it up now."

Carl's eyes dropped to the floor. His foot straddled a yellow line of tape running across the corridor. Ahead, plastic sheeting covered the hall, sealing it. "Thank you."

In the cafeteria, he ate an egg salad sandwich that tasted so much like cellophane he wondered if he'd remembered to unwrap it. He washed that down with dark bitter liquid from the coffee dispenser, which bore more resemblance to crude oil than coffee.

Full, unsatisfied, and a little disgusted, he decided to check in on Silva and Sampson. On his way, he tried to figure out what day it was. He worked eighteen hours on and six off, but couldn't remember how many times he'd bunked down in the on-call room.

Another patient lay where Silva had been. On the other bed lay Sampson. His hollow eyes looked through Carl, rather than at him. The skin on Carl's arms prickled, and his breathing quickened. The man's icy stare made him feel like running from the room. There was darkness behind Sampson's eyes. Carl stared back, trying to pin it down. Define it. Reduce what was wrong to clinical terms. He wanted to give the feeling of horror a scientific name attributable to some condition. But as he stared, the shadow vanished like a monster in the closet when the lights came on, leaving only a vague menace.

"Ummmm nnnaaaaattt sss-ssssam, uummm mm-aaawwkkk!" Sampson raised his fist off of the stark white hospital sheets, then punched the bed in frustration. His face was red, and his lips curled into a malevolent down-turned crescent. "Ummmm Mieeekkkkke."

It took Carl a moment to puzzle out what Sampson was trying to say. He put it together in his head: 'I'm not Sam. I'm Mike.'

"I'm going to help you fix that," Carl said. "I know about Silva, and I know what happened to you. Right now, I think it's happening to the rest of the world. Do you remember me? From Beachwood?"

"mmmuuuww,"

"I'm not surprised. You probably weren't even aware of Beachwood. Well, I helped care for you there. I'm not actually on your care team here," Carl said, "but I'm going to help you get your identity straightened out. Your speech is coming along remarkably. You're doing much better than I expected. Mike, it's good to see you doing so well. I'm going to check in on Dr. Silva now."

Sampson's eyebrows drew down in the middle, and the malevolent sneer returned. "Um guwa kiwim. Um guwa kiwim! Um guma kiwim!" Sampson shouted over and over.

Carl dashed from the room and leaned on the wall outside.

A nurse rushed down the hall. She looked at Carl accusingly, then darted in.

He stayed put, trying to regulate his breathing. Regain his professional composure. Shake off the willies.

The nurse emerged a few minutes later. She fixed him with a stern look from under thick, unkempt brows. "What the hell was that about?"

"I helped care for him and Dr. Silva at the nursing home. I just stopped by to check up on them."

The nurse's attitude changed, and she leaned in toward Carl. "There's something not right with that one," she whispered. "Did you mention Silva to him?"

"I mentioned I was going to look in on him," Carl whispered back.

The nurse motioned Carl over to the nurses' station, but she still whispered. "He wants to kill Silva. That's why we moved Silva to another room. Any time anyone mentioned Silva's name, or the curtain was open, and he could see Silva, he started shouting. It took almost a week for his speech to be intelligible. You said you helped care for Sipkomen and Silva at the nursing home. Do you know what this beef between them is about?"

"I have pieced together some of it," Carl said. A thought struck him—so obvious it embarrassed him not to have seen it sooner.He'd been so buried in the day-to-day grind, he hadn't looked up in what—days?He had to find the chief of medicine or the CDC guy on site and tell them what he knew. Immediately.Maybe someone with real authority could force the military to acknowledge a link between Silva's work and the smiling flu.And if they couldn't? Then every minute he kept quiet, more people might pay the price.

"I'm sorry, there's something urgent I must attend to," he said and started toward the elevators.

"If you don't want to tell me, you could just say so, Doctor!" The nurse called after him.

The Chief of Medicine's door stood open. Inside, a thin-lipped, thin-boned redhead of about sixty sat behind a large ornate, carved wood desk. A middle-aged bald, bespectacled man sat behind a cheap pressboard desk, plopped haphazardly at the far end of the room with a hand-lettered sign taped to its side reading CDC. It featured a telephone whose cord ran like a tripwire across the carpet to the wall outlet.

The chief of medicine, Dr. Stephenson, was in a heated conversation. "I don't give a good God damn! If you don't get them here by sundown, I'll call a press conference and throw you to the wolves!" She looked at Carl suspiciously as she listened to the other end of the conversation. She neither invited him in nor dismissed him. "Let me do the math for you," she said. "I've got three hundred and fifty patients on four liters a day. They should be on six to eight liters a day. That means I'm burning through fourteen hundred units every twenty-four hours, and my patients are still dehydrated. All I can do is barely keep them alive. AND the number of patients is growing by the hour. Now get those IV bags, NG tubes, and OG tubes over here." She listened, red-faced. "I don't care what everyone else is going through. Patients will start dying if I don't get those supplies! Get them here! Now!" She slammed the phone down. Her eyes turned to Carl. "What do you want?"

"I have something to tell you. It may seem far-fetched, but please hear me out."

"First, who are you?" Stephenson said.

"Sorry, I'm Dr. Parks. I started here four days ago."

"Why the hell are you bothering me, then? Talk to your resident, or the attending, or someone, you know, closer to your level." She looked down at the papers on her desk.

"You're going to want to hear this. So is the CDC."

She looked at Carl and frowned. Then she glanced at the CDC man. He had his phone to his ear and was writing furiously.

"You have one minute to convince me this is worth listening to."

Carl looked at the CDC man.

"Never mind him. If he needs to know, I'll fill him in," Dr. Stephenson said. She looked at her watch. "Go."

Carl told her about Sampson, Silva, and Fort Johnson. Then that Fort Johnson bordered the farm on which patients zero and one lived. Next, he talked about the nature of Silva's work and Sampson's coma. Then, finally, Silva's efforts, now successful, to wake Sampson.

"So," Stephenson dropped her pen. "This thing might be connected to Fort Johnson, and this Silva might have a treatment if it is, but Silva had a stroke?"

"Yes."

"Where is he now?"

"Sixth floor?"

"In this hospital?"

Carl nodded.

"Come with me." She turned to the CDC man. "Dr. Singer, hang up the phone and come with me. We may have something here."

The CDC man looked surprised. He stood up, the phone still to his ear, and said, "I'll call you back."

"Tell him what you just told me," Stephenson commanded as they walked to the elevator.

Carl repeated his story for the CDC man as the elevator beeped and rattled its way to the sixth floor. He finished just outside Silva's room. Dr. Stephenson and Dr. Singer examined Silva while Carl stood by the door. Silva mumbled or nodded in response to some of their questions, but not all.

Stephenson said nothing to Carl when they finished. They simply walked down the hall to Sampson's room. They examined Sampson, asking him questions to which he mostly didn't know the answers. He mumbled responses with lips, tongue, and teeth that had long ago forgotten how to speak and struggled to learn again.

Stephenson marched to the nurses' station when they were done, with Singer and Carl trotting along behind. "Gather your people here right now," Stephenson called to the head nurse.

The nurse did. A few minutes later, they stood in a silent semicircle.

"Listen up, people," Stephenson barked. "Two patients on this floor, Sampson, and Silva, may have information on the smiling flu. Silva is post-stroke and non-verbal. We need him to talk. He may have successfully treated the other patient, Sampson, for the smiling flu or something like it. We need Sampson to fill in the blanks. I want a complete workup on Sampson. I mean everything, any test you can dream up, run it. I want to know what happened in his body, in his brain, in his breakfast! I want everything tested, from dandruff to toenails. These two men are the key to solving this thing.

"Now, we can't have the flu up here. We can't take any risks with these two. As of now, this entire floor is under quarantine. I'm going to get as many other patients out as I can. Specialists will be consulting via video chat. These two patients are your highest priority."

Stephenson turned to Carl. "Dr. Parks, you are on this now. Get me the treatment Silva used on Sampson, or you will never leave the sixth floor again, and neither will they. Normal recovery time for a stroke like Silva's is eighteen to twenty-four months. I need Silva reciting the Gettysburg address by tomorrow. Get to work, all of you!" She turned and walked back towards the elevator with Dr. Singer. Carl was going in that direction and overheard their conversation.

"How high in the government can you get?" Stephenson asked.

"My boss can get pretty high up, I think," Singer answered.

"Start working that end of it," Stephenson said.

Carl wondered if the CDC man resented being ordered around.

"We need to know what was done to Sampson at Fort—what was it?" Stephenson asked.

"Johnson," Singer supplied.

"Right. If that's where the extra virus protein came from, maybe we can reverse engineer a treatment or vaccine."

"Yes, that was my plan," Singer said. "You know, you're less like a doctor and more like a steamroller."

"I know. I made my peace with it a long time ago." Stephenson replied.

Chapter 19

Sarah

September 6-7, Bitter Butte, Montana

Sarah sat on the porch as Mike from the feed store unloaded sacks of oats, kibble, birdseed, and groceries. He set everything down in the driveway, a safe distance from her house.

"Never delivered people food before," Mike said. He wiped his forehead with the sleeve of his blue work shirt, then adjusted the white mask that covered his nose and mouth. "The paper sacks are dry goods. The plastic bags have the refrigerated stuff. You must be in pretty good with Mrs. Werner. This isn't what we do," the man called to Sarah.

"Yeah, must be," she said absently. Her eyes followed him as he put the rails back on the end of the truck. But she didn't really see him. Instead, her attention focused inward. In her mind, the sheriff shot the poodle. Again.

And, again. She shook herself. "Hey, Mike," she called as he walked towards the truck's cab.

He turned. "Yeah?"

"How bad is it? In town, I mean. I've been watching the news, but Bitter Butte doesn't get any coverage."

He walked back and stood near the groceries. "It's bad, Miss Sarah. They turned the high school into a hospital. If someone in your house is sick, you go to the cafeteria. If you've already got 'the smile,' they put you in the gym."

"Are there a lot of people there?"

"I'm not. That's all I know. The town is pretty deserted. You don't see people walking around; if you do, they're wearing gloves and masks. The hardware store sold out of both. Hell, when I go out in public, I wear my Ma's pink dish-washing gloves. I feel like a damn fairy."

"Shit," she said. "Thanks. Take care, stay well."

"You do the same. See you next week."

"I'll be done with quarantine by then."

"Well, see you when you get out." He got in the truck and drove away. A cloud of dust marked his wake.

Sarah rolled her two-wheel ranch cart, an oversized wheelbarrow with gray wooden sides, up to the pile of supplies. She loaded the groceries and pulled the cart up to the porch step. As she put away the groceries, she imagined all the families locked away at the High School. Their houses not quite empty.

When she finished putting the groceries away, she called the police. A recorded message played: "We are experiencing high call volume. Please stay on the line. Your call will be answered in the order it was received." It took fifteen minutes for her to get the operator. When she did, she asked for Sheriff MacFarlane.

"I'm sorry, the sheriff is very busy. Do you have an emergency?"

"Not exactly. Can you pass along a message for the sheriff to contact Sarah Sampson as soon as he can?"

"Okay, regarding what, exactly?"

Sarah knew that her thing would be near the bottom of Ralph's to-do list. But she also knew that if she made something up, he would see through it, and she would get nowhere. Best to tell the truth and rely on their personal connection as a motivator. "Saving the animals," she said.

"I'm sorry?"

"Just please tell him that."

"Okay, goodbye."

Sarah went back outside and spent an hour hauling the supplies for her rescue animals to the barns and enclosures. Then she spent another two hours feeding all the animals. She was just finishing up when Koontz started barking. Dickens joined him. The flat chirp of a police horn sounded in the driveway. When she came around the side of the horse barn, she saw Ralph MacFarlane's police truck in the driveway. Ralph stood next to the open driver's door.

"Hello, Sarah," the sheriff said when she was close enough to hear him, "you had me worried."

"I did?"

"Yeah, you called about saving the animals. I figured you meant the ones here. Then you didn't answer your phones. So naturally, I had to haul ass down here to check on you."

Sarah felt in the back pocket of her jeans where she usually kept her phone; the reception at the ranch was a little spotty, but she usually carried it anyway. It wasn't there. "Sorry, Ralph, I must have left my cell in the house. I've been out here doing chores since I called."

"Sarah, I'm not a young man and not particularly fit either. I know I'm not your father, but with the state of the world, do you think you could try a little harder not to give me a heart attack?"

Sarah stifled a smile. She never ceased to be amused by the giving and receiving of the Sheriff's devout Catholic guilt. "I'm sorry, Ralph. I didn't mean to scare you. I wasn't talking about the animals out here. Mike from the feed store told me about the high school, all those people leaving their homes with their pets unattended. I'm sure animals are dead or dying in some of the abandoned homes in town. People quarantined at the high school will be worried sick."

"Sarah, those people are worried sick about their own lives. Anyway, we have stopped using the high school as quarantine. We are telling people with sick family members to hang a red cloth on their door. Then we get the sick person to the high school."

"Why are you doing it that way?"

"We needed more room for the sick."

"Shit. What about having Todd from animal control pull the licensing records from city hall and cross-check them with the list of people at the high school?"

"Can't. Todd is at the high school."

"I'll do it."

"You are still under quarantine."

Sarah put a hand on her hip. "Come on. Animals are dying out there."

"*People* are dying out there. A lot of them."

"I thought the CDC folks said the mortality rate was zero?"

"Come on, Sarah, think. Haven't you been watching the news? They don't die from the flu. They die because they can't drink for themselves, and there are not enough IV bags to give everyone fluids. Not enough feeding tubes. Not enough trained people to put them in. They die of dehydration. If they live alone it might as well be the flu that kills them. They're just as dead."

"Let me go rescue the animals."

"I understand your priority is the animals. My priority is the people of this town." He paused and sighed. "I'll see if I can get you a list you can follow up on when your quarantine is done in a few days. It's going to take some time. I'm running around like a fool, day and night."

Sarah let out an exasperated grunt. "The animals are running out of time!"

"So am I, Sarah. I don't know how to stop this thing, and it's eating this town alive. Besides, never mind quarantine. The best, safest place for you is right here. You stay put, and you'll outlast all of us."

"So this isn't just about quarantine. You're doing that father figure thing again."

"Well, maybe I am. Maybe if I was better at it, you wouldn't be so damn antisocial and argumentative." He climbed into his truck and slammed the door.

Sarah smiled despite the situation. He really meant a lot to her, and she rather liked the crusty curmudgeon side of his personality. They shared that trait, and she could relate to it. A thought struck her as the sheriff started his truck: he was probably exposed to this flu every minute of his job. It was likely that he would get sick. Every time she saw him could be the last. There was so much between them that was never said. She never got to say good-bye to her father, and now...

The sheriff stopped in the middle of a three-point turn in the driveway. He leaned out the open window. "Don't do anything stupid, Sarah. Stay here. Wait for me to get you that list."

"Ralph," she called, "Be careful."

"I always am." He started to turn the truck again.

"Hey!" she called.

Ralph stopped the truck again and leaned out the window to face her. "What?"

"I... I don't know if I ever really thanked you, you know, for all you did for me. I wanted to say so, just in case."

"Now, don't you start getting all mushy on me. Then I'll know something's wrong with you for sure. And..." he shook his head.

"What?" she asked.

"Jiminy Christmas, it took you thirty dang years to say so. I'll see you in a few days."

Sarah stood in the middle of the dirt track and watched him drive away until the truck was lost to sight. The lump in her throat wasn't going away. That annoyed her. Ralph was right, of course. No sense in getting all sentimental now. He was also right to tell her not to do anything stupid because she was already plotting her next stupid move. "C'mon, boys," she said to the dogs, "let's blow this pop stand."

The dogs followed her over to where her truck and Laura's Jeep were parked. She raised the hoods of both vehicles. Then she laughed. She looked down at Dickens, wagging his tail beside her. "He must have forgotten everything he taught me about cars."

She located the coil and the distributor on her truck. Sure enough, Ralph had removed the wire between them. She found the same in the Jeep. Sarah knew there was nothing special about that wire. Any spark plug wire could do the job. So she went to Laura's Jeep, pulled out the longest wire, and used it on her truck. It took less than a minute. Then she turned the key. The pickup fired right up.

"Ha!" She clapped her hands. "Suck on that, CDC quarantine!"

Dickens barked at the open truck door. He put his front paws on the jamb.

"Not yet, buddy. We'll give Ralph twenty-four hours, then we are rolling." She shut off the truck and headed into the house to make dinner.

Microwave dinner in hand, she sat on the couch and put her dinner on the coffee table. "Don't even think about it, Dickens," she admonished the Lab. He sat a foot away, eyes traveling from Sarah to the food and back. "Go lie down," she said, then clicked on the TV.

The news anchor didn't look good. Pale and pasty. "... has now been confirmed in seventy countries worldwide and every continent. At this hour, the acting president has ordered the US borders closed. Air travel is suspended indefinitely."

"You hear that, Dickens? They're ready to close the barn doors now that the cows are all sick."

The TV report continued: "All troops stationed on foreign soil are ordered home."

"Here comes the cavalry Dickens!" Dickens came back to the coffee table at the second mention of his name and began licking the crumbs Sarah dropped. Sarah was too dumbfounded to notice.

The footage was of people ransacking a grocery store. Police were firing tear gas into the crowd and shooting their guns. "Rioting and looting have broken out in several US cities," the announcer said, "and the acting president is said to be federalizing all the state national guard units as we speak."

Dickens licked Sarah's plate clean, then nuzzled his head against her leg. She reached down and patted his head absently. The screen switched back to the anchorman in the TV studio. "We now have some smuggled footage from within one of the National Guard flu treatment centers erected outside hospitals in many cities around the country. With us to help explain what we are about to see is Dr. William Todd, our medical correspondent."

The image on Sarah's TV screen switched to a view of the inside of a tent. The walls were lined with rows of cots, all occupied by figures with IVs in their arms and masks on their faces. At the end of each cot was a patient in a wheelchair with an IV and a face mask. Three white biohazard-suited figures moved back and forth among the cots and wheelchairs.

"Dr. Todd, what are we seeing here?" The anchor asked.

"Clearly, we are looking at a facility that is way beyond capacity. There are not enough beds, so patients are strapped into chairs. The staff must be struggling to keep all those patients alive."

"Struggling in what way, Dr. Todd?" The anchor asked.

"Well, all those patients must have IVs or feeding tubes to keep them alive. We are looking at a ratio of three caregivers to two hundred patients. Just keeping the nutrients flowing must be a Herculean task. Not to mention catheters and the patients' elimination needs."

"I'm sure it is, Dr. Todd. We have reports of overcrowding at facilities across the country. Can we expect conditions to improve any time soon?"

"Well, with an increasing number of people needing care, and a limited amount of medical personnel, it will be difficult to—"

Sarah shut the TV off. "Holy shit," she said. "Holy shit, holy shit, holy shit." She felt numb, like she was in a waking dream. Dickens sensed something was wrong and began licking her hand. "What the hell is happening, buddy?" She hugged the dog tight. Usually, Dickens would shrug her off. Affectionate as the Lab was, he did not suffer hugs for long, but this time he let her hold him tight for several minutes. Koontz and King, who were lying in their usual places by the doorway to the front hall, stood, shook themselves in unison, and came over to nuzzle her too.

Eventually, Sarah took down her meds and the bottle of tequila from on top of the fridge. She put her daily dose of Laetanol on her tongue and chased it down with three long pulls from the bottle. Then gagged. After a chaser of juice, she went upstairs, stomach burning, and collapsed on the bed. The dogs piled on with her.

The morning required an extra cup of coffee and an extra glass of water. Sarah did her best to keep her mind off the animals trapped in empty houses across the country and here in town. Instead, she busied herself running the animal rescue ranch alone. With Laura gone, many maintenance chores and cleaning had slipped off the edge of her plate full of responsibilities. A typical operation this size would have a staff of four. But Sarah didn't like people much, so she did the extra work herself.

Initially, she'd had a tough time bringing herself to hire Laura. There was something about the girl that overcame Sarah's reservations. As Sarah completed the tasks Laura usually did, she couldn't help thinking of her friend. Sarah pretended she was immune to Laura's sunny can-do personality. Instead, she rationalized hiring Laura because the girl was fearless with animals. Laura would walk right up to a barking, snarling dog, take the leash, tug it, and just say, "Now, now, that's enough of that." It usually worked too.

Sarah mucked out the bird barn, her heart heavy. Her chest tight. She wanted to call someone to check Laura's condition, but there was no one. Laura represented a Sarah that never was. Laura was a young and beautiful girl, a small-town innocent. Innocence the foster care system stole away from Sarah. The tears came and wouldn't stop. She dropped her shovel and covered her face with dirty hands.

Tears soaked into the dusty ground as Sarah stomped off to the house. A phone call to the police yielded the "high call volume" recording again. This time, it took forty-five minutes to get someone on the line. When she did, she asked for Sheriff MacFarlane. Silence. Finally, the woman said: "the sheriff is unavailable. Is there something I can help you with?"

"No," Sarah said, "I need Sheriff MacFarlane."

There was another pause, then: "I don't know when you will be able to reach him."

Sarah's heart hammered in her chest. "Did he go to the high school?" As soon as the words left her throat, she chanted in her head, please say no, please say no, please say no.

"I... I can't give you that information."

"No!" she wailed and sank to the floor in the hall in front of the urn of her mother's ashes. "No! I just saw him yesterday. He was fine."

"I didn't say he did," the woman said, but the catch in the woman's voice said exactly that.

It made sense to Sarah. Of course, the woman couldn't say the sheriff was out of commission. You couldn't tell people that law enforcement was failing. It would be a free-for-all.

"There's quite a long backup of calls I need to answer. If there is nothing I can do for you—"

"Wait, wait," Sarah said. "He was going to get a list of the people at the high school who have pets at home? I could try to rescue them, take care of them until their owners get well."

"Well, I'm an animal lover myself," the woman said. "That is a good idea. Let me see if there is a note. Can you hold?"

"Yes,"

"Okay."

The hold announcement told people to stay home and hang a red flag on their door for medical help and a black flag for help with the deceased. It told people to wash often and avoid all personal contact. It said that masks and gloves were required for all persons in public places. Then the woman came back on. "I found a list on the sheriff's desk with 'pets' written in highlighter at the top and certain names and addresses highlighted in the same color. I bet this is what you're looking for."

Sarah sighed. At least there was one good thing happening today. "Thank you. I'll come get it."

"Anything else?"

"No, thank you."

"Goodbye."

Sarah didn't know whether she should smile or cry. She did both as she loaded up the truck with crates, blankets, jugs of water, plastic bowls, the electrolyte solution, kibble, leashes—anything that seemed useful.

As she drove, she tried not to dwell on Laura or the sheriff. Instead, fixating on the high she'd get from saving animals.

A dust mask and thick rubber gloves lay by her side on the seat. She felt a little like a criminal, breaking out of quarantine, but the sheriff was among the smiling now, and the doctor from the CDC, Dr. Willis, hadn't answered her phone or returned Sarah's calls in five days.

She rolled down the window, enjoying the wind until the chilly Montana evening made her close it. Her smile faded as she thought about the logistics of saving these animals. How was she going to get into these houses? She would risk her life not only from hungry or vicious pets, but from neighbors with guns who'd think she was a looter. Once inside, the environment would be toxic with invisible death — covered with flu virus. So, death by germs, death by hungry dogs, or death by bullets. Those were just the ways. There were lots more. And that thought put a gaping chasm in the pit of her stomach.

As Sarah entered town, a lump formed in her throat. Black flags made from shirts, shorts, and fabric scraps were tacked or taped to door after door, porch after porch. Many more houses flew makeshift flags in red fabric. Some homes were boarded up entirely. The downtown shops featured more plywood on the windows than glass. More padlocks than 'open' signs. On Main Street, once the bustling heart of Bitter Butte, there were no pedestrians and plenty of empty parking spaces.

Sarah parked haphazardly in front of the police station. There were no other cars. No one would be handing out tickets, maybe ever. A sign taped to the glass door read: *Face masks and gloves required. No exceptions.* Sarah let out a dry, empty laugh. Three weeks ago, a person might have been shot for entering the police station in a face mask and gloves. Now that same person risked getting shot for entering without them.

She put on her face mask and gloves and went into the police station. The station was quiet and devoid of civilians or cops. The sole occupant was a woman in plain clothes sitting behind the front counter. She wore a headset and sat in front of a computer. She was speaking into the headset, but she met Sarah's eyes. The woman held up her hands, then pointed at Sarah.

It took Sarah a moment to realize what she wanted.

Sarah held her hands up, showing the woman her gloves.

The woman gave her a thumbs up, then held up her index finger. Her cheeks curled up and bunched up under her eyes — a masked smile.

Sarah nodded and waited a polite distance from the counter. She looked down at her gloved hands. Had the woman's smile been about Sarah's gloves? She'd grabbed the first rubber gloves that came to hand as she left the ranch—elbow length thick black rubber. Sarah used them to clean up bodily fluids and excretions from the animals she rescued.

"Okay, I'll send officers as soon as they are available," she heard the woman say. "I don't know. They are going from call to call as fast as they can. Goodbye." The woman looked up at her. Sarah could tell she was smiling under her mask again. "Oh honey, those gloves. You walk around like that—people will think you cooked this whole thing up in your lab."

Sarah was taken aback by how cheery the cop operator was. She had a sunny, joking, casual tone.

The silence stretched.

"Did I offend you? I'm sorry. I'm trying to keep the old attitude positive. Gallows humor. It's a cop thing. Keeps me sane."

"No, it's okay. I was actually thinking the same thing. They are supervillain gloves. I'm Sarah. I think we spoke on the phone about the pets list."

"Oh yes, God bless you. I'm Gladys. I can't bear to think what's happening to all the sick people's pets. So, before I give you the list, we'll have to talk about how you'll do this. You need to be safe both from germs and twitchy members of the public."

"Yeah, I was thinking about that on the way over."

"You'll also have to gain entry into the various homes and apartments. You may have to break in."

"What do you suggest?" Sarah asked. She hadn't thought about that part. The idea seemed simple initially, but now...

"Well, I think we will have to deputize you."

"Um, what?"

"I think," Gladys began, "that the community would be best served if I deputized you. We'll get you a uniform. Then you can identify yourself as a deputy. It would at least protect you from trigger-happy citizens. I can't give you a car or a weapon, you understand, but the uniform will help. I can give you a radio so you can call in when you're working a house or if you get into trouble."

"Sounds good," Sarah said.

"I'll take your oath, but I think it would be best if we said the sheriff took it before." Gladys's face fell.

Sarah felt a lump swelling in her throat at the mention of the sheriff. Though she always did her best to distance herself from people, she couldn't with Ralph. He took her in as a sixteen-year-old, very damaged runaway.

Silence again.

Gladys cleared her throat and sniffed. "I silenced the ringer on the phone because I was losing my mind, but there are a lot of people out there in trouble. The calls are backing up."

"Yes, of course," Sarah said. She realized Gladys was right. There was important work to be done. Unfortunately, sentiment would just have to wait.

"There are uniforms in the locker room closet. Second door on the left. Change in the closet. No germs in there. We don't give out uniforms very often. Come back here when you're ready."

"This day keeps getting weirder," Sarah said.

"You have no idea," Gladys muttered, then took another call.

Sarah came back a few minutes later wearing a deputy sheriff's uniform.

Gladys finished the call she was on and looked at Sarah. "Not bad," she said.

"I feel ridiculous," Sarah said. "I'm not cop material."

"You care, and you want to do right by your community. Sounds like cop material to me. Before I swear you in, I want to emphasize that your authority is strictly limited to entering homes and rescuing animals. You are not a regular deputy. If I hear otherwise, you are going home."

"I understand," Sarah said.

Gladys took her oath and then told her where to get a radio, flashlight, and some pepper spray. Once Sarah was loaded up, Gladys gave her some final instructions in between telephone calls. "Okay, when you start on a house, call in on the radio. Your handle will be Sierra eight. When you call in, say, *Sierra eight to base*, then wait until I say, *go ahead, Sierra eight*, then you give me the address and say, *working*. When you're done, call in the same as before. When I give you the go-ahead, you say, *Sierra eight clear*. Got all that?"

"Sierra eight. Got it."

"Okay, last but not least, there are disposable gloves and masks on that desk over there." Gladys pointed. "Do you know how to don and doff gloves without contaminating yourself?"

"Yeah, I took some veterinary classes."

"Good. Remember, the whole world is swarming with virus right now."

"That's pretty hard to forget," Sarah said.

"Okay," Gladys said with the wink of a round brown eye, "Good luck, Deputy."

Chapter 20

Erica

September 10-11, Marilyn County, Idaho

Erica followed the yellow line on the floor back from the shower, surveying the stricken faces behind each plastic-sheeted cubical as she went. Mostly, they were new faces. In her estimation, only five in one hundred lasted more than a few days before they were smiling and drooling. Erica kept track of the comings and goings for her story. But as patient after patient became idiot vegetables, her notes dwindled to a line or two of prose before she closed the file and cried.

The astonishing rate of people getting sick made every tickle in her throat, every sneeze from some dust particle, and every sniffle a sword of Damocles. Each tiny physical disturbance could be the first on the path to becoming a smiler.

As she approached her tiny plastic cubicle, a mother wept while trying to get her infant to breastfeed. Stringy blond hair hung limp around the edges of her pimply face, and tears rained down on the child as she looked down. The young mother held the infant like a football, its tiny head in the crook of a sallow-skinned arm. She used her other hand to manipulate her breast. No matter how she moved, the baby wouldn't latch on.

Erica turned into her area and sat on the bed. The scrubs still clung to her wet skin. She pinched the fabric away from her thighs as she sat to keep it from chafing. Erica pulled out her laptop but left it turned off, using it instead as a hazy mirror to watch mother and child superstitiously.

The mother continued to struggle, moving baby and breast to different angles. The dull computer screen washed away all detail from the scene. It could not penetrate the layers of milky plastic curtains between them. Giving up discretion, Erica turned and sat facing the aisle, her laptop in front of her.

The mother's lips moved continuously and became frantic, along with her manipulation of the child. Finally, she switched breasts and tucked the infant into the crook of her opposite arm. This continued for several minutes until a nurse stopped in front of the woman's cubicle.

"Is there a problem?"

"No," the woman replied in a trembling voice. "Everything is fine. Just a little trouble getting her to latch, that's all." But her wide-eyed terror showed through the layers of plastic between them.

"Maybe I can help," the woman in the bio-suit said.

"No!" The breast-feeder turned her body aside, hiding the infant from view.

The white-suited woman drew the plastic curtain back and stepped into the cubicle.

"No. She's okay. We're okay. It's fine," the woman said, rising to her feet and backing up against the fabric wall of the quarantine tent.

"It's all right," the medic said. "I'm just going to check the baby."

"No, stay back!" The woman said.

"Does the baby seem to be getting sick?" The medic asked.

"She's fine! Go away!"

"I need to examine the baby," the medic said. "If she is getting sick, we need to get fluids into her right away."

"NO!" The mother was practically screaming now. "She's not sick. She's not sick!"

The medic reached down and touched a small square box on the hip of her suit.

"No!" the mother screamed. "We are fine. There's no trouble here. Leave us alone!"

Another figure, this one in a baggy camouflage one-piece suit with a gas mask, walked down the aisle and stopped outside the cubicle. The camouflage figure said something to the medic.

The medic nodded.

The camouflaged person pulled the plastic aside, entered the cubicle, and stood behind the medic.

Erica abandoned all pretense of looking at her laptop.

Someone started shouting two cubicles over. "Don't hurt the baby. Don't, no! That's mean! You leave her alone, you monster!" The voice had a thick, slurred quality. A man with Down syndrome stood at the edge of his cubicle, pointing at the camouflaged figure. "Stop it, Army man! You go away. Don't hurt the baby!"

The medic turned toward the intellectually disabled man and touched the box at her hip again. With the medic distracted, the mother climbed over the bed and made for the aisle.

The camouflaged figure stepped in front of her and reached for the baby.

The medic was stuck behind the Army man and could only watch the struggle.

"No! Leave us alone, you fucking bastards!" The mother screamed.

The soldier snatched the baby away from the woman. Then gingerly handed it to the medic.

The mother clawed at the soldier's suit.

The guy with Down syndrome barreled through the plastic at the end of his cubicle. Another white suit and another camouflage suit jogged down the aisle. Camouflage number two grabbed the unruly man, struggling to hold him while the medic gave him an injection.

"Leave that baby alone!" The man shouted. "You make that mommy sad and mad! Hey, leave me alone! Don't poke me! Don't poke me!"

In the cubicle, the mother continued to scream at the medic and the soldier who held her wrists.

"Your baby has the smiling flu, Ma'am," the medic said. "I'm sorry. We need to start her on fluids and nutrients right away."

"No! You can't take my baby! You can't take my baby!" The woman screamed.

"If you don't let us care for your baby, you'll both go to the sick tent. And you'll get sick too. When your baby recovers, you won't be able to take care of her." The medic said.

"No one recovers!" The woman screamed. "Do you think I'm stupid?! No one recovers!"

"This is your last chance. Settle down, or you are both going to the sick tent."

"Then take us. Just fucking take us. Give her back to me. Give my baby back to me, please!"

Tears ran down the woman's cheek and joined the string of spittle hanging from the corner of her mouth. She wailed in despair, staring at the medic with wet red eyes, "Give her back!"

"You'll have to go to the sick tent."

"I'll go with her. Just give her back."

The medic held the baby out.

The soldier let go of the mother's arms so that she could accept the child.

"Come on, follow me," the medic said.

Erica couldn't see the medic's face, but she could tell the white-suited woman was crying too. Medic, mother, child, and soldier exited the cubicle and walked down the aisle toward the front of the tent.

Behind them, the man with Down syndrome slumped into the soldier's arms. The soldier dragged the drugged patient back into his cubicle and laid him on his cot.

When the second medic and soldier walked away, and the tent turned quiet, Erica allowed herself to cry. She wept for a long time.

"Hey," it was Ed Hargrave's voice in the next cubicle.

Erica lifted her face from her hands.

Ed lay on his side, propped up on one elbow, looking at her.

"Not now, Ed, okay? Can I have a little fucking privacy?" she asked.

Ed snorted.

She wiped her tears and looked at him, eyes narrowed. "What?"

"I'm sorry," Ed said. "It's just that we're in a tent with a hundred other people, and you're asking for privacy. It struck me funny. I didn't mean to be insensitive."

Erica smiled a little. It was funny when you looked at it in context. His words seemed a little too collegiate for an Idaho farmer: 'struck me funny,' and 'I didn't mean to be insensitive.'

She was glad to be thinking of something else. Anything but the scene that had just played out before her, but that thought made her thin smile fade. She grasped at this distraction, saying: "You don't talk like an Idaho farmer."

Ed sat up and gave her a wry smile. "And how are Idaho farmers supposed to talk?" He slackened his jaw and pretended to look into the distance. "You ain't got no privacy in this here crowded tent." He looked back at her. "Does that meet your expectations?"

"C'mon Ed, that's not fair, you know what I mean."

Ed grinned at her. "Maybe not, but it's fun to poke you a little. Anyway, I was an English major at the University of Idaho. I went home to help take care of the farm when my dad got cancer. Then I stayed to take care of my mom after he passed. Jamie was studying Classical Languages. She came with me. Turned out she liked the life of a farmer's wife."

Erica thought of his daughter, Aella, and what an unusual name that was. She was going to ask, but thought better of it. Ed was in a good mood. Bringing up Aella right now would ruin that for both of them. She changed the subject.

"Actually, there aren't one hundred people in here," she said, looking around and taking in the empty beds. "There are only ninety-four."

"I noticed," Ed said, "that's got to be good news, right? Things must be getting better out there. The epidemic must be coming under control if there aren't new people coming in."

"Must be." That was the good news. The bad news was—no one left quarantine. At least not through the *front* door. No one got better. Just like that hysterical mother said, everyone got sick.

A medic in a white bio-suit pushed a cart of military rations down the aisle and left one outside each plastic sheeted cubicle. The rations—MREs or Meals Ready to Eat—weren't bad. They just weren't good.

"Is there a chance we can get some internet in here?" Erica asked when the medic got to her cubicle. "Or a phone call, anything?"

"Miss Goldman, we've been over this. It's better for morale if people aren't watching the news. Concentrate on staying healthy. Your time is up tomorrow. Then you can have all the internet you want."

"Better for whose morale?"

The man in the bio-suit faced her. Only his eyes were visible above the mask he wore under his hood. They bored into her, their expression secret, inscrutable. On the breast of his suit, a piece of masking tape said, Tom Parker, RN.

"Miss Goldman, it's better for people not to know what is happening in here, and vice versa."

"Okay, but things are getting better, right? I mean, look at the empty beds! This thing is burning itself out, right?"

Parker sighed. Erica couldn't hear it, but she saw him deflate. He stepped close to the plastic curtain of her cubicle. Only several inches and a couple of layers of plastic separated their faces. "This facility is being transitioned into care for the sick. People are being asked to quarantine at home."

"But it's getting better, right?"

"Enjoy your spaghetti, Miss Goldman." He set the box on the floor outside the plastic curtain and then pushed his cart down the aisle.

Ed was already eating his meal. "Not bad," he said around a mouthful of pasta.

Erica looked at him. The man's goofy smile took the edge off of her anger. "It's good to see you smile, Ed."

"It's good to feel like smiling." When he met her eyes, his smile died. "Erica," he paused as if searching for words, or maybe courage, "I want to thank you for everything. For coming to my house, for telling me the truth, but especially for your encouragement these last few days. I've never..."

She wondered if he could say the words she knew most drunks couldn't; detox, DTs, sobriety. Using these words indicated there was a problem. Drunks couldn't do that.

"... I've never had to detox before. I've never needed to. A couple of days ago, when you told them not to take me to the sick tent, and said I didn't have the flu... How did you know what was happening to me?"

"I've seen it before. My father was an alcoholic. You were drunk at ten AM the day I met you. Doesn't take Sherlock Holmes."

"Well, anyway, you have been so kind. Thank you."

"Of course, Ed. I can't imagine what you are going through."

"Yeah." He looked down. "Tomorrow, I'm going to get one last update on Jamie. Then I'm going to find a way to Washington. To Aella. I need to be there when she gets better." He turned away, reached into his shaving kit, took out a prescription pill bottle, and took one. For a moment, Erica thought maybe he had a pill problem, too.

Then Ed turned back. He must have guessed her thoughts because he said, "it's okay. It's just Laetanol. It's an antidepressant."

"I know," she said, "I take it too."

"You?"

"Yeah, though I've been thinking of stopping. I went through a long rough patch. Now I'm not sure I need it. When I get back to Washington, I'll talk to my therapist.

"Ed, I think I can get my editor to pay for your trip to Washington if you let me write about your family. It would have to be only me. An exclusive. Otherwise, I don't think he'll go for it."

Ed looked at her for a long moment, so long that she thought he would call her an opportunistic bitch, capitalizing on his family's suffering to make a lackluster career finally shine. But he couldn't know all that. It was just her guilt talking. He might not be wrong if he did call her an opportunistic bitch.

"That would help a lot," he said at last. "I have no idea how I can afford to go otherwise. Hitchhike, I guess."

"Well, I won't let it come to that, Ed."

"Thank you."

The next twenty-four hours were excruciating. Time seemed to slow. Every twitch of her nose and tickle in her throat made Erica sure she wasn't going to make it. That she wasn't going to be the first leaving by the front door. Instead, they'd roll her out the back, smiling and drooling.

Ed did calisthenics, paced, and talked about Aella. He went on about her grades, her softball team, and her drawings of pop stars. Then he grew sullen as he described the warmth and weight of her head on his chest as they sat together watching cartoons on Saturday morning, her squeals of delight as he pushed her on the swing in the backyard. Then he sat on his cot and stared at nothing, silent.

In the morning, a nurse took blood samples from each of them. By lunchtime, they were ready to tunnel out of the tent with their plastic forks. Erica watched the clock on her laptop. Time seemed to stop. Enough time for entire civilizations to rise and fall before the minute numeral advanced by one digit. The shuffling of feet in the aisle, low conversations, and rustling of lunches and bedclothes echoed in her head.

At 2:07 PM, Nurse Parker returned. He stood just outside and between their plastic-clad cubicles. "I have good news and bad news," he said.

"Oh Jesus," Erica gasped.

Parker smiled under his mask. "You are both cleared to go home. That's the good news."

"Oh, thank God," Erica said.

"And the bad news?," Ed sat forward on the bed. "Are Jamie and Aella okay?"

"I double-checked on that before I came and got you; your wife's condition remains unchanged. I couldn't get an update on your daughter's condition from Washington. Communications are a little hit-and-miss. The last update is the one I gave you yesterday. Her condition is unchanged."

Ed looked away. His shoulders shook.

"So," Erica asked, "what's the bad news?"

"I'm afraid the discharge procedure is a bit undignified," Parker said.

"More undignified than living in a plastic fishbowl in front of one hundred strangers for two weeks?" Erica asked.

"I'm afraid so. Both of you, come with me, please."

Erica and Ed picked up their bags and brushed through the plastic curtains. They followed Parker out through the back of the tent.

"So much for leaving through the front door," Erica muttered.

Two low platforms sat to the right of the shower tent, tucked between the quarantine tent and the hospital buildings. They were knee high and curtained on three sides with army-green tarps. In front of the platforms were two folding banquet tables.

"Please put your bag on the table in front of your platform, Miss Goldman on the left, Mr. Hargrave on the right. Follow the instructions of the staff. Goodbye, and good luck." Parker started to turn.

Ed held out his right hand.

Parker shook his head and held up both hands, clad in purple gloves this time, taped tightly to his wrists. "Mr. Hargrave, that is a habit you should break as soon as possible."

Four people were standing by the tables. Instead of full bio-suits with hoods and face-plates, these four were only wearing surgical gowns, masks, and plastic face shields. "Okay, Miss Goldman, please place your bag on the table."

Erica did. Then turned to see Ed doing the same at the other table to her right.

"Please step on the platform. Remove all your clothing," the masked woman behind the table said. She was short, the same height as Erica, and their eyes met, but Erica got nothing from them. The woman tossed her head toward the platform.

"What? In front of God and everyone?" Erica didn't move, "but we're virus free."

"You are virus free on the inside. Now we're going to make sure you are virus free on the outside, and we're going to disinfect your be-longings."

Erica walked slowly to the platform as if it were a gallows. She always made sure she was made up and coiffed in public. Now, she was neither. The real indignity was that she didn't have a razor in quarantine. Not that she would have been able to conduct the proper personal grooming in the two minutes allotted for showering, but the fact remained that she hadn't shaved her pits, legs, and bikini area for two weeks. It mortified her to let another human being see how hairy she was.

The second woman, Erica hoped it was a woman, stepped forward. She had a yellow tank on her back. A hose ran from the tank to a nozzle in the woman's hand.

"Please remove your clothes now." A woman's voice. At least there was that.

"I haven't been able to groom properly in weeks. This is humiliating!"

"No one has. Not the patients. Not the staff. Christ, I've got a fucking redwood forest between my legs. Now please take your clothes off."

Erica pulled off her scrubs, suffering the dual humiliation of public nudity and the shame it made her to feel about her vanity.

"Throw the scrubs in that barrel." The woman with the sprayer pointed at a barrel with a red plastic liner near the platform.

Erica stripped out of her scrubs and threw them into the barrel. She stood on the platform naked, with her hands covering her crotch.

"Arms up."

"Perfect, the ultimate humiliation." Erica raised her arms over her head, displaying the dark hair under her arms, and... lower down.

The woman sprayed her with the cold, stinging fluid. It smelled of alcohol and had a freezing effect on her skin. Goosebumps rose all over her body. Once she was drenched, the woman said: "Please rub the solution vigorously into your skin."

Erica did as she was told. When she was done, the woman handed her a small scratchy hospital towel. She dried herself and tossed the towel into the barrel with her scrubs.

The woman at the table handed her a plastic bag. In it were the clothes she was wearing the day she came to quarantine. "These have been sterilized."

Erica dressed quickly. When she turned, all of her things were out of her bag on the table. The woman there wiped each item with what looked like wet wipes. Erica stood by the table and waited. A dozen yards away, Ed stood by his table.

Further on, the bicycle rack-like barriers making up the hospital perimeter were now chain-link fences. Soldiers with dogs and machine guns walked along it. Two Humvees went by. Soldiers manned the big guns sticking out of the top.

Something tugged at her mind, a thought that lay just below the surface.

Ever since she stepped out of the quarantine tent door... "How does everyone know our names?" She asked the woman wiping down her belongings. "There are hundreds of patients in these tents."

The woman stopped her work. She looked at Erica for a moment, "you are celebrities. You're the first people to leave the compound... healthy." She returned to wiping Erica's things.

A Humvee turned the corner and idled a short distance from Ed. Medical staff drifted out of various tents and the hospital building itself. They stood a respectful distance from the tables and whispered in small knots.

"Here you go," the woman said, handing Erica her bag.

"Thank you," Erica tried to smile pleasantly, her heart pounding in her chest

A soldier got out of the Humvee and walked to Ed's table. "Miss Goldman, Mr. Hargrave, this way." He turned back toward the Humvee.

"Wait!" a voice called out, accompanied by running footsteps.

Erica turned.

A man ran up with a stack of surgical face masks in one hand, their strings wagging as he ran. In the other, he held a fist full of purple rubber gloves like a bouquet of dead latex flowers. He stopped in front of Erica. "You will need these pretty much wherever you go," he said, catching his breath. "Good luck."

"Thank you," Erica said, putting the masks and gloves in her bag.

"Put them on." The man said.

"Okay." Erica's shoulders sagged. She thought the danger would be over when they got out. Realization dawned. The threat wasn't gone. It surrounded her. She put the mask and gloves on. They were too big. The tips hung flaccid from the end of her fingers. She gave a mask and gloves to Ed.

"This way," the soldier said. He walked toward the Humvee.

As they made their way to the Humvee, applause broke out among the hospital staff gathered around the discharge area. Erica gave a small wave as she ducked into the vehicle. Her stomach churned. Rather than feeling encouraged or exhilarated by the applause, it made her want to cry or run and hide. The fact that the staff gathered to applaud their release drove home how unique an occurrence it was and, in so doing, how dire the situation was.

The Humvee pulled away.

When they arrived at quarantine, there were three big tents in the hospital parking lot. Now, there were six, along with smaller tents, Humvees, and pallets of supplies. They approached a gate. Razor wire topped the fence on either side and snaked away in either direction like a malevolent slinky. Soldiers crouched behind great bunkers of sandbags, weapons trained on a crowd Erica estimated to be about a thousand people. Erica heard their indistinct shouts over the engine noise of the Humvee.

"Don't worry," the soldier shouted over his shoulder, "it's bulletproof glass."

"What!" Erica cried, horrified to think that they might *need* bulletproof glass.

"Things have changed somewhat," the soldier shouted. He spoke into his radio, and another Humvee pulled in front of them. A soldier behind a big gun protruded from its roof. The gate rolled aside as the Humvees approached.

The crowd pressed against the concrete highway barriers lining either side of the road leading to the gate. Some held signs saying "Obama's Muslim plague" or "bring Trump back." One sign said, "not a plague, a military coup."

A bottle of red liquid smashed against Erica's window. "Oh, shit!" She jerked her head away from the glass. Angry screaming faces flashed by her red-smeared window. The Humvees picked up speed. She looked out of Ed's window instead, unsettled by the red goo.

On that side, people formed a long line behind the highway dividers. Some stood behind wheelchairs holding smiling, senseless occupants. Others sat in lawn chairs or looked out of small tents, their faces desperate and sullen.

The concrete barriers and the crowd dropped away behind the speeding Humvees, leaving only the line of people beside them. An old woman lay sprawled atop a mattress balanced on a child's wagon. A man sat senseless, propped against a tree. A young girl wearing long kitchen gloves wiped his nose. A weeping man squatted, cradling a limp, smiling little girl in a princess dress. An old man leaned heavily on the back of a kitchen chair. A middle-aged woman in a housedress sat tied to it.

"Are these people all waiting to get into the hospital?" Erica asked.

"Yeah, the ones this far back are goners," the soldier said. "When people get in, they stay there. No new beds open up unless they die from something else. One bed might open up every day or two, but these people... best not to think about it too much."

"Why don't you put up more tents?"

"Oh, we got more tents. Sure, we're setting up two more sites in the area, but it won't help much."

"Why not?"

"Not enough medical supplies and personnel. You need biohazard suits, IVs, feeding tubes, and people to place them. They are broadcasting appeals for anyone with medical experience to volunteer. But so many are already infected that not many make it through screening. The ones who do, well, they're replacing others who got the flu. The real problem, though, is IVs and feeding tubes. Everyone who is sick needs one or the other. They can't eat or drink, you know, not in a coma like that. It's an international crisis. You gotta have the bags and the machine to fill them, the nutrients, and the staff to prepare the stuff. Lots of places are making up their own IV solutions and are punching holes in the top of the bags to refill them.

The images blurred into vague impressions as the Humvee continued to pick up speed, and then the line was gone, replaced by all but empty city streets. The few people they saw were masked, gloved, and rushing as if to outpace the flu. A foot patrol of soldiers walked down an empty street, masked, gloved, weapons at the ready.

As the city center gave way to residential neighborhoods, Erica noticed shirts, tablecloths, or bits of fabric hanging from doors, windows, and porch rails. Some were red. Others were black. She didn't ask the driver about these. She could guess their purpose. Her guess was confirmed a minute later when they rolled past soldiers in MOPP gear carrying a body bag from a house with a black flag. Another soldier opened the doors of a white semi-trailer. Inside, Erica could see similar bags stacked like firewood. "Oh my God," she raised a gloved hand to her mouth but thought better of it before her hand touched her mask. "Why are the soldiers using civilian trailers?"

"Refrigerated trailers," the driver replied, "slows decomposition and dampens the smell. Not to mention everyone is trying to stop this thing. The mission is containment and control. There aren't the resources to spare for body disposal. Right now, we're just struggling to get the infectious bodies out of the community and on ice. They're just parking the trailers and getting empty ones. There's a crew just refueling the cooling units of the parked trailers.

"This is unbelievable," Ed said. "Erica, I have to get to Aella. I have to get to Washington."

"I know. Let me call my editor right now. It's time to check in, way past, actually." She tried several numbers at the paper and ended up on hold every time. Then she tried to check her email, but her phone just said no data service. When she looked up, fields of green vegetables slid past her red-smeared window instead of suburbs. She called the emergency number for her editor, his private cell phone.

"Miss Goldman? Erica?"

"Yes, it's me."

"I thought you were... uh, it's good to hear from you."

"I just got out of quarantine. They started jamming communications the second day I was in there."

"That doesn't surprise me. Do you have a story to file?"

"Yes, and another I need to write up. Apparently, Mr. Hargrave and I are the only ones to walk out of that quarantine unit."

"Send me the story as soon as you can."

"What's the deadline for tomorrow's edition?"

"There is no tomorrow's edition. We're not running a print edition."

"Why not? There's probably more news than we could print in a month of Sunday papers."

"No one to print it. No one to deliver it. The staff is getting smaller and smaller. Each day, fewer and fewer people come to work. We're online only. I have to go. Send the story as soon as you can."

"Wait, I told Mr. Hargrave that the paper might pay to fly him to Washington if he gave us an exclusive."

"Air travel has been suspended worldwide. Get back here any way you can. Bring Hargrave. The paper will reimburse you... if there still is a paper. Stay well." He clicked off the call.

Erica stared at her phone. This was all so hard to believe. The world was closing in on itself, shrinking around her.

Fat tears ran down Ed's cheeks. He gave no other sign he was crying. No sobs or convulsing shoulders, just salt water threading through a dark two-week beard, and a red-rimmed stare out the window. She felt terrible about the frank nature of the conversation she had with the driver. She hadn't realized until now, they'd been talking, albeit obliquely, about the fate of the man's wife and daughter. She could think of nothing to say. No words of comfort she could offer would come across as anything but weak platitudes. She reached across and took his hand.

Ed jerked his hand away from the unexpected touch, then smiled faintly and took the offered hand, latex on latex. "I saw a sign back at the hospital about bringing back Trump," Ed spoke loudly and leaned toward the driver. "Where did he go?"

The driver turned his head to look at Ed for a moment, then turned back to face the road. "I forgot about the information blackout in the hospital zone for a minute. You don't know yet. I guess the Girl Scouts, the ones who started all this, took a tour of the White House. What with senators and congressmen going there for meetings, well, the smiling flu ripped through the federal government. The Secretary of Defense is the acting President now. But that's a little shaky because no one signed a letter abdicating the presidency. All the others above him in the constitutional line of succession are still alive. At least that's what they are telling us. So technically, Trump is still President even though he is a grinning, drooling idiot like everyone else."

"How is that different than normal?" Erica asked.

"Show some respect. That is my Commander-in-Chief."

A few minutes later, the escort Humvee in front pulled off to the side of the road. They turned down the dirt track to Ed's farm. Ed looked out the window, scrutinizing his crop. "If I don't get it harvested right away, I'm going to lose a lot of it. And maybe the farm." He pulled his hand away from Erica and put it on the thick window glass.

"Ed, look!" Ahead, there were cars and trucks parked all over Ed's front yard.

Ed turned. "What the fuck?"

Two semi-trucks blocked the barn. A third sat jammed into the space between house and barn. Half a dozen cars squatted around them, blocking in Ed's pickup and Erica's rental car like steel guard-dogs. The Humvee came to a stop behind the menagerie.

"Okay, folks," the driver turned to look over his shoulder, "this is your stop."

"Thanks," Erica said, "good luck."

"You too."

Erica got out and gaped at the scene.

Ed stood beside her, mouth open. They looked from one semi to another. The trailers had doors, stairs, slide-outs, and windows. The CDC logo emblazoned on them cantilevered over the grass.

A man emerged from the trailer closest to the house. He wore a blue windbreaker, surgical mask, and gloves. "Mr. Hargrave!" He called over the noise of the departing Humvee, "I'm Dr. Billings with the CDC. I'm sorry about the lawn."

"The lawn? The fucking lawn? I don't give a shit about the lawn. What the fuck is all this? What the fuck are you people doing here?!"

"Let me start again. I'm sorry there is," he paused, looking around, "... a circus on your farm. Please come to the operations center and let me explain."

"Look, mister, uh..."

"Doctor... Billings."

"Whatever. I just spent two weeks in a cot behind a plastic sheet. with a hundred-plus people. All I want is a shower, a change of clothes, and a decent cup of coffee at my kitchen table.

After that's done, we'll discuss how fast you can get all this shit off of my farm." Ed turned toward the house.

"I'm sorry, Mr. Hargrave, but, uh... you still can't do those things. I—"

"Why the fuck not?"

"If you'll follow me to the operations trailer, I'll explain. The coffee's not bad either."

"Urrrrrrg!" Ed stomped his foot like a petulant ten-year-old.

Erica put a hand on Ed's shoulder.

He shrugged it off.

They followed Dr. Billings up the steps of the trailer.

Billings stopped at the door. "You went through a decontamination process when you were released from quarantine, correct?"

"Extensive and humiliating," Erica said.

Billings nodded.

The inside of the trailer smelled of burnt coffee and antiseptic. Desks laden with laptops, radios, phones, and papers lined the walls. Some had people behind them. Most didn't. Off to the side sat a table encircled by folding chairs. Billings flipped his gloves into a red trash can by the door and lowered his mask. Erica and Ed did likewise.

Billings directed them to a coffee station, and all three made cups in silence. Erica could feel the heat of Ed's boiling anger as she stirred the powdered creamer into her coffee next to him.

As soon as they sat down. Ed said, "Now, tell me what the fuck is all this about?"

"We came to investigate your farm, Mr. Hargrave," Dr. Billings began, "because patients zero and one both came from here. We're trying to find the source of the epidemic. We found it in the soil—"

"My soil? You found the source of the flu in my soil?"

"Please, Mr. Hargrave, if you let me explain, this will become clear much faster."

Ed grunted.

"As I was saying, we found a protein in the soil, on the corn, on the floor of your house, probably tracked from outside. The protein is normally found in the brain. It is the protein that triggers the pleasure response. It is wrapped in a chemical jacket we've never seen before, but we think it keeps the protein from being absorbed by the body before it gets to the brain. This same protein and its chemical jacket are found on the smiling flu virus. The protein causes the smiling flu victims to smile like that and become catatonic."

"How can a pleasure response cause a catatonic state?" Erica asked.

"Think of it as a massive dose of heroin. Addicts call it being 'on the nod.'" He made air quotes.

Erica hated people who made air quotes. She always imagined them making air quotes around the word 'douchebag.'

"The pleasure response is so powerful that it blocks out all outside stimuli," Dr. Billings finished.

"So, where did it come from? How the hell did it get on my farm?"

"There's a lot we don't know yet. We don't know how that protein got onto your farm, but we're working on some leads."

"What leads?!" Ed banged his fist on the table. "I'd like to have a little chat with whoever did this."

"I'm sorry. I can't share that information with you at this time."

Ed rose, leaning in toward Dr. Billings. Erica clamped a long-nailed hand on his shoulder and dug in, pulling him down into his seat.

"Um, yes," Dr. Billings pushed his chair back from the table away from Ed. "We, uh, as I was saying, we don't know a lot, but we are learning fast. We know the smiling flu acquired this protein, but we don't understand how the protein went from the soil to being incorporated into the flu RNA.

"You see, flu virus is just genetic material in a protein shell. There are typically two kinds of proteins that make up the shell. One protein helps the virus get into the cell so it can hijack the cell into making more copies of the virus. The second protein helps the virus punch its way back out of the cell, killing the cell and releasing all the new copies of the virus. Smiling flu has a third protein, the one we found on your farm. This protein allows the virus to pass the blood-brain barrier, enter the brain, and plug into the pleasure center.

"That's what we know. We don't know how the virus acquired the protein. It should be all but impossible. We think it may be due to the chemical jacket around the protein. We also don't know why or how the flu continues to overstimulate the pleasure center. It should just wear off, but it doesn't. We are working hard on that too. That's why your farm has been invaded. And that's why there are two mobile laboratories and a command center here.

"The highest chemical concentrations are on the side of your farm by the burned forest. We just discovered that this morning. A large swath of the corn has already been harvested there. Mr. Hargrave, it is vital that we track that corn. Can you tell me what became of it?"

Ed told Dr. Billings about the fire, the early harvest, and the sale to the restaurant chain.

"Jesus," Dr. Billings breathed. "Excuse me for a moment." Billings went to a desk on the other side of the room and banged away at the laptop. He took a cell phone from the desk. Then punched a number and repeated the details of what Ed had just told him.

"I know," he said into the phone, "Do your best. Track it and shut down any restaurants that are sill open." He listened for a moment, "... you can try. Credit card receipts will help, but not with the cash customers. It was two weeks ago. All the contact tracers we have couldn't put this genie back in the bottle... Okay, keep me posted."

Billings put the phone down and pinched the bridge of his nose. He sighed and returned to the table.

"We were having trouble figuring out how the virus spread so fast with just two initial carriers. The restaurant that bought the corn has franchises in several airports. Anyone who ate at those restaurants may have been exposed, so possibly thousands of carriers. It makes our efforts to find the link between the chemical and the virus even more critical."

"What does this mean for my farm and my crops?" Ed gripped the edge of the table.

"Mr. Hargrave, this farm is contaminated, as are your crops and your home. It is uninhabitable. As far as the long term—I really don't know."

Erica remained mostly silent until this point in the conversation, but she couldn't stand to see Ed get screwed out of his farm, especially after all that had already happened to him. She especially hated this kind of government stonewalling. "We know this came from Fort Johnson. We know about Dr. Silva's secret happy weapon. And we know about Mike Sampson. If you're leaving that out for a government cover-up, you're wasting your time." Erica's face reddened.

"I work for the CDC. I'm here to solve a mystery and stop the global spread of a horrible disease. I have no authority to disseminate classified information. Or tell you what to do about the farm. If I were Mr. Hargrave, I would hire the most aggressive, bloodthirsty lawyer you can find and sue the shit out of the US government.

"In the meantime, it isn't safe to live here. You can gather some things from the house, but you can't stay. I'm sorry, I truly am."

To Erica, it looked as if the spirit Ed found in himself after detoxing purged itself from his body in one long exhale, leaving him slump-shouldered and slack-jawed. He stared at some point to the right of Dr. Billings and said nothing.

Erica put a hand on top of Ed's.

Ed didn't move.

"Mr. Hargrave?" Billings asked.

Ed cleared his throat. "This will help my wife and daughter? All this? You taking our farm; is it going to save them?"

"We are trying, Mr. Hargrave, very hard. I don't know if this will save them. But I don't think they can be saved without our efforts here. Your wife and daughter are the first two patients, as you know. That's a good thing. Not that they are ill, of course, but because no two people out of the millions now infected are being taken care of better than they are. Your wife and daughter are being monitored, tested, scanned, treated, and tested again. An entire world full of doctors and specialists is reviewing their cases, developing hypotheses, and making suggestions. Mr. Hargrave, if anyone has a chance of beating this thing, it's your wife and daughter."

Ed nodded. "Okay, please have those cars cleared out from behind ours so we can go. I

just need to grab a few things from the house."
He turned to Erica, "C'mon, we're going to
Washington."

Chapter 21

Sarah

September 11, Bitter Butte, Montana

Sarah dropped the crowbar. Her arms were too tired to jam it between the door and the frame. Her eyes were dry and cracked. Halfway to rubbing them, the purple blur of her rubber glove reminded Sarah what a terrible idea that was. She looked at the distance between the window beside the door and the knob. Close enough. Sarah picked up the crowbar and rammed it through the small ornamental window. The shattering glass echoed through the silent neighborhood. The smell of dog shit emanated from the broken window and assaulted her nose through her face mask. She ran the crowbar around the edges of the window, knocking away the shards of glass clinging to the caulk. She reached through, unlocked the door, and stepped into the kitchen.

On the floor, five feet inside the door, lay a little brown mixed terrier. The dog whined feebly; its fur was matted and far too thin. Its tail twitched as she approached. Sarah ran her purple-gloved hand over its body to check for injuries or tenderness and found neither. She spoke soft, reassuring words to the dog as she took the baby bottle of sugar water digging into her ass out of her back pocket and began feeding the animal. The dog greedily drank about half of the bottle before Sarah pulled it away. "Slowly, little guy, slowly," she cooed.

She took a black plastic bag from the pocket of her police windbreaker and unfolded it on the floor, then scooted the dog onto the bag. Gathering the edges, Sarah picked up the dog in her arms with a protective layer of plastic between the animal and her jacket. The dog didn't have the strength to struggle. As she held it, it whined louder, pleading.

"You'll get some more in a minute." After carrying the plastic-clad dog to her truck, she gently slid him into an open pet carrier on the tailgate. Sarah wrote the address in black marker on a disposable collar and slid it around the terrier's neck. She fed him some water, then shut the crate, strapped it into place, and closed the tailgate.

Sarah sighed, steeled herself, took out her flashlight, and headed back into the house. She walked from room to room, swinging her flashlight beam into corners, closets, and the floor to avoid the piles of dog shit. She called out her name as she went, identifying herself as a sheriff's deputy. The house was otherwise empty. A good way to end the day. One live animal rescue, no infected persons to contend with, no gun-toting crazy rednecks, no decomposing bodies.

Out front, Sarah picked up a can of spray paint on the porch underneath the red slash she painted on the white clapboards to indicate a search was in progress. She added another slash to form an X, sprayed the date at the top, her sheriff's department call number on the left, BIO, indicating a biohazard on the right, and finally, a zero on the bottom, indicating no persons or bodies inside.

When she finished, she tossed the spray can on the floor of the truck, pulled off her gloves, and tossed them onto the lawn. She checked that all was secure in the pickup bed, pointed the truck toward the ranch, and keyed the radio mic on her shoulder. "Sierra eight to base."

The radio crackled. "Go ahead, Sierra eight."

"I'm calling it a day. Catch you in the morning."

"Good night, base out."

Sarah settled today's sole surviving pet in the temporary enclosure she had cobbled together from pallets and scraps of chain-link fence she had on the ranch. She fed the dog and gave him fresh water, then set about feeding and caring for the other animals that lived in the Sampson Animal Rescue Ranch. Koontz, King, and Dickens followed her from enclosure to enclosure, wagging their tails and nuzzling her legs. "Come on, Dickens, you're going to knock me over." She set the five-gallon bucket of bird feed on the ground and bent down to pet the dog. "I know I haven't paid much attention to you guys this week. It won't last forever," she said, scratching the black fur under the lab's upturned head. "It's almost over. I only found one today. All the others were..." She grabbed the dog in a tight embrace. "Anyway, buddy, it's almost over." The lab wiggled free from her hug. Sarah stood and grabbed the bucket of bird feed. "C'mon, boys, let's finish up so we can eat."

When she finished with the chores, she was practically staggering with exhaustion. She scrubbed out in the slop sink in the dog barn. After that, her three dogs in tow, she went into the house to wash. Again. Then she fed her dogs and made herself a frozen dinner. By the time she sat down on the couch with her meal, her eyelids drooped to half-mast.

The TV screen showed a building with several enormous tents in front. A fence ringed the whole compound, and a sea of angry people ringed the fence. The shot shook slightly with the movements of the helicopter holding the camera. The label at the bottom of the screen said: Abraham Lincoln Memorial Hospital, Washington, DC. There were vast crowds outside the fence by what looked like a gate. The camera zoomed in on the mob. People were throwing things over the fence. It was night there. Sarah couldn't make out what they threw. Inside the perimeter, flashes lit the night. A moment later, smoke billowed at several points inside the crowd. The announcer said: "It looks like the military is firing tear gas into the rioters." There was an audible "pop, pop, pop." The announcer continued. "It sounds like weapons fire. We can only hope that it is just the military firing rubber bullets."

Sarah sat transfixed, her dinner forgotten. The crowd moved back from the fence in a shadowy black mass tinted orange by the streetlights.

"It seems to be working," the announcer said. "People are moving away from the fence. Recapping what has happened now for those of you just tuning in: Earlier today, a source inside the hospital claimed that this man," a picture of an old man with a short gray buzz cut appeared on the screen, "Dr. Anthony Silva, the inventor of the antidepressant drug Laetanol, and an expert on the brain's pleasure and reward systems, may have found a cure for the smiling flu, and tested it on this man, Michael Sampson." A picture of a young Sampson in his Army uniform appeared on the screen.

Sarah dropped the glass of water she was holding. It smashed on the coffee table. She didn't look down. She couldn't look away. Her mouth hung open, her hands clenched and released, then clenched again. "Can't be," she breathed. She hugged her knees to her chest.

The announcer went on, "Sampson, a source inside the hospital claims, was sick with the smiling flu and given an experimental cure by Doctor Silva. Our source says that Sampson is still very ill but is slowly recovering. He is speaking and can move his body." The image switched back to the crowd. "Crowds began gathering outside the hospital shortly after the news broke. People arrived pushing sick loved ones in wheelchairs, grocery carts, wagons, and anything with wheels, demanding to be let in, demanding the cure. At this time, there may be as many as ten thousand people outside the hospital compound."

"Dad..." Sarah was only half listening to the TV now. Memories, once so foggy, so obscured by the passage of time, came roaring back in full focus. She remembered him pushing her on the swings at the park. She remembered him kneeling next to her bed, reading her bedtime stories. She remembered hugging him goodbye, his stubbly face scratching her cheek. The weight she'd carried in her chest all day threatened to break free. She bit her lip. Dickens jumped up on the couch and licked her face.

All the years of missing him, of anger and loss, of hugging her mother while they both cried—happened again in bits and flashes.

The TV babbled on. "We have Dr. Stephenson, Chief of Medicine at Abraham Lincoln Memorial, live on Skype. Good evening, Dr. Stephenson. Can you tell me what the conditions are like inside the hospital? Is there any move to evacuate because of the gathering crowd outside?"

On Sarah's TV screen, Stephenson's thin lips pressed together while the anchor spoke. When it was her turn to speak, the words exploded from her mouth with surprising vehemence. "Before I answer your questions, I'd like to make a statement. There is no cure for the smiling flu, not at ALM, not anywhere. Everyone in the healthcare industry, as well as all the world's governments and NGOs, are working around the clock to stop and cure this global health catastrophe. The CDC, WHO, NIH, private labs, and health agencies worldwide are putting all their resources toward finding a treatment. But I say again; there is no cure, no effective treatment, and no vaccine at Abraham Lincoln Memorial Hospital."

"What about Dr. Silva and Mr. Sampson? Is the rumor that Dr. Silva cured him, true?" The anchor asked.

Sarah raised her head from behind her knees at the mention of her father's name. The TV showed a split screen with the red-haired doctor on one side and images of the crowd outside the hospital.

"That story is a total fabrication. Mike Sampson was in a coma at Beachwood Assisted Living Center for years, not a recently infected smiling flu patient. He was a coma patient. When Sampson emerged from his coma, we rushed him to the hospital for analysis and treatment."

"And what about Dr. Silva?" The anchor asked.

"*Doctor* Anthony Silva"—Dr. Stephenson almost spat the name—"is retired. He was also a resident at Beachwood. A patient, okay? He was not a doctor in a lab working on a cure. He was an old, frail man working on gumming down green Jell-O from a plastic cup." The woman was silent for a moment. Even in her emotional state, Sarah could tell the woman regretted what she had just said.

Before the anchor could cut in, Dr. Stephenson barreled ahead. "Whoever spread this lie about a cure, and whoever first reported it, is responsible for the exposure of thousands of people in that crowd on your screen, to the smiling flu. That crowd is a Molotov cocktail of virus, and it is on fire. There are sick people in that crowd right now, infecting others. This will cause thousands of direct infections. Then those people will bring it home and infect their loved ones, resulting in thousands more infections. We are watching a devastating tragedy in slow motion right before us. We are working hard to find out who spread this deadly misinformation—"

"How long was Dad in a coma? When did they find him? When did he come back from Vietnam?" Sarah screamed at the TV.

"I'm sorry, Dr. Stephenson, it looks like something is happening outside the hospital now." The doctor's image went away, and the picture of the crowd went full screen. Four black helicopters flew in over the compound. Ropes dropped from each, and soldiers with guns on their backs slid down. When those helicopters flew away, four more flew in and did the same. And then four more. The commentator yam-

mered on about reinforcements. Flashes riddled the crowd around the hospital's perimeter, and smoke billowed in their wake.

Sarah didn't care. She changed channels
again and again, trying to find out about her
father. *Just a few more minutes,* she kept
telling herself, *until they talk about him
again.* Hours passed. Dawn found her hopping
just one more channel, and she'd know how
long he'd been in a coma. She wanted, *needed,*
to believe he'd been comatose since he left.
Otherwise, he'd abandoned her... on purpose.

Chapter 22

Carl

September 11, Washington, DC

"Which one of you *IDIOTS* leaked the Silva/Sampson thing to the press?! Do you have any idea of the magnitude of this screw-up?! Right now, the military is choppering in reinforcements to defend the hospital from an angry mob!" On the screen, the Chief of Medicine paused. Her lips tightened, and her nostrils flared.

"Men and women are now putting themselves in harm's way because one of you couldn't keep your mouths shut. Worse yet, that crowd will expose thousands of people to the virus. They'll go home and deliver the flu to their loved ones.

"Besides the implications of all that, let me add that the hospital is already fifty percent beyond our surge capacity. While you princesses prance around in a nearly empty sealed ward I set up for you, your colleagues are treating patients in broom closets! That is going to change. The Girl Scout troop, including patient zero, has been declared virus-free, yet they are still in persistent vegetative states. They're coming to you after the military gets the situation outside squared away. Which, by the way, is also a result of the leak and, therefore, your fault." Stephenson paused, closed her eyes, and rubbed her temples.

The sixth-floor staff gathered around the computer screen at the nurse's station, shuffled restlessly, or looked down. Carl saw some lips moving in prayer.

"We are gathering the first cases along with the cases you already have so we can better follow the progression of the illness, and, God willing, pioneer some treatments. If those patients are the canaries in the coal mine, you are just the ones holding the cages. That's it. Don't have any illusions about being the best, or special, or chosen for your skill. The only reason that any of you are on this, is that you were on that floor when I shut it down. You were sitting on a winning lottery ticket. The world is crashing down around this building. You are riding it out in a virus-free environment. Do you know how many staff we've lost to the virus so far? Thirty-nine, THIRTY-NINE! Thirty-nine of your friends and colleagues are now sitting in the waiting room because we have no beds, strapped in wheelchairs, drooling on their scrubs, with some of the last IV bags we have dripping into their bodies.

"Now, princesses, get your act together and prep your floor to receive the ten Girl Scouts and their parents. Oh, one last thing. Since we can't have leaks like that in the future, the military is shutting down the Wi-Fi and jamming all cell and data channels. In the next hour, the

Army is going to send up computers for you to use to communicate with the specialists and doctors that are advising you on your patients. Only those communications are allowed. All others will be blocked. Now get back to work!"

"She really knows how to pump up her team," Carl said, pulling a melted candy bar from the pocket of his lab coat.

"Hey, where'd you get that?" the plump, pimply young nurse next to him asked.

"I bought it from the vending machine the day before yesterday. I forgot about it until now." He broke off a third of it and handed it to her with messy chocolate fingers.

"Thanks, Dr. Parks!"

"Sorry, it's melted."

"That's okay. I'll savor it. It might be the last candy bar we see for a while. It's not like they're going to refill the machine."

"Maybe we should call Dr. Stephenson back. Get her to send some up."

The nurse laughed. "I'm glad you are here, Dr. Parks."

"That's right." He pointed to himself, "I'm all the chocolate you need, baby."

"You're playing for the other team. I couldn't get at that chocolate even if I wanted it."

The joviality drained out of Carl. This silly little innuendo made him think of the one person who *could* have his chocolate, Brian. Carl tried not to see the mental image of Brian, a dead smile on his face, marooned in some Greek hotel. A second image followed of Brian strapped to a wheelchair in the waiting room of a Greek hospital, smiling and drooling with an IV sticking out of his arm.

He turned and walked to Sampson's room. The man lay in a bed, inclined to almost sit upright. Sweat dripped from the man's gray temples. Sampson grunted, his upper body coming about an inch off of the mattress, then two inches before he collapsed back onto the bed. He banged his fist on the mattress in frustration.

"Don't be discouraged, Mr. Sampson. You are making excellent progress. Thanks to the care you received at Beachwood, you have a little muscle to work with. They're small and weak, but they're there, and they are working."

Sampson looked at Carl, "Not fffassst enough." Then he lifted his upper body again.

"Your speech is progressing remarkably, even faster than your physical rehabilitation. There are very few coma cases like yours, but of the ones that I've studied, you are light years above the curve."

"Gweat, phthe bessht offff phthe cwiipp-lesshhtt." Sampson grunted and sank back to the bed after another try at sitting up.

"Mr. Sampson, I think it's time we talked." Carl took a few steps toward the bed.

"We... awrre."

"Yes," Carl took out his phone and hit record on his voice memo app. "I want to have a conversation with you of a more serious nature."

Sampson looked at him blankly.

"I know you have been watching the news. How do you feel about it?"

"Whasss... what... are... you... talking about?" Sampson slowed way down.

Carl realized that when the man concentrated and took his time, his speech was much easier to understand. "I mean, does it make you feel frightened or depressed or happy?"

"I," Sampson began. Then, he inserted long pauses between words as if figuring out how to form them in advance, "don't... care."

"Mr. Sampson, millions of people are sick and dying because they can't get medical care. The ones that can are hooked to IVs, going through the same thing you did. You are the only person on earth who understands what that feels like."

"Sssso... what?"

"So, tell me about it. Tell me what you remember, how you felt. Tell me anything I can use to help them." It seemed to Carl like a shadow settled behind Sampson's eyes, as if he were looking out at Carl from some horrible place.

Again, Sampson spoke slowly, concentrating on each word. "You... whhhant... to ...hhhhelp... them." His dark, brooding eyes bored into Carl's, "kkkill... themmmmm."

"Why would you say that? How would that be helping them?"

Sampson lay back and closed his eyes. "I... awmosht... canmpt... we-re-rememba," He took a sharp, deep breath like he was in pain. "Jusht... a... sh-sl-iver... of... time. I... don't... know... how... long. You... can't... tw-tell... time." Sampson's words came a little faster, as if not concentrating was better for his speech. His jaw clenched. "It was like... making... love... at fwurst. Feews... good... awl... over... but... it... kept... going... feewing... better... and... better... until... it... huwrt... and... kwept... going... untiw... it... wasss... h-horrible... paaaain." Sampson's voce dropped, his hands clawed the bed sheets.

Sampson opened his eyes and looked at Carl with the same expression that had chased Carl from the room the first time he visited. Horrible darkness swirled in the man's eyes, a shadow of some malignancy. Then Sampson spoke again. His voice had a strange timbre and wobbled as if he were speaking through a throat full of insects, all scuttling legs and hard carapaces. More disturbing still was that Sampson's speech cleared to a point where Carl couldn't help thinking that something terrible had taken him over. The only reason Carl didn't bolt from the room was that Sampson couldn't get to him—not physically.

"It sssstarts to turn. At first, it's too mm-much pleasure, pushing, burning, c-consum-ing you. Y-you can scream ffforever in that place. N-no n-need to breathe, no w-words, just the ssscream, foreverrrr. You wish for death so long... y-you believe you're dead. You're in hhhhell, alone. White. Hot. Paaaaain s-squeez-ing and s-suffocating. I forgot the wooooorld. Forgot everything. T-two dreams broke the pain. M-my faaamily. Aaannd the t-test that ended my old liffffe. Ssssilva's drug. Ssssssilva did thisss.

"W-when I w-woke up, I c-couldn't re-memberrr—o-objects, s-sight, s-sound. Every-thing... terrifying. What Silva d-id to me... m-onsterous. I'm ssstill trying to u-understand the h-horror of what I-I am now."

Sampson seemed to be looking through Carl. Goosebumps stood out on the brown skin of his arms. He suddenly wanted to be anywhere else but in this hospital room with this malignant man. This was the most Sampson had spoken since he woke. Everyone, up to that point, was operating under the assumption that Samp-son didn't have all his mental faculties. Now, hearing Sampson talk about his life, Carl knew Sampson retained his intelligence. "And what is that, Mr. Sampson? What are you now?"

"A monster," he said. The sound of insects in his throat seemed to grow louder. A thou-sand hooked legs vibrated at once. "I'm h-here in this world now. B-but not all of meeee came back. T-the part of me that... knew... something," Sampson's speech faltered and regressed, words and pronunciation came hard again, "... happiness... ma-maybe... didn't... c-come... back."

"It will come back too, like your speech and your muscles. Give it time." Carl tried to project confidence he didn't feel while simultaneously hiding his revulsion.

"Time," Sampson closed his eyes, "I... forgot... time" Whoever or whatever had possessed Sampson, that spoke through him so well, deserted him, "i-in... thhhhat... h-hell. I-it'ssss... a... relief... k-knowing... thisssss... w-will... all... e-end... in t-time."

"It will get better in time, Mr. Sampson."

"Y-youuuuuuuu... don'ttttt... k-know... tttt-that," Sampson croaked. The scuttling sound in his throat elongated and emphasized the word "you." "L-leaveeee... m-me... a-lone...nowwwwww. I h-have... workkk... t-to... do." He began trying to sit up again.

Carl stopped recording. Unable to think of anything comforting to say, he turned and left the room.

Trying to shake off the encounter, he headed for the coffeepot but stopped short. It was late now, and he suspected he'd have trouble sleeping as it was.

After a few laps of the sixth floor, which served as both his prison and his lofty tower of salvation, he found himself in Silva's room. Dr. Silva had a laptop open on the table that overhung the hospital bed. Carl couldn't see the screen, but he could hear the speech therapist on the other end making vowel and consonant combinations and asking Silva to repeat them.

Carl watched for a while, then wandered to the waiting room that served as the staff's living room. There was no point in trying to pantomime with Silva. If there was a cure in the old man's head, there was no way to get it out yet. Based on his conversation with Sampson, suddenly, any cure that Dr. Silva had given Sampson seemed almost as inhumane as Sampson himself.

Through the waiting room window, Carl watched the flashes and smoke. The military launched a fresh round of tear gas into the crowd around the gate. Finally, the gate opened, and soldiers and Humvees rushed out. The crowd drew back. Carl could make out muzzle flashes unleashed from the soldier's weapons. The TV in the waiting room was turned down low, but the obnoxious chirps of the Emergency Alert System caught his ear. He turned away from the scene unfolding six stories below. On the TV a message crawled across the screen, and the scratchy voice said: "Acting President Joel Watkins has placed the District under martial law. There is now a dusk till dawn curfew in Washington, DC. Anyone out after curfew will be arrested." The message repeated.

Outside, bodies littered the street. The crowd was on the run. Within a few minutes, it was all over. The crowd was gone except for those willing to risk getting shot or arrested to stay in line with their sick loved ones. The line wrapped around the hospital compound. Finally, a white semi-trailer pulled by an olive drab military tractor drove up in front of the hospital gate and idled.

Soldiers made a large V-shaped formation outside the gate. Inside the V, several soldiers went up to the bodies and started working. An ambulance pulled out of the gate, and they loaded one figure into it. They loaded others into the semi-trailer. Once the casualties at the gate were gone, the truck and the soldiers moved down the line of waiting people. Each was checked in turn. They loaded some into the semi-trailer. Carl realized the trailer was for the bodies of those who died in line. "They're out of body bags," Carl whispered. "How many have died that we're out of body bags?"

Seeing people shot and loaded onto a truck churned Carl's stomach. It was like a World War II documentary scene, but it was happening right before him. He felt guilty, standing above the death and carnage, safe in his ivory tower. He should do something. Anything to earn his place and privilege, but there was nothing. Sampson was doing physical therapy, Silva was doing speech therapy, and the support staff had already finished preparing the floor for the arrival of the Girl Scout troop.

Carl was about to turn away. But when two Humvees drove up and positioned themselves at either side of the gate, maybe fifty yards out, he stopped. Soldiers opened the gate. More headlights cut the darkness. Another Humvee led two school bus-sized ambulances toward the hospital.

"They're here," Carl said to the empty room.

It took almost twenty minutes for the first patients to come up in the elevator. Carl assumed there were lengthy decontamination procedures taking place downstairs.

They rolled the patients one by one onto the ambulance's wheelchair lift, lowered, and brought into the hospital lobby. There they were stripped, sprayed with a disinfectant solution, dressed in sterile hospital gowns, positioned in disinfected wheelchairs, and placed, four at a time, in the freshly sterilized elevator car.

They wheeled Aella into the elevator first, then her friends Jane and Bronwyn, and finally Mrs. Thompson, all four smiling at nothing. The soldier guarding the elevator on the first floor radioed the guard on the sixth. "Patient on their way up."

The stainless-steel doors closed. The four catatonic people sat alone and unaware under the ghoulish glow of the elevator's fluorescent lights.

The elevator was silent except for the faint whirring of machines high above, and the chirp indicating another floor going by. There, in the relative silence, unobserved, Aella made an almost imperceptible "mmpphh," and moved the tip of her right index finger just two millimeters before it sank back to the fabric of her hospital gown.

Chapter 23

Erica

September 11, Destination, Idaho

Erica pulled her rental car into the Sleep Titan Motel parking lot and parked in front of the room she hoped still contained her carry-on bag. After two weeks away, she had her doubts. Ed pulled his truck into the space next to hers. She dug in her shoulder bag for the old-fashioned metal key with the large red plastic diamond-shaped tag. The key still turned the lock. Inside, she found all her things right where she had left them. Even though she'd "showered" when leaving quarantine and wore her own freshly laundered clothes, she wanted *her* soap, *her* lotion, and most of all, her razor. She emerged from the room a little less than half an hour later, a real rush job by her standards, fresh and ready for the trip to Washington.

Ed leaned over the side of his pickup, throwing junk from one side to the other. He grumbled unintelligibly. His head rose when he heard the motel room door close.

Erica walked toward the office to return the key and maybe negotiate the bill down. The intervening two weeks weren't her fault. Quarantine.

"Don't!" Ed called after her.

She turned. "Why not? I have to return the key and pay my bill."

"Just don't." He turned away.

"I don't..." Erica stood staring at his back.

He dug around in the truck bed for another minute. The metallic scraping punctuated the parking lot's perfect silence. Then Ed came away with a largish black rag. He leaned into the cab and pulled out with a roll of duct tape. He walked over to Erica and held out his hand. "Key."

She handed it to him, half puzzled and half dreading what the black rag was for. "Oh no," she whispered.

Ed said nothing. He just opened the office door, tossed the key inside without aiming, and slammed it shut. The tape coming off the roll made a cloying, dreadful sound. When Ed finished, a black cloth fluttered from the motel office door. He returned to the truck without meeting Erica's eyes.

"She used to babysit me when I was a boy. My parents would drop me off here when they went out. We would lie on her bed and read books. She had lots of books. I learned to love books because of her." He cleared his throat. "If this is going to be how it is now, all this death... watching everyone you love get sick and die... one by one by one... Fuck. Let's get out of here."

Erica agreed. She wanted to get the hell away from Destination. Get home. "We can gas up across the freeway at the truck stop."

Ed looked across the empty blacktop at the truck stop with its attached old-style diner. "Jamie worked there, you know. If all this hadn't happened, she'd be there right now. Pouring coffee for some trucker and pretending not to notice him looking at her legs. She's got great legs," he didn't look away from the darkened diner. "Let's drive awhile before we gas up," he said in a choked voice.

"Yeah, of course." She moved to get into the rental car.

"Are we taking two cars to Washington?" Ed frowned.

"I thought we'd drop off the rental car in Twin Falls or somewhere with a car rental place."

"Look at the gas prices," Ed pointed to the truck stop marquee, $7.13 for regular unleaded gas. "They've doubled since we went into quarantine. Doesn't make sense to take two cars anywhere."

"But it's in my name. They'll report it stolen, ruin my credit, charge me for the whole thing."

Ed laughed. It was not a pleasant laugh. "The world is crashing down around us, Erica. They took my wife and my farm. My daughter all but killed the President apparently. My childhood babysitter is right behind that door being eaten by maggots," he pointed, "and you are worried about your *credit rating*? Get in the truck." Ed got in the truck, started the engine, and sat stone still looking straight ahead.

Erica stood between car and truck, between optimist and pessimist. Part of her refused to believe that things were so bad that a missing rental car would go unnoticed and unreported. But the other part, the reporter, saw the world as it was, and knew Ed was right. She gathered a few things from the rental car, tucked the key above the sun visor, and locked the doors. Erica, only a head taller than the fender, had a hard time lifting her carry-on bag over the side of the pickup. It landed in the back with a thump. Finally, she climbed into the truck and slammed the door.

Ed didn't meet her eyes. "I'm sorry. That was uncalled for."

"It's okay. It's been that kind of day. You're entitled."

"No, I'm not." He put the truck in reverse and laid his right arm across the back of the bench seat.

Erica felt him brush the back of her neck, accidentally intimate. His hot breath washed the side of her face as he turned to look out the rear window.

"No one is entitled. Not anymore. We're all equally fucked."

They drove in silence. The traffic varied from light to nonexistent. The old cracked pavement was patched with tar, giving the impression of writhing black snakes squirming across the street in the twilight. Two lanes ran to the horizon in each direction, separated by a long, grassy ditch. Night came quickly. The color drained from the world.

Police lights appeared in the distance. As the pickup drew closer, Erica saw a Destination Sheriff's truck on the shoulder, crashed into the guardrail. Ed pulled up behind it and just sat there.

"What are you doing?" Erica asked.

"Making sure we're not rolling up into the middle of a situation. I'm going to see if the sheriff needs help."

Erica fidgeted in her seat and squinted into the lights.

Ed waited a little longer, then got out, approached the driver's side of the sheriff's truck, and disappeared from view. He reappeared a minute later. The red and blue flashing lights silhouetted his grim face. His mouth was drawn as tight as a ratcatcher's kill sack. He climbed back into the truck, put it in reverse, and backed away.

"Well?" Erica asked.

"Nothing I could do. The sheriff and his wife have the smile." Ed put the truck in drive and gunned the engine.

"Let's find out what's going on." Erica reached for the radio.

"Okay."

There were very few stations. Erica couldn't tell if that was because of the smiling flu or just the fact they were deep in the boondocks. She stopped scanning when she heard the grating chirps of the Emergency Alert System.A voice buzzed to life—metallic, warped, unmistakable.

"The United States is now under martial law. The Chairman of the Joint Chiefs has ordered a national dusk-to-dawn curfew for the duration of the health crisis. The public is advised to shelter in place and avoid contact with others.If a person in your household is infected with the smiling flu, place a red cloth in a visible location on the front of your home. If someone in your home passes away, place a black flag in a visible location on the front of your home.Wait for nelp. Do not treat the sick or dispose of the dead on your own."

That horrible mechanical voice—and the words—landed like a one-two gut punch.A chasm opened in Erica's stomach. The world was unraveling, and there was nothing she could do. No report, no in-depth story, no amount of fact-finding could fix this.

The message repeated. Erica listened again, not because she didn't believe it—but because she couldn't accept it."It's getting dark," she said. "Maybe we should get off the road."

Ed sighed. "It *is* getting dark... in a lot of ways."

The silence stretched.

Finally, he said, "There's a big crossroads a few miles ahead. Couple hotels there. We'll be alright until then. See if you can find some actual news."

Erica switched stations. The next one was broadcasting the same message.She clicked over to AM and found a news station out of Boise:

"...declaration of martial law without a clear end to 'the health crisis' could cause a constitutional crisis. This comes on top of the uproar over Joel Watkins, Secretary of State, assuming presidential authority while everyone above him in the line of succession remains alive.Some are calling it a coup d'état and demanding his arrest.Meanwhile, the Nuclear Regulatory Commission has advised shutting down all US nuclear power plants due to a critical staffing shortage. Acting President Watkins has signed off on the order.And the hits keep coming, folks. In a statement this morning, the Chairman of the Joint Chiefs confirmed that military personnel are being dispatched to safeguard key infrastructure and set up checkpoints to isolate the infected."

"Holy shit, this is grim," Ed muttered. "I wonder what it's gonna take to get to Washington."

"I don't know." Erica shook her head.

They rolled into a sea of brake lights. The highway had become a crawl.

"Think this is a checkpoint?" she asked.

"I doubt it. Not this fast."

The traffic inched forward. Orange cones appeared on the right, squeezing traffic into the fast lane. Flashing lights bathed the cars ahead in momentary bursts of blue and red. As they crept forward, Erica could make out a tangle of vehicles. Behind the wrecked cars, an ambulance the size of a school bus idled.

Erica rolled down the dusty window to get a better look. Ahead of the vehicles, she saw a semi-trailer on the shoulder with its rear doors open. The interior of the trailer was dark, and Erica couldn't make out what was inside.

The traffic crept forward, half on the road and half in the median grass. As they passed the ambulance, four figures, two in white baggy suits with hoods squared off against two in camouflage suits with gas masks dangling from their necks. All the figures had gloves taped to their wrists. One of the camouflaged figures had a pistol trained on a person in white.

The other white-suited person shoved the second camouflaged guy. "They're—" he shoved the soldier. "Not—" shove. "Dead!" Another shove.

The soldier easily repelled the man in the white suit and shouted back, "do you have any IVs? No. Any NG tubes? No. Anything to help them? No! They are a biohazard, and they go in the truck!"

Erica couldn't hear the rest. She craned her neck, but the semi blocked the figures from view. A sob pushed past Erica's lips. She turned back in her seat and rolled up the window.

Ed mumbled behind the wheel. It took her several moments to decipher his words.

"I've got to get to Aella. I've got to get to Washington. I've got to get to Aella. I've got to get to Washington." He chanted this grim mantra over and over.

They drove in silence, punctuated occasionally by Ed's new mantra. Erica had trouble digesting the reality. Things were so bad, living people were being stacked among the dead in refrigerated trucks on the roadside. And those who were supposed to help were engaged in fisticuffs.

Ed turned off one exit short of the interstate crossroads. Ubiquitous blue signs for food and lodging grew from the tall grass on the verge. The surface streets were all but empty. The usually bustling area where hotels, gas stations, and restaurants vied for travelers' business was still and quiet.

Ed pulled into the parking lot of the first hotel. A cardboard sign taped to the glass lobby doors read: Closed. The cars in the parking lot were spaced out. No car was parked next to any other. People sat in their vehicles, resting their heads awkwardly on pillows pushed against the glass.

"Let's try the hotel across the street," Ed said.

At that hotel, a paper taped to the lobby doors fluttered in the evening breeze. Just inside, a uniformed man gazed at them through the glass. Erica couldn't make out the words on the paper at this distance.

"Want to check it out?" Ed asked.

"Yeah, okay." She climbed out of the pickup and approached the doors. The man inside the hotel tapped a sign written in pen on the back of a flyer. The ink on the back bled through. Erica squinted at it.

The man in the hotel yelled through the glass in a thick Indian accent, "Mask and gloves required!"

She turned and went back to the truck. "Mask and gloves required," she said, rummaging around in the accumulated clutter of the truck.

She found them, donned them, and went back to the door.

"Let's see your cash!" The man yelled through the glass.

"What do you mean?" She yelled back.

"The rooms are one hundred and fifty dollars plus a one-hundred-dollar biohazard fee. Cash in advance."

"That's fucking ridiculous!" Erica yelled back. "This is a big national chain; this room should be like seventy bucks."

The man behind the glass shrugged. "Not anymore. Two hundred- and fifty-dollars cash. Let's see it!"

"Fuck you!" She turned and started for the truck.

"Hey, fuck you too, lady!" The man yelled after her, "I'm taking a big risk letting anyone in, washing their sheets..." his voice, muffled behind the lobby doors, receded behind her.

"He wanted two hundred and fifty bucks cash," she said, getting in the truck. "I don't even carry cash."

"Jesus, I guess we should have expected something like that. I've got five hundred bucks of cookie jar money and maybe a thousand in the bank because I haven't paid the bills this month. That's all the money I have in the world. Everything else is tied up in the farm." Then in a whisper, "...and the harvest that's never coming. After that..." Ed stared out the windshield into the night.

"Well, I've got some money in the bank. Without new paychecks, it won't go far."

"Yeah, I'm sure as shit not paying two hundred and fifty bucks to lie in a bed and wonder if I'm sleeping with the virus."

"What do we do?"

"Looks like we sleep in the truck."

Erica looked over her shoulder at the junk-filled bed of the truck. "Back there?"

"No, in the cab."

"Terrific."

"Just for tonight. Tomorrow we'll see if we can't get to a store, pick up some camping stuff, and hit an ATM. We'll clean out the bed so we can sleep there tomorrow night."

"I was hoping to sleep in a hotel tomorrow night." Erica frowned.

"You can if you want, but with limited cash and gas at eight bucks a gallon, an expensive hotel doesn't make sense to me."

"I've never spent a night camping in my life."

"Well, then it's about time."

Ed drove the truck back to the hotel with the closed sign on the doors and backed into a space adjoining a field full of tall weeds. "Best bring anything you care about into the cab in case it rains or something."

When Ed said, "or something," Erica pictured infected people crawling out of the tall grass, snot running from swollen red noses onto dirty faces, hands reaching out to infect her. She shook it off and put her shoulder bag behind the seat. Ed helped her get her bag from the bed of the truck. Then she squashed it into the passenger's footwell and, stacking some of its contents on top, made a little L-shaped bed. Erica was never so glad to be short. With a balled-up sweatshirt under her head and her body curled into a fetal position, she was almost comfortable.

Ed dug things out of the truck bed, too. He returned with a duffle bag. "Before you get too comfortable, put these in the glove box." Ed handed her two small boxes.

"What are these for?"

"For these," Ed said. He pulled first a rifle and then a shotgun from the bag and stood them up behind the seat. He wedged some stuff against them to keep them standing, then hid them under a flannel.

"What do we need two guns for?" Erica asked.

"Three," he said, pulling a pistol from behind his back. "This thing has been digging into my ass all day."

"Okay, why do we need three guns?"

"The pistol is for close in offense and defense. The shotgun is for medium-range, multiple targets. It fires in a cone shape. The rifle is for long-range offense. Take out a target before they know what hit them."

"Do you really think we need all that?"

"I hope not. But as they say, hope for the best, plan for the worst. Besides, I wasn't going to leave them home for the CDC guys to have. Try to get some sleep."

"It's like nine o'clock," Erica said, looking at the dashboard.

"We'll be rolling at first light. We've got errands to do, and I want to get as far as we can by dusk tomorrow."

Erica slept in little naps. Her dreams featured all kinds of horrors crawling from the tall grass behind the truck. Each time she woke, she looked up to make sure Ed was still there. She couldn't tell if he was asleep or awake. He didn't move, save for the rise and fall of his chest, head leaning on an old shirt against the window.

Chapter 24

Sarah

September 12, Bitter Butte, Montana

Sarah spent the night watching TV and studying the few pictures she had of herself, her mother, and her father, as if the faded dog-eared images held some long-overlooked answer. She looked out the window as the sun came up. The orange light played across the weathered wood, setting the barns full of rescue animals ablaze with color.

She'd been thinking about jumping in the truck and heading to Washington off and on all night. Beyond the glass, the barns beckoned. Inside, animals to care for. A myriad of chores to do. Her responsibility was to the animals.

But part of her needed to know why he never came back. Needed it very badly.

"It's ridiculous," she said to Dickens as she dressed. "I'm a grown woman seriously contemplating dropping everything and running across a plague-ridden country to find an old man in the middle of all this madness, just to ask him why he ran out on me and my mother. Father or no, MIA or no, that was then. What the hell is wrong with me? Why does it matter now? It doesn't."

In answer, Dickens cocked his head and wagged his tail.

She started in the bird barn, distributing feed and seed to the various enclosures and individual cages. Checking the watering systems. The whole time trying to convince herself that she didn't care why her father never came back, that it didn't matter. But that was a lie.

A lot of things needed doing. She did her best to put all these thoughts out of her tired mind. Later, at the kitchen table with a pad, pen, and a fresh cup of coffee, she made a list. Item one: a call to the feed store to place her monthly order.

She placed the call. The phone rang for a long time before anyone picked up.

"Bitter Butte, Sweet Feeds, this is," a fit of coughing came over the line, "this is Ted."

"Ted, it's Sarah. You sound terrible."

"I am terrible. I'm locking up."

"Locking up? Where is everyone?"

"Where do you think?"

"Shit, sorry. I was calling to place an order."

"We're not taking any orders," more coughing, "most suppliers aren't answering the phones. The ones that are, don't know when they'll ship. Everyone's sick."

"Fuck. Ted, I'm sorry. Can I come and pick up whatever you have on hand?"

"Sarah, there's fuck all on hand. Anyone with animals who isn't already sick came down here this week and cleaned us out."

"What about my animals?"

"I don't know. I'm sorry, Sarah. Look, I need to go lie down."

"Okay, Ted, feel better."

Ted laughed a little too long. "Yeah, feel better. Right."

The line went dead.

She sat, stunned, turning things over in her mind until her coffee went cold. Then she made the rest of her list and put her boots on. Just do the chores. Do the tasks right in front of you, then worry about the big picture.

While caring for the horses, her mind gravitated not to the animal feed crisis, but back to her father. She tried to convince herself that she only cared why he never came back because of her mother.

After finishing with the horses, she found herself doing an angry speed walk to the dog barn. She slowed her pace and concentrated on slowing her breathing. A few lazy white clouds floated in the otherwise deep blue sky. The smell of hay and horse lingered pleasantly in her nose. The peace from deep breaths and the mindfulness of her surroundings didn't last.

After her mother died, she blamed her father for everything. If her dad was around, she wouldn't have been in foster care. She wouldn't have been raped. She wouldn't have needed to run all the way to Montana. It was wrong, but she couldn't help feeling that way.

After a shower and some clean clothes, Sarah sat at the kitchen table with a fresh cup of coffee, crossing off the completed chores on the pad. She crumpled the page and threw it across the room. "Fuck!"

She started writing again: No more feed. Options.

1 Animals starve. She crossed this out right away.

<u>2 Scavenge feed from nearby ranches.</u> This was no good either. Even though there would probably be some hay; no way they'd have all the dog food she needed, or bird feed.

<u>3 Scavenge dog food from the houses in town.</u> No good for the same reason. She didn't take pet food from the houses where she rescued the dogs. It was likely contaminated. And even if she went back to town—house to house—there were so many houses and so little food, it wouldn't get far. A day or two, maybe. It would take that long to round it all up.

The numeral four stared blankly at her for some time, alone on a separate line of the list.

She knew what number four was—the only option left:

<u>4 Let them all go.</u>

It was the only way to save at least some animals. Some would make it in the wild. Most would die. She sobbed. Just once, before straightening and tapping the pen on her list.

Dickens came over and rested his soft black chin on her knee. She dropped the pen, took his head in her hands, and pressed her face to his.

"This is so hard, buddy. It's like all the work I've done is for nothing." "We're dying. Everyone is dying." An errant tear escaped her control, sliding cold down her skin. "All our pets—they never had a chance. I've just been spitting in the wind. I don't know why I'm not sick." Holding Dickens close, Sarah let a wave of despair wash over her. King and Koontz sat beside them, King resting his flank against her opposite thigh.

"If I get sick, then all the animals die. If I don't get food for them, then they die anyway. I have to at least give them a chance," she said.

She imagined the animals milling around outside the door to the house or out in the yard, barking, starving, dying. No way could she bear to watch that happen.

"I think we have to go," she said. "We can't stay here."

Dickens whined and licked her face.

Her stomach rumbled. Sarah wasn't hungry, but she had to take care of herself—for the animals.

"Get tough, lady," she said. "You can take care of yourself. Start acting like it!"

She fixed herself a microwave meal and sat down in front of the TV. "If we're thinking about leaving, best to see what we're headed into," she said to Dickens, who had stationed himself at her side to catch any crumbs.

When she turned on the TV, the news desk sat empty on the screen.

A man in blue jeans sat on a chair in front of the set. He read from a paper. "... just a copy editor here. There aren't many of us left at the station. We'll keep you updated as best we can. If anyone in charge of picking up the sick is watching, please come to the station. We've moved everyone to the lobby.

"There was another riot in downtown Manhattan last night. We do not know how many dead. But we do know that the National Guard troops are using live rounds. Several fires were set, and only two fire trucks responded. I'm sorry we don't have any video. We're rigging cameras on the roof to get you a shot of the city. Right now, the fires are burning out of control."

Sarah switched the TV off and finished her meal in silence. She could only bring herself to eat about half of it and set the plastic tray on the floor for the dogs to finish.

Her most sturdy clothes and blankets went into a duffle bag. She stuffed a pistol from the nightstand in the pocket of her Sheriff's Deputy windbreaker and dumped the box of bullets in the other. Then she turned on the taps and left them running at a trickle so the pipes wouldn't freeze when the cold weather came. She laughed at herself for thinking she would ever make it home; it was a bitter, dry laugh.

She threw the duffle in the back of her truck along with a tarp, several bags of dog kibble, and nonperishable food from the house. Last, she took the urn of her mother's ashes from the front hall, careful not to let her father's dog tags fall from it, and placed it behind the seat, then packed it in with some jackets.

One by one, Sarah opened every door, every gate, every cage, and every crate. She dumped what food she had left in the middle of each barn. Her eyes never met the eyes of the animals. Her tears fell on the dusty ground. She refused to wipe them away.

Sarah made a last walk through the house looking for things she forgot; toilet paper, her bottle of Laetanol (she dry swallowed one of these before throwing the bottle in the bag), and a bottle of tequila.

When she finished, she grabbed the dogs' bowls and called them to the truck. Dickens rode shotgun, as always. King and Koontz rode in back.

One big burning pull from the bottle of tequila later, she drove down the driveway. In her rearview mirror, it was bedlam. Dogs chased each other around the yard. Some chased birds that flew in confused circles. A few chased the truck down the road. The horses seemed content to stay in their pasture, avoiding the chaos.

Sarah hit the gas.

She had stopped crying when she drove through the outskirts of town. Her handiwork was spray painted on the fronts of many of the houses. Numbers in dripping red paint representing the number of sick or dead, each accompanied by a gruesome image. Dead owners, starved pets, and houses full of the smell of dog shit and death flashed through her mind. She drove faster. All those people. All those pets. Unsavable because of a lack of IV bags and feeding tubes. They just died in their homes. Dehydration and starvation in houses with pipes full of water and cupboards full of food.

Too late, she remembered the sheriff's department radio on the kitchen table. Maybe she should stop in and let them know she was leaving town. No point. Just another person gone quiet.

The deserted downtown streets sped by in a blur of boarded-up storefronts. Past that, red or black pieces of cloth hung from almost every home. No more tears came. As she passed the last homes and drove into the rangeland, Bitter Butte's ghosts followed her.

She could almost forget what was behind. The fields were silent and still, as always, behind their barbed wire fences. No cars on the road. No contrails in the sky, just the sound of tires on the asphalt and wind through the open window. The yellow lines disappeared beneath the truck, their monotony unbroken as the sun sank.

A few cars appeared on the road as she approached Roundup. Rangeland gave way to scattered pines as the shadows lengthened. Occasional houses on either side squatted in too-tall grass, most with red or black bits of fabric flapping half-heartedly in the evening breeze. The squat concrete block grocery store sat silent and empty behind plywood-covered windows.

The gas station she pulled into seemed deserted, but the lights were on. The windows weren't boarded up.

As soon as she got out of the truck, a voice came over the loudspeakers. "All we have left is premium unleaded."

Sarah looked at the price on the pump: $9.22 a gallon. She figured she could get half a tank for a hundred bucks. She sighed and started for the store. Even though she brought food from home, she knew it wouldn't last long. Best to stock up while she had a chance.

A man in jeans, rubber gloves, and a dust mask stood inside the glass doors. He held a shotgun. "No one comes inside. Tell me what you want. Slide the money under the door. Then step back. I'll set the stuff on the ground and tell you when it is okay to come get it," he yelled through the glass.

It took about five minutes of "go fish." Sarah came away with two cans of vegetable soup and a gallon of unsweet tea. It cost her twenty bucks.

Sarah and used her credit card at the pump. Her heart was pounding as she slid the card through the reader. She half-expected the man's voice to come over the loudspeakers, saying "cash only." But the transaction went through. She put in eight gallons. She could have filled it, but it was just too offensive to pay that much. Maybe it would be cheaper, closer to Billings.

After pumping the gas, she pulled off to the edge of the parking lot, let the dogs do their business, then loaded them up and kept driving. She knew there was a dusk 'til dawn curfew, but she pushed on a little further. She wanted to be a long way out of town before pulling over for the night. Darkness closed in around the truck. The headlights cut yellow slices of light into the night. It was hard to see good places to stop.

She chose a stand of pines way off the shoulder and drove through the tall grass to park underneath them. Then, after letting the dogs out, she walked back up to the shoulder. The tall grass and shadows of the trees hid the truck reasonably well.

The kibble pinged loudly into the stainless-steel bowls, making her feel conspicuous in the stillness. Dogs fed, she set about feeding herself. She rummaged around the truck in vain for a can opener and found none.

"Twenty bucks for canned soup and some tea," she said to Dickens. He stood in the grass looking up at her eagerly, "and no can opener." She laughed, "I guess that doesn't matter. There's no way to heat it, anyway. Your mama is a dipshit sometimes."

Her hand found a crinkling package among the bag of food, and she withdrew a package of ramen noodles. She opened the top, poured in a little tea, then sprinkled the flavor packet in. She crunched them down, eating carefully from the wrapper, and washed them down with bitter tea from the gallon jug.

Sarah opened the cab's rear window so she could hear what Koontz and King were up to, then did her best to settle in on the truck's bench seat. Dickens insisted on sleeping on the seat with her. There simply wasn't room. After several minutes of struggling, Sarah put an old shirt on the passenger floorboard and wrestled the seventy-pound dog onto it. She lay on her back, staring up at the pines through the windshield until sleep took her.

Only three cars passed during the night. Sarah woke with each, then settled back to sleep.

Sometime after the third car, she woke to Koontz's low growls.

"What is it, buddy? You smell a coyote?"

Koontz's growls became more insistent, the low noise growing in his throat to a crescendo that ended in a series of barks. Dickens joined him, his deep barks echoing around in the cab, making it sound as if a chorus of dogs were barking. Sarah slowly cranked her window down, grateful for the old truck's manual windows. She tried listening, but with the two dogs barking, it was useless.

A voice drifted through the darkness, the source maybe twenty yards away by Sarah's estimation.

"Nice doggies. Yeah, good doggies." It was a male voice, not too deep, with no discernible accent.

"King, go," she whispered out the back window.

The ping of paws on metal answered through the barks of the other two dogs.

"That's as close as you should get," she called.

"Sorry, Ma'am, I didn't know anyone was home."

"What do you want?"

"Just a little gas, so I can get home to my family, is all."

"I don't have any gas to give!"

She rummaged for the pistol in her coat pocket. After this, she would find a better way to carry it.

"Now see, I'm betting you do. I'm betting you've got plenty, and you can let me siphon off a few gallons. No harm done." The voice was slowly getting closer.

"If you get any closer, I'm gonna shoot you."

"You're gonna shoot me over a couple gallons of gas? I don't think so."

"Try me," she said, trying her best to sound tough. Her heart hammered in her chest, and her mouth was a desert. She couldn't hear, couldn't think with all the barking. "Dogs, quiet!" Koontz and Dickens subsided into low growls.

"It doesn't have to be like this. No one needs to get shot. I just need a couple gallons of gas."

Sarah doubted very much that the man would stop with just a couple of gallons. A man who would creep up in the night, who was undeterred by vicious dogs, or the threat of getting shot, might try to take more than gas from a woman alone. She'd die fighting that.

"Last chance, fucker!"

"That's not very nice. I haven't done anything to you but ask for some gas." The voice was closer still.

Sarah unlatched the driver's door as quietly as she could. then turned so that her head faced the passenger door. She took a breath, steeled herself, then kicked the driver's door open.

There was a shot. The door swung back toward her with a hole in it.

"King, dubya!" Sarah yelled.

The man screamed.

She jumped into the grass and squinted into the night.

Three more shots boomed into the darkness.

Sarah saw the muzzle flash arc toward the sky. She rushed forward.

Another shot.

King stood on the man's chest, chewing on his gun arm. The man struggled to throw off the hundred-pound dog. He punched King's side with his free hand. Sarah was glad the darkness obscured the worst of the gore.

She stood above the man's head, away from the pistol that wagged with the vigor of King's gnawing jaws.

"You're gonna wanna stop punching my dog before you really piss him off." Her hand shook. The pistol barrel wobbled in the darkness.

The sound of the punches that pelted King became feebler. Sarah kicked the man hard in the temple, not trusting the aim of her shaking hand.

The blows stopped.

He went limp.

She kicked him again, then crouched beside him and took the gun. King let go of the mangled arm and stood at her side, panting, his mouth dark with moonlit blood.

Bile rose in Sarah's throat. She fought it back down. She checked the guy for more weapons, careful to keep her eyes from lingering on the gory mess that was his arm. Black blood pumped into the pale grass, and as she watched, ceased.

Worms of half-digested ramen noodles rose in her throat, and she was powerless to stop them. She turned and wretched. All three dogs stood at her side now. Dickens sniffed at the vomited noodles.

"Dickens!" Her stomach heaved again, producing nothing, "... don't you fucking eat that!" She looked at him sternly, then wretched again.

When she had herself under control, she squinted in the direction the man had come. Something lay in the grass about twenty feet away.

"Dogs, come."

They were at her side as she approached the area of flattened grass with the shadow in it. Sarah pointed her gun at the shadow and stepped closer. She swallowed hard, trying to wash away the taste of vomit even as the bile rose in her throat again. The dogs neither barked nor growled. Their silence gave Sarah the confidence to move closer. Even with the dogs' silence, she dared not put her gun away to turn on the light from her phone. The sky was just starting to lighten over the hills to the east.

Another step closer revealed the shape to be a container and something roundish with a hose coming out of either side. She bent to look. It was a metal five-gallon gas can. Empty. And the round shape was a siphon pump.

Down the road, about a hundred yards away, a beat-up pickup truck sat on the shoulder, dark and quiet.

Sarah figured if the dead man had anyone with him, they would have come to his aid during the fight.

No sense in taking risks.

She left the siphon and gas can where they lay.

"Dogs, come," she said again. They did. She approached the truck in a crouch, gun in hand. Once even with the tailgate, she popped up like a jack-in-the-box, looked, and ducked again. The truck bed was empty except for some strewn trash. She crept forward and did the same jack-in-the-box trick. The cab, too, was empty except for a small gray backpack on the seat. Sarah took one more long look around, opened the door, grabbed the backpack, and ducked down to examine its contents: a dirty sweat-fouled set of clothes and a baggie half-full of white powder. She thought about taking the backpack, sans contents, but she suspected she would feel the bile rise in her throat every time she saw it. A further search of the cab turned up nothing.

It didn't take long for Sarah to figure out the siphon. She took four gallons of gas from the dead man's truck and added it to her own. Then tucked the confiscated pistol under her seat.

Her stomach was still too upset to eat. She took a cigarette from the pack in her glove box and smoked it while she drank tea from the gallon jug. Smoking again after so many years—she shook her head. It had been a rough couple of weeks, and besides, who cared about longevity anymore? She fed the dogs breakfast, loaded them into their usual places, and pulled out onto the road.

Chapter 25

Carl

September 12, Washington, DC

Carl stared out the window of the sixth floor waiting room. Smoke billowed into the sky in several places on the horizon.

Movement caught his eye. A dog ripped into one of the many piles of garbage on the street below, disturbing a colony of rats who'd claimed that pile for themselves. Little gray forms scattered from the black bags and ran down a nearby sewer.

Occasionally, a biohazard-suited figure moved among the array of army tents. Outside the compound, a car weaved through the stalled vehicles on the DC streets. The traffic signals went through their cycles unobserved. No lines of the sick waited outside the hospital.

The TV, whether by design or attrition, Carl couldn't tell, showed only the same Emergency Alert System message: Shelter in place for one to two weeks, hang a black flag for body pickup, a red flag for medical help. He flipped channels angrily. He needed to know what was going on out there... and what was being done about it. How many still alive? How many dead? What was on fire? Was the virus finally burning itself out?

There was no news. Not on any channel. He sipped his tepid coffee. The power went out. Alarms beeped across the ward. Carl walked down the hall and checked in at the nurses' station.

Nurse Crippin sat behind the counter in purple scrubs, slightly too small for her bulky middle-aged frame. Her short hair, normally parted perfectly, shot out from her scalp at odd angles. "We're okay for now," she told him. "The critical systems are on UPS."

"Package delivery? I don't understand."

"No, Uninterrupted Power Supply; a giant bank of batteries in the basement somewhere. The orange outlets in the rooms run to it. The generator should have kicked in by now."

"How long do we have on generators?" Carl asked.

"Well, the confabulated aerolite grunphies will eventually bandle the linchpin and score the frogging on the bushings."

Carl frowned at her.

She made a wry face. "How the hell should I know? We had a power outage once, they were fine for a few hours."

He didn't know what to do with that. Humor was scarce these days, but hers implied he was stupid, and he liked her, so he ignored it. The lights came on just as Carl turned to check on his patients.

"There," the nurse said, "one less problem."

The video conference line began ringing. Carl turned back.

"HU-HA, Nurse Grippen!"

Carl recognized the voice as that of Dr. Stephenson, chief of medicine, but not the tone. Dr. Stephenson was never friendly, certainly not jovial. He walked around the counter to look at the screen.

"It's Crippin," the nurse mumbled.

"How're things on the fabulous sixth floor?"

Carl saw Dr. Stephenson on the screen, her thin lips in a wide grin. He stood open-mouthed.

"We lost power for a minute," Crippin said.

"I know!" Stephenson said it like it was the best thing ever to happen. "We got it back too!"

Crippin and Carl exchanged a look. Carl nodded. Smiling flu.

"So listen, Pippin, we have been stock-piling diesel for the generators, AND we've even got a couple of Army guys to keep it going. Soooooooo, you have twelve days to solve this before you lose power," Stephenson laughed. "The Army tells me you should go easy on the water too. We don't know how long that will work. The Army put a shitload of MREs, that's Meals Ready to Eat, to you and me, on the fifth floor for you. When the..." she had a bout of giggles. "When the power runs out, so will the Army. Your time will be up, just like mine is. So, I guess that's it."

"Dr. Stephenson, I think you should go to the ER and have them take a look at you," Crippin said.

"The ER? Nurse Pippin, the hospital is shut down except for the sixth floor. There is no ER."

"What?!" Carl's mouth hung open a little wider.

"Where is everyone?" Crippin asked.

"Don't you know? They're in the tents," her smile faded, "they're all in the tents."

"Don't you think you should go to the tents too? For treatment?"

"Oh yes. I've been avoiding it," her jovial tone returned, "but when you're right, you're right, and you, Nurse Pippin, are right! I need to go to the tents for some special penguins treatment."

"Penguins treatment?" Carl asked. Why weren't they informed if there was a new therapy?

"Goodbye, Nurse Pippin, goodbye Dr. Whatsis. Good luck. The whole world is counting on you. No pressure, though."

The call ended.

Crippin turned to Carl. "Penguin treatment?"

"I have no idea. I'm going to look out the window. See if she makes it to the tents."

"Okay," Crippin was sobbing.

"Hey," Carl said softly, "What?"

"I know she was a bitch, but she was our bitch. She looked out for us. Without her, it's like we're alone. We have no contact with the outside world anymore. If there even is an outside world."

Carl hugged her. He had no words of comfort to offer, no platitudes. "I'll be back in a few minutes. I need to see if she makes it."

"Yeah," Crippin wiped her eyes. "No need to check back in. I'm good."

"I know you are. If I check back in, it will be for me, not you. You, and these people," he waved an arm at the entire floor. "I think you might be the last people alive that I know."

"Yeah." Crippin busied herself with a chart.

Carl walked back to the waiting room. Before, there was almost nothing going on in the fenced parking lot below. Now there was a bustle of activity.

Soldiers were doing something to the treatment tents closest to the gate. Carl couldn't tell exactly what. A moment later, an army truck pulled a camouflaged trailer out and drove it out of the compound. Then, a second trailer, this one a white civilian trailer with a refrigerator unit on the front, pulled out of the tent and drove to the corner of the lot. As soon as the second truck was gone, soldiers collapsed the tent. Carl gaped. There were no cots. No patients, medical equipment, or staff, just an empty tent. The trucks must be full of the cots and equipment.

A figure in a white lab coat stumbled out of the hospital and fell on the pavement. Her red hair wavered off of the pavement in the breeze. She tried to get up, then lay still. Two soldiers in MOPP gear came over and carried the figure not to the tent, but to the white truck that idled in the lot. They set Dr. Stephenson on the ground and opened the truck doors.

"Son of a fucking bitch! No! No!" Carl banged his fists on the window.

The truck was full of bodies, not in bags, just stacked like books at a garage sale. They laid Dr. Stephenson inside it and closed the doors.

"She's still alive! You fucking bastards, she's still alive! SHIT, SHIT, SHIT!" Carl pounded on the thick glass.

He watched, tears rolling freely down his face as another white truck parked next to the one Stephenson was in. Another tent collapsed. The whole world was collapsing.

"What are you shouting about in here?" Nurse Crippin asked behind him. "Did she make it?"

Carl turned to look at her. He wanted to share the horror of what he'd seen. Instead, he looked at her, searching for the right truth to tell, or the right lie. She had puffy red eyes. He imagined his own looked the same way and decided the truth served no real purpose. No good would come from it. "She made it," he said. "Last ambulance out. Looks like they're moving the facilities out of the city."

"Shouldn't we go too?"

"No, too much virus out there. Too much death. It's safer here."

"Right, of course." She paused, took a deep breath, then let it out slowly. "We have another problem. I can't get any specialists on Skype or the phone. Brain specialist, speech pathologist, physical therapist, all unreachable."

"Is it the network?"

"No, the network is fine. They're just not there."

Carl sighed and rubbed his eyes with the tips of his fingers. "Well, we've seen enough of what they do to carry on for a while. Why don't you canvas the rest of the staff? See who is most comfortable doing what? We've got to come through on this. I'll be with you for rounds in a few minutes."

"Okay, Doctor."

Carl turned back to the window. The soldiers below were still packing up the tents. The smiling flu won. The military was in full retreat. Virus, seven billion. Humankind, zero. Everyone paid the cost now, just like Silva, but everyone else paid with their lives. He kept watching the soldiers, wondering what it must be like to abandon your humanity and load the living into trailers full of the dead because there was no hope. No doctors left to help them, no medical supplies to keep them alive. Then just turn and fold the canvas.

To Carl, the white trucks full of bodies signified the end of the effort to save the species. If the fight against the virus had come to this... If there was so little hope that people had given up on the living, it was all over. Nothing left but this tiny enclave on the sixth floor, pushing on the ocean.

He thought about the troop of Girl Scouts under his care. So beautiful, so innocent... Maybe it was more humane to just let them go, unplug everything, and let them slip away.

He ran the scenario in his head. If everything worked perfectly and he got the formula out of Silva, what then? Rouse the girls and scout leaders to find a dead world where all they loved was gone? Dead parents, dead friends, dead teachers, and relatives. Then turn them loose thousands of miles from home in a city full of corpses with no way back. Just a bunch of scared little girls and a couple of soccer moms in a landscape of death so vast that Carl himself had trouble comprehending it.

He stood at the window and stared vacantly at the evacuating military, at the smoke in the distance, at the cold, empty skies. He knew what he had to do. Now, he was just procrastinating in favor of bathing himself in pity.

A little gray sedan came around the corner of the street below. Belongings were piled on its roof. The car swerved for one hundred yards before crashing into a light pole. The severity of the crash swung the car sideways on the pole like a 'ringer' in horseshoes and left it longways across the street. No one got out. No one went to help. He watched for several minutes, then turned away.

Time to end this ridiculous charade. In the closest scouts' room, a nurse was turning them, sponging them, and leaving them in a new position, so they didn't get sores. He nodded to her but said nothing. If he spoke or engaged with her, he couldn't do what needed to be done. He would be forever damning these girls, if they ever recovered, to a life of misery. They'd be picking off the bones of a dead world they would scarcely remember. They would know only rot and decay.

"Are you okay, Doctor?" The nurse studied his face.

Carl nodded.

She left.

Carl stood, leaning on the doorframe, looking at the little girl in the bed closest to him. The macabre smiling flu grin on this girl, as on some others, was gone, her mouth a thin line turned up slightly at the corners. Carl couldn't help thinking that she was someone's little angel. So peaceful, as if she were just sleeping. Brown curls ringed her face. She lay on her side now that the nurse had turned her. The feeding tube snaked away from her nose and into the shadows.

Carl walked to the bed. The fastest way to end her suffering was to smother her, but he wasn't that far gone, not yet. He couldn't do it. He looked down at her sweet little face and felt evil. Darkness filled his insides. He touched the pillow next to her head, steeling himself to grab it and hold it over her face. His slender brown fingers grasped the white fabric. He knew if he did it, he would be smothering a piece of himself, the piece that made him human. He grabbed the pillow in his fingers, then stopped.

Did she just move? Carl could swear the girl's finger twitched against the sheet. Was it possible? Was she reacting to the sound of his fingers on the fabric near her head or the movement of the pillow as he grasped it? He moved the pillow again. Nothing.

Leaning close to the girl's ear, he fixed his eyes on her finger. "Can you hear me?"

There! The finger twitched again. He strode to the wall to check the chart. This was her—patient zero. Aella Hargrave. He returned to her side. "Aella, tap your finger if you can hear me." The small pink index finger of her right hand tapped the sheet.

"Aella, my name is Carl. I'm going to help you," words caught in his throat. He cleared it. "I'm going to help you get better."

He dashed into the hall. "Nurse Crippin, come quickly!"

Crippin trotted toward him from the nurses' station. "What is it?"

"Get Dr. Patel, get everyone!"

"What? Why?"

"I think the Hargrave girl is waking up!"

Chapter 26

Erica

September 12, Declo, Idaho, I-84 Snake River crossing

Erica clenched her jaw so tight her teeth hurt. Red nails dug into the vinyl seat. She was sure that Ed's truck was going to explode. A horrible clanking came from under the hood. Black smoke billowed out. A steady rain pelted the windshield. She looked at Ed, his face grim, his jaw set. A gray SUV sped past. Erica glanced at the truck's speedometer. They were only doing fifty.

"That makes six since Twin Falls," she said.

"Yeah," Ed agreed, "only six."

"The engine sounds like it's getting louder."

"It is." Ed white-knuckled the steering wheel. "We're on borrowed time."

"Then let's turn back to Twin Falls and get another car."

"No turning back." Ed's eyes were fixed on the road. "Besides, I think our ride just passed us."

"What?"

"That guy in the gray SUV, he's weaving pretty good. Won't be long now, as long as he doesn't crack it up too bad."

"That's awful. It makes me feel like a vulture." Erica's eyes dropped to her long nails.

"That's the way it is now, I guess. We're all vultures. It should make you feel alive. We're lucky to be alive, and any resource we can use to get us to Washington is a resource we take, period. Something's going on up there." Ed squinted into the rain. "Can you make that out?"

"Looks like a pileup." Orange diamond signs showed the lanes shifted ahead. Another said: Bridge Closed. In the rain, Erica could barely see a pile of cars on the other side of the highway. Broken orange-and-white barriers littered the road ahead, a gray shape slumped just beyond them. "Looks like the gray car missed the lane shift."

"C'mon, God, we could use a change in our luck here," Ed said.

As they drew closer, Erica saw that the gray SUV had run into one of two big piles of gravel sitting in the roadway. She guessed Ed saw it too, because he looked at the ceiling of the truck cab and said, "Thank you!"

"Let's not count our chickens just yet," she said.

Ed pulled up behind the SUV. "Looks okay," he said. "Don't think the stop in the gravel hurt it much."

"You know what we didn't get on our little shopping trip?" Erica asked, looking out at the rain.

"Raincoats?"

"Raincoats," she agreed.

Ed reached back behind the seat and produced a shotgun. He handed it to Erica.

"What am I supposed to do with this?" she asked. It was heavier than she expected, and unwieldy.

"Just stand outside the truck behind the open door. Point it at the passenger door of that SUV, and look tough."

"When the door's open, I'll barely be able to see over it. Your truck is too tall."

"No, you're too—"

"Don't say it..."

"—short."

Erica grunted in frustration.

"It'll work. Gloves and masks." Ed said, reaching for the box on the seat.

After sliding white rubber gloves over her long red nails and fixing a mask over her face, Erica opened the door. She gagged as the stench of rotting bodies overpowered her. "Shit! Oh, God." She gagged again.

"Christ, that's awful. It shouldn't be that strong from just a few cars," Ed said.

Erica heard him gagging, too. She rolled down the window and hoisted the shotgun up so that it rested on the sill. The rain soaked her hair and ran down her face, wetting her mask and making it hard to breathe. She glanced at the wreck while Ed advanced on the gray SUV. A white tractor-trailer had jack-knifed across the road, blocking the bridge. It was the same kind she saw bodies loaded into on the drive out of quarantine.

Ed crouch-walked carefully up behind the SUV. He looked in the windows as he moved to the driver's door. "Shit."

"What?"

Ed shook his head and motioned her over.

She withdrew the shotgun from the window, walked up next to Ed, and peered through the glass. The woman's hands rested on her large, round, pregnant stomach. She turned her head very slowly and raised dark, wide-set eyes up to Erica's.

"Oooolla," she said.

Erica could barely make the word out through the window glass. "Well, what do we do now?"

"I know what I think," Ed said. "I want to know what you think."

"Well, I'm not really sure."

"Okay, we know there's no help for her. She's as good as dead."

"We do? How do we know that?"

Ed pointed to the pile of cars resting against the jackknifed truck. "I-84 is shut down. The only bridge across the Snake River is blocked. There are no cops, no tow trucks, and from the smell, it's been like that for days."

Erica looked at the white trailer. It had a refrigerator unit mounted on the front. "Ed, this accident is probably only a few hours old."

"Not with that smell. Come on, Erica, wake up. The world is fucked. Face it!"

"The smell isn't from the wreck. It's from the trailer."

Ed looked over at the trailer. "Yeah, but it was probably working when it crashed. I say it's been there a long time."

"I'm getting soaked," Erica said. "Can we talk about this out of the rain?"

"Okay."

They walked back to the truck and climbed in.

Erica reached behind the seat, pulled out the first piece of cloth she found, one of Ed's shirts, and toweled her face and hair dry with it.

"Hey!" Ed reached for the shirt.

Erica held it up out of his reach. "*This* is what you're choosing to be upset about?"

"Yeah, okay. What do we do now?"

Erica checked her phone. No service. She didn't really expect any, but still, she hoped. "No way to call for help."

"Of course there isn't. There hasn't been for..." Ed looked toward the white truck and the pile of cars.

"What?"

"Not any way to call on a phone."

"Out with it, Ed."

"That truck might have a radio we can use—if the battery is still good. But I don't want to walk into that cloud of fucking stink."

"Worse than the stink of your conscience if you don't do everything you can for that woman and her baby, then steal her car and leave her on a pile of gravel in the rain?"

"I wasn't going to leave her out in the rain."

"Ed."

"Yeah, I know. I have to try." He sat unmoving, staring at the truck.

"The smell isn't getting any better, Ed."

"Yeah. If anything happens, fire a shot."

"What's going to happen? We're alone in the middle of nowhere."

"The way our luck is running, anything could happen."

Ed got out of the truck, hurried across the highway, and into the grassy median. He hopped over the growing creek at the bottom of the ditch, slipped, and landed ankle-deep in the brown, stagnant water. On the westbound side of the highway, Ed stood surveying the pile of cars. Then he circled around the wreck, disappeared into the ditch on the far side, and was lost to sight.

A few minutes later, Ed emerged and crossed the highway again. He made no attempt to jump the swampy ditch water this time, instead sloshing through the knee-deep runoff.

"Radio's dead," he said, squelching into his seat and slamming the door.

"Well, now what?"

"All I can think of is to put her in this truck with a sign in the window; *help, pregnant.*"

She didn't like this idea at all. It seemed wrong to her, but so did walking out of there in the rain when there was a perfectly good vehicle. "Okay, I can't think of anything else either."

It was a long, sopping wet process. Erica stood in the rain helping Ed get all their things out of Ed's truck, then stood on tiptoes to help pull a tarp over it all. While Ed worked, she made the sign in the back window with duct tape.

She stood next to Ed, ready to assist as he opened the driver's door of the gray SUV.

"We're going to put you in our truck until help comes," Ed said to the woman.

Erica was doubtful that the woman could understand English or, for that matter, anything at all. She seemed pretty far gone.

The woman turned her head slowly, "L... la niña..."

"Yes, we're trying to help you and your baby," Ed's voice quivered.

He pulled her gently from the car, and together they helped her stumble to Ed's truck. It was much higher than the woman's SUV. There was nothing graceful or dignified about the way they pushed, pulled, and prodded her into Ed's truck. A process made much more difficult by the gentle way they had to work around the woman's enormous belly.

Erica was about to close the door when the woman, who seemed to be slipping away, suddenly grabbed her arm.

"... la... niña..." the woman croaked, then slumped back into the seat.

"Yes," Erica cooed, "la niña."

The woman smiled a little.

Erica closed the door and sobbed. "This fucking sucks, Ed."

"Yes, it does," he said. She heard him sigh, the wind catching in his throat. Then he cleared it and said, "Let's get this done."

They walked together toward the SUV. A gallon bottle of bleach swung from one of Ed's hands, a fortuitous purchase from their shopping trip after the night in the hotel parking lot. Erica held a fist full of red gas station rags. There were no wipes or paper towels at the grocery store they'd shopped at, so they'd picked up some rags at the auto parts store along with a siphon pump.

They doused the rags in bleach and prepared to wipe down the inside of the SUV. Erica noticed after soaking her rag that her gloves left red smears on the white handle. "Terrific," she groaned. "Now the whole inside of this thing will look like we wiped it down in blood." She opened the rear hatch. Her gloves left red smears on the latch. "Oh no, no, n—" She burst into tears.

"What?" Ed stopped cleaning to look back at her.

"La niña," Erica managed between sobs. She touched the back of her wrist to her face mask. The red rag hung limp from her red-smeared glove.

Ed dropped his rag and hurried to her side. Together, they stared down at a little girl, maybe four or five years old. Brown curls fell against the white sheet enfolding her. The child's small brown arm clutched a pink stuffed dog. She lay on her side as if asleep, legs bent under the sheet. But she wasn't sleeping. Instead, her eyes stared unblinking at the molded plastic wheel well.

"I..." Ed shook and made a sound, half sob, half shudder, "I saw Aella's face. She has the same hair..."

"I'm sorry, Ed."

"Honestly, I feel like I keep getting punched in the gut. I'm so sick of this never-ending parade of the dead."

"Me too."

"I've never wanted a drink more in my life." He took a deep breath, let it out, then turned to Erica. He took her gloved hand in his, the red stains mixing together. "I'm glad you're with me."

"Me too," was all she could think to say. She was glad not to be alone. Ed wouldn't be her first choice. And she wouldn't be his. For both, it was better than nothing.

Ed reached down and closed the girl's eyes, then scooped her up and started for the truck. Erica picked up the pink stuffed dog and hurried to open the truck door for him. She stood helplessly behind Ed as he wrestled the child's limp form onto the truck seat with her mother. Hot tears mixed with the cold rain.

When he stepped back, Erica saw the smears of red from Ed's gloves on the white sheet. She sobbed and leaned in to place the stuffed animal on the girl's chest. As she did, she noticed the red stains from Ed's gloves on the girl's eyelids. She sniffed and wiped her nose on the back of her drenched shirtsleeve. Ed shut the door, and they stood in the middle of the silent highway. The only sound was the staccato of rain hitting the pavement.

"I'm not sure what to do." Ed looked at the ground. "I feel like I should pray, but I'm not sure I still believe in God. Not after this."

"Come on, Ed, before we catch pneumonia."

"Yeah."

It was well after dark before they finished wiping down the gray SUV with bleach. Red rags mixed with the bleach left the interior looking like they washed it in dried blood. Ed folded the seats down, and together they transferred the things from the back of Ed's truck to the new vehicle. The rain diminished to a drizzle.

Erica lined up some dry clothes just inside the rear passenger door. "Don't look, Ed. I'm changing."

"Same here."

She stripped to bare skin, then removed her gloves and mask. Shivering and covered in goosebumps, she did her best to balance on top of her sneakers while she changed into dry jeans and a T-shirt, the only one she owned.

Neither of them spoke as they drove encased in the bloody-looking interior.

Chapter 27

Sarah

September 13, Billings, Montana

Only a handful of cars passed Sarah as she drove into Billings. She craned her neck but found no hope in the drivers' faces, only despair metered in brief flashes as they sped by. The traffic lights were out. Sarah crept slowly through the intersections, empty except for the occasional car. Some abandoned, some full of the dead. The number of stalled vehicles increased as she got closer to the highway. They appeared in random formations. Some crumpled together in accidents. Others just stopped in the travel lane as if frozen in time. In a few places, she squeezed through partially cleared accidents. Something big had apparently bashed the cars out of the way.

She passed a gas station with a sign taped over the logo saying: No Gas. She looked for an open store. Someplace she could get some food and maybe a can opener. Further down the road, she pulled into a gas station with no visible signs and shut off the truck. A newspaper rustling in the breeze made Sarah jump. The eerie silence gave her goosebumps. The dead electronic displays on the pumps stared at her with lifeless yellow eyes as she passed to let the dogs out. They scattered, sniffing out their surroundings.

The doors to the store rattled but didn't open when Sarah shook them. But on the side of the building, the ladies' room did. Sunlight spilled onto the grubby white linoleum. King and Koontz sniffed in disapproval. Dickens pissed on the tire of a car parked nearby. The open door shed enough light for Sarah to see and do what needed doing. When she finished, she went to the sink to wash. No water came from the taps. "Shit! Oh, shit, shit, shit! Dickens, why didn't you remind me to put on my gloves?"

Dickens poked his head in and lowered it in remorse.

"Damn it. I'm so stupid. This place is probably swarming with virus." She walked back to her truck, hands held out as if they might turn and attack her. Using the water jug in the back of her truck would contaminate it. There had to be some other way of cleaning her hands. She caught sight of the windshield washing stations mounted to the gas station poles, black squeegee handles sticking out of brown bins. Windshield washer fluid contained alcohol to keep it from freezing and should make a serviceable disinfectant. The squeegee in the bin closest to her truck clattered to the pavement when Sarah tossed it aside, sending echoes around the intersection. She peered at the dark liquid in the bin. "That doesn't mean anything, right Dickens? They could have changed the fluid right before the station closed for the last time. I mean, the container is brown, so..."

Dickens stood at her side and wagged his tail.

"Thanks, buddy, very reassuring." She tried not to think about the amount of road filth, bug guts, and bird shit likely to be hidden in the dark fluid. The reassuring presence of paper towels in the receptacle gave her just enough courage to plunge her hands into the dark liquid. She pursed her lips in disgust and tried to ignore the random clumps of filth she felt between her fingers as she scrubbed her hands. She scrubbed vigorously, counting to thirty in her head. When she reached thirty, she yanked her hands out and reached for the paper towels, deliberately not looking closely at her hands as she did. She dried her hands, letting wads of wet paper towels fall on the cement.

Engines rumbled in the distance.

"Dogs, come!" All three dogs trotted to her side as the noise grew louder. Sarah fumbled for her pistol in the pocket of her windbreaker, vowing she'd find a better way to carry it, again. The rumble deepened and separated itself into the roar of many engines.

In the distance, metal crashed. Glass shattered.

Sarah ducked reflexively behind the gas pump. Two snowplows roared into the quiet intersection. The lead snowplow bashed a blue Toyota out of the road. The second smashed it up onto the sidewalk. They thundered through the crossroads and kept going. A giant army-green front-end loader followed. After the front-end loader, ten army trucks went by with metal freight containers on their trailers. Then several trucks full of people went by. Those in the back stared out from under the canvas roofs.

Sarah stood.

After the trucks with civilians came half a dozen more, full of soldiers in camouflage, weapons propped between their legs.

Then, finally, a line of Humvees.

Two of them pulled out of formation and into the gas station next to Sarah's truck.

Koontz and Dickens barked at the intruding vehicles. The rear door of the second Humvee opened. A soldier stepped out with a piece of paper in his hand. Koontz and Dickens stood at her side, barking. King circled around to the side of the soldier behind the Humvee.

"Hello, Ma'am, I'm Lieutenant Miller with the Montana Army National Guard. Are these dogs with you? Are you in a safe situation?"

"Yes, to both," she said.

Lt. Miller raised a hand and motioned toward the gas station. At this signal, the first Humvee drove around the parking lot. "Would you mind calling off your dogs so we can talk for a moment?"

Sarah wasn't sure.

"I just want to talk and give you this flyer."

"Why do you want to talk to me?"

"I'm just here to give you some information, that's all."

She didn't trust the military, not after her dad. This guy was too young, and so clean-cut you could eat off of him. His uniform was crisp. His boots polished to a mirror finish that reflected the midday sun.

Lt. Miller nodded and bent down to Dickens, who barked at him from a few feet away. Miller slowly extended a closed fist. Dickens sniffed it, wagged his tail and allowed Miller to gingerly pat his head.

"Well, Dickens likes you. Dogs, heel!"

Koontz stopped barking, and King returned to her side.

"Good dogs," Miller said.

"Yes, they are."

"Well trained. An attack dog," he pointed at King, "a watchdog," he pointed at Koontz, "and" he looked at Dickens.

"A friend," she said. "How did you know?"

"I used to train dogs for a living. I could tell because that one didn't bark, just took up a flank position. The other made lots of noise. This one," he patted Dickens one more time, "I couldn't figure." He stood up.

"A friend, and a good judge of character."

"Well, I'm glad I passed muster. Unfortunately, Ma'am, we don't have much time. We need to rejoin our convoy, but I saw you over here, and I wanted to stop and give you this." He handed her the paper. "It says that the military is gathering willing people at military bases to clean up and get organized. These military colonies are voluntary, and civilians enjoy all the freedoms and rights of the constitution. You wouldn't happen to be an engineer or a doctor, by any chance?"

Sarah folded her arms, dangling the flyer between thumb and forefinger as if it were something nasty. "No, why?"

"Some special privileges go with those professions as an incentive to join us. We really need engineers."

"Why are you pulling out of the city?"

Miller shook his head. "Too spread out for effective law enforcement—too many bodies, chemical factories, lack of power and sanitation; lots of reasons. What do you think?"

"Sounds like a good idea."

"Will you join us?"

"I'll go my own way for now."

"Why? If you don't mind me asking?"

"I've got to find my father." Sarah gazed east.

"Where do you think he is?"

"DC."

Miller frowned. "I strongly advise you to stay here with us. It's the Wild West out there."

"I can't," she said, but she knew she could.

"I'm sorry to hear that. Are you armed, at least?"

Sarah nodded.

"Good. Stay away from the cities. Don't travel at night. Remember, there's a lot of bad guys out there right now."

"Okay."

"Good luck, uh, I never got your name."

"Sarah."

"Good luck, Sarah." He smiled.

"You too."

Lieutenant Miller got back in the Humvee. Together with the second that idled in the intersection, they rumbled off to rejoin the convoy.

Sarah stood for a long time, looking at the flyer while the engine noise died away. She considered jumping in the truck and chasing after the convoy. Instead, she folded the leaflet and put it in her pocket.

The car outside the bathrooms yielded six gallons of siphoned gas. She stopped, looked around, and listened intently several times during the operation. The talk she had with Lieutenant Miller kept echoing in her mind. *It's the Wild West out there.* While she spoke to Lieutenant Miller, she felt strong and determined. Now, standing by herself in a place that used to be bustling with people, she felt alone and exposed.

Sarah wanted to get into the store part of the gas station. She circled it again. The back door was steel and probably bolted. The only thing she could think to do was break the glass on the front doors. Shattering that glass would be loud and might draw bad guys.

Dickens let out a small, muted woof. She had been standing there too long, she supposed. "Well, what do you suggest?"

Dickens wagged his tail.

"Yeah, you're a plethora of good ideas today. Maybe we can break the lock with the truck bumper? The glass might hold." She thought about backing into the doors, but decided against it. If the glass did shatter, it would fall into the truck bed and get into everything. Best to attack it straight on.

She drove the truck up to the front doors, popped the front wheels over the curb, and brought the bumper against the door frame. For a moment, nothing happened after she feathered the gas pedal. She gave the truck a little more gas, and BANG. The lock holding the two doors together popped, sending echoes around the intersection. The glass on the doors shattered with four dull pops, but stayed in place, spider-webbed with cracks. Sarah put the truck in reverse and backed off of the curb.

Afraid the noise would attract unwanted attention, she jumped out and pushed the door. It grudgingly opened a few inches on its bent hinges. Not enough. She tried to pull it outward with a little more success. The broken bolt that fastened the door closed at the bottom retraced the groove it made in the linoleum when she bashed the doors inward, then stuck on the metal threshold. With a lot of shoving, yanking, and lifting, the battered door swung open enough for Sarah to squeeze through.

A wall of stink assaulted her nose as soon as she was inside. The dogs followed, snuffing and sneezing. The place smelled of moldering frozen dinners, rotten bananas, and sour milk. A cloud of flies buzzed around the counter. Cockroaches scurried across the floor.

Sarah bypassed the aisles of sugary crap and ran to the one where there was actual food. She grabbed an armload of soups, crackers, peanut butter, and whatever was within reach of her sweeping arm. Some items fell on the floor. Some dropped as she dashed for the truck. She dumped the goods in the truck bed, stopped, looked around, and listened. Nothing. Dickens on her heels, Sarah made another trip. To him, it was just another game of chase. He bounded after her, tail wagging. She made another grand swipe at the food aisle and nearly tripped over the dog. "Damn it, Dickens, OUT!" He scampered back outside. Once again, she dumped her groceries into the back and ran in for another trip.

Sweat ran down her temples and back. Load after load of bottled water, tea, bread, and sundries tumbled into the truck bed. She cleaned out the pharmacy section and even grabbed a few things from automotive. After her fifth trip, she stopped to listen again. Still nothing. It took less than five minutes of running back and forth for her to get a good amount of supplies, but each second lasted an eternity while the danger of approaching bad guys grew. Lieutenant Miller's words echoed in her head: *It's the Wild West out there.*

She forced herself to slow down and walk the aisles to make sure there was nothing else useful. There was. Sarah grabbed a can opener, some batteries, and a couple of flashlights. She stood for a moment, sweating next to the glass case of petrified donuts at the end of the aisle, then dumped her last haul into the truck. "Dogs, IN," she called, and the dogs jumped into their accustomed places.

A string of smashed-in cars left in the wake of the National Guard convoy led to the highway. Sarah rolled her window down and unzipped her windbreaker to dry the sweat. She leaned over Dickens, retrieved the pack of cigarettes from the glove box, and pushed in the dashboard lighter. When it popped, she took a cigarette from the pack and brought the glowing coil to its end. As she pulled the cancer stick from her lips, she noticed her hand had a brownish cast. "Fuck!" She'd forgotten to grab hand sanitizer and hadn't cleaned her hands since the windshield washer fluid. "Well, Dickens, the damage is already done. Might as well smoke it."

Dickens wagged his tail once at the sound of his name, opening his eyes and looking up at her without lifting his head, then closed them again.

The cars on the road weren't moving. Some were stopped in the passing lane, some half in the ditch. Most had bodies in them; whether living or dead, she couldn't tell, not that it mattered.

Sarah tossed the cigarette, rolled up the window, then rubbed the mid-September chill from her arms. The nights were likely to be cold all along the I-90 corridor. She wanted to get south and take 80. The weather might stay mild longer. That route would avoid some of the big rust belt cities as well. At the interchange, she slowed for the curve and the five-car pileup that appeared around the bend. No smoke or steam rose from the wrecks. No police cars spun their gumballs. And no drivers wandered around, confused. A little boy, maybe ten or twelve, his pants torn and bloody, sat with his hands pressed to a large red stain on his stomach. His back rested against a crumpled compact car, his face grimacing at the sky.

"I fucking hate this, Dickens." She knew, dead or alive, there was nothing she could do for the kid.

Southbound, the odometer ticked off the empty miles. Sarah kept her speed low enough to dodge the stopped cars littering the road.

When the shadow of her truck stretched off the road and into the tall grass, she began looking for a place to stop for the night. Ahead, a big green moving truck blocked all three lanes, jackknifed across the road with two cars wedged underneath it. The cab pitched down into the median, but the trailer and the cars underneath it formed a perfect roadblock. No one coming down the highway could see past it.

She crept by on the grassy shoulder and carefully peered around the other side. Nothing. The air held no scent of death, so she pulled her truck back onto the road behind the trailer and got out.

"Dogs, come!" They did.

A quick walk around revealed no one in the semi's cab and no one in the cars. Rubber gloves and bloody gauze littered the ground. "This one happened when there was still help to be had, Dickens. Wonder why they never moved the wreck off the road. Whaddaya think? Good place to spend the night?"

Dickens wagged his tail.

"Me too."

The tanks of the crushed cars yielded ten gallons of gas. "Not bad, Dickens, not bad at all." She organized her haul from the gas station in the fading light. In the pile, Sarah found she had grabbed a bottle of hand sanitizer after all, and a bar of soap. After washing her hands twice with the water from her five-gallon container and a generous smear of hand sanitizer for good measure, she stripped and washed her body. Clean clothes and skin lightened her mood, but her thoughts turned morose again when she realized this luxury wouldn't last. She left her filthy clothes on the pavement.

As Sarah went about the task of choosing dinner, she realized she had a can opener, but no stove. And someone might see a fire. So dinner comprised peanuts, granola bars, and dry cereal.

After she fed the dogs, they lay together in the grass between the wide ribbons of blacktop. Dickens and Koontz lay on either side of her, King at her feet. She examined the flyer Lieutenant Miller gave her, shining her flashlight back and forth across it. "Seems like a good idea," she stroked the fur on Koontz's back absently.

The flyer read:

Fort Harrison Restart Camp

Purpose: To restart American civilization consistent with American values and the laws set forth in the Constitution of the United States.

Goals:

1 Create a safe perimeter for the inhabitants of Fort Harrison to live and work in.

2 Create a sustainable food and water system.

3 Create a sustainable power system.

4 Secure and dispose of hazardous materials in an ever-expanding perimeter around Fort Harrison for the health and safety of all area residents.

5 Continue expanding the perimeter to include Helena and eventually all of Montana.

6 Re-establish communications with other communities.

7 Work together with other civilian and military communities to rebuild America.

Incentives provided for engineers, medical personnel, and farmers.

Sarah turned off the light and laid back in the grass, resting her head in her hands. The ground's cold grip clawed into her clothes, but the grass felt good. She couldn't remember the last time she had just laid in the grass looking at the sky. More stars than she had ever seen winked down at her from the closing curtain of night.

She thought about Fort Harrison. It wasn't too late for her to go. She could be sleeping in a bed tonight. Her gaze fell on the dogs lying peacefully in the grass. "Why would we want to do that, boys? So I could work, grow old, and die trying to rebuild a world I didn't fit into in the first place? I guess it's not crazier than driving across a thousand miles of country that has descended into anarchy to find a man who abandoned Mom and me forty years ago. If he's even still alive."

She closed her eyes. The crickets chirped a monotone song. A night bird called out in the darkness. She thought of the birds outside the apartment she shared with her mother, how they sang in the morning, reminding her with their throaty cries to check the valve on her mother's oxygen bottle.

After her father went MIA, her mom just checked out. She worked her shifts as a waitress, then came home, sat in front of the TV, and smoked. She never smiled. Would her mother have smoked herself to death if her father had come home? Would Sarah have gone into foster care? The unbroken string of events, the rest of her life, seemed to key off the question: *What happened to Dad?* In that light, it wasn't so foolish to find the answer. Except what difference could it possibly make now?

Sarah learned to make herself hard in foster care, like pouring cement into the holes in her life. She cemented over the hole that her father left in her life. She cemented over the hole that her mother left. She cemented her psyche after she was raped by her foster father. The thing about cement was that it never stopped getting harder.

Chapter 28

Carl

September 13, Washington, DC

"Okay, Carl," Dr. Patel said, shuffling through the papers in front of them on the break room table. "Let's go over this again. There must be something here we're missing. Why do the girls begin to recover but the adults do not?"

"I don't understand it either. The treatments are exactly the same. And the dates of infection were roughly the same."

"Yet on the brain scans, the girls are now showing signs of increased neurological activity. It makes no sense."

"They're growing."

Carl and Dr. Patel turned to see Nurse Crippin standing in the doorway, munching a bag of chips.

"My God," Dr. Patel said, "Of course! Not only are they growing and forming new neural connections, but most likely, they are also using other parts of the brain to substitute for the damaged areas. I wish we could get new scans."

"Me too. How long has it been since we heard from the CDC or WHO? I've lost track."

"Three days?" Crippin balled up the empty chip bag and threw it in the overflowing trash.

"Can you go get someone on the line? We need to communicate this." Dr. Patel said.

"I'll do my best," Crippin said, then hurried out of the room.

"I'm going to look in on Silva and Sampson. Silva put a sentence together today," Carl said.

"That's remarkable, considering how recently he had the stroke."

"It was only three words."

"What did he say?" Dr. Patel asked.

"I am sad."

Patel wobbled her head—an Indian shrug. "Okay," she said, rising, "I'm going to check on the other patients.

Carl walked down the hall and stood outside the door of Silva's room.

The old man stared at a fuzzy broadcast of a man in jeans and a T-shirt reading from slips of paper. "... all citizens needing aid in the form of food, clothing, shelter, and medical care should make their way to the nearest military base. The Army assured me that despite martial law being in effect, all citizens still enjoy all the freedoms provided for in the Constitution.

"The WHO reports a suspected link between the drug Laetanol and immunity to the smiling flu. So far, no reported cases of smiling flu have been found in Laetanol users."

"Did you do that on purpose?" Carl demanded, stepping into the room.

The TV droned on... "a team led by Dr. Anthony Silva, who is implicated in the emergence of the smiling flu developed Laetanol."

Carl put himself between the screen and Silva. "*Did you do that on purpose?!*"

"—The CDC reports that the last accurate figures, as of ten days ago, show that upwards of ninety percent of the global population have been infected with smiling flu, with numbers in the US estimated to be even higher."

"You hear that? Ninety percent. Ninety!" Carl stabbed the air in front of Silva. "You've killed ninety percent of the world's population with your pet project!"

A single tear rolled down Dr. Silva's cheek.

"Did you develop Laetanol as a hedge? An antidote? Did you know about this?"

Behind him, the TV kept going. "That's all the news I have fuel for. If you have a story, you can catch me on CB channel 19. God willing, I will broadcast again at six PM tomorrow. Stay healthy, everyone, and I guess, take your Laetanol." Static blasted into the room. Carl reached behind him and shut off the TV.

More tears made wet tracks down Silva's gray-stubbled cheeks. Although he had a vocabulary of about fifty words, it wasn't clear to Carl how much Silva understood. Clearly, he understood enough to make him cry.

Carl looked down at him, so far away from the sweet old Englishman he remembered from Beachwood. It was like cognitive dissonance: he was the man Carl knew at Beachwood, but he was also a modern-day Dr. Mengele, accidentally creating the smiling flu, then keeping it quiet for years while he experimented on Sampson to fix it. Silva left Sampson to twist for forty years.

Still, in a different light, here was a man who dedicated his life to improving the human condition. He tried to make a weapon that, instead of killing people, made them happy. When it became clear that there was a problem, he advocated for the destruction of the project, losing his job for his troubles. Then he went on to invent Laetanol, saving many people from suicide and depression. Now his newer invention, Laetanol, was saving people from his old one, the weapon, the smiling flu. Carl couldn't help feeling that maybe Silva knew.

"So, you understood at least some of that?"

Silva nodded. He looked up at Carl, eyes pleading. "My," he made strangling sounds in his throat. "My... nnnodblood."

"What?" Carl asked through gritted teeth. He wanted to grab silva by the neck and shake him until the answers fell out. "Did you know about the effects of Laetanol on your old Army weapon?"

"My... my nodblood."

"What? Nodblood isn't a word." Carl crossed his arms over his chest.

Silva looked at his lap like a child being scolded.

"My nodblood. My... nnod... blood."

Carl bent down to Silva's eye level, "If I find out you knew Laetanol could stop this... I might forget I'm a doctor."

He straightened, then left the room to gather himself. This man was a patient. There was no room for emotion.

Sampson was in his room with an orderly on either side, steadying him as he stood next to the bed. Sweat dripped from his face onto the white floor tiles.

"Enough!" He barked through clenched teeth.

"Five more seconds, Mr. Sampson," one of the orderlies said.

"Enough!"

"... and relax." The orderly said, easing him into a sitting position on the bed.

"You're doing remarkably well, Mr. Sampson," Carl said from the doorway.

Sampson looked up at him, eyes narrowed.

"We didn't expect you to be working on standing so soon."

"Again!" Sampson grunted, raising himself up. The orderlies grabbed him by the armpits and extended his arms out. "I've got a mission," he grunted through clenched teeth. He stood, knees bent slightly, arms spread like the wings of an angry albino bat.

Carl shivered. Sampson gave him the creeps. He never smiled, never laughed. He seemed to be just a hate machine. His physical and mental recovery were off the charts. The experts who used to Skype, said he might never walk again, or function above a two-year-old level. One by one, the experts stopped Skyping, but Sampson remained, getting smarter, getting stronger, and they were gone.

"I want to talk to you about that," Carl said, trying to shake off his revulsion.

"I—" Sampson's teeth clenched so tightly that the words whistled, "—don't."

"You brought it up," Carl said in his best implacable doctor's voice. "Do you understand what is happening out there?" Carl realized as he said this that 'happened' might describe it more aptly.

"Enough!"

"Just a few more seconds, Mr. Sampson," the orderly said. The man's big, dark hands gripped Sampson tighter.

"Uuuurrrggggg!"

"You're looking at me like you want to kill me, too. Do you?"

"No," Sampson sighed as the orderlies helped him sit, "just Silva."

"The answer to all this is locked away in Silva's head somewhere. We need it. The world needs it."

"I don't need it."

"You *do* need it. You *did* need it. Without it, you would still be a vegetable locked away in your own private hell."

Sampson shuddered.

"Think about that. If you kill Silva, everyone left alive, and everyone going through what you went through, is doomed to live there forever. And you will be an even bigger monster than Silva, than Hitler, than Stalin. You will be the biggest monster in the world's history. You will kill humanity."

"I'm already a monster. Look at me! I can't remember what it felt like to hug a child. To make love. To laugh. That part is gone!

"If you get your cure from... him... you sentence all those people to this," he flung his hands down awkwardly, indicating his body. "You yank them from the screaming hell of constant pleasure to the cold, hopeless hell of none at all. They would wake, as I did, to a world where everyone and everything they love is withered, dead, useless. It's not worth giving them the cure. They don't need it. Only a bullet. The same thing Silva needs. If you want your precious cure from him, you'd better get it before I have the strength to walk down the hall and wrap my hands around his neck." He wiped the sweat from his forehead with the back of his arm. "Again!" He pushed off the bed violently, taking the orderlies by surprise. They scrambled to grab his arms.

Carl's hands clenched into fists. "We can't study your brain anymore. The techs who ran the machines and the specialists who interpreted the scans are gone. We don't actually need you for anything." He turned and stomped away, angry with himself for letting his emotions show in front of a patient, even a monster like Sampson.

There was no coffee in the break room. Carl sighed and made himself a cup of tea. What he needed was to do something positive. At the nurses' station, he grabbed the notebook tracking Silva's speech therapy and returned to Silva's room. He stood in the doorway, flipping through the pages. The few words Silva had left were random. Echoes of a once brilliant intellect rattling around in a damaged brain.

"Nodblood!" Silva shouted, pointing at Carl. "Nodblood!"

Carl looked at Silva, then at the notebook in his hands. "Notebook?"

Silva nodded vigorously, "nodblood!"

"You want this notebook?" Carl tried to hand it to him.

Silva batted it away with his good hand. He pointed to himself, "My nodblood!"

"You want your notebook?"

Silva nodded.

"Everyone in the world wants your notebook. We looked for it. No one can find it." Carl sat down on the bed next to Silva. "I know the man that I knew is in there somewhere." He took the old man's hand. "If there is any hope for anyone anywhere, I need him, just for a moment."

Silva sobbed.

"Help me understand."

The old man looked around the room. His eyes came to rest on a red plastic water pitcher; he pointed at it. "Blood."

"The pitcher?"

"Blood," Silva said again, shaking his finger at it.

"I don't understand."

Silva shook his finger at the pitcher. "Blood," he said, then he pointed at the notebook in Carl's hand. "Nodblood, blood Nodblood."

Carl looked at the notebook, then at the pitcher. "I still don't—"

Silva looked around the room wildly. He pointed at a red biohazard bin in the corner. "Blood," he said. Then he pointed at the notebook: "blood nodblood."

Red. Silva associated the word blood with the word red. Carl scooted closer to him and took his hand. "Concentrate, you are the great Dr. Anthony Silva, inventor of Laetanol. Tell me, where is the red notebook?"

Silva looked at his lap.

"Is it here in the hospital?"

Silva shook his head.

"Is it at Beachwood?"

Silva looked up and crinkled his brow.

"The nursing home."

"H-h-home. Home." He nodded.

"We looked many times. We didn't find a notebook in your room, or anywhere."

Silva shook his head. "Grn" he choked, then shook his head again. He pointed to the wheelchair. "Go."

"You can't go to Beachwood. We're quarantined up here. It's too dangerous." Silva probably didn't understand.

"My go. My go!" Silva pointed to himself, then the wheelchair.

If there was a chance to find the notebook, to find a cure, Carl couldn't justify not taking the risk.

"Okay," Carl said. He ran back toward Sampson's room. "Steve," he called, rounding the corner. The orderlies were just laying Sampson down. "Steve, I need you in—" he was about to say 'Silva's room,' but caught himself, "six fourteen right away." He didn't wait for a reply and dashed back to Silva's room. Steve showed up a few moments later, and together they helped Silva into the wheelchair. Carl covered him in a blanket and wheeled him toward the elevator.

As they passed the waiting room turned living room, Silva pointed excitedly at a fake plant just outside the archway. "Tree!"

"Yes, Dr. Silva, that's a tree, a plant." Carl tried to keep going, but Silva put a hand on the wheel, slowing the wheelchair. "Tree!"

"Yes, it's a tree. Let go of the wheel. We have to go. Every minute could save lives."

"Blood nodblood... tree!"

Carl looked down at him. "Your red notebook is in a tree?"

Silva held out his arms in a wide semicircle. "Tree."

"A big tree?"

Silva raised his hand high, palm parallel to the floor, then lowered it.

"A short, big tree? Like a bush?"

Silva nodded. "Tree." He pointed at the plant again.

"Your red notebook is in a bush at the nursing home."

Silva nodded again, smiling. "Blood nodblood tree home."

Carl pushed the wheelchair to where the MP stood next to the elevator. "Sergeant Welsh, we need to get to Beachwood Assisted Living Center in Bethesda. It's urgent. Life or death."

"My orders are specific, Dr. Parks. No one comes. No one goes. I'll radio my commanding officer." He spoke into his radio, then listened to the reply. "It'll be a minute. My commander has to radio Andrews Air Force base."

"Andrews? Aren't you Army?"

"All armed forces in the area are consolidated at Andrews." His radio crackled. He listened and then spoke into it. "They can't spare a detail right now."

"Tell them it might be a cure."

The Sergeant perked up and relayed the message on his radio. They waited. The radio crackled to life again. "There will be a detail here in twenty minutes to take you."

"Thank you, Sergeant." Carl turned the wheelchair around and headed back to Silva's room. Now that he had an idea where to look for the notebook, he was loath to take Silva with him. "You're too valuable to risk. I'm sorry, Doctor, you can't go."

Silva started squirming in his chair. "My go! My go!" He banged his good fist into the padded armrest of the wheelchair.

Carl dropped him at the nurses' station and asked Nurse Crippin to get him squared away, then headed back down the hall.

"They're sending up protective gear for you, Dr. Parks," Sergeant Welsh said. "I'll show you how to put it on."

The suit was heavy and smelled of charcoal, which Carl found reassuring, not only because it would keep out contaminants but also because no one could smell his sweat.

"Okay," the Sergeant said, "they're here. Put your mask on like I showed you."

Carl donned the mask. It felt like the world shrank into two foggy discs and smelled only of rubber and alcohol cleaning wipes.

"Try to breathe through your mouth," Sergeant Welsh said as the elevator doors opened. "It won't fog up as much. Good luck, Doctor."

Carl hit the "G" button, and the doors closed. When they opened again in the lobby, Carl gasped. The corridor of plastic hung in tatters from the suspended ceiling. Beyond it, he caught glimpses of past chaos. Gurneys sat smashed into one another. Cast-off gloves and masks littered the floor. Boxes of supplies lay tipped on their sides, and piles of plastic packaging from all manner of medical devices were strewn about.

A Humvee idled in the horseshoe driveway under the portico. An MP stood outside it, waiting. The hospital doors were locked. Carl banged a gloved fist on the smeared filthy glass.

The MP trotted over and unlocked the door. "Sorry, Doc," came a gas mask muffled voice.

"Okay," Carl said. His voice had its own rubbery echo inside the mask. The world he observed as he walked to the Humvee was not the world he stepped out of when he went into quarantine on the sixth floor. Gone were the crowds, the lines of the sick snaking around the fences. The enormous tents were gone, and thank God, the white trailers full of bodies. Now, there was only the idling Humvee and bits of trash blowing in the light breeze. Apart from that, nothing moved. There were no cars, no planes, no city noises, just footsteps, and the Humvee motor.

He got into the back and the MP closed the door. He leaned forward. "Have you been told where we are going?"

"Yes, sir," the driver said through his gas mask.

"Beachwood Assisted Living Center, Bethesda," Carl said it anyway.

"Yes, sir."

"Okay, let's go."

A light rain fell as they drove through the empty streets. Rivulets of water ran down the thick window. Piles of garbage, abandoned cars, and feral dogs went by, their images distorted by the water as if through a funhouse mirror. Once in a while, a face appeared in a darkened window, nose and eyes peering over a sill.

On the outskirts of DC, a few people shuffled along, carrying heavy bags or backpacks, skirting their way through the tangles of cars and trash. They turned their masked faces to stare at the Humvee, then put their heads down and trudged on.

Carl leaned forward. "Why are we wearing these gas masks? A surgical mask would protect against the virus."

The soldier in the passenger seat turned towards him. "It's the smell. These buildings are full of bodies. No one to clear them out. It could be years before we get them all. Not so dangerous, but the strong smell will make you barf all over everything. Also, it's a morale killer."

"I see." Carl sat back. Jesus. Years? Intellectually, Carl knew that there would be no going back to normal any time soon. But experiencing it like this, driving through it, brought it all crashing down in a great wave. Would there be anything like the world he knew in his lifetime?

The Humvee weaved around cars left haphazardly in the streets, many occupied by corpses, their grinning faces staring at their laps or leering at him through rotting lips, foreheads pressed against dirty glass. He sobbed. His chest heaved. He brought his hand up to hide his face and wipe the tears. Instead, rubber gloves bounced off of his gas mask. There was nothing for it. His tears ran down his face and pooled where the mask met his jaw.

The passenger turned and saw him. "You all right?"

Carl shook his head.

"Concentrate on your breathing. In and out. Stop looking out the window. Think about the mission. How to conduct it. How to win."

Carl did, but it felt like someone was squeezing his chest. He began to hyperventilate and reached up to unhook his mask.

"Keep your mask on! I'm not cleaning your puke out of the Humvee. You'll be doing that yourself!" The soldier shouted. "Put your arms above your head, look at the ceiling, and breathe slowly."

Carl did what the soldier told him and tried to clear his mind, slowly bringing his breathing under control.

"You ready to make the big move, Doc?" the soldier in the passenger seat asked.

Carl, still gasping for breath, could only incline his head in reply.

"They didn't tell you?"

Carl had to concentrate to understand the soldier's words between the layers of rubber mask he wore over his ears and those of the mask over the soldier's mouth.

"Yeah. We're shutting down the hospital and moving everyone over to Navy Med. Doesn't make sense to split our forces anymore, I guess, but what the hell do I know? Funny, all those Girl Scouts on the sixth floor came from Navy Med. Now they're going back. Typical Army."

The logistics involved with moving all the comatose patients made Carl's mind reel. He was breathing almost normally when they pulled up in front of Beachwood.

"How you feelin' Doc?" the soldier asked.

"Better. All that stuff about moving the hospital... was that true? Or just designed to distract me?"

"Yes," the soldier said, then exchanged a few hand signals with the driver and got out.

Carl reached for his door handle.

"Wait, Doc." The driver said. "Stay here until we've checked things out."

"Expecting trouble at an abandoned nursing home?"

"It's a brave new world."

A minute later, the driver opened his door and motioned for Carl to get out.

They stood under the portico, looking at the front doors.

"What's the deal, Doc?" the driver asked.

"We're looking for a red notebook, possibly stuck in a tree or a bush. This notebook may contain vital information about a smiling flu treatment."

"And it's stuck in a tree? Are you fucking kidding me, Doc?"

"I wish I was."

"Is that it?" The other soldier pointed at a bush to the right of the front doors, just outside the protection of the portico roof. There was a splotch of red amid the leaves.

They walked over to the bush together. Carl reached into the foliage and fished out a red notebook. Raindrops ran down its warped, waterlogged cover. Rust from the spiral metal binding left brown spots on Carl's gloves. He opened it. The ink on the first page was smeared, illegible

"Is that it?" The soldier who pointed it out asked.

"I don't know yet," Carl said, turning the pages, looking for one he could read. Page after page of blue smears passed through Carl's gloved fingers. Towards the middle, some pages were half and even three-quarters legible. After finding the name Sampson, he read about an injection that had no effect. He kept turning pages, but as he approached the back of the notebook, where, presumably, the successful treatment would be noted, the pages became totally smeared again. He let the book dangle by the spiral from his gloved fingers. His stomach churned.

"Well?" the soldier asked.

"We're all fucked."

Chapter 29

Erica

September 13, I-84, Utah

Erica rubbed her eyes as the first hints of twilight revealed the desert scrub in shades of blue and black. The SUV sat backed up against a chain-link fence separating the rest area from the featureless plain beyond. She fought the urge to sleep by looking left, counting to a prime number, then right, and counting to the next highest prime number. Her thin sweatshirt did little to fight the chill. She rubbed away the gooseflesh on her arms and cast a baleful look at the heater controls. But no. Gas was getting hard to come by. They couldn't spare any for the luxury of using heat. When the sky began turning blue over the distant hills, Erica decided that was close enough.

"Ed?" She turned her head so she could look into the back at his dark hair poking out of the sleeping bag. "It's dawn, and I'm cold and tired."

There was a grunt from the back.

"C'mon. Let's get going. It's a long way."

"No shit, really?" He unzipped the sleeping bag, opened the back door, and stepped barefoot into the grass. "Shit, that's cold!" He jumped back into the SUV.

Erica turned around and faced the front while he struggled into his shoes.

"You're up for some bunk time," Ed said.

"I want some breakfast and a real bathroom. Then, I want to get changed standing up."

"And I want a million dollars."

"Well, we can go get that after I use the bathroom." She pointed at the rest area building. "And have something to eat."

"Okay, okay."

She gathered her things and stuffed them in her shoulder bag.

"You really need all that?"

Erica looked down at her bulging shoulder bag, then back at Ed. "Yes." They walked together toward the restrooms. Ed held the shotgun. They both wore gloves and masks.

Outside, Ed picked up a handful of stones.

"What are those for?"

"A diversion, a decoy."

"Why?"

"Just stay behind me, okay?"

"We need a diversion to use the ladies' room? You've been watching too much TV."

Ed ignored her. He threw the stones in, waited a few seconds, then entered. "All clear."

"That was a little paranoid," Erica said, advancing to the sink with her bag.

"Maybe. But there's no police. No ambulances. No nothing. So it's just the bad guys and us, and I don't think they announce themselves. Speaking of paranoid, what if there's virus in here?"

Erica pulled a spray can from her shoulder bag. "See?" She sprayed down the sink. "I do need all this stuff. Now, if you will excuse me," she stood looking at him until he closed the door and left her alone. Ed stood leaning on the SUV in front of her when she emerged. He mimed looking at his watch.

"Oh, fuck off." She unpacked her shoulder bag, leaned into the SUV, and put things away in their proper places. "Okay, now breakfast."

"It's on the passenger seat."

"Really? What?"

"A banana and cereal."

"Milk?"

"Hold on, let me just pull some out of my ass."

"You don't have to be a jerk about it." Erica slammed the hatchback.

They got in. Ed drove. Erica ate the mini box of dry raisin flake cereal, washing it down with gulps of bottled water. Apart from her munching, the car was silent. She looked at Ed; his jaw clenched, nostrils flared. "Are you mad at me?"

Ed's lips tightened, but he said nothing.

"Why don't you tell me what's going on with you? Why are you keeping it all bottled up?"

"Because it won't make things better."

"How do you know?"

"Because I do."

"It might."

"It won't."

Erica peeled the brown spotted banana and took a bite. "This might be the last banana I get to eat for a long time." She regarded it thoughtfully. "Too bad it's turning already."

Ed was silent.

"C'mon, Ed."

"Fine, you want to know what's bothering me? I'll fucking tell you. We have two thousand miles to cover. I'm trying to get there as fast as I can to see my little girl who is in some kind of fucked up coma, and you're stopping to shave your legs and put on makeup! For who? Everyone else is fucking dead!"

Erica dug in her shoulder bag for a travel pack of tissues. She sniffed and padded her eyes, careful not to smear her makeup. "We don't have to travel together if you don't want to," she said, looking straight ahead. "There's no reason to anymore. When there was a newspaper story, and travel expenses there was, but now... well, there's not even a newspaper, much less a story for it."

"I'm sorry," he said, "I can't stop thinking about Aella, all alone in some hospital room, eating and drinking through a tube. What if she wakes up, and no one is there? What if the doctors get sick and there's no one there to take care of her? What if..." Ed sobbed, rubbed his shirtsleeve across his eyes, and took a deep breath. "Anyway, I'm sorry."

Erica nodded. She was about to explain the makeup. But when she looked at Ed, he was staring fixedly in the rearview mirror. "What is it?"

"Car coming up very fast. Too fast, lots of obstacles and abandoned cars on the road. He'll never be able to react at that speed."

Before Ed finished speaking, a white minivan whooshed by them, its engine screaming. Erica only got an impression of a curly-headed woman at the wheel and a sleeping passenger.

"Shit," Ed said, "wonder what that is all about." They watched as the car grew small and disappeared on the horizon.

"Ed, I'm sorry I slowed you down this morning. I just... I haven't showered in days, and, well, I just couldn't face the world dirty and disheveled. As for makeup—"

"Forget it."

"No, please, let me finish. The makeup and the clothes and the hair, it's like," she paused, looking for words, "it's like armor. If I'm put together, you know, on the outside, it helps me feel put together on the inside, like I'm in control. I need to feel that today, Ed. In control. After the pregnant lady and the little girl... everything is so out of control. Anyway, I don't want to slow you down."

"I'm not leaving you behind. After you helped me with the DTs in quarantine and your kindness before and after, I figure I owe you."

"I was using you to get a story, to advance my career," she looked away from him, out the window.

"You were kind and genuine. You weren't faking that, were you?"

"No."

"Anyway, we are a good team, and I like your company. It helps. Talking to someone helps me take my mind off of Jamie and Aella."

"I like your company too, Ed. I'm glad we're working together."

They rounded a slight curve, and down a gradual slope in the distance, smoke rose. As they got closer, a white minivan came into view. It had smashed into the end of a bridge. It impacted the abutment head-on, crumpling the whole front end right to the windshield. Thick white smoke rose from the wreck.

"That's the minivan that passed us," Erica said.

"Yeah. Something about this isn't right. I'm not sure — wait, there are no skid marks."

"Maybe the brakes went out? Or the driver was sick like... like yesterday."

As they passed, a fat woman with a big perm and fashionable clothes staggered out of the driver's door. Blood ran down her face. She stamped her foot and clenched her fists like a toddler having a tantrum, and then the scene was behind them.

"We're not going to stop?" Erica asked.

"No. Something's not right."

"She didn't seem sick or incapacitated. She seemed pretty angry."

"What do you want me to do? Invite her to ride with us? What if she's infected, but not sick yet?"

"I want us to do the humane thing, the right thing. I want to see if we can help somehow," Erica folded her arms across her chest.

"We have to get to Washington."

"What's the point if you're not a human being when you get there?"

Ed looked straight ahead, jaw clenched.

"What if Aella was in the car with us? What would you want her to see you do?"

"Don't try to manipulate me." Ed kept looking straight ahead, then, after a few seconds.

Erica crossed her arms and scowled.

"Fine!" He stomped on the brakes, sending all the supplies in the back crashing into the back of their seats. Then he turned the SUV around, tires squealing. Then stomped on the gas again, speeding down the highway in the wrong direction.

"Ed!"

"We're going back. Don't tell me *how* to go back."

The woman stood next to her minivan using a napkin to wipe blood from her face.

Ed stopped just past the wreck. He tucked the pistol into the back of his pants.

When Erica saw him reach for the door handle, she said, "Ed, mask and gloves."

They both donned masks and gloves, got out, and walked a little way toward the woman. Ed stopped halfway to the wreck.

Erica frowned but stopped, too, standing at his side.

"Thank you for stopping," the woman said. She took one last swipe at her face with the napkin, then looked at the blood on it.

"What happened?" Ed asked.

"Oh, I swerved around that abandoned car up there and lost control." She dabbed at the blood oozing from a gash on her cheek and inspected the napkins.

Erica didn't believe her. Apart from Ed's observation about the lack of skid marks, there was something not right.

Erica's experience as a reporter made her a pretty good judge of when people were lying to her, and this woman was full of shit. Still, there wasn't anything menacing or dangerous about her. The whole thing was just wrong somehow. She began to regret pushing Ed so hard to stop. Maybe she could get to the bottom of this by asking some innocent questions. "Is everyone in your car okay?" She couldn't see into the minivan's tinted windows.

"Oh, they're fine. Just resting. I'm trying to get them to the hospital."

"If they're fine, why are you trying to get them to the hospital?" she asked.

"Oh, no, I meant they didn't get hurt in the crash. They have the smiling flu. The hospital in Twin Falls wouldn't take them. They said maybe Salt Lake, so we're going there."

"We can't give you a ride. I'm sorry," Ed said, "maybe we could help you get that car going." Ed pointed to the abandoned car up the road.

"Oh, I really wouldn't want you to go to all that trouble for us. I'm sure highway patrol or someone will be along."

Erica felt a pit forming in her stomach. Something was really wrong here. The woman drove down the same road they did. She had to know that there was no highway patrol, no one coming.

"Well," Ed said, "We can send help as soon as we see someone."

"Yes, thank you. I want to stay here with my husband and son. I couldn't live without them." She looked at the ground.

"Do you need any food or water?" Erica asked. She wanted to toss the woman a couple of water bottles and try to outrun the sense of foreboding creeping into her heart.

"No, no, we're fine. There is one thing, though."

"What's that?" Ed asked.

"I'm worried about being out here alone. My husband can't help right now, and, I uh, I can't figure out how to work his gun. Can you show me?"

Alarm bells clanged in Erica's head.

"I suppose we shouldn't leave you out here unarmed," Ed frowned.

Erica put a cautioning hand on his arm.

"I'll just get it."

"Slowly," Ed said, hand behind his back.

The woman turned and reached into the minivan, her ample rump stretching her expensive-looking slacks. She emerged holding a small black pistol.

When she emerged with her pistol, Ed pulled his, pointing it at the ground in front of him.

"It's all right," the woman said. "It doesn't work. Anyway, I'm not going to hurt anyone."

"Then why do you want it?" Erica asked.

The woman ignored her and held the pistol out to Ed in her open palm. Ed took it in his free hand and tucked his gun back into his pants with the other. He removed the clip. Checked it, then racked the pistol. The chamber was empty. He inserted the clip and handed it back, safety on, chamber empty.

"So," Ed said, drawing his pistol again, "I'm going to show you what to do, but don't you try it until we're gone. You might give me the wrong idea. And I might make a mistake that could never be set right in your lifetime."

"Dickens," Erica murmured. She turned and looked at Ed in surprise.

"Don't worry, don't worry," the woman said.

"You're gonna hold it like this, finger off the trigger, and pull the top part back 'til it clicks, then let go and let it slide into place. Mine already has a bullet in it ready to fire, so that bullet is just gonna pop out. Yours won't cause there's no bullet in there yet." Ed racked the pistol and deftly caught the bullet that popped from the ejection port. "Then, when you flick the safety switch on the side, it'll be ready to fire. But don't do it. I'd take it the wrong way."

"What if you're gone, and it still doesn't work?" the woman sobbed. "How 'bout if you train your gun on me, and I just try it? Just to make sure. Please! Please don't leave me out here like this without knowing the gun works."

"Well—"

"Ed, no!" Erica grabbed his arm again.

"It'll be all right." Ed pointed his gun at the woman. "If that gun points anywhere near us, I'll end you."

"I promise, I mean you no harm," the woman said. She turned so that the pistol pointed at the other side of the highway. "So I pull the top back like this 'til it clicks, then let it go?" She did. "And I flip this safety switch?" She did.

"Whatever you do right now, do it slowly. You are making me nervous," Ed said.

"I'm just going to fire it over there." The woman had her gun pointed at the hills across the highway, ninety degrees from Erica and Ed. She squeezed the trigger. The shot was loud in the relative silence of the empty highway. "Wow, that was louder and jumpier than I thought. Thank you."

"Now, just set the gun down on the ground and get back in the car until we're gone. Erica, you are cutting off my circulation and limiting my range of motion."

Erica found that she was still squeezing Ed's arm, though he was aiming his pistol at the woman. She let go, bunching her hands into fists.

"Sure, I'll just put it down," the woman said, but she didn't.

"Go on!" Ed widened his stance.

"Ed!" Erica saw the woman raising her pistol.

"STOP!" Ed yelled.

The woman froze.

"I'm not going to do anything to you," the woman said, almost to herself.

"Ed!"

"This was your idea."

"Not getting shot with a gun you fixed," Erica said out of the side of her mouth.

"Well, what do you want me to do now? Shoot her?"

"I just want you both to know I really can't live without them." The woman started raising the gun again. It was not pointed at Erica and Ed.

"Don't you do tha—" Ed yelled.

In one fluid motion, the woman raised the pistol to her ear and fired. Red chunks of her head splattered all over the side of the white minivan. The woman fell across the dotted white line. The impact shattered the rest of her skull and splattered her remaining brains in an arc, radiating from her body like a Japanese folding fan.

Ed stood, gun still pointed at where the woman had stood.

"Oh God." Vomit rose in Erica's throat. The woman's blood splattered brilliant crimson across the white line. "Oh fuck. Ed, why did you do that? Why did you show her that?" Erica put a hand to her mouth.

"You wanted to stop and help, so we helped." Ed straightened and lowered the weapon.

Erica ran to the back of the SUV. She had just enough time to lower the mask before she vomited. The slippery white chunks of banana plopped onto the pavement at her feet and sprayed onto her sneakers. Ed's hand touched the small of her back. She wiped her mouth on the back of her hand. "Leave me alone."

"Okay. Get a drink of water and get in the car. Try not to look. I'm going to check something."

She wanted to ask him what the hell he was going to check, but more banana worked its way up her throat, and she vomited again. After dry-heaving a few times, she cleaned her face with her mask and threw it and the gloves in the puddle of banana vomit. She got a water bottle from the back and got in the SUV doing her best not to look up.

Ed came back a minute later, started the SUV, and turned them around.

Erica looked at her lap until she was sure they were past the horror on the road.

"What... what just happened?" She took a long pull from her water bottle.

"Her family was long dead. She tried to kill herself by driving into that bridge, I think. But the minivan was engineered too well. When we passed her, she wasn't angry. Then she crashed and was angry she wasn't dead. She probably tried the pistol first, but couldn't make it work. Lucky we stopped. Now she's with her family."

Erica couldn't tell if he meant it or if he was being sarcastic to spite her. Her stomach roiled. She decided to let it go for the moment. Just concentrate on her breathing and try not to throw up again.

"You were right. We had to stop and help. She would have died of thirst or exposure eventually, after days of agony. She just wanted to be with her family. She didn't have any fight left in her soul. It was the humane thing to do."

She still couldn't tell if Ed was saying all this to fuck with her, like some kind of passive-aggressive 'I-told-you-so.' Either way, she had all she could stand. "Humane?"

"Yeah. Think of it like assisted suicide. What I don't get is—why she didn't wait until we were gone. That's what I thought she'd do."

"You knew?"

"I suspected. It was the lack of tire tracks."

"Maybe she wanted a witness, someone to see her last act of love." Erica wiped her eyes. The SUV was silent for a while. "Funny that her whole family died of it, and she was fine."

"Just like us," Ed said, steering with his knee while he dug in his pocket. He came out with a pill bottle. "This was in her purse."

"Laetanol?"

"Yup."

Chapter 30

Sarah

September 14, Crow Reservation, Montana

S arah drove less than an hour down US 87 before coming to a whitewashed highway sign. Hand-lettered in neat black script read: 'Entering the Great Crow Nation Toll Road. Prepare to STOP.'

What kind of toll? Certainly not money. Sarah's stomach turned. She slowed down and took the pistol from the seat beside her, tucking it into the back of her jeans. Her long flannel shirt should help cover the bulge. A little ahead, right near the exit sign for a town called Hardin, two dump trucks blocked the road with 'STOP' painted on their sides in large block letters. Men with guns stood in the back, pointing their weapons over the side. Beyond the trucks, two large campers sat parked under the overpass. To the left on the shoulder, a man sat in a lawn chair under a free-standing shade tent.

Sarah pulled to a stop, even with the man in the lawn chair. He was about forty, pudgy, with a jolly round pockmarked face and a long black ponytail. The man waited for her truck to stop, hands folded on the generous belly of his green t-shirt, then motioned for Sarah to roll down her window.

"Ma'am, I realize your hand is on the window crank, but now please put both hands where my friends in the trucks can see them, and don't make any quick moves."

Sarah put both hands on the wheel.

"That's good, thank you. Anyone else in the truck? Ducking down or hiding in the back?"

"Just my three dogs."

"Three dogs? That's a lot of mouths to feed in these times. What do you need three dogs for? Hunting?"

"They're my dogs."

"Okay," the man sighed. "How are you feeling? Any cold or flu symptoms? Have you been in contact with any infected persons in the last few days?"

"I'm fine, and no, I haven't."

"Good." He raised an eyebrow. "You armed?"

"I prefer not to answer that."

"Well, that's a smart way to play it these days. But I don't want to get shot, and my guess is neither do you. So best be honest."

"Yes, I am."

"Good. Honesty is the best policy. Old Indian proverb." He chuckled. "Anyway, welcome to the Crow Nation toll and inspection station. I'm Russell Black Eagle."

Sarah nodded.

"And you are?"

"Sarah Sampson."

"Well, Miss Sampson, leave any weapons on the seat of your truck where the guys can see them. Then, come on over, and we'll have a chat about the toll while they inspect your vehicle."

"The dogs won't like that."

"It's got to be inspected, Miss Sampson."

"For what?"

"Drugs, heavy weapons, infected persons or corpses, things like that. Do you have leashes for those dogs?"

"They don't need leashes."

"I hope you're right. Come on out slowly, leave your weapons, and keep those dogs under control."

Sarah saw two men with assault rifles hop out of the back of the dump truck and start toward her. She didn't like the look of them. They were serious-faced, dressed in jeans and t-shirts, not professional soldiers. Koontz started barking first. Then Dickens joined in. "Dogs, quiet!" she yelled. Koontz subsided into growls and occasional soft barks. Dickens let out one more good bark, then looked at Sarah. "Good boy," she said.

When the dogs started barking, the men advancing with the guns stopped and leveled their weapons.

"Twitchy," she thought. She decided it was best to announce her next move. "I'm going to reach behind me and lay my pistol on the seat," she called out the window.

"Slowly," Russell Black Eagle cautioned.

Sarah did it slowly, trying to control her shaking hands. "I'm coming out," she called. She got out, and Dickens bounded after her.

One man tracked Dickens with his rifle.

"Dickens, come! Koontz, King, come!" On command, the big dogs leaped over the tailgate and joined Dickens at her side. She reached down and patted their heads. "Good boys."

"Good dogs," Black Eagle said. "Guess they don't need leashes after all. Come on over and chat with me here in the shade." The man got up with a show of effort and picked up a camp chair that lay folded in the grass of the median behind him. He set it opposite him, then sat back down and beckoned Sarah to join him.

Sarah sat down, and the dogs took up stations on either side of her. Koontz growled in the direction of the men rifling through the truck. "Koontz, quiet." She looked at Black Eagle. "Koontz says they should be careful with our things."

Black Eagle smiled. "I'll bet he does." He looked over at the men searching through the truck. "Make sure we are respectful of our guest's belongings." He turned back to Sarah. "There now, about the toll."

"Yes?" Sarah's heart pounded a staccato rhythm. She was acutely aware she was a woman alone, surrounded by men with guns. If there were trouble, the dogs would help. Her Wushu would help. But none of it enough for her to escape with her life or her honor.

"You look nervous. Try to relax. If you are honest and deal honestly, you will get the same in return. None of these men is a stereotype. Are you a stereotype? Self-absorbed middle-class, middle age white woman?"

Sarah stayed silent, unsure if the question was rhetorical and not liking the tone of it at all.

"Of course not. See, we want you to leave here and tell people you meet that the Crow Nation is a sovereign nation. That gives better than it got—a fair deal that stays made." He looked directly into her eyes. "Things being as they are, I guess we could say every person walking is a sovereign nation unto themselves."

Koontz barked, and Sarah turned to see the man approaching. "Good boy Koontz, now be quiet."

The man, tall and thin, had short dark hair and a gold hoop earring in his left ear. He was handsome, and he smiled easily. "Hello," he said, raising a hand in a semicircle wave. "I'm Nate Begay. Is Russell talking your ear off?"

"I'm Sarah Sampson, and no, he isn't."

Nate smiled knowingly. "Did he get around to talking about the toll yet?"

"We were just getting to that," Black Eagle said.

"Sure you were." Nate looked at Sarah. "Let me guess, sovereign nations and fair deals? All that?"

Sarah just smiled at him.

"Our friend Russell here is a talker. Says us Indians got a PR problem. Do you think we have a PR problem, Sarah?"

"Not anymore. No more public."

Nate smiled. "I guess not." He turned his gaze to Russell Black Eagle. "Well? Are you going to keep Sarah here hanging around all day, or are you going to get down to it?"

"Mr. Begay, do I come over there and tell you how to do your job?"

Nate grinned.

"All right then." Black Eagle turned to Sarah. "Miss Sampson, we have cleared the highway all the way through the reservation, and we guarantee safe passage all the way. No highwaymen or bandits. You can go as fast as you like, BUT you are in another country. You are subject to the laws of that country. The penalties for lawbreaking are quite... unpleasant. Do you understand?"

"It's hard to say yes when I don't know what the laws are."

"Of course. Nothing that common sense wouldn't tell you. All you really need to know is: stay on the road. Take no exits. If you have trouble, if you break down, if you need help stay on the road. Do you understand?"

"Stay on the road. Got it." Sarah stroked Dickens's head absently. She wasn't sure what the big deal was, and she didn't care. She just wanted to be on her way. All this talking was making her anxious. This guy didn't belong at a toll booth. He belonged in a coffee shop.

"Now, about the toll. Because we maintain the road, which was and is a lot of work, and because we provide security, we require a little compensation. Obviously, money is no good anymore. We'll have to trade. You've heard what you are getting. What can you offer in return?"

Sarah didn't know what they wanted. She didn't really have anything in the truck she didn't need. "Like what? I'm traveling pretty light. I don't have much to spare."

Russell Black Eagle looked up at Nate Begay, who nodded. "Well, what about one of your fine, well-trained dogs?"

"No way." Sarah gripped the arms of the chair. The thought squeezed her chest.

"Let's start a little smaller, then. How about information? We're pretty isolated here, and since the radio and TV have stopped broadcasting, well... where did you come from?"

"Central Montana down through Billings," she said.

"And how was the trip?"

Sarah told him about the clerk she paid through the gas station door and about Roundup and Billings being all but deserted.

"What about law enforcement, the military, any of that?"

She told him about the military withdrawing from Billings and the flyer.

"That's excellent information! Do you still have the flyer?"

"I think so." She stood a little too quickly to dig into her front pocket. Nate Begay twitched a hand on the strap of his rifle. Sarah saw him run his eyes over her body and pause where her hand reached into the front pocket of her jeans for the flyer. She didn't much like it. She took the flyer out, handed it to Black Eagle, and sat back down.

Black Eagle read it aloud, commenting on this and that, but Sarah wasn't listening. She was looking at Nate Begay, and he was looking at her, smiling pleasantly. She figured he was in his twenties, and he was handsome. As he and Sarah looked at each other, she found that rather than resent his roaming eyes; they flattered her. She smiled back, then worried that she might lead him to believe in an impossible possibility. She frowned and tuned back to what Black Eagle was saying. They talked back and forth about her encounter with Lieutenant Miller and her impression of him. She couldn't help glancing at Nate from time to time, standing there smiling and darting his eyes away every time she looked up. *Nothing's changed*, she told herself. *It's not like this handsome Indian has penetrated my soul, and I'm suddenly a sexual creature ready for a whirlwind romance.* This situation was ridiculous. She drew strength from the fact that there were no butterflies in her stomach; she was not weak in the knees, and there was no magic sensation between her legs. Still, there was something about the guy. He looked into her like a bottle he picked up at a party to make sure there were no cigarette butts in it. She wondered if he saw them. She knew they were there.

Black Eagle was looking at her expectantly. Sarah realized she hadn't been listening for some time. "What?"

"I said, I think the flyer and the information you have provided are enough for the toll. You are free to be on your way."

"Almost," Nate said.

"What?" Black Eagle looked up in surprise.

"What?" Sarah echoed.

"You'll need an escort," Nate said.

Sarah looked at Black Eagle. He smiled knowingly, but remained silent.

"If you're providing security and making the highway safe, why do I need an escort?"

Black Eagle shrugged.

"It's just part of the service we provide," Nate grinned.

Sarah frowned. What was to stop this guy from forcing her into something once they were alone on the road? She could just go around the reservation. It would be a long detour, but doable. She looked at Nate again. He seemed harmless enough, but in her experience, bad guys didn't come equipped with a warning label. Still, it was only about an hour to the other side of the reservation, and if he rode in the back with King and Koontz, it should be safe enough. "Okay, on two conditions: one, you ride in the back, and, two, Dickens has to approve."

Black Eagle let out a good-natured laugh.

"Dickens?" Nate asked.

At the mention of his name, the dog's ears perked up.

"Go," Sarah said.

Dickens popped up like a four-legged jack-in-the-box. He was usually timid when first meeting strangers, sniffing a hand, and then backing away, especially with men. But the dog trotted right up to Nate, who squatted down to meet him and extended a hand. Dickens quickly sniffed the hand, then ignored it, instead putting his paws on Nate's shoulders and licking the man's face, almost knocking him over.

Sarah was stunned. She had never seen Dickens take to anyone so quickly. She looked at Nate to see what he would do. Nate hugged the dog before pushing him back, then patted the dog's head.

Black Eagle looked at her face and laughed again. "Well, I guess that's settled."

This was not the way Sarah expected this to go at all. She sighed. "Okay, let's get going."

"Let me get my bag," Nate said, sounding more like a school kid being taken out for ice cream than a grown man with a rifle on his back. He jogged off toward the dump trucks. She watched as he handed his rifle to the men, exchanged a few words, then ran out of sight toward the campers parked under the overpass.

Sarah and Black Eagle exchanged goodbyes. Black Eagle called to her as she walked toward her truck. "It's all right, Miss Sampson. He's my sister's nephew. He's a good boy."

Sarah nodded, then turned and loaded the dogs into her truck. The dump truck on the left backed up onto the grassy median, and the man in the back waved her through. She inched her truck forward until it was under the overpass and stopped in front of the campers. After a few seconds, Nate emerged with a large, faded green army duffle over his shoulder. He dropped the bag into the back and climbed in after it. Once he settled in with his back resting against the rear window of the truck's cab and stretched out his legs, Sarah hit the gas.

There were no cars in the rearview mirror. There wouldn't be, maybe ever again, so Sarah adjusted it to keep an eye on Nate. He'd taken off his work boots. His white stockinged toes wiggled in the breeze. King rested his head on Nate's thigh while Nate scratched between King's ears. Not only was King letting Nate touch him, but the dog's eyes were closed. As far as Sarah knew, no one but her had ever touched the cool and aloof pit bull. Not even in Sarah's bed did King deign to be affectionate. Instead, he curled up in a corner by himself. Koontz curled up in a ball, his head resting against Nate's other leg, asleep.

The truck shuddered and shook. A loud "ggggrrrrrr" came from the passenger's side wheels. Sarah turned toward the road again and realized that she had drifted onto the rumble strip on the edge of the highway. "Shit," she said, cranking the wheel to bring the truck back onto the road.

"Everything all right up there?" Nate called.

"Fine," Sarah said over her shoulder.

"I can drive if you're tired."

"I'm fine."

Nate shrugged in the rearview mirror.

Who the hell was this guy? Some kind of Indian dog shaman or something? Did he have bacon in his pockets? It bothered her. What also bothered her was that the guy wasn't talking. The way he looked at her when they met, she expected him to talk her ear off, to try to get somewhere with her, but he wasn't talking. Then, a minute later, she heard him singing. It sounded like "On the Road Again," the Willie Nelson song, but the words were different.

"The apocalypse. I'm driving through the apocalypse. The life I love is singing with some dogs, and I'm just driving through the apocalypse." Nate kept singing.

Sarah strained to hear the verses. They were dark and funny, like Nate himself. And she appreciated his gallows humor. And what of that? Usually, Sarah eschewed the company of people. She didn't trust their intentions and didn't like trying to guess when they would try to screw her, figuratively or literally. So, she pushed everyone away. They called it universal precautions in vet school—treat each animal as infectious. But this guy seemed to breeze right past her defenses without acknowledging they were even there.

She had driven for an hour before stopping at the Crow toll station and picking up Nate, and it had only been fifteen minutes since he got in. Even so, she was ready for a break. Maybe if she stopped and talked to this guy, she could put him into a neat little category in her head, dump him, and forget all about this foolishness.

"Hey, Nate?"

"Yeah?"

"Was Black Eagle telling the truth about safety and security on the reservation?"

"Pretty much. There's always going to be troublemakers. Nothing anyone can do about that. But there's so little traffic on 87 now, it just wouldn't be worth hanging around. Plus, the Rez was a pretty empty place before the flu."

"You in a big hurry to get where you're going? I want to stop and let the dogs do their business."

"I'm never in a hurry."

She pulled the truck onto the shoulder, took the pistol from the seat, and tucked it into the back of her jeans. She saw Nate looking at her as she tucked the gun. He opened his mouth, then shut it and just shrugged. She dropped the tailgate, and the dogs leaped into the tall grass of the roadside. Nate pulled on his boots without lacing them, climbed out, and stood, resting his butt on the edge of the tailgate.

"What are your dogs' names again?"

"The Lab is Dickens, the Shepherd is Koontz, and the pit bull is King."

Nate watched the dogs sniffing around in the grass. "Are they named for the authors?"

Sarah was filling three stainless steel bowls with water from her five-gallon container. She stopped and looked at him.

"Hey, I'm not just some dumb Indian. I'll have you know I have attended three colleges and universities."

Sarah raised an eyebrow.

Nate smiled. "And dropped out of all three. I had good grades, but I wasn't built to sit in a classroom."

"I'm sorry," she said, "It's not like that. So few people make the connection. It's got nothing to do with you being an Indian."

"I'm sorry too. It's an old habit. An old trick. You make light of the stereotypes and prejudices, play on the middle-class white guilt, and keep them off balance. Helps you get your way sometimes. I'll try not to do it again with you."

"Okay," she said, returning to filling the bowls. She set them down on the pavement. The dogs came running to the sound.

"Who's your favorite?" He asked.

"Dog or author?"

"Author."

"Stephen King is my favorite overall. That said, the first few passages of 'A Tale of Two Cities' are my favorite passages of prose ever."

"Never read that one, but that explains why the third dog is named Dickens."

"Why wouldn't he be? What's wrong with Dickens?"

"Well, King and Koontz wrote horror and supernatural stuff. I just don't see Dickens that way."

Sarah was rummaging around in her food stores. "You hungry?" she asked.

"I could eat."

"How much Dickens have you read?" she asked. She picked up one food item after another, then threw it back in the pile.

"Well," he paused, "um, Great Expectations in high school. Oh, and I tried to make it through Bleak House in college, but I couldn't — too dense."

"What about A Christmas Carol? You must have seen it or heard it read somewhere; that's riddled with supernatural stuff, almost the whole thing. And Great Expectations, the milieu of the graveyard scene, and Mrs. Havisham's house. Anyway, Dickens is right at home on my shelf next to Koontz and King. Peanut butter and jelly okay with you?"

"Love it, thanks."

There was a comfortable silence between them as they made their sandwiches on the back of the tailgate. Sandwiches made, they sat on the tailgate, eating. Nate produced two cokes from his duffle bag. Afterward, Sarah got the cigarettes from the glove box and offered one to Nate, who took it.

As the cigarette burned down between her fingers, Sarah's head dipped. She jerked upright.

"That right there is why you shouldn't smoke in bed," Nate said, breaking the long silence.

"Shit. Must be the sugar from the coke and the jelly." She took a last drag, then stood, crushing the cherry between her boot and the blacktop.

"When was the last time you got a decent night's sleep?"

"It's been a few days," she admitted.

"Seems like you could really use one."

The voices in Sarah's head were contradictory. One said: here it comes. He's working up to proposition you. The other said: three nights ago, you stayed up all night watching the news. Two nights ago, you kicked a man to death in the middle of the night. Last night you slept fitfully, camouflaged as a car accident. He's right. You could use a good night's sleep.

"Yeah, I guess I could at that. Do you have a good hotel on the reservation, one with room service and a good concierge?"

"Well, I don't know about that, but the view is pretty cool here. It's quiet and safe. You got armed guards in front and behind. I don't know how it is off the reservation now, but I bet you sleep with one eye open out there."

"I don't know..." The idea of relative safety was appealing. Losing half a day of travel wasn't.

"Think of it this way: if you can get a good night's sleep in here, you are in a much better position to leave alert instead of nodding off with a cigarette in your hands."

She knew he was right, of course. Despite that, though, this guy was a question mark. What was his motive? Was there a bottle of chloroform in his bag? Best not to risk it. "No, I think I'd better get moving."

"Okay, but I'd stand watch for you."

Sarah frowned. "I don't know you. How do I know you won't, I don't know, knock me out and steal my stuff?"

Nate shrugged and gave her a funny little half-smile. "No offense, but your stuff isn't that great."

She softened. "Better than your stuff."
Charming as Nate was, Sarah wasn't all that
reassured. "Seriously though, how do I know ʼ
you won't hurt me in the night?"

"The dogs don't think I will, and neither do
you, if you're honest with yourself."

"I'm just gonna keep moving."

"Suit yourself." Nate reached down to pat
Dickens, who was nuzzling his hand. "What are
you in such a hurry for? Where are you going?"

"I don't know you well enough to tell you that
yet."

"Okay." He hopped off the tailgate and threw
a stick for Dickens. All three dogs ran after it.

Sarah packed up the food and dog bowls,
feeling like she was being rude and hard on the
kid. She did think of him as a kid, though he
was probably near thirty. There was a wonder-
ful boyish quality about him. She caught herself thinking of him in those terms and reminded herself that he was a man and a stranger.
Not to be trusted, no matter how handsome
and charming he was. "Dogs, get in the truck!"
She called. They did. So did Nate.

Tall brown grass waved gently in the breeze,
stretching away into featureless plains on either side of the empty road. The tires made a
low moaning sound, and the wind in the open
rear window faded. The world grew dark.

"Hey!" Nate yelled.

The truck rumbled and shook. Sarah jerked
the wheel, then steered with one hand and
rubbed her face with the other.

"All right, that's it. You're going to kill us.
Either let me drive or pull over and get some
sleep," Nate said through the window.

Sarah pulled over and turned to face him.
"No bullshit. I sleep with three attack dogs
and a loaded gun, so don't even think about
messing with me."

"Three attack dogs?" Nate grinned. "Are you honestly asking me to believe that Dickens is an attack dog?"

Sarah smiled despite herself. "Okay, would you believe two attack dogs and a neurotic Lab?"

"I'll watch over you. Honest Injun," Nate raised a hand in a mock oath.

The way he mocked the stereotype made Sarah uncomfortable. White guilt? She bit the feeling back by going on the offensive. "You're kind of a goober, aren't you?"

If her insult phased Nate, he showed no sign. "Took you long enough to figure that out. I've gotta shake the dew off the lilies. No peeking." He jumped out of the truck.

Sarah coaxed Dickens into the passenger's footwell, then stretched out on the seat. She raised her head, looked out the side mirror, chided herself, and then fell asleep.

Tapping on glass.

Sarah opened her eyes. Wires drooped down from under the dashboard, their form visible in the deep shadow. She sat up. It was dusk. The tapping was back. She turned to see Nate's knuckles on the driver's window.

"I hope you don't mind. I made us some soup." His hand was wrapped in cloth, and he held up a blackened can.

"What time is it?"

"Soup time."

She grunted.

They sat on the tailgate, eating soup from cans with plastic spoons.

"How did you do this? I don't have a stove."

"Simple," he said, swallowing a mouthful of soup. "Heated a rock in the fire and set the soup can on it. It took a long time, not much grass to burn here, but I found enough sticks to do the trick."

"Well, thanks. I had no idea how I was going to cook this."

"We make a good team."

She looked at him, still an enigma to her. What did he want? Did he want a traveling companion? A fuck buddy? A girlfriend? If any of that was true, he was going to be disappointed.

"So, do you know me well enough to tell me where you're going now?"

"Washington."

"Sta—"

"DC."

"That's an epic journey. Or is it a quest?"

"I wouldn't say that. It's not like I'm taking the ring to Mount Doom."

"Well, you must have a good reason. That's a long, dangerous trip these days. Some might even say an epic one."

She sighed. "The short version is: my father was missing in action in Vietnam forty years ago. I saw him on the news a few days ago. Back when there was news. I guess he was in a coma for a long time. I'm going to find him. Find out why he never came home."

"Are you mad at him?"

"What is this? The Inquisition?"

"It's okay if you don't want to talk about it."

Sarah had to admit it felt just a little bit better to talk about it. The realization unnerved her. She was a loner, a unit of one. How dare this guy just show up and penetrate her defenses? "I don't know. I just need to know what happened."

"Sounds pretty epic to me."

They ate the rest of their soup in the same companionable silence they'd shared at lunch.

"Has it been hard so far?" Nate asked.

She saw herself kicking the man in the grass. "Yes."

Nate convinced her it wasn't a good idea to leave the reservation until morning. No telling what they'd be driving into. So, she agreed to keep watch while Nate slept.

The stars moved slowly overhead. She battled with herself over Nate. She liked him, a rarity in and of itself. And she felt safe with him, even though she had known him less than a day. Part of her, the small part she couldn't entirely kill, wanted him to stay with her. The bigger, badder part of her, protected under a mountain of emotional scars and sealed like NORAD behind massive blast doors, wanted him gone, wanted things back to normal: her and three dogs.

When it was her turn to sleep, the siphon man troubled her dreams. He got up after she kicked him to death and ran by the side of her truck, screaming, "You killed me! You fucking killed me over a few gallons of gas. You'll burn that before you make Billings. I'll be dead forever!"

She woke shivering. Gray light silhouetted the edge of the distant hills. Nate sat on the tailgate, his back to her. Just for an instant, the smaller part of her wondered what it would be like to hug him. The big bad part of her brought its boot down on the thought. She stretched, then got out of the cab, Dickens at her heels.

"Mornin'," Nate said.

"Mornin'—I'm going up in front of the truck, don't look."

"Okay, I'm goin' the other way, don't look either." He smiled.

Sarah looked, but only, she insisted to herself, to see if he looked. He didn't. Afterward, she set the dogs' food out on the edge of the pavement in stainless steel bowls. The sun rose bright and warm over the hills.

"I was thinking of trying to find my aunt and uncle. They were headed to a powwow in North Carolina. I figure we could travel together for a bit, if you don't mind. At least until I help you replace all the food I've been eating. I feel bad about that, like a houseguest that invites himself to dinner."

There it was. Sarah knew it was coming. Yesterday she would have said 'no' out of hand. But today, after last night's dreams... it was good to fall asleep knowing someone had her back. She knew he would let her down. Everyone let everyone else down. Maybe if the arrangement were left open with the understanding that he would definitely leave, that would be okay. The dogs liked him. "Okay, until we resupply."

"Great!" was all he said.

When the dogs finished eating, Sarah packed up their bowls. "I suppose you'll want to ride in front now." Her voice sounded harsher than she meant it to. She chided herself for her lack of social graces. God, this was turning into a pain in the ass already.

Chapter 31

Carl

September 15, Washington, DC

C arl watched through the window of the
military bus as they approached Walter
Reed National Military Medical Center. A single pale tower stood vigil over a dying world
like a splinter of bone. At the top, a large dark
opening whose purpose Carl couldn't guess
gaped at the silent city.

In his lap rested the backpack he had hastily thrown together as he left his apartment
almost a month before. His companions on
the bus were, as far as anyone knew, the
last functioning civilian medical personnel in
DC. There were six of them: himself, Dr. Patel, Nurse Crippin, Nurse Chen, and orderlies
Steve and Dave.

The bus stopped in front of the tower, and
they all climbed out under an American flag
fluttering at half-mast.

A man in crisp fatigues waited until they'd all disembarked, his head hairless around his cap with the notable exception of bushy gray eyebrows that stood watch over intense gray eyes. "Ladies and gentlemen, welcome to Walter Reed. I'm Colonel Giels, director of the facility. I wanted to come down and welcome you personally."

A short, dark man in battle dress uniform came into view around the corner of the bus, wheeling a large cart in front of him. He stopped and saluted the Colonel.

The Colonel whipped a quick salute back to him and motioned him forward. "Please give PFC Davis your things. He will place them in your quarters. I will give you a quick tour of the Civilian Medical Unit, then PFC Davis will show you to your quarters."

When everyone's belongings were tagged and stowed on the cart, the Colonel led them around the side of the tower to a squat white three-story building. They entered through the glass doors and stood in the spartan white tiled lobby. Once they were all inside, the Colonel turned to address them. "The first floor is the children's flu ward. The second floor is for civilian adult flu cases, and your quarters are on the third floor. Your patients from A.L. Memorial have all been settled in and are stable. I must stress that this campus is under strict quarantine. No exceptions.

"Right now, we are over capacity. The unit was a two-hundred-bed surge capacity facility. We currently have one hundred and twenty-five pediatric cases and one hundred sixty adult cases. This way."

The Colonel pushed open the double doors, revealing a new-looking ward with pristine white floors and taupe walls. A thick plastic crash rail ran down the hall at waist height, and against it, gurneys with children on them lined the corridor. Their little faces featured feeding tubes snaking from tiny noses presiding over ubiquitous grins. Carl rubbed at the gooseflesh on his arms as they passed child after child, each grinning maniacally at nothing.

"Excuse me, Colonel," Dr. Patel said. "I don't see any young children here."

"Yes, Dr. Patel, the children are arranged in descending order of age. The youngest are closest to the nurses' station." He walked a little further down the hall and gestured at a doorway. "We have four children who have awakened within the last week. There is some brain damage. But the hope is that the impact will be minimized as they continue to develop because they are so young."

Carl peered into the room. Infants sat in car seats, three to a bed. Plastic tubes crept like vinyl vines into their tiny nostrils. They lay, little arms in their laps, horrible toothless grins on their faces, and drool on their chins. A nurse went from infant to infant, swabbing the insides of mouths and noses with something. Written on white tape affixed to the car seats were names, most of them presidents or prominent women from history. Andrew Jackson was there, and so were Susan B. Anthony, Harriet Tubman, Rosa Parks, and Alexander Hamilton. A few seats, ones without recognizable names on them, had red tags with numbers. "Excuse me, Colonel, can you tell me about the President's names and the red tags?" Carl asked.

"I was just getting to that. Many children came to us from strangers who found them with incapacitated or deceased family members. We needed names for the children. Numbers just didn't seem right somehow. So, we chose prominent names from US history. It's that simple. Roughly eighty percent of the children under our care have unknown names. As for the red tags, they indicate a connection to a patient upstairs in the adult ward. Some are indeed the children of those patients. Others were merely found with an adult in unclear circumstances.

The Colonel moved down the hall. "In this room, we have the children who recovered on their own."

Carl squeezed into the semicircle around the open doorway. Inside, there were three playpens and one large play enclosure. Two nurses sat in chairs, each holding a child. One child, a little black girl of about two, cried softly into the nurse's shoulder. Her bare legs extended down from a pink nightdress and dangled into fuzzy pink slippers.

The second nurse held a boy of about three or four, also crying, but his eyes drooped, almost asleep. He was dressed head to toe in gray sweats. One playpen held a bundle, unmoving. Carl guessed it was a sleeping infant. The large enclosure was thigh high for an adult, made of tan plastic outlining symmetrical round holes. Through them, Carl saw a little boy, maybe four years old, throwing blocks at the enclosure wall. Bang, bang, bang. Occasionally, one would make it through and bounce onto the floor on the other side.

"Scans show a total lack of activity in the pleasure centers and reward circuits of their brains. So far, they seem incapable of pleasure. No smiles, no laughs, or any other positive behavior. However, they respond to touch and are calmed by physical contact. We have a team devoted specifically to this form of therapy."

The Colonel paused and met the eyes of each of the people gathered around the doorway. "The next thing I have to tell you is going to seem extraordinary and far-fetched. I assure you it's the truth. When a child emerges from the persistent vegetative state, they... vocalize."

The Colonel, who, in Carl's estimation, was Army all the way from his crisp cap to his spit-shined shoes, seemed rattled and at a loss for words. Carl thought he knew why. He still remembered Sampson's horrible gut-twisting screams when he came around. If he heard that sound coming from a child, well, he preferred not to think about it.

"Vocalize?" Dr. Patel asked.

"Clinically"—Colonel Giels cleared his throat—"uh, clinically, we are referring to the phenomenon as Synchronized High-Volume Vocalization. In plain English, it seems that when one patient emerges from their vegetative state, they scream. Each time this happens, the other awakened patients scream too. I know this is difficult to believe, and we have no medical explanation, but I assure you, it is real."

The short hairs on Carl's neck crackled with electricity. He shivered, thinking about a chorus of 'Sampson-like' screams coming from a group of toddlers. As he heard it in his mind, he pictured himself bolting from the hospital. He hoped that if it happened, he could retain his professional composure.

"We can't predict when the next child will wake," the Colonel continued, "and we don't have the resources to split all the children up. We're running tests. Analyzing the few brain scans we have the resources to perform. But as of right now, there is simply no explanation."

A dull thrum came from the middle of Mike Sampson's head. It was as if a monstrous heart was beating, turning toward him. The pounding grew louder and closer, like the footsteps of an approaching giant. This was the second time he had felt this sensation since arriving at Walter Reed. He had felt it before, at the other hospital. There it was, faint, fleeting, an impression rather than a sensation. Now, it was enveloping, overpowering, inescapable. He sensed a coming, an arrival of a dark presence. This time was worse than the last. Stronger, closer, as if he were in the epicenter of an earthquake.

The thrumming made him clutch at his buzzed gray hair and push down hard on his scalp. He was grateful that he was alone in his hospital room. If he ever wanted to get out of here, he was going to have to hide this... whatever this was. Otherwise, the doctors would poke and prod him forever.

Still not strong enough to walk or transfer himself to the wheelchair, he turned over onto his stomach and buried his face in his pillow against what was coming next. The urge welled up from the depths of his chest. He was powerless to deny it. His mouth opened on its own. He released the scream into his pillow.

The Colonel went on about the condition of the recovering children. The doctors hypothesized only children were emerging from the grip of the smiling flu because young brains develop rapidly and form new neural connections around damaged areas. A hypothesis Nurse Crippen had come up with a week ago, but it wasn't worth pointing that out at the moment.

"We are limited in our ability to conduct brain scans because of the—"

The Colonel stopped mid-sentence and gazed into the hospital room full of toddlers. Carl followed his gaze. All four children, including those asleep, stopped what they were doing, raised their heads, and looked at a spot on the wall.

"Colonel, I think it's happening!" the nurse holding the little girl said.

The nurse holding the boy looked at the crowd in the doorway. "Could one of you hold the baby, and another hold Ryan?"

Dr. Patel strode into the room and picked up the bundle in the playpen.

Nurse Crippin went to the boy throwing blocks. "Can I give you a hug?"

"I don't want a hug," the boy said in a monotone. He never took his eyes from the spot on the wall.

"Are you Ryan?" she asked.

The boy nodded.

"I had a boy about your age," her voice caught in her throat. "He liked hugs. Do you like hugs too?"

"I guess." He raised his hands to his head and clutched it.

A terrible sound that started in hell and ended in a little girl's mouth echoed down the hall. Before anyone could turn their heads toward the noise, the four children in the hospital room screamed, low and mournful at first, like the first note of a funeral dirge. It grew in volume and intensity until it reached a crescendo of desperate agony made more macabre by the children's tiny, high-pitched voices. All four children paused, drew a breath in unison, then started screaming again. Nurse Crippin leaped over the little fence, deftly for a big woman, and grabbed up Ryan in her arms.

A lump formed in Carl's throat. His chest heaved with a repressed sob. The screaming children and the sound's awfulness made him shiver and rub at the goosebumps that broke out on his arms again.

"Colonel!" a shout came from down the hall. "Room one-twenty-four!"

The Colonel ran. Carl followed, with the others running like a school of out-of-shape fish.

When they arrived at room 124, Carl recognized Aella. She sat bolt upright, screaming. The nurse who'd arrived first sat next to her in the bed, holding her hands. Carl covered his mouth to keep from screaming himself. The sight of this little girl screaming in agony cracked what was left of his professional veneer. The wailing went on forever. Carl prayed for it to stop.

Chapter 32

Sarah

September 15, Denver, Colorado

The rain bridged the gap between the cold gray sky and the cold gray pavement of Interstate 25. Sarah sat with Nate on the tailgate of her truck, dry under an overpass. The cigarette was stale and tasted of metal. Her exhaled smoke mixed with Nate's and drifted out to dissipate in the falling water.

Nate stared out at the rain. "We need a more practical vehicle."

"It would be fine if I weren't picking up hitch-hikers," Sarah blew more smoke into the gray-ness.

"So, you're saying that without me, you could fit three dogs, and all the supplies into the cab? Let's see, that's dogs, dog food, people food, clothes, blankets, lights, and batteries... hmmm, yeah, I bet that would all fit."

"It might," Sarah smiled.

Nate gave her a wry look.

"I hate to leave this truck. She's been good to me."

"I get it. But even if we go down to seventy to cross the country, the nights will be getting a little cold for sleeping outside."

"Yeah," Sarah sighed.

They sat listening to the water drip from the bridge above onto the pavement. The dogs, bored now from running and sniffing, lay in the pickup bed with them. Dickens rested his head on Sarah's thigh.

"Well," Nate said, breaking the long silence. "I guess we could wade into the traffic jam and see if there is something suitable we can drive."

"No point in getting wet. There's nothing to build a fire. No way to dry off except sitting in the truck in front of the heater burning gas."

Nate stood and looked at the highway in front of the truck. Sarah turned and followed his gaze. The traffic jam started just one hundred yards past the overpass and stretched into the distance. Tracks scarred the roadside. Evidence of vehicles that had escaped or been salvaged by travelers like themselves. The rain drowned all but the faintest smell of the bodies rotting in the cars.

"We've had a pretty clear run until now," Nate said.

"I should have known our luck wouldn't hold." Sarah flicked her cigarette butt into the rain. "Isn't there some kind of stop-the-rain dance you can do?"

Nate went red. "Okay, I've overlooked some of the casual comments you've made about my ancestry. I'm a pretty easygoing guy, but let's get some things straight. When I was ten, I left the reservation with my mother. I was a city boy until just a couple of years ago, and when I moved back to the reservation. The

Crow Reservation, not the Navajo. I've lived in a house all my life. Not a teepee or a hogan. I've never been to a sweat lodge, rain dance, or any other kind of dance except at a powwow, and that's totally different. I'm not a chief, or a shaman, or medicine man or a warrior. I can't hunt or track, and I have no magic Indian power of sneaking up on people. I can't shoot a bow or even ride a horse. And I don't have some secret well of ancient Navajo wisdom. Okay? I'm just not that kind of Indian. I'm just a guy, okay? I'm just a regular guy."

"Okay," Sarah said. Her hackles up now, too. "As long as we're laying it all out, let me clue you in on a few things, too. I'm not some helpless woman. I don't need a man around. I'm not interested in love, sex, romance, or any of that crap. I'm not a lesbian, either. I don't understand why you came with me. I don't buy your story about finding your aunt. I like having you around. It's easier to travel with two of us, but if you're looking for love, or a fuck, you will strike out." She paused and looked at him.

The anger from a moment ago drained from his face. Now he just looked kind of sad.

"I think you knew all that on the first day," Sarah went on. "Even though I never spelled it out exactly. So why are you here, Nate?"

Nate wore a stoic, inscrutable expression. Silence hung between them for several long seconds. Then he let out a breath. "The truth is, I don't have a good reason. I just do what comes into my head. I just do what's next."

He sat down on the tailgate next to her. "I was working for my aunt and uncle, making blanks for wood flutes they sell at powwows. I watched over their house, made the flutes, then shipped them out to whatever city the powwow was going to be in next. Then the flu hit. No one was going to need any more flutes, so I volunteered for guard duty on the edge of the Rez. I stood in the back of that dump truck for a week with the other guys. But I'm not Crow. I'm an Indian, but I'm not one of them. They've known each other, each other's families, all their lives. I was almost as much an outsider as you. They were nice enough to me, but it just wasn't my place."

"I thought you said you were Navajo? What was your uncle doing on the Crow Reservation?"

"He's a Crow, and my uncle by marriage. My Aunt is a Fancy Dance champion, and she ran a fry bread stand at the powwows. She met my uncle, they married, and now they do the powwow circuit together.

"Anyway, I'm up in that truck wondering what the hell I'm going to do next. I definitely wasn't going to spend the rest of my life in the back of a dump truck.

"Then you showed up with your dogs, and I thought, *She looks interesting. I like dogs. Guess my ride's here.* Simple as that. So I made an excuse to come along. Although my aunt and uncle are out on the East Coast somewhere, I don't think it'd be worth trying to find them."

She felt better having it all out in the open. It looked like Nate didn't. He looked at the ground.

"I didn't really lie, but I wasn't exactly straight with you. If you want me to go, I'll go," he said.

"As long as it's not some misguided notion of helping a damsel in distress or any romantic crap," her words sounded harder than she meant.

"I told you, I'm not that kind of Indian."

"Okay, you're not that kind of Indian. And I'm not that kind of girl."

Nate smiled, "okay."

Sarah stood and stretched. She turned, looking out over the parallel lines of cars that ended where a tractor-trailer jackknifed across the road, blocking her view.

The rain tapered off, and patches of sunlight glinted on wet chrome and glass. She took the pistol from the truck seat and tucked it into the small of her back. "Let's take a look. I'll take the right side."

"I'm going to hang back a bit and cover you, just in case."

Sarah walked along the shoulder, trying not to look into any cars she wasn't interested in taking, trying not to see the desiccated, grinning corpses. Her four-legged phalanx of dogs formed up around her.

A crow fluttered out of an open window.

Sarah shrieked.

Dickens barked.

"Everything okay?" Nate called.

"Fuck. Yeah, just startled."

There were no useful vehicles on this side of the jackknifed truck. She rounded the truck and stood in between the lines of cars.

Koontz let out a soft "woof."

Sarah ducked. What is it, boy?

Koontz woofed again and shifted his weight from one front paw to the other.

She stuck her head around the bumper of the car she crouched behind. Several cars ahead, the door of an odd-looking orange car stood ajar. It was a suicide door. The kind that opened backward. It masked what went on behind it, but Sarah knew.

A man stood in the open door, pants around his hairy ankles. Through the window glass, she saw a little, bare foot in the crook of his arm. The foot, too flaccid to be attached to someone consenting, and too small to be an adult, flopped obscenely in time with the man's pumping motions.

The cold Colorado day became the hot Florida sun. Beads of sweat tickled her upper lip. The smell of slow rot from the cars surrounding her became the smell of a fetid Florida swamp. Sarah smelled stale nicotine fingers covering her mouth. She felt the putrid beer breath of her foster father on her neck. The time and distance between that moment and this one shrank to nothing. She heard his voice in her ear.

"You shut up now and take it, or I'll feed you to the gators. Ain't no one going to come looking here. Ain't gonna be no search parties opening up no gator's stomach. Ain't gonna be no search parties at all. No one's gonna wonder what happened to poor little Sarah. You just gonna be another white trash runaway."

Her body jerked at the memory. She was there... and she was here; the memory overlaying the present. She shook off the ghostly feeling of her foster father's weight on her and rose to her feet on the Colorado highway. Then she was running. The dogs kept pace.

Koontz barked a battle cry.

The man turned his craggy face toward the noise, dropped the leg, and reached for his pants.

Sarah rushed around the open door and sent a savage kick into the side of his hairy ass. He bounced into the door and fell sprawling onto the pavement.

"What the fuck!" He yelled, fighting to untangle his legs from the pants at his ankles while covering his penis with one hand.

She glanced at the back seat. The limp body of a young boy hung half out of the car.

Rage boiled inside her. A molten lava of pent up hurt and horror took over her actions. Sarah sent a savage kick to the rapist's head.

He screamed and tried to turn away.

Sarah let out an answering primal howl and kicked again.

His head snapped to the side. He stopped trying to pull his pants up and instead tried to roll under the car.

"No, you fucking don't!" She grabbed a handful of greasy hair. Lithe, trained muscle and animal fury allowed her yank the fucker into the open. She kicked again, connecting with his cheek with a wet crunch.

The man screamed again, more feebly this time.

"FUCK YOU! YOU PIECE OF SHIT!" She delivered another kick.

The man's penis sent threads of clear fluid across his thighs. He moaned and rolled onto his belly.

She let him. She didn't want to see that shit. She wished she hadn't.

He clawed at the pavement, trying to belly crawl away, his pants acting like shackles around his ankles.

"How could you do this to me?" She screamed and kicked him repeatedly before he could disappear under the car.

The man stopped moving.

"How   could you"—kick—"do"—kick—"this"—kick. Bone cracked against her toe—"to me?!" Blood trickled from a tear in the skin above the man's ear.

She kicked again.

And again.

And again.

The man's head caved in like a jack-o'-lantern left on the porch long after Halloween.

The dogs stopped barking.

"Okay, okay, it's over," Nate's voice came from behind her as his hand came to rest on her shoulder.

Sarah shrugged him off. Her animal self in full control. And kicking again.

"Sarah, he's dead. It's over." Nate's voice was a little stronger and louder now. It broke the spell. Florida was gone. There was only Colorado. She looked down at the mess of the man she'd killed. Bile rose, and she vomited on the pulpy mess of the man's ruined head.

Nate put his arm around her shoulders, guiding her toward the grass on the roadside.

She let him. Her breath came in ragged gasps. The puke worked its way back up her throat. She squatted down and threw up again in the grass. The smell of sick and blood mixed with the stench of the surrounding dead made her sicker. She heaved, but there was nothing left in her to come out. Leaning back on the car's front tire, she cried, quietly at first, then louder and stronger as the vomit cleared from her mouth and the magnitude of what had happened sank in. "Oh God," she sobbed. "Oh my God."

Nate crouched next to her. "Hey, it's over. It's all over now."

"It's never over. Not ever. It just keeps happening in my head. Over and over."

"Shhh, yes, it is. That's it now. It's gonna be okay."

"It's not okay, and it never will be."

"Yes, it will. If you can find a way to let it." He put his arm around her shoulder again.

She turned, her knees coming down from in front of her face to the pavement at Nate's feet. Nate put his other arm around her neck. She let him hug her.

They stayed like that for several minutes. Nate rested his cheek on her head until her sobs diminished to sniffles.

She straightened, coaxing Nate back. "I want to bury the boy," she said.

"Okay, wait here a minute. Let me cover... the other body."

Sarah spat bile, then nodded without looking up.

He was gone for a minute. She heard him rummaging around in the car. He came back and held out his hand to help her up. She ignored it. She shook with spent adrenaline.

"There's a sleeping bag in the back seat with him. We can put him in that," Nate said.

"All right."

He fished out the "Hulk" sleeping bag and handed it to Sarah. "I'll pick him up," Nate said. "You slide the sleeping bag over him."

She stepped over the blanket covering the lump on the pavement, trying not to think about what it hid.

Nate leaned over the boy to pick him up. "He's still alive."

"Oh God," she said. She didn't know if that was better or worse. "Okay," she whispered.

It was an awkward job, but they managed to get the limp boy into the sleeping bag. "Let's get him away from here," Sarah said.

"Yeah." Nate cradled the boy in his arms and followed Sarah down the edge of the break-down lane toward the overpass.

They laid the boy at the slope's edge so that his upper body inclined a little. Sarah sat down on the wet grass next to him.

"I'll be right back," Nate said.

Sarah nodded. She sucked on the cuff of her flannel overshirt, the bitter taste of the fabric a welcome change from vomit. Using the moistened cuff, Sarah cleaned the mucus and spit from the boy's face. Too late, she realized she wasn't wearing gloves, and neither was Nate. This boy was crawling with the virus. Nothing she could do now. She took off the shirt and threw it in the grass down the slope. Her eyes came back to the boy's face. His wide, round blue eyes were starting to dull. He didn't have long. She brushed his long brown bangs from his freckled forehead. He was beautiful. Someone's beautiful baby. And he would join them before long. She pushed his cheek muscles a little to relax the weird smiling flu grin.

"It's all right now," she said, wondering if the boy could hear her. Dickens came up behind her and licked her ear. Koontz and King laid down at her side. She stroked them each in turn, then looked back at the boy. "At times like this, my mother always used to say, *this too shall pass*, and it always did. But she never told me you have to *let* it pass. I'm not so good at that part."

Nate's footsteps swished in the grass behind her. He had his backpack on. For a moment, she was afraid he was coming to say goodbye. Maybe her display of savagery convinced him she was crazy. "Are you leaving?"

Nate stood next to her, looking puzzled for a moment. "Oh, the backpack. No, I'm not going anywhere. I just needed something to carry stuff in." He set the bag in the grass next to Dickens, reached in, and handed her a bottle of hand sanitizer. "Here. Start with this."

She took it and rubbed it into her hands and face.

"Now this." He handed her a bottle of water. She drank it all.

"Good." He took a trash bag from the pack and placed it on the wet grass and sat on it.

"What about me?"

"I think you should go wash up and change. I'll stay here."

She looked down at herself. Her shins were covered in drying blood and gore. "Yeah, right." She got up and walked to the truck. Dickens got up with her. "Stay with him." She knew the kid probably did not know what was happening. But she liked the idea that the boy had a dog during his last hours on earth. She gave Nate a thin smile. "Thanks."

Sarah stripped naked under the bridge. The cool dusk hardened her nipples and sent goosebumps rippling along her skin.

She had one leg into a fresh pair of jeans when she stopped to listen. It was a flute. The sound was rich and mournful, the notes long and slow. Nate was playing. Though the song sounded sad, it made her feel better somehow. The smooth notes chased the horror from her mind. The tension in her jaw eased. She walked back barefoot. The grass was wet and cold underfoot. It was good to touch something alive.

She sat down on the trash bag next to Nate. When he saw her bare feet in the grass, he stopped playing.

"No, don't stop. It's beautiful."

"You'll catch a cold or pneumonia or something."

"I'm from Montana," she said, "play."

Nate rested the flute between his knees and dug in his duffle bag. After a prolonged struggle, he produced a pair of beat-up sneakers and a pair of socks. "Put these on."

"That's ridiculous. They're way too big. Plus, wearing someone else's old shoes is disgusting."

"Would you agree that we've done everything pretty much your way since we met?"

"I guess."

"Have I ever asked you for anything besides a ride?"

"No."

"Then please put the fucking shoes on." He elbowed her playfully.

"Fine, now play the fucking flute." She elbowed him back, then put the shoes on.

Nate played until the light faded entirely from the western sky. "My fingers are getting cold."

"Those were beautiful songs. Were they Navajo?"

"I don't know any Navajo songs, or any other songs. I just find a theme and improvise."

They stared into the night for a long time. The stars reflected off the glass of a hundred cars, making a second star field on Earth. Somewhere in the distance, coyotes yipped and howled. The dogs' ears perked up, but they didn't bark.

"Sarah," Nate was looking at the boy.

"I know. He's gone." She sniffed and wiped a tear.

"You did right by him."

"I want to bury him." She looked at Nate, daring him to object or point out the futility of the gesture.

Instead, he said, "I think we should eat first. The dogs are hungry."

On hearing the word hungry, the three dogs leaped to their paws and wagged their tails.

"Yeah, okay."

Nate sat with the body while Sarah made sandwiches and fed the dogs. After they ate, Nate freed a shovel from a Jeep he'd seen on the highway, and they dug at the bottom of the slope at the foot of the overpass. After they interred the boy, they stood looking at the heaped dirt.

"Will you play the flute again?" Sarah asked.

Nate played soft and slow while Sarah thought about how, as she buried the boy, she buried a part of herself. Though it was not her foster father she killed, she felt she had avenged her young self.

Nate finished his song.

"Thank you," she said. "Let's get some rest. I want to go shoe shopping in the morning."

"Great." Nate rolled his eyes.

The sleeping arrangements were different that night. Sarah made a nest in the truck bed. She arranged the supplies around the edges and then stacked clothes, blankets, and soft items in the middle. She climbed in and called the dogs. Nate stood on the pavement, looking uncertain.

"C'mon, Nate, get in."

He smiled and climbed into the midst of them.

She lay awake thinking mostly about Nate's kindness, the way he hugged her and helped her with the boy; no grumbling, no questions. She rolled over and reached for his hand in the darkness. "You awake?"

"Yeah," he sighed.

"I think you *are* that kind of Indian."

Chapter 33

Carl

September 17, Washington, DC

Carl sat on the steps of the hospital eating spaghetti from an MRE package. "I wonder how long the supply of these will last."

Nurse Crippin sat beside him, picking at her food. "I was just getting used to fresh food again. Now we're back to this junk. It pisses me off that the Army won't tell us how bad things are or why the fresh food stopped."

"Well, you can bet the second outbreak is bad enough to cut the Army's supply lines, at least the ones bringing fresh food."

Carl regarded his spaghetti for a moment, then raised his eyes to the empty road. "I've hardly seen any vehicles coming and going today."

"Quarantine's extra tight now. Probably trying to keep it from spreading to Andrews."

"If it isn't there already." She looked down at her food. "I can't eat any more of this crud."

"One thing I've learned since this started: eat when you can, sleep when you can."

"Want it?" she held out the MRE toward him.

"God no," he smiled.

She chuckled and set it down on the cement.

"How are the kids doing?" he asked.

"The last of the Girl Scouts woke up yesterday. God, I hate the screaming."

"Me too. I heard Sampson howling in the stairwell again yesterday. He still does it every time one of them wakes up."

"They all do, even the babies. It makes me want to run away, especially when the babies do it. Carl, I'm afraid."

"Who isn't? Babies that act like Sampson. Jesus." He took another bite of spaghetti. "How are they *doing*, though?"

"They're angry and scared. They're angry their parents aren't here. That candy doesn't make them feel good. They're angry that they can't be happy."

"Can't blame them. I'd be pissed too. Does Aella know her mom is upstairs?"

"No, no point in telling her. Not until there's a way to wake her mom." Crippen looked out at the vast lawn and the military roadblock. "You know what's odd, though?" She looked at Carl.

"Be quicker to list what isn't odd," he said through a mouthful of spaghetti.

"They stick together. You'd think with no joy, no reward circuit, they wouldn't really be social. No incentive. Yet they sneak into each other's rooms at night and just lie together."

Carl swallowed the cold noodles. "Maybe the feeling of comfort is totally separate from happiness. Could be the same reason they all scream together when another wakes."

The front door of the hospital burst open. Dr. Patel looked down at them. "I have been looking everywhere for you two! The CDC is on the radio. They have a treatment!"

"What?" Carl couldn't get his mind around what she said. He must have heard wrong.

"A treatment for the smiling flu, you idiot!"

"Holy shit!" Carl dropped his MRE and took the steps two at a time.

"Praise God," Crippen said, right on his heels.

They raced after Dr. Patel. The entire staff gathered around the radio. Two nurses and a doctor scribbled furiously in time with the instructions coming through. Carl had a hard time making out the words between the cacophony of conversations. Units were receiving orders. Supplies were being located, and transports arranged.

Nurse Timms turned the civilian radio down. Her thin, dark fingers twisted the knob all the way to the left. She picked up the phone, spoke for a time, then addressed the crowd at the nurses' station. "The supplies needed to formulate the treatment will be here within the hour, as well as additional supplies for patients that are awake. Toothbrushes, toilet paper, and rations."

Dr. Maxwell, the chief of medicine for the Civilian Unit, a large meaty man of about fifty with a pockmarked face, held up a hand. "Okay, people, we are going to divide into two teams. Those formulating and administering the treatment, and those distributing supplies. Adult patients with children down here are first. Then patients in ascending order of age, this way patients requiring fewer resources are first, leaving more time and personnel for the recovery of difficult cases."

"No one recovers," a dull voice said from the back of the crowd.

All eyes turned to Sampson. He stood in an Army shirt and sweats, leaning on a cane.

"Anyway," Maxwell continued, "let's work out the exact order and get tags up outside the patient's rooms.

Chapter 34

Jamie

September 17, Washington, DC

Whiteness. Fading. Otherness. Something more existed, but it couldn't remember. There was pain building, building, and fading, then building again. Darkness now. Confused. Darkness and pain. A change. It remembered that darkness and pain were ways of describing, explaining... words... it... no—she, she remembered all at once: words, self, family, the shape of the world. The world, the thing that existed outside the pain of endless burning pleasure. The pleasure burned out, had burned out, leaving only the pain.

She opened her eyes before she was all the way back. All the way free from the burned-out pain. She remembered sight and eyes and walls and ears and sounds. She screamed.

Screams answered.

Jamie. She was Jamie. Fog rolled over her mind, erasing the pain and dulling the shock.

It was a fog of otherness, of others. She could feel them holding her mind. Holding it up, holding it back. Then the fog receded, and the others receded.

She was in a white room. How the place looked meant something to her. She couldn't remember what.

A thin black man in a white coat leaned over her. "Jamie? Can you hear me?"

Words. Words went with talking. This man was talking to her. She must respond, reply, with words, with talking. When she tried, there was just a low croaking in her throat.

"That's good, Jamie. Just relax and rest now. You have been through a lot. My name is Dr. Parks, and I'm going to help take care of you." A white smile stood out from his dark face.

She worked her mouth to make sounds, make words. What words? "Words..." she croaked.

"It's the morphine. It helps when you are waking up. Recovery can be quite difficult."

The world was thick. Too thick to make words through. She was drowning in that world. Too much, too much. Too many sounds, and too much feeling. Something was touching her, every part of her. The sheets, clothes, air, all pushing down on her. Down, down, down... She fought it. It was important to fight because... because... she needed to know... something important.

Aella. She needed to know about Aella, her daughter. Where was Aella? She pushed against the thickness. She fought, and she struggled, and she forced her mouth to make the sounds. "Where?"

"Try to relax," the man said. "You are at Walter Reed Military Medical Center in Washington, DC."

The man didn't understand her word. It didn't penetrate the thickness right. "Aella," she tried again. It felt like there were bugs in her mouth.

"Aella is here. You will see her soon. Rest now. I'll check on you in a little while." The man rose and walked out.

Darkness.

Unfamiliar sounds. Step, click, step, click.

She forced her heavy lids open into the thickness of the world. The noise was an old man with a cane. A cane. An old man. Words and memories and pieces of the world began to resolve and fall into place...

The old man limped closer. He sat on the edge of her bed. He wore gray clothes with a word on the shirt. Army. Pale blue winter sky eyes stared down at her. He took her hand.

"It's confusing," he said. "The pieces are there...but not all of them. There are holes. Don't worry. It will make sense soon. There are others. Can you feel them?"

She looked at him through the thickness, trying to comprehend.

"They gave you morphine. You may not feel the others right now. You will. When you feel their presence, it will be... not better, but less confusing. More comfortable. Say nothing about this. Don't tell the doctors and nurses. That is important. Unless you want to spend the rest of your life locked in an army hospital, or a padded room, don't tell them. They won't understand. Rest now, Jamie. I'll check in on you later."

The man let go of her hand and limped from the room.

She slid back into darkness.

Light.

Awareness.

The old man was there. His dry papery hand closed over hers. Silver stubble stood out on his face. She felt more than his hand. There was an otherness in her head as if she weren't alone inside her skull. The presence was like a hand smoothing the wrinkled sheet of her thoughts.

"Hello, Jamie. I'm Mike Sampson. Do you feel us?"

She shook her head slightly.

"Do you feel a presence? Something soothing?"

She nodded.

"That's us. We are the hand, smoothing, soothing."

The... fuck? She pulled her hand away. "I don't understand."

"No one truly understands, but you will come to accept it, as we have."

"Who is we?" She tried to sit up, then lay back.

"The others that have woken up from the smiling flu."

"Where is my daughter? Where is Aella?"

"She will be here soon." The man took her hand again. "Do you feel different than you did before?"

"Before what?"

"Before the smiling flu."

She could remember the time before—her life, and Ed, and Aella. She remembered it all, but it felt different... "Something's missing inside me. I feel... sad."

Sampson leaned closer. "Below that lies the darkness. It's a bottomless pit best not explored. What you are missing is happiness. I'm sorry, Jamie, it's lost to us."

She thought about that. She couldn't feel happy. Even thinking about things that used to make her happy. There was an empty hole there. "I feel that."

"That place, where the joy used to be, that's where the darkness comes from."

"I want the happiness back."

"We all want those feelings back." He squeezed her hand. "But the smiling flu burned that out of our brains."

"Will it come back?"

"No one knows. But I don't think so."

She closed her eyes. Hot tears ran down her cheeks.

Someone took her hand.

She opened her eyes. Aella sat next to her. "Hi, Mom."

Chapter 35

Erica

September 17, Denver, Colorado

Erica slowed as they approached a massive traffic jam of abandoned cars. Ed's head popped up in the rearview mirror. She sighed. He'd been hitting the bottle hard. She hoped he'd sleep it off and leave her in peace.

"This is exactly why I didn't want to travel on the interstate." The hand rubbing his face distorted the words.

"We can just go around on the westbound side." Even as she said it, a lane opened up on the right. A truck parked across the road had a sign painted on its side. White stenciled letters proclaimed: US military supply route. DO NOT BLOCK. Large cities unsafe. Use 470 to avoid Denver. Survivor Colony at FT Carson in Col. Springs. All welcome. Food, Clothing, Shelter, and Medicine available. INFO at 570AM.

Erica stopped the car and read it several times.

"Well, look at that," Ed slurred.

Erica shook her head and turned on the radio.

"What are you shaking your head at?"

"You. You detoxed in quarantine. You had a second chance. You have a responsibility to Aella. You have a responsibility to me. To us. We have to get to Washington."

"I don't know what you're talking about."

"Yes, you fucking do! What if we're attacked? You can't shoot straight. You can't even think straight. You are useless to everyone right now."

"I can take care of business."

"Bullshit."

"My wife is dead or dying. My daughter is in God knows what condition a thousand miles away. The government took my farm. I've got nothing. Nothing but some bitch ordering me around."

"Ed, get out of the car."

"What? No!"

"I said," Erica put her hand on the pistol in the center console, "get out of the car."

"What are you going to do? Shoot me? That's not who you are."

"That's not who I was. You don't know who I am now. Get out."

"You're going to kill me for having a few drinks? Go fuck yourself."

"Get. OUT!"

"No."

"Then shut the fuck up for the rest of the day. Not a fucking word. I had to deal with drunks like you when I was a kid, and I swore I would never put up with it again."

"Screw you, you uptight—"

Erica picked up the gun and fired it into the roof of the SUV. The unbearable noise almost made her drop it. She coughed on the smoke but couldn't hear herself through the ringing.

Ed made a drunken grab for the gun.

Erica looked down the barrel at him. His lips moved, but the ringing consumed all sound.

Ed grabbed for his shoes and opened the door, his mouth still moving as he got out. She saw him grab a half-empty pint of vodka and clutch it to his chest.

"Perfect." Her voice sounded as if it were coming from under a stack of pillows. "Grab the booze before you even think to put shoes on."

"You are a fucking piece of wo—"

She didn't hear the rest. She sped away with the door open. The acceleration closed it for her.

Once away from Ed, she slowed down to pilot the car through the narrow channel between the ruined vehicles. Someone had come through with a heavy truck and just bashed things out of the way. Erica crossed her fingers that the pieces of metal and glass left in the wake of that violence wouldn't pop her tires.

In her rearview mirror, Ed made obscene gestures at her.

Fuck that guy. Even if Aella recovered, she'd be better off without that drunk.

The gauntlet of ruined cars ended in huge black arcs of rubber on the road leading to a tractor-trailer. It began to rain. Big fat drops fell intermittently at first, then built into a deluge. Water trickled through the bullet hole in the roof and pooled in the gooey residue of the change tray.

Erica thought about Ed—out in the rain. She pulled over, her anger spent; guilt seeped in. It would serve that drunk right to catch a cold.

She realized she had severely overreacted. She didn't want anything bad to happen to him. So what to do? Drive back? He was still drunk. She didn't want to deal with that. Maybe what she needed, what they both needed, was a cooling-off period. They had been together 24/7 since they went into quarantine weeks ago.

She thought of the sign. Maybe a stop at Fort Carson was what they needed. A break from each other and from the road. The sign said to tune to an AM station in the 500s. She didn't remember the exact number. She turned on the radio and scanned. A voice came in through the pops and whines of the AM band.

"... to your nearest military base. Your nearest military base is" the voice changed, "Fort Carson in Colorado Springs," the voice changed back to the original speaker, "food shelter and necessities are available there. Those requiring aid may be asked to work if they are able. Help us rebuild America, join your local survivor's colony at," the voice changed again, "Fort Carson in Colorado Springs," then the original speaker was back, "God bless you, and God bless the United States of America. This message will repeat... Hello Americans! This is Admiral Charles M. Cox, Commander of the Joint Chiefs of Staff. It is with great pleasure and relief that I report to you today the Centers for Disease Control in Atlanta has developed a successful treatment for the smiling flu. This treatment is a series of timed injections and must be administered by a medical professional.

"Most hospitals are closed now, but the treatment is available at your local military base and survivors colony. Let me repeat that. The treatment for the smiling flu is available at," the voice changed, said "Fort Carson in Colorado Springs," and changed back, "We are rebuilding America. Those

wishing to join a safe, productive commu-
nity are urged to report to your nearest
military base. Your nearest military base
is..."

She had already heard the rest. They had a
cure? Except they didn't say cure, they said
treatment. Why? She had to find Ed. Make
things right, and get to Washington.

She swung the SUV around and headed
the wrong way down the highway. The rain
slowed. She drove back through the tunnel of dead and damaged cars. Her head
swiveled left to right, looking for Ed. When
she reached the spot where Ed had gotten
out, she rolled down the window. Icy rain and
drips from the roof spattered her arm. "ED!"
she yelled into the storm. "ED!"

Silence.

She got out and climbed onto the roof. Her
sneakers slipped on the windshield, and her
instantly sopping clothes clung to her body.
"Ed, there's a cure! A CURE!" She heard only
the sound of rain clinking off of the surrounding cars. She climbed down again and
opened the door, leaned in, and beeped the
horn. "Ed, there's a cure for the smiling flu...
I'm sorry... c'mon, let's go!"

She heard a car door open, and Ed's head
popped out about eight cars to her right.

"Are you going to shoot me?"

"No. They said on the radio that they have
a treatment."

"Really? A treatment?"

"Yes, for the smiling flu!"

"This isn't a trick, just so you can shoot
me?"

"No, Ed, I wasn't ever going to shoot you."

Ed walked over to where she stood, soaking
and shivering in the chilly rain. He looked at
her chest. She looked down and saw her erect

nipples poking through her sopping shirt and bra.

"Up here, Ed," she pointed at her face. The apology that had been on her lips died.

"Hey," he said, "I'm a man." He looked at her. Rain fell between them. "No kidding, a cure."

"They used the word 'treatment' on the radio, but yes."

"I want to hear."

"Get in."

He stood looking at her.

"Ed, I'm sorry, I... I just don't do well with drinking, okay?"

He nodded.

She hugged him. "My God, they have a treatment," she said into the shoulder of his denim jacket.

He hugged her back. They got in the car. Ed picked up the gun that was in the passenger seat.

"Ed, give me the gun."

"Are you nuts? You just tried to shoot me."

"No, I didn't. Don't be dramatic."

"I'm dramatic? *I'm* dramatic? You're the one who was yelling and shooting guns, and you're calling *me* dramatic? No way am I giving you this gun."

"Ed, you're drunk. You can't be trusted with a gun."

"Oh, and you're the poster child for gun safety?" He pointed to the hole in the roof. "You've got a chip on your shoulder and an itchy trigger finger."

"Ed. Give me the gun."

"No." He looked at her for a second, then ejected the clip and racked the pistol so that the round in the chamber fell out. Ed made a grab for it, trying to look cool, but bobbled it twice before it fell on the floorboard.

Erica laughed.

Ed laughed too.

"Okay, I'm taking us to Fort Carson."

"What? Why?"

In response, Erica turned on the radio so that Ed could hear the message. She let it play twice before shutting the receiver off.

"Let's get right to Washington. I have to get to Aella."

"Maybe we can get information about her right now at Fort Carson."

"Yeah, okay, quick stop, though."

Erica nodded.

Erica slowed the SUV at another sign for Fort Carson and the Colorado Springs turnoff. Vast lines of dead cars blocked the highway except where one lane had been bashed clear, just like the last traffic jam. Erica took it slow. The rows of cars stretched out in front of her to the horizon. Dark clouds of flies buzzed black in the twilight. The smell of death seeped into the car through the closed windows. Nothing else moved. Stretched out in the back, Ed snored.

Worried about some kind of ambush or attack, Erica kept her head on a swivel as she drove through the chokepoint. The sign earlier about cities being unsafe justified a certain amount of paranoia. And she knew if there was trouble, Ed would be worse than useless—a liability. She crossed her fingers and concentrated on making Fort Carson.

The base wasn't hard to spot. Lights shone out in the distance, an oasis of light in a desert of growing darkness. Erica pulled up to the guard post just past the sign for the base. The uniformed men with guns were reassuring, like the sign itself. Black letters affixed to a stone wall, solid, permanent, strong. Fort Carson.

Bright lights on metal poles turned the night around the gate into high noon. Erica stopped the car at a crash bar with a stop sign blocking the road. A masked and gloved soldier stepped within five feet of Erica's window and motioned for her to roll it down.

She did.

Two more soldiers stepped forward on the other side of the car.

"State your business, ma'am," the soldier said.

"Um, we are traveling, and we saw the signs. We wanted to get some information."

"We?" The soldier bent down, looking for someone in the passenger seat. "How many are in your vehicle?"

"Two."

The soldier's hand went to the butt of his pistol. "Where is the second occupant?"

"Ed's asleep in the back."

"Is anyone sick or injured?"

"Um, no."

"Any weapons in the vehicle?"

"Yes, we have a couple of pistols, a rifle, and a shotgun."

"All weapons have to be checked with us at the gate. They will be returned when you leave. All vehicles are subject to search. Please unlock your doors and slowly exit the vehicle. Leave all weapons inside."

"Okay." Erica hit the unlock button and stepped out. Her clothes were dry now except for her bottom, which grew cold and itched instantly. She fought the urge to pull the wet fabric away from the skin of her ass.

The soldiers opened the hatch and made a groggy Ed get out and stand barefoot on a red line next to Erica. He shifted his weight from foot to foot. "A little heads up that we were coming to the gate would have been nice."

She smiled a little and bit back the words, 'suck it, drunk.' The search took about ten minutes, after which they were directed to the big imposing brick building that surveyed the base through suspicious narrow windows.

They followed the signs in the empty, echoing halls to the quarantine intake room. Several chairs faced a glass wall with an intercom on its surface.

Ed shot Erica a groggy, questioning look.

She shrugged, then sat.

A woman entered. She was small and trim, her camouflage uniform crisp, and her brown hair was pulled into a tight bun above her pale, angular face. "I'm Lieutenant Anderson. I'll be conducting your quarantine intake interview. May I have your names, please?"

"I'm Erica Goldman, and this is Ed Hargrave."

The woman stopped writing their names on her clipboard and looked at Ed. "Did you say Ed Hargrave?"

"Yes, that's me," Ed said.

"Are you any relation to Aella Hargrave?"

He gaped at the woman. "I'm her father. How do you know that name?"

"She's patient zero. Everyone knows that name," the woman said.

"That's actually why we're here," Erica cut in. "We heard about the treatment on the radio. We're heading to Washington so that Ed can be with his daughter. But we wanted to stop and see if there was any information on her."

"Also, my wife, Jamie," Ed added.

"Oh, I thought you were looking to join the survivor's colony. Of course, you're not." She looked down at her clipboard for a moment, then back at Erica and Ed. "It's late in Washington, but I'll get on the radio and see what I can find out."

"Thank you," Ed said, his voice thick, "thank you."

Erica reached out and squeezed his hand.

"I'll be back in a few minutes." Lt. Anderson got up and exited through the door on the other side of the glass.

The seconds seemed to march by with increasing slowness. Erica felt through Ed's clenched hand that he was a coiled spring. He looked at the floor. His lips moved silently in what Erica could only guess was a prayer.

The door opened silently. The intercom was off. Lt. Anderson entered with a smile.

Erica tapped Ed on the shoulder, not wanting to let go with her other hand.

Ed looked up.

"I was able to reach Walter Reed. Aella and Jamie are awake and recovering!"

"Jamie?" Ed's eyes went wide. "Jamie is in Idaho. There must be some mistake."

"No. The information I have is that she is at Walter Reed with Aella. And they are recovering."

"I don't understand. How did Jamie get to Walter Reed?"

"I'm sorry, Mr. Hargrave, I don't have that information."

"Can you find out?"

"I'm sorry. Radio traffic is restricted right now. I wasn't really supposed to make the call in the first place."

"In God's name, why?" Ed asked.

"I can't disclose that."

"But you're sure Jamie is there too, and they're both recovering?"

"Yes," Lt. Anderson smiled. "I hope you don't mind, but I took the liberty of passing on the fact that you're on your way."

"No," Ed said, "that's great. Thank you. Is there a way I can talk to them? Get them a message?"

"I'm sorry. As I said, radio traffic is currently restricted."

"It's okay," Erica said, squeezing Ed's hand. "We appreciate you sticking your neck out for us."

"Yeah," Ed looked through the glass. His cheeks were wet. "Thank you." He turned to Erica, letting go of her hand. "Let's go."

"Wait," Erica wished she had her notebook with her. "Is the country still under martial law?"

"Yes, Admiral Cox is the commanding officer."

"What about the President?" Erica asked.

"I don't have that information."

"How many dead? How many survivors?"

"I don't have that information either."

"How many survivor colonies?"

"I don't have," Lt. Anderson sighed. "We're just getting reorganized. The smiling flu hit the armed forces the same way it hit everyone else. There's at least one survivor colony per state, probably more. I'm sorry I can't answer all your questions. Some things I don't know, others I'm not allowed to share."

"How many survivors at this colony?"

"So far, about one hundred. We expect that to keep growing."

"How about the rest of the world? Survival rates and so on?"

The Lieutenant frowned. "It's a global pandemic."

"What about our armed forces? Is the country being defended?"

Ed stood up. "Who cares about that right now? Let's go! My family is waiting."

"The country is being defended," Lt. Anderson said.

Erica held up a finger. "Hang on. We can spare one more minute. Lieutenant Anderson, what about the cure? How is it working? Does everyone who gets the cure recover?"

The lieutenant looked uncomfortable. She shifted in her chair. "As far as I know, everyone who receives the treatment wakes up."

Erica stared at the woman, trying to use the reporter's trick of letting silence loosen sticky tongues. It didn't work.

"Come on," Ed said.

Erica ignored him. "There's something you're not telling us."

The Lieutenant cleared her throat. She looked at Ed. "So far, no one that has awakened has fully recovered."

"What the hell does that mean?" Ed folded his arms across his chest.

"Well, I'm not a doctor, so—"

"Don't mess around with me. I want to know what's happening to my wife and daughter. What do you mean they haven't fully recovered?"

"Well, they have some mood problems."

"Stop mincing words. What's wrong with them?"

"Ed," Erica put a hand on his arm, "It's not her fault."

"It's okay," Lieutenant Anderson said. She looked at Ed, her knuckles white on the clipboard. "I don't feel like I should be the one talking to you about this, but... they don't smile. Those recovering seem to have a diminished capacity for happiness."

Ed grabbed Erica's hand and tried to yank her out of the chair. "I've got to get to Washington."

Chapter 36

Sarah

September 17, Lawrence, Kansas, I-70

Nate's smile threatened to touch his ears. "Can I just say again that this is a nice fucking car?"

"Oh my God, you're killing me."

Nate sang: "Killing me softly with his mouth, killing my whole day with this car, Ki—"

"Please stop!" Sarah covered her ears.

Dickens stuck his head between the seats and licked Nate's ear.

"No, Dickens! You'll only encourage him." Sarah smiled and dropped her hands.

Nate's smile went undimmed, a canyon of bright white teeth between the rolling brown hills of his cheeks. "Hey, before, if people saw a guy like me behind the wheel of a giant shiny new Cadillac Escalade, they'd call the cops. But now, hell, I'm King of the Road." He sang that song.

"Please, enough with the song parodies." She laughed. "If I agree with you one last time that this is a really nice car, will you shut up about it?"

"Maybe."

"How about for the day?"

"Okay."

"This is a really nice car... being driven by a Navajo pimp."

"Hey!"

"You could pull off the snakeskin boots, but that 70's shirt, and the leather blazer—" she flicked the collar of his coat.

"It's not my fault you can't appreciate high fashion," Nate took a hand from the wheel and straightened the collar she'd ruffled.

"Oh, brother."

Dickens licked Nate's ear again.

"See, Dickens likes it."

"Dickens likes everything. It's not an endorsement of your fashion sense."

"Don't you feel better, though? A day of shopping around Denver, and you're a new woman. I know I'm a new man. A new man in a new car."

"New doesn't always mean better."

They rolled through the vast, flat plains of Kansas. Sarah watched for other cars, movement, and signs of life. There was almost nothing. Occasionally, they saw a vehicle moving. Most were going the other way. The driver's heads craned to look. Nate and Sarah did the same. Other motorists were a novelty. And maybe a threat.

"Look," Nate pointed, "another military sign. Looks like they want us to take 435 around Kansas City."

"Okay, I guess. I wish we knew for sure that it was the military. Could be some group of assholes setting up an ambush."

"Well, so far, the roads have been cleared, at least one lane anyway. Who else but the military would bother to clear hundreds of miles of highway?"

"I guess so."

The dead cars grew as thick as the clouds of flies buzzing from their open windows. Even with one lane open, Nate had to slow down and occasionally swerve around some car that wasn't bashed all the way out of the lane. He slowed almost to a stop near the front of the line of cars. Big steel pipes and plywood boxes from a flatbed truck spilled across the road and onto the shoulder.

"How'd that happen?" Sarah asked.

"Probably messed up the straps on the load when they bashed it aside. Guess we get to see how Black Beauty here handles off road." Nate patted the dashboard.

"Black Beauty? You've named the car now?"

"Yeah, why not?"

"You know Black Beauty dies at the end, right?" She tried to keep a straight face.

"No, he doesn't!"

"Yes, he does!" Sarah grinned into her hand and had to turn away to hide it.

"No, he doesn't. Shut up." He turned the wheel and drove into the deep grass on the side of the highway.

As they passed the pipes on the road, the car lurched and sank a little. There was a pha-pha pha-pha sound from under them.

"Oh, man!" Nate yelled.

"What happened?"

"Flat tire."

"Which one?"

"All of them, I think." He stopped the car, and they got out.

Both tires on Sarah's side had triangles of black steel sticking out of them.

"Fuck!" Nate yelled. "How's that side?"

"Both tires are flat." Sarah sighed, walking around to the back. Metal clinked off of Sarah's new work boots as she walked. She bent down and picked up one of the little black triangles. "What are these?"

"They are spikes that get welded to the top of a wrought-iron fence. Must have spilled from one of those boxes on the truck up there."

Sarah dropped it and looked at the cars up on the road. "Think we could find tires to replace them from one of the cars?"

"Maybe." Nate followed her eyes. "But the lug pattern would have to be the same. We'd have to find another big truck, maybe a Chevy or GMC. I'm not sure which ones would match."

"That would take all day," Sarah sighed.

"Probably, if we're lucky. Might not even find something that matches. We should probably just look for a new ride. Damn shame. This thing doesn't even have a thousand miles on it yet."

"That's just fucking great." Sarah opened the door and let the dogs out. They ran around in the grass while she rubbed her temples.

"We should look ahead. I don't remember seeing anything useful behind us."

They walked along the median, surveying the cars. The sickly smell of rotting bodies hung in the air. A crow flew from the open window next to Sarah.

"Oh Jesus," she grabbed her chest.

Koontz barked. Dickens chased the bird across the median, then gave up as it soared away.

They saw no big Chevys. There were a few candidates for a new ride, but as they approached, they found corpses in each. The dogs sniffed at the cars and snorted. No words were exchanged. They understood battling the germs, and the smell was not an option. They walked on.

"Hey, look at that." Nate pointed to a white minivan in the ditch on the side of the road.

As they approached, Sarah held her arm out in front of Nate to stop him. "Hear that?"

"What?"

"It's still running."

They stood looking, watching for movement in the minivan, but the sun was bright, and the minivan's windows reflected the cars on the road.

"I don't see anything," Nate said. "Let's take a look."

"I'll look. You cover me."

Nate pulled the pistol from the waistband of his designer jeans. "Okay, be careful."

"Yeah, thanks for the advice." Sarah walked directly behind the minivan the way she'd seen Sheriff MacFarlane do a hundred times. The dogs formed up around her, keeping pace, tails at half-mast, ears pricked. She peeked in the rear window. There were bags, blankets, and the backs of heads in the seats. She moved to the side door.

Nate stood in the street several feet away, his gun trained on the van but away from Sarah.

She peered in. A woman and a baby, both unconscious, were in the seats. She moved to the driver's window, and Nate sidestepped with her. A man sat in the driver's seat, still breathing, grinning at the strings of mucus that ran to his chest.

Sarah gave a thumbs-up and told Nate what she saw.

"Shit. I thought this part was over. I didn't think there was anyone left to get infected."

"Well," Sarah said, "there's us."

"That's a cheery thought, thanks."

"Anytime."

Sarah moved back and inspected the woman and the baby. She was in a ruffled nightgown with little pink flowers that rose and fell with her breathing. Blond curls obscured the smile and mucus Sarah knew were on her face. The baby remained strapped into the car seat. It was a girl, dressed in pink under a white teddy bear blanket, head down, mouth open, eyes closed, dead.

"I'm so tired of this, Nate. Rapists and dead babies, and just all of it. FUCK!" She turned away. Faces of all the corpses she'd seen these last few days flashed across her mind. She kicked a rock in the road. It clinked off of a car on the other side, sending a cloud of flies buzzing from the window.

"Yeah, me too." Nate lowered the pistol. He walked closer to the minivan. "Engine sounds good. The tires look okay. I want to check under the hood."

"We should glove up."

"Good idea. I'll drive the truck over on the flats."

Nate drove the Caddy over, flat tires flapping on the pavement. They donned masks and gloves and stood looking at the minivan, reluctant.

"Well," Nate said finally, "what do we do with them?"

"Before we get carried away, why don't you check the engine first?"

"Right." He opened the driver's door, popped the hood, looked around, and closed it. "Looks all right," he said. He reached in and turned off the engine.

"Okay. I guess we just lay them out on the grass. There's nothing anyone can do for them."

"Yeah." Nate nodded. "Let's start with him."

They struggled with the chubby man, laying him on the grass. They did the same with the woman. She, too, was still breathing. Sarah almost tripped over Koontz as they set the woman down.

"Dogs out, damn it!" Sarah yelled.

Then they stood, looking into the van at the baby.

"I think it's dead. It's not smiling anymore."

"She," Sarah corrected softly. "She's dead... I fucking hate this! I fucking hate it!" She felt anger rising in her chest. Anger at the situation, anger at what? God? Anger was the only way she could cope. The only way to keep from breaking down. Giving up. The only way she could deal with disposing of a baby's body. What kind of fucked up world was it where she had to even think the phrase *dispose of the baby*, let alone *do* it?

"Do you want me to—"

"No! I'll fucking do it." She leaned in, tugged on the straps that held the car seat, but she couldn't figure out how to unfasten it. She straightened, rubbing her lower back. "Do you have a fucking knife?"

"Yeah." Nate handed her a pocket knife.

She leaned in once again and cut the straps. She grabbed the back of it and began hauling it out of the van.

A dry, rasping, plaintive sound made Sarah stop.

A cry.

Wide blue eyes looked up at her.

Dickens wagged his tail and barked softly.

"Oh my God," she gasped, setting the seat on the grass.

The baby let out a weak and hoarse cry.

Sarah moved the blanket off the child and unbuckled the straps holding her into the seat. Dickens nosed in and tried to lick the baby.

Sarah pushed him back. She picked up the little girl and held her. "See if there's a diaper bag in there somewhere?"

"On it."

Sarah rocked the crying infant while Nate searched the van.

"Got it," he held it out.

"She's weak. Probably hungry and dehydrated. Is there a bottle or formula in there."

"Are you sure it's safe to hold it like that? It's probably crawling with virus," Nate said as he emptied the diaper bag's contents onto the grass.

"I don't care anymore. If I get the smiling flu from this baby, then that's how I die. I've had it with this shit."

Nate unzipped a lunch bag he found and pulled out two eight-ounce bags of yellowish liquid. The liquid inside had separated, watery stuff on top and chunky white stuff on the bottom. "I don't think these are any good. They're pretty warm."

"That's breast milk. Homogenized milk doesn't separate like that. Open one and smell it."

Nate did, then shook his head.

"Hold her while I check out the mama."

Sarah went to the mother and pulled the woman's nightgown up, rocking the woman's hips to get the fabric past. She pulled it up over her breasts and looked at the bra. It had clasps in the front. "Nate, bring her here." Sarah unclasped the bra on one side, exposing a light pink nipple.

"How do we do this?" Nate asked.

"How the fuck should I know?" The baby's weak cries were going right up her spine and into her brain. She couldn't think straight with that awful noise. It had to stop. She had to make it stop. "I'm sorry. The crying... God damn. I can't stand it."

"Hard to believe you don't have any kids."

"All right, super-dad, what's your idea?"

"Let's sit her up and put the baby in her lap. You hold mama. I'll hold baby."

Sarah hauled the woman up by the armpits, heavy and limp like a sack of feed. The woman slumped away from her. She tried again from behind, bracing the woman upright with her knees.

Nate positioned the baby this way and that, trying to get the angle right. The child just wouldn't latch on. Her tiny mouth sucked at the nipple in vain.

"Well, this isn't fucking working," Nate said, cradling the baby to him.

"No shit, Sherlock."

"Well, you think of something, if you're so smart."

Sarah thought of nursing animals. They almost always lay on their sides. "Let me get her on her side."

"The baby or the mother?"

Sarah shot him a look. "Really?"

"Well, how the fuck should I know?"

Sarah laid the woman down and then rolled her onto her side. Her exposed breast lay in the grass. "Lay the baby here. I'll position the breast."

Nate set the child gently on the grass and scooted her toward the nipple. Sarah lifted the breast to the baby's mouth.

"Scoot her a little closer."

Nate did.

The baby latched on and began to suck.

"Oh, thank God," Sarah said, slowly letting go of the breast. The baby's latch held. She continued nursing. "The crying was killing me."

"Me too. Now what?"

"Now we get her fed and cleaned up."

"I mean after that. Are we taking her with us?"

"Nate, are you honestly contemplating leaving her by the side of the road to die?"

"No. But how are we going to feed it? Are we bringing its mother along to nurse until the woman dies? Then what? Are you keeping the baby? Are we dropping it off somewhere?"

"Her."

"What?"

"You keep calling the baby 'it,' Nate, it's a girl."

"So, are we dropping *her* off somewhere?"

"Hell, Nate, I don't know. I just got into this. Same as you. I'm not contemplating the nature of post-plague orphan etiquette. I'm just trying to keep her alive for now. We'll figure it out. Why don't you get the van cleaned out and give the dogs some water?"

"In other words, get lost for a while."

"You're getting to know me pretty well."

He walked away, shaking his head.

She listened to him rummaging through the van and throwing things into the grass. The baby let go after a while. She cried stronger and louder than before.

"Done on that side, huh, little one?"

Nate poked his head around the side of the hatchback. "Everything okay?"

"Fine, just gotta switch sides. I think I can handle it." She rolled the woman onto her back, unclasped the bra on the other breast, then rolled mama onto her other side. She set the baby in place, and the infant latched right away. Sarah looked down at the nursing baby. The full weight of an instinct dormant motherly instinct pressed her chest. How much of the urge to care for this child was straight-up biology? How much was because the child somehow reminded her of her mother? There was no use denying she wanted to keep this baby and raise the little girl as her own. Totally crazy thinking, but still...

The baby finished nursing on that side and began crying again. Sarah caught a whiff of something awful. "Do you need a change now, little girl?" She cooed. "Nate, can you bring me the diaper bag?"

"Yeah, be right there. Most of it is all over the grass."

Sarah struggled with every part of the process. It took her a minute to figure out that the girl's garment snapped at the crotch. She fought and cursed with the diapers and wipes. At one point, the baby kicked, getting shit all over her foot. When Sarah finished, soiled wipes littered the grass. The dirty diaper lay beside the child, who grabbed it and got shit on her little hand. Sarah cursed again and threw the diaper, getting baby shit on her shirt in the process. "Oh, for fuck's sake." Sarah spat.

There was laughing from behind her.

"Yuk it up, Mr. Mom. It's your turn next time. We'll just see how you do." She cleaned her shirt, hands, and the baby one more time, then picked her up and held her. The little girl rested her head on Sarah's shoulder and stopped crying. "There, that's better. It's all right now, little one. What's your name, sweetie? Huh? What does mummy call you?" Sarah couldn't believe how good it felt to have this little life resting on her shoulder. She was so beautiful.

"I'm going to call her Penelope after my mom a — hey! Get out of there!"

The dogs shooed away from the dirty diaper and wipes on the grass.

"So now what?" Nate looked at the van.

"Now we disinfect the van, load up, and go shopping."

"Shopping?"

Sarah lifted the top of the diaper bag up with a finger and peeked inside. "Shopping."

Chapter 37

Mike

September 19, Washington, DC

Sampson shuffled into the conference room. He picked a spot where he could still see the front and leaned on the wall. Most of the staff were there. An ominous sign. He caught Carl's eyes, bloodshot over bags that weren't there just a few weeks ago.

He was the only patient there because he'd appointed himself the de facto advocate for the recovering smiling flu victims, making rounds and checking on each patient in both the adult and children's wards.

"Okay, everyone." Dr. Maxwell held up a hand. "Let's make this fast so we can get back to it. The Army has informed me that because of another outbreak of smiling flu, it's shutting down operations in DC. Including this campus."

"What does that mean, exactly?" Carl asked.

"Well, you know, it's the Army. So, of course, they aren't saying. But you can bet that they just don't have the resources to keep things going."

"Jesus. When will it end?" Carl looked at the floor.

Silence descended on the room.

"What is the timeline?" Dr. Patel asked.

"Starting now. That's not the biggest concern. The biggest concern is that they are pressuring us to release patients. They are worried about running out of supplies before they can bring additional supply sources online."

"Release patients? To where? To go do what? Root around in the empty cities like dogs?" Nurse Crippin's face was as red as her hair.

"I can speak to that." Sampson extended his cane and stepped forward. "I've spoken to all the unrecovered, and—"

"The... unrecovered?" Maxwell's brow furrowed.

"That's how we refer to ourselves, because though we are awake, articulate, and even ambulatory, no one recovers from the smiling flu.

"As I was saying, I have spoken to the rest of the unrecovered. We're going to travel south, where it's warmer in the winter. Then start a farm or take one over. We made a list of the things we'll need from the Army." He passed a packet of papers to Dr. Maxwell.

Maxwell flipped through it. "There's no way the Army is going to let you have all this."

"It's on the last page. We're gonna make a trade. They won't have to feed us. They give us the supplies on that list, and we'll start sending recruits once we're established. I already have volunteers."

"How are you going to accomplish that? You can hardly walk." Maxwell pushed his glasses up on the bridge of his nose and peered at Sampson. "Most of them can't walk at all."

"I can't walk because I was in that state for most of my life. Most of *them* have only been off their feet for a month, tops. They'll be on their feet in no time."

Dr. Patel raised a finger in the air. "Even if this goes as you plan, we still have the problem of the children. We have to start thinking long term."

"We will take the children," Sampson said.

"What?" Dr. Maxwell shook his head.

"No!" Nurse Crippin said.

"That's a bad idea," Carl said.

Sampson turned to him. "Is it? How many times have you lost your temper with a patient you couldn't please, a patient you couldn't make feel better?" His eyes went to the faces around the room. "Same question for all of you. You've been doing your best. No one can say you didn't do an excellent job with us, but let me ask you: how many times have you lost your temper? How many times have you asked yourself, why do this for people who will never be happy? Have you ever cried at the end of the day? Wept for sad, angry children who don't know joy? I know you have. All of you. I may not understand happiness anymore, but I know sorrow and despair.

"So, if it's like that now, how will it be out in the world? Who's going to have enough joy and patience to raise a child that never smiles or laughs? A child who is either sad, angry, or nothing at all. Who will raise a child that can only return love with heartache?

"There are also half a dozen children whose parents are among the unrecovered. What would you do? Separate them? No. The children will come with us."

Crippen crossed her arms. "What about modeling behavior? We think the children will recover fully in time. How will they understand their feelings if the adults around don't know how to deal with their happiness?"

Sampson sighed. "We'll cross that bridge when we come to it. We're not monsters. We want what's best for the children."

Dr. Maxwell glanced at the list again. "I'll take it to the Admiral. It's his call."

"Thank you," Sampson said, and carefully stepped back. "Do you have anything else for me? I've got things to do."

No one spoke.

The crowd of stunned faces parted for Sampson like the Red Sea as he hobbled through a gauntlet of scrubs and closed the door behind him. It was all such bullshit. He missed most of his life behind a curtain of excruciating pleasure. Now that he was free, they were going to take away the only thing that made life tolerable, the comfort of the others. Even as he walked down the hall, he felt the slight otherness in his mind and the comfort it brought.

Fucking Silva. He wanted to take the man by the neck and ring all the arrogance out. He found himself standing in Silva's doorway, staring at the back of the man's head. Silva sat in his wheelchair, gazing out the window at the birds flitting by outside.

"You like that?" he asked, stepping into the room. "Looking at the unmowed grass, the birds picking at the scraps of a dead civilization?"

Silva turned in his chair. When he saw Sampson, his eyes widened into brown pools of terror. "No, please."

Sampson wished he could feel some joy or even morbid satisfaction that the man was terrified of him. It was odd. He still remembered where the missing feelings should go. He just couldn't feel them. "It always surprises me—yes, I can still feel that emotion—how much you want to live. If I was responsible for the deaths of seven billion people, I don't think I could live with it."

"Please... no... I... I fi..." Silva struggled with every word. "I... fixed... you."

"YOU BROKE ME!" Sampson screamed.

Silva lurched violently in his chair, nearly falling out of it. "I... sorry."

Sampson dragged a chair across the linoleum. The legs made a sound like metal nails on a chalkboard. He sat beside Silva, resting his hands on the cane between his legs. "You can relax for now. I have sworn not to kill you in a written document to Admiral Cox. But, honestly, I wish I could feel the pleasure of scaring and humiliating you."

Silva's eyes were still wide. His knuckles were white on the arms of his wheelchair.

"I wonder how much you understand? I wonder how much brain damage that stroke really caused..." He leaned in to examine Silva's eyes. Not that he expected to find answers there, but because it would make the old man uncomfortable. "...and how much is an act. Are you faking some of it, Dr. Silva? I would. If I were responsible for the horrors you are, I would absolutely fake it. Drool on my shirt—anything to avoid facing the responsibility and the consequences. I guess we'll never know, or maybe there's a way...

"I came here to tell you something. I have sent a request to the Admiral that you be released into my custody when this facility is shut down. Won't that be fun? Well, not fun for me because you saw to it that I could never have fun again. And not fun for you either, for pretty much the same reason.

"If I have my way, your punishment for crimes against humanity will be to live out your days in a place with no happiness. No smiles, and no laughter. I'm asking the Admiral to hand you over to the very people whose lives you stole. Whose brains were permanently damaged by your work. Your little toy took the joy, the love, and the laughter of everyone in the world who survives. And so, I intend to steal yours."

Silva's face, the right side anyway, trembled. Tears rolled down his shriveled cheeks.

"I guess the only thing you can take comfort in is knowing that I won't enjoy it. I'll take no pleasure in it at all—because I can't."

Sampson stood, slowly pushing up on his cane. He turned toward the door, then stopped. He put a hand on the handle of Silva's wheelchair and leaned down so that his face was right next to Silva's.

Silva didn't turn. He looked straight ahead, like a child afraid to look at the closet door in the dead of night.

"What's really going on in there, I wonder?" Sampson said in his ear.

"I-I just... I just... w-wanted... t-t-o make peoplessss happy." Silva struggled and stumbled over the words.

Sampson rose again. "Nice work," he said, and limped from the room.

He stopped next in Jamie and Aella's room. Mother and daughter sat on the bed next to one another, brown curls touching, hands clasped, expressions blank, like grim dolls waiting to be played with.

"Can I come in?"

"Yes," they answered as one.

"I have news. I asked to be the one to deliver it."

They looked at him, brown eyes betraying no expectation, no hope.

"The military received a radio call at Andrews. Your husband is looking for you. He was in Denver. He knows you are here. He is coming."

Aella sobbed. She hid her face in her mother's breast. Jamie only nodded.

He stood in the doorway, still looking at her, then nodded in understanding. It would be better if her husband didn't know they were here, didn't think they were alive. Better if the man had died or become unrecovered himself. The woman and child he knew never recovered from the smiling flu. These two joyless creatures were like their former selves, only in appearance. "I'll leave you then."

"No," Jamie said, "I'd like to talk to you privately."

"I can come back," he said.

"Please stay."

"All right." Sampson limped into the room and sat on the gold-framed banquet chair.

When Aella's shoulders stopped shaking with sobs, she sat up. Wet spots stood out on Jamie's Army shirt, bracketing the 'Y.'

"Will you go downstairs and sit with Bronwyn and the other girls? I want to talk to Mr. Sampson?"

"Okay, Mom," she said and rose to go.

"I'll be down when I'm done," Jamie said.

Aella nodded and left.

"She's getting strong," Sampson said.

"It would be better if we died," Jamie said. "What is left for us in this world? What point in going on? Just because? Just out of habit? Nothing good can come from it. Even if it did, we can't enjoy it."

"The doctors think the children may recover in time."

"The doctors think. Let them think. Look what has come from that. The world is dead because the doctors thought. They thought up the drug that mixed with the flu. They thought up the treatment that has left us in this cold purgatory. Don't tell me what the doctors think."

Sampson said nothing. He stared at his pale hands on the cane handle between his legs. They should be young hands, he thought. "Why did you ask me to stay?"

"I wanted to talk. I wanted to hear your plan for the unrecovered colony. You seem to be thinking more clearly than the rest of us. You seem smarter somehow. Do you have some kernel of hope or joy that the rest of us don't?"

"I'm almost certainly insane." He looked down and adjusted his hands on the handle of his cane. "No one could stand to be in that place—if it is a place—for so many long years of pain, and not go insane.

"As for my plan? It's not a plan, really. It's a necessity. I can't be around people. I can't look at them laughing and smiling without wanting to take these hands," he rested the cane on his thigh and held up his hands, "and wrap them around someone's neck and squeeze."

"I understand."

"No, you don't. You can't. Your experience stopped so quickly. You barely scratched the surface of agony. I have stared into the deepest abyss of agony. I know its name."

"Why do you go on? Why not just end it?"

"There are two reasons: comfort and justice."

"Are you comfortable?"

"Yes, or a version of it. You are too. You feel the others, their presence on the edge of your mind, don't you?"

"I feel it. Is that comfort? I don't think it is."

"Imagine being without it. Try, close them out."

"I don't want to," Jamie shuddered, "it's... it's all I have."

"Yes, exactly. That's the feeling. It may not be comfort in the old sense, the pre-smiling flu sense, but it is comfort in the unrecovered sense. It's better to have it than not to, don't you think?"

"Yes, I suppose it is. You mentioned justice?"

"The colony will incarcerate, or perhaps encapsulate is a better word, Dr. Anthony Silva. He will never see another smile, never hear laughter. That, I think, will be far worse than the strangling I want to give him."

"Do you find some kind of pleasure or reward in that? Is that why? Like a little piece of pleasure you can't get any other way?"

"No, Jamie, I don't have anything special, nothing extra, except maybe more time spent in hell than anyone else and more time unrecovered. There is no pleasure in justice, at best, a grim comfort."

"I was thinking of taking Aella away, living alone, just the two of us."

"What about your husband?"

"He'd be no good for Aella. Certainly, he'd be no good for me. And what about him? It would be a horrible prison for him, just like you describe for Silva. He's going to have to find his own way, just as we are."

"Give the colony a chance. Consider the comfort you feel from the others and your reluctance to give it up. Then, consider what will happen if Aella does not recover. You will need the help and comfort of the others."

"I'll consider it."

Sampson rose and leaned on his cane. He looked at Jamie for a moment.

She looked at him.

There was a momentary connection, mind to mind. He could tell she was comfortable. He nodded and hobbled from the room. Over the last week, he had experienced that connection once or twice. The link between the unrecovered was growing stronger with time. Would they share thoughts eventually? ESP in a real sense? He decided these thoughts were useless. What was going to happen would happen. Still, he wondered if these connections he'd been feeling really happened, if Jamie really felt easier just now, or was he, as he'd told everyone else, insane?

Chapter 38

Erica

September 19, I-70 East of Columbus, Ohio

Erica was done. She was done with everything, starting with driving and ending with Ed. She drove, as usual. Ed lay in the back, sleeping off a bad drunk—the new usual. Each time he swore it was the last. He'd say some variation of, "I'm going to sober up now, for Jamie, for Aella. I want to be right when I see them."

He'd said that right before he climbed in back and passed out. He'd said it the time before too, or something like it. It was all the same alcoholic bullshit she'd dealt with all her life. First from her father, now from Ed.

She really wanted to leave him, just stop the car and walk away while he slept. The only thing stopping her was the story. She had a one-track mind now, a singular purpose. It didn't matter that there was no newspaper anymore. It didn't matter that there was no website to publish to, no internet even. *The story* was there, and she had to have it. It was all there. Patients zero and one, a family torn apart by plague, a chase, a reunion (she hoped) with the father who lost it all. It would be easy to romanticize Ed, leaving out the booze and moodiness. But she was a reporter, and this was going to be lauded by those left alive as the definitive history of this time, not a romance novel.

Just east of Columbus, the gas needle hit 'E.' Ahead, a double line of dead cars stretched out like a frozen river of plastic, glass, and steel. Erica looked for a good place to stop and siphon some gas. Siphoning was routine now. It was the best, easiest way to get gas. Their hose wasn't long enough to reach the tanks at the gas stations, and Ed said it was dangerous working around such a large quantity. The best place to find lots of fuel in the tanks was at the back of a traffic jam. The last cars to get in line hadn't burned all their gas while waiting to move.

She pulled up behind a dinosaur of a Buick, stalled in the fast lane.

"Ed," she said over her shoulder.

"Mmmph."

"ED!"

"Mmm... what?"

"It's your turn to siphon."

"Mmmphhh."

"Ed, get up."

"Let me sleep."

"Ed!"

"In a while. Why don't you take a nap or something?"

"Ed! Damn it! We'll never get there like this!"

No response.

"Oh, for fuck's sake!" She picked up the pistol, opened the door, and stood on the edge of the grass-covered median sloping down to the ditch.

Silence.

No cars coming and going.

No planes overhead.

No bird calls.

Just the faint clinking of the cooling engine.

She tucked the pistol into the small of her back and stretched the long miles out of her joints.

The rear hatch creaked as she opened it, but the lump of Ed in the sleeping bag didn't stir. All manner of items banged around inside the SUV as Erica sought the siphon. She slammed the hatch and jumped on the bumper, shaking the car as she unhooked the bungees that held the gas can in place.

Her footfalls were loud on the silent highway as she stomped over to the old Buick. The fuel door was on the rear driver's side of the car. She opened it, took off the cap, and dropped it on the pavement.

"Don't move," a deep sleep-husky voice said from inside the car.

Erica froze. She moved only her eyes to the left. A gun stuck out of the rear window, and a grizzly gray beard on a pockmarked face behind it.

"You can't just come up and steal a man's gas." he slurred, but Erica noticed—rather, couldn't help but notice—the gun remained steady. He opened his lips into a gap-toothed jack-o'-lantern grin. "Look at you. All dolled up, hair, makeup, and mmm-mmm, tight jeans. None of this down-home cornpone poontang I've been runnin' into lately."

"Fuck off," Erica said. Her hands trembled on the red plastic gas can.

"That's not a nice thing to say. We just met. Plus, you was stealin' from me. Now, set them things on the ground real slow."

Erica did.

"Good. Now, stand up and turn around slow, slow, slow, like a model in a runway show."

Erica turned slowly away, reaching as she did for the pistol. She whipped it out, speeding up her turn and pointing it at the man.

"Drop it."

Her trembling hands made the gun barrel jitter. If she fired, it wasn't a guaranteed hit.

"I'm not gonna do that, and you're not gonna shoot, 'cause if you do, that muzzle flash is gonna ignite those gas vapors comin' out o'the tank and blow us both to kingdom come."

Erica glanced at the open fuel door

"That's right, honey. Now, bend down and set that pistol on the ground real easy."

She bent. Heat, noise, then nothing.

Chapter 39

Sarah

September 19, Columbus, Ohio, I-70

Sarah lay in the back of the minivan, cradling Penny to her. The dogs lay in a cramped semicircle around them. She rubbed her eyes and adjusted the pile of clothes that served as her pillow. Penny kept her up most of the night. Perhaps for want of the scent and familiar touch of a woman dead in the grass by the side of the road. She hoped, in time, the little girl would forget, would come to see her as mommy. And she hoped to live up to the title. She knew, too, that formula was a poor substitute for breast milk. Maybe Penny cried for that.

"Trouble up ahead," Nate called from the front.

"Please keep your voice down. I just got Penny to sleep."

Koontz and Dickens raised their heads and looked toward the front.

"Car fire or something," Nate said in a loud whisper.

She got up on one elbow, careful not to disturb the baby's cocoon of blankets. Craning her neck to look out the windshield, Sarah saw a column of smoke rising into the gray evening sky.

"Be careful. Go around," she whispered. "We have Penny to think about now." Then she laid back down.

"Yeah, thanks," Nate said in a tone that betrayed no thanks at all. "I almost forgot."

The minivan slowed.

Sarah sat up, picked her way around the sleeping baby and the dogs, and climbed into the front seat. They approached a line of dead cars blocking all but one lane of the highway. At the back of the line, flames engulfed the second to the last vehicle. Debris smoldered in a wide circle around it. A man staggered from the ditch of the median strip. He looked around, dazed, then looked their way.

"Go around him. Don't stop."

The man stumbled out in front of their minivan.

Nate hit the brakes.

"What are you doing? I thought we agreed not to get involved."

"No choice."

Sarah heard rustling in the back. All three dogs were up. "Lie down," she hissed, "dogs, quiet." They obeyed, but their heads were still up alert.

The man didn't move out of the way. He stood several feet in front of their windshield. "Please," he yelled, "my partner is hurt bad. The car exploded. Please help me! Please! She needs help... and I don't know what to do."

"Go around him," Sarah said.

"I'm not that kind of Indian," he said.

"Aw shit," Sarah banged her fist into the door handle.

Penny stirred.

Sarah swung her head around and looked at the bundle of blankets. Penny lay still. The dogs were on their feet again. She looked at Nate. "Okay, what's your plan?"

"Plan? I plan on helping the guy."

Sarah crossed her arms. "How?"

"I don't know. You're the vet."

"I'm a vet school dropout," Sarah said.

"Please!" the man shouted.

Nate held Sarah's eyes, not blinking. "Still makes you more qualified than me."

"Could be someone else out there. Could be some kind of trap."

"I'll cover you," Nate said.

"You stay here with the engine running. Watch over Penny."

"I can do both."

"My ass," Sarah said, fishing around behind the seat for her boots.

She looked up as she pulled them on. The man just stood there swaying, looking at them.

"This guy's not right," Nate said.

"Yeah," Sarah said through gritted teeth. "This is exactly why I wanted us to go around." She reached for the door handle.

"Mask and gloves," Nate said, pointing at the box resting between the seats.

Sarah put them on and got out. The man started to speak, but Sarah held up a finger. She got the first aid kit out of the back as quietly as she could manage. It was under a pile of baby things they took from a baby store. Sarah hadn't known exactly what to get, so they got everything. "Dogs, come," she whispered, then gently closed the hatch after them.

"Down here!" The man ran into the ditch.

Dickens barked.

"Quiet, Dickens." Sarah followed, head swiveling, looking for hidden shooters. King and Koontz fanned out along the line of cars, sniffing the air and giving the burning vehicle a wide berth.

A woman lay in the grass, arms and legs splayed awkwardly. Pieces of metal, wires of some kind, stuck out of the woman's cheek. Half of her face was a raw, burned mass. White pustules stood out of red flesh in the places where the skin wasn't black. Sarah put her finger on the woman's neck. It took several seconds for her to find the pulse, but it was there.

The man hovered over her, asking questions. "What's wrong with her? Is she going to be alright? What should we do?"

"What's her name?"

"Erica."

"Was she sick before this happened? Does she have it?"

"No, she's fine, was fine." The man's words were slow and thick.

"Were you in the car?" Sarah asked, thinking maybe this guy was injured too. He was acting like he was in shock.

"Yes."

Sarah looked up at the burning wreck. She realized that was a dumb question. If the guy had been in that car, well, he'd still be there. "You were in that car?"

"No, the one behind. What should we do?"

"Get the emergency blanket out of the first aid kit and cover her." Sarah rechecked the woman's pulse, feeling for a change.

The man fumbled with the emergency kit, unable to open the latches.

Sarah grabbed it from him, opened it, and covered the woman with the blanket. "Erica, can you hear me? Erica?" Sarah said, focusing her attention on the woman's closed eyes.

"What should I do now?" The man asked.

She needed to get rid of this idiot. "Go get some water and something to drink it from. Preferably something with a straw."

The man tottered off.

"Erica? Erica?"

"Yes," her eyes blinked open.

One of the woman's eyes was a seething red mess. Sarah tried not to look at it. "Can you tell me where it hurts?" Even as the words left her mouth, she felt stupid. She didn't know what else to say. She'd never worked on a patient that could talk.

"My head, all of it. I... I can't feel anything else."

Sarah's stomach churned just looking at the woman.

"Oh God, oh God, it hurts," Erica moaned.

"I know," Sarah said, "I'm sorry."

Dickens padded over and sniffed at Erica. Sarah shooed him away.

"Is that man your husband?"

"Man?"

"He, he called you his partner when we pulled up."

"Ed?" She tried to raise her head.

"No, don't move," Sarah said.

"God no," Erica coughed.

"Did he do this to you?" Sarah didn't like the man. Didn't trust him.

Erica's good eye focused on Sarah. "No, I don't think so. Accident." She winced. "It hurts so bad." Her face contorted. "Am I dying?"

Sarah didn't know what to say. She was pretty sure the woman was dying. She could provide comforting words, offer platitudes, and tell Erica that everything was going to be alright. But if it was her dying in the grass, she'd want the truth. "I-I don't know, maybe. I'm sorry."

"Me too," Erica said, "there's a notebook—" she gasped, "—in my shoulder bag. It's—" another gasp, "—it was a newspaper story, a history. Now... a legacy... I guess." Erica's eyes closed.

Sarah checked for a pulse. Still there. "Erica?"

Erica opened her eyes. "What's your name?"

"Sarah."

"Thank you, Sarah."

"For what?"

"For being here." She closed her eyes again. "Don't let him have it."

"Okay." Sarah wasn't sure what Erica was talking about.

"He... give the book to someone... who will finish it."

"I will."

"Not him,"

"Who is *he*?"

"A drunk. A walking newspaper story." Erica wheezed. "The father of patient zero."

Ed came back with water. He knelt down on the other side of Erica, holding the water bottle out to Sarah.

"I don't want it. The water was for you. Drink it," Sarah said.

Ed blinked at her, dumbfounded. "What? What about Erica? Why haven't you done anything about her face?"

"Because the shock would most likely kill her," Sarah said. She held his eyes. He looked away first.

"Are you still there?" Erica's voice was just a whisper.

"Yes, I'm here," Sarah said.

"Would you... hold my hand?"

"Of course." Sarah took the woman's hand. It was cold.

"Please, just hold my hand."

Sarah looked down at their clasped hands. "I am."

"Oh."

Ed looked down. He was crying. "Erica, I'm sorry. I'm so sorry. It was my turn to siphon."

"Sarah."

Sarah bent closer to the woman's mouth. "Yes, Erica, I'm here."

"Help him."

"Help Ed?"

"Help him."

"Okay." She didn't know what she agreed to. Who was she supposed to help? If it was Ed, what kind of help did he need beyond a swift kick in the ass?

Erica went still.

"Erica?" Ed sobbed. "ERICA!"

"Hey," Sarah looked up at him, eyes narrowed. "Get it together. Don't let her go listening to this!"

"Oh, gawd!" Ed bawled.

"Shut up," Sarah said.

Erica's lips moved.

Sarah leaned in, so close Erica's lips almost brushed her ear.

"I... I just wanted to see how it ended..." Erica's whispers were so faint Sarah could barely make out the words. "... I just wanted to see how it ended."

The world was quiet except for Ed's sobs.

Sarah put a finger on Erica's neck. She couldn't feel a pulse.

Erica took a racking, shuddering breath. Just one.

"She's not breathing. Shouldn't you start CPR or something?"

"No."

Erica inhaled.

Sarah thought the woman had passed. It was easily five seconds between breaths.

"Hurts,"

"Sssshhhh, Erica. It's okay. Let go, and the pain will go," Sarah whispered.

Again, Erica wasn't breathing.

"How can you tell her to let go? Tell her to fight. Tell her to live!"

Sarah looked at Ed. He was drunk. He was guilty. He was everything she hated about men, about her foster father, about people. She wanted to shut him up.

Sarah punched Ed hard in the solar plexus.

He toppled over backwards.

King stood off to the man's left, ready to enter the fray. Koontz and Dickens stood by her side, panting.

Erica took another shuddering breath. They were coming even further apart now.

"I'm here, Erica. I've got your hand. It's okay. Let go."

There was no sign that Erica was alive. Ed gasped in the grass, clutching his chest.

Erica drew in another breath, this one very weak. Sarah started counting in her head.

"It's okay, Erica. It's okay." Eight, nine, ten, eleven.

"What the fuck, lady?!"

"Shut up, or I'll knock you the fuck out this time. She's going. If you want to say good-bye—now's the time." Nineteen, twenty.

Erica shuddered—not really a breath.

Ed bent down to Erica's ear. "I'm sorry, Erica, I'm so sorry." He put his face next to hers and wept.

Seven, eight, nine. "Erica? Are you still with us?"

No response.

Fifteen, sixteen, seventeen. Sarah still couldn't find a pulse, but it must be there. Erica had drawn several breaths since she lost it. Twenty-one, twenty-two.

"Erica, I'm sorry. I'm so sorry." Ed sobbed.

Thirty. "Erica?" Sarah whispered.

No response.

Sarah let go of the woman's hand. Her throat tightened. Her fists clenched. She didn't know how that car exploded, but she was sure, from Ed's guilt, that it was his fault. This woman just died in front of her. The victim of one more drunk asshole. The world was all but dead, but this shit still kept happening. Drunken fucking idiots still hurting women. Women like her. She rose and shifted into a fighting stance. Her foot came up, a loaded spring, ready to strike. To exact vengeance for Erica, for herself, for all women.

King crouched, ready.

"Sarah," Nate's voice came from behind her. She heard Penny's cries. She looked down at Ed, weeping over Erica's body.

"Sarah!"

Nate stood at the edge of the road, a bundle of crying blankets in his arms. He shook his head.

She turned back to the pathetic man kneeling in the grass. Then planted her foot on the ground again, and walked up the slope. The dogs formed up with her.

"NO!" Ed cried behind her.

Sarah stopped without turning and unclenched her fists. "She's gone, Ed. Let her go with some dignity. She seemed like the kind of person who would have wanted that."

She flipped her gloves onto the grass, pulled her mask down, and took Penny in her arms.

Chapter 40

Carl

September 20, Washington, DC

Carl watched the curtains of rain sweeping across the waiting convoy, borne on a cold whipping wind. Twigs and leaves smacked and scratched at the windward side of the impervious military vehicles. He stood in the vestibule at the front of the hospital between the two sets of glass doors, close enough to the outermost door that his breath created rhythmic circles of fog on its surface.

"We could wait a day," he said. "It's going to be hell loading up in this."

"Every day we wait is a day we aren't gathering resources for winter. It's a day all these people are lingering in purgatory, mourning their old lives," Sampson said. "No. We need to get going. We can wait an hour or two more, but that's it. If the hospital staff and the rest of the patients want to stay, that's on them. The unrecovered are ready."

Carl was silent. He wondered how in the hell this creepy old bastard worked himself into a position to call the shots. The *doctors* should call the shots. "Two hours then," he said.

It wasn't a military operation. The Army furnished the vehicles and equipment Sampson had requested to Sampson himself. There was no distinction made between vehicles furnished for the unrecovered and those furnished for the evacuation of the hospital. They shut down military operations at Walter Reed, and the last of the Army medical staff evacuated.

Carl turned to go.

"I still don't understand why you want to come with us. I don't understand why you would choose to live among the unrecovered," Sampson said, "you and the staff."

Carl turned back to face him. "I'm not saying we'll live among you, but we will be close by. We can't stay here, and you are still our patients until you fully recover. You will need doctors."

"We will never recover. We are unrecovered. There are doctors among us, nurses, and construction workers. You know this."

"Regardless of what you think of Silva, he's still my patient, too," Carl said.

"You still don't trust me not to kill him?" Sampson looked out at the rain.

"Not entirely, no."

Sampson nodded once, still looking away. "Fair enough."

"Still planning on making your stop?"

"Yes."

"You got everyone to agree?" Carl asked.

"The convoy will go ahead. We will catch up."

"Taking Silva?"

"He needs to see."

"He had nothing to do with the war."

Sampson spun around, pivoting on his cane, his eyes narrow and cold. "He had everything to do with it!" He jabbed the air with his cane. "Instead of spending money on helping our guys in Vietnam, or spending it on getting them home, we spent it funding Dr. Silva's wet dream. And look what it brought us!" Sampson lowered his cane. "Besides, I'm not taking him just to see The Wall. I'm taking him into the city. I want him to see, hear, and smell what his work has done to the world."

"I'm going with you."

"I'm not taking him to execute him at the fucking Vietnam Memorial."

"I'm still going."

"Fine then. A witness." Sampson turned, staring out at the storm. "It's going to take some time getting everyone loaded up. Maybe the rain will be over by the time we're done. Let's get started." He left the vestibule, the clacking of his cane muted, then vanished as the glass door closed behind him.

Carl couldn't remember when he last smiled or laughed. *Smiling flu,* he thought, only granted smiles until death, or recovery... or un-recovery. There was no joy in this new world. Uninfected and unrecovered alike had lost it.

Looking out at the rain, his thoughts turned to Erica. Did she ever get to the bottom of it all? Confirm the connection with Fort Johnson? Had she succumbed to the smiling flu after being in the Hargrave's house?

Ed was on his way. There was no mention of a woman with him.

He thought about Brian and whether he ever got to a hospital. Or whether he was rotting in a hotel room overlooking the Mediterranean. Silent tears streamed down his face.

It took the better part of an hour to get everyone loaded up. Only about a quarter of the
unrecovered adults walked on their own. The
ones who got infected late in the epidemic.
Their comas were short, their muscles not yet
atrophied.

Carl, Sampson, and Jamie argued about
leaving a sign for Ed. Jamie and Sampson
were against it. They insisted it was better
for Ed not to know where they went. Not
to know what Jamie and Aella had become.
Carl insisted on the sign, saying the man had
traveled all this way to help his family—they
owed him that much.

He duct-taped a sign to the doors under
the tower detailing their route. Then he got
behind the wheel of the last Humvee with
Sampson, Silva, Aella, and Jamie.

Jamie and Aella separated themselves from
the rest of the unrecovered. Everyone treated them differently. There were always veiled
glares and whispers. Though Aella was just
an unwitting vehicle for the smiling flu, she
was the one who brought the bug to the
world. She was the one who started the chain
reaction that killed everyone, and so Jamie
and Aella stuck close to Sampson, the leader,
the actual patient zero—someone who had
nothing to blame them for.

The convoy rolled out at ten AM. It comprised two leading Humvees, four buses,
three supply trucks, a fuel truck, and two
Humvees at the rear.

Carl looked at the lonely jagged spire of Walter Reed in the side mirror as they drove away, the duct-taped cardboard sign on the door incongruous with the clean, austere lines of the tower. The convoy moved slowly through the city. Most of the drivers had never driven a truck. None had driven a military truck without all the creature comforts.

The Army gave them a clear route south out of the city, and at Sampson's request, a route that came close to the Vietnam Memorial. They rumbled down 495, the engines loud on the empty highway.

Carl turned away from the convoy as planned. His single Humvee, a lone intruder in the silence. At Memorial Circle, Carl did his best to avoid the helter-skelter of cars. Some crashed, some just stopped. He turned onto the wide bridge and inched his way forward, straddling the double yellow line in between the cars full of corpses on either side. Three-quarters of the way across, he had to stop. Even the Humvee couldn't push through the stalled cars blocking the bridge.

"If you still want to go, we are on foot from here," Carl said. He turned off the engine. The silence was perfect.

Chapter 41

Sarah

September 20, Maryland, I-68

Sarah read by flashlight lying in the back of the minivan, cuddling Penny, squished by the dogs. Her clothes still stank of the funeral pyre they built for Erica. No one could bear the thought of just leaving her. Though she tried to concentrate on reading Erica's notebook, her argument with Nate about taking Ed with them rang in her ears. Nate didn't understand, not in any real sense, the connection made between the two women in the last moments of Erica's life, and her plea to help Ed. It was a tough sell. For all she knew, Ed had done this to the woman and might do it to them, too. But now, reading the notebook, her mind changed about Ed a little more with each page.

A lump rose in her throat when she read about Dr. Anthony Silva and the experiments and... her father. "Dad," she whispered. The riddle was solved. The reason for her trip. A lifetime of anger, wondering, and sorrow answered in just a few pages, written in the handwriting of a dead woman. It was a gift, she realized, from Erica to her, and she could never tell Erica how much it meant, how much it answered.

There were still questions, though. Why was her mother never told? Why was her father still listed as MIA? Did he abandon them? Did he volunteer to be Silva's guinea pig? She believed her father wanted to come home. She needed to believe it. The anger didn't leave her. It merely transferred to Silva. Without Silva's drug, her father would have been there. Her mother wouldn't have smoked herself to death. She wouldn't have been orphaned, raped, and thrown away. All because of this Dr. Silva's hubris. Tears flowed, for herself, for her mother, and for her father.

When she had control of herself, she read on—about her father waking, screaming, the soldiers in the chem suits at the base. She read about Ed. In the bitter gray twilight of dawn, Dickens licked at her tears.

"I can't drive anymore. My eyes are closing," Nate said.

Penny stirred and began to cry. She reached her tiny arms out to Sarah. Sarah was never so glad of the touch. She held the little girl, this great gift, and smelled the sweet scent of Penny's hair. "Let's stop. Penny's hungry, and we could all use a break."

"Sounds good," Nate said. He pulled up behind a six-car pileup on the highway, got out, and opened the tailgate for Sarah and the dogs.

The three dogs leaped from the car and ran off.

"Where are we?" Sarah asked.

"Frederick, Maryland. We're close now, just an hour or so out of DC depending on tra—" Nate laughed. "I almost said, depending on traffic." He looked at the deserted highway. "I mean, depending on how clear the roads are."

"Good," Sarah said. She watched as Ed wandered off into the trees beside the road. "I'll be glad to be rid of him."

"I still don't understand why we let him come with us," Nate said, following her eyes.

"Let's not have this argument again, okay? It's only for a few more hours."

"You hope."

"Smells like someone needs a change," she said, wrinkling her nose at Penny. "Can you lay the diaper stuff out for me?"

"Sure," Nate said. He arranged a changing pad, wipes, and a diaper at the back of the minivan's open hatch.

Sarah laid Penny down and undressed her. "Oh God, there's shit everywhere. These diapers suck. It leaked out the leg hole and up the back. Can you dig out a new onesie?"

"Yeah. If this keeps up, we're going to have to raid a baby store like every few days."

"Hold still, sweetie, uh, hold still. No, no—uh—damn it!" Sarah managed to get shit on her fingers, the changing pad, and Penny's kicking feet. There was laughter from behind her. Sarah turned to see Ed standing there, covering his mouth with his hand.

"You think this is funny?"

"No," Ed said, dropping his hand. "I think it's hysterical."

"Oh fuck off, Ed. I'm a beginner, okay?"

"Do you mind if I—" he pointed at Penny and her mess.

"By all means!" Sarah waved him forward with a poop-covered hand.

"Hi, little one," Ed cooed. "Hi, cutie. Uncle Eddie's gonna help Mommy get you all cleaned up." Ed was fast, efficient, and gentle. "Do you have a trash bag or something? And another for the dirty onesie and diaper pad?"

"Uh, I can find one," Sarah said.

"That would be great. The best way to do this is to have those open and ready beside you. That way, you don't get poop on everything else."

"Nate, could you get a couple of bags? I've still got shit all over my hands," Sarah said.

Once the bags were there, Ed finished the change in less than a minute. He picked up Penny and rubbed her nose with his. "There, all clean and ready for Mommy." He kissed the top of her head. She smiled, a few tiny teeth peeked out of empty gums.

"You're so good with her," Sarah said as she cleaned her hands with baby wipes.

"It's been a long time, but I was quite good at it when Aella was little." His voice grew thick and unsteady. "I miss having a girl this age around." He hugged Penny.

Sarah couldn't help the way her heart softened as she looked on. She couldn't imagine what it must be like for Ed, knowing Aella was sick, that she was out there somewhere. She finished cleaning her hands and took the baby from Ed. "We need to get you a bottle. Yes, we do." She saw Ed frown. "What?"

"How old is she?"

"I don't know. I thought maybe a year."

"That's probably about right. You're just giving her bottles?"

"Yes, I, we, um, we didn't see any baby food in the diaper bag where we found her, and the mother was breastfeeding still. Admittedly, neither of us knows what we're doing."

"No new parent does. How long have you had her?"

"Just a couple of days."

Ed smiled. "Under the circumstances, I think you are doing a great job. She should be eating solid food, baby food, puree, stuff like that."

"I feel another baby store raid coming on," Nate said.

"You should be able to find that stuff at almost any store. Even convenience stores will probably have some." His chin wrinkled, and he swallowed hard. "She's lucky people like you came along and found her." Dickens sniffed at Ed's leg. Ed reached down and patted him.

Sarah startled. She never thought of herself as a desirable parent or friend, except for the dogs. But, looking at Penny, Sarah knew she was the lucky one.

They ate a meal of cereal in powdered milk from plastic bowls. Nate fed Penny a bottle. When they finished, Nate took Penny into the grass. She stood, grasping his fingers in her tiny hands. Then she let go and stood, wobbling. Dickens came over and licked her face so hard she fell over laughing. No one said a word about the day before. They piled back in the van and headed for Walter Reed.

Ed sat in the back with Penny and the dogs this time. Sarah kept looking over her shoulder to see if Ed was sneaking drinks from anywhere, but she didn't see any sign. He seemed stone-cold sober to her, but she knew you couldn't trust a drunk.

Penny found a playmate in Dickens. She learned quickly that King only growled in irritation and batted her away with a meaty paw, and Koontz would only tolerate the inevitable ear and tail pulling for a few seconds before moving out of her reach. Sarah smiled as she watched Dickens put up with the painful consequences of Penny's love with only the occasional 'yip' of pain. In return, he licked the toddler ferociously, sometimes knocking her down to get to fresh salty skin. Ed joined in and gave Penny a raspberry, sending both into peals of laughter.

Sarah relaxed. Ed was doing fine with Penny, and she put her worries about him out of her mind. Best to take it minute by minute in this new world.

As they drew closer to Walter Reed, the crumpled cars on the road became thicker and closer together. The wind whipped up and buffeted the van. The rain came in a sudden torrent. The wipers couldn't keep up. Nate cursed softly, leaning forward and squinting through the windshield. It took nearly three hours to reach Walter Reed. Besides navigating the snarls of cars, Nate now had to swerve around tree branches and debris in the road, and flooded streets above clogged storm drains. Finally, they pulled up to the base of the white tower and saw a cardboard sign taped to the door.

The sign read: Ran out of supplies here. Heading south on 95.

"Well," Nate said, "that's anticlimactic. Now what?"

"It lays out the route," Ed said. "We follow it."

"Not long on information apart from that, is it?" Sarah asked. "Doesn't give a destination. What kind of vehicle. How many people, or even when they left." And it doesn't say who is with them.

Nate twisted his hands on the steering wheel absently. "My question stands. Now what?"

"Now we follow them. Try to catch up," Ed said. He bounced Penny on his knee.

"I guess so," Sarah said. "I have to make a stop first."

"What stop?" Ed asked. "Who knows when they left? We need to get on their trail right now!"

"I'm driving." Sarah motioned Nate out of the driver's seat.

He shrugged, cast a look out the window at the storm, and struggled into the space between the seats to let Sarah pass.

They pulled away from Walter Reed. The storm slackened. Penny fell asleep in Ed's arms.

"Do you know where you're going?" Nate asked.

"Yup. Studied the map all morning," Sarah said.

"Want to tell me?"

"Just a quick stop. I may never see DC again. I want to find my father's name on the Vietnam Wall."

Nate nodded.

"We don't have time for that. I'm trying to find my family, who are still alive!" Ed said.

"Anytime you want to get out and go it alone, you let me know and I'll pull over." Her voice sounded harsher than she meant. "Besides Ed, it won't take long." It took longer than Sarah intended. It took two tries to get close to the memorial. She finally gave up and parked the minivan behind a Humvee in the middle of the Arlington Bridge. The rain stopped, and the wind died down to a light breeze.

"According to the map, it's an easy walk from here. I'll be right back."

"Bad idea," Nate said. "You shouldn't go alone. We don't know who or what is out there. You might need backup."

"Then come with me."

"We'll all go," Nate said, looking at Ed.

"She's asleep. We'll wait here."

"No offense, Ed, but I don't trust you with my baby and all my worldly possessions. You're in a hurry to leave. I don't want you taking off without us. Nate's right. We'll all go."

"Come on. I wouldn't do that."

"I just met you yesterday, Ed. Do you remember yesterday? Not a good first impression."

Ed rubbed his chest. "Yeah, I remember. You punched me."

Nate opened the hatchback. The dogs jumped out.

"I'll take her," Sarah said. She put Penny in a fabric sling around her neck.

The bridge smelled like death. Sarah hurried forward to get away from the smell and the desiccated grinning faces in the cars. Ten cars ahead, the bridge cleared into a broad, open paved avenue that looked like it ran right up to the Lincoln Memorial. Their footfalls scraped loud in the silence.

Chapter 42

Sarah

September 20, Washington, DC, Arlington Bridge

Dark shapes appeared at the end of the bridge. They came forward a bit, then stopped. Koontz let out a bark but remained by Sarah's side along with King. Dickens barked and raced ahead.

"Dickens, come!"

The dog came back and joined the pack.

Sarah, Ed, and Nate stopped. The wind died.

"Can you make them out, Nate?"

"What? Am I supposed to use my super Indian vision or something?"

"Don't be an ass, Nate. I'm asking because you are the youngest and probably have the best eyes."

"Well, there's one in a wheelchair, and one behind him, a short one, and a dark one, and one more, so five."

"Anyone pointing guns?"

"Can't tell from here."

"Let's go back," Ed said.

"Sure," Nate said, "how do you want to do that? Should we walk backward all the way? Or turn our backs on them to find out if they intend to shoot us?"

Ed frowned.

"What do you think?" Sarah asked.

"There's no cover here. Even if we could dive for cover, that would just invite a fire-fight. So I guess it comes down to your world-view. Do you assume everyone is out to get you? Or do you assume that most people are basically good?"

"Oh my God, Nate! I don't give a shit about philosophy. I just want to get off this bridge alive."

"Then I say we walk on. No one looking for trouble brings a man in a wheelchair."

"Okay by me." Sarah walked forward again.

"Don't I get a vote?" Ed asked.

"No," Sarah and Nate said at once.

The other group on the bridge moved forward, too.

"There's something weird about the way they're moving. They're kind of lurching, all except the black one. It's like they're zombies or something," Nate said.

Sarah looked at him. "Zombies? Seriously?"

"Hey, I just call 'em like I see 'em."

"Terrific, all this way to end up in a bad sci-fi movie."

They closed the distance, walking slowly, hands at their sides. Sarah noticed what Nate was talking about; the others had a strange gait. When they were close enough to make out the faces of the people coming toward them, Ed broke into a run.

"Aella! Oh my God, Aella! Jamie! Jamie!" He reached the girl and scooped her up in his arms. She hung limp for a moment, then put her arms around Ed, stiffly, mechanically.

"Hi, Daddy," she said.

The child's words had all the warmth of day-old fish.

Ed wept.

Sarah looked over the line of people facing her. The child was obviously Aella. The woman behind her, most likely Jamie, though Ed had yet to embrace her. She didn't know the old man in the wheelchair, but the one pushing the chair had a familiar face...

Aella cried too. Ed put her down, and she backed up until she rested against her mother.

"Jamie?" Ed sobbed, reaching out.

Jamie didn't move to embrace him. Instead, her hands rested on Aella's shoulders. "Hi, Ed."

"I love you so much. I'm so happy to see you!"

They stood looking at him, mother and daughter. Tears rolled down Jamie's face, but apart from that, she betrayed nothing. No sobbing, no shuddering. Just still deep sorrow.

"Aren't you happy to see me?" Ed wiped his face on his shirtsleeve.

"No," Jamie said.

Sarah's heart broke for Ed. To come all this way, to fight so hard, and lose everything else, hoping to save this one thing, his family, only to find it and lose it in the same instant.

"I... I... I don't understand."

"Oh, Ed," Jamie whispered. "We are not the same."

"Not the same as who?"

"As we were before," Jamie said.

"I still don't understand. I have imagined this moment a thousand times over the last month. This moment seeing you both, this is the only thing that has kept me going, and now..."

"The smiling flu burns out the pleasure center in the brain, destroys the reward circuit." It was the old, spooky-looking guy behind the wheelchair talking.

A shiver took Sarah as his eyes swept over her and landed on Ed.

"They're not happy to see you because they can't be. They are physically incapable of it."

"Who are you?" Ed asked.

"I'm the real patient zero, not Aella. I am the first of the unrecovered. My name is Mike Sampson."

"Dad?" Sarah whispered.

Sampson's head snapped like a flicked switch, focusing on Sarah.

She looked at him, recalling a face foggy in memory, foggy from time. She tried to subtract the intervening years from that old face.

"It can't be," Sampson breathed.

"Dad?" Sarah asked, a little louder, more sure it was him.

Sampson mouthed the word 'dad' as if turning them over in his mouth would help him turn it over in his mind. "Sarah?"

"Yes!" She brushed a tear from her cheek. Dickens sat down and pressed his weight into her side. Penny shifted in her sling, but stayed asleep.

"How?" Sampson asked and then mouthed the word again.

"I saw your picture on the news. I came to find you." She fought it down a lump in her throat and said, "I came to find out why you never came back."

"How did you know I was here? On this bridge?"

"I didn't. I came to see my father's name on The Wall."

Sampson nodded. "I just came from there."

Sarah opened her mouth to ask all the questions she'd been saving all her life, but when she looked into her father's ice-blue eyes, she found her mouth empty, her voice frozen.

"You have questions," her father said.

She nodded. The way he said it, the way he looked at her, made her feel that the answers might be more terrible than not knowing.

"The burning question you already asked. Why didn't I come back? Why don't you walk with me? I'll show you where my name is. I'll explain what I can."

"No. I need to know right now."

Sampson nodded. "It was the end of my tour, one month to go. The Army offered me a chance to come stateside early, get out of combat, and earn a fat bonus. All I had to do was go to Fort Johnson and take part in some kind of test. I thought I'd surprise you and your mother and take you to Disney World."

Sarah stifled a sob, wiped her tears on the back of her hand, and sniffed.

"This man," he showed Silva with a wave of his hand like a leggy game show model, "was testing a new weapon. It worked too well. As I understand it, the cold I had at the time interacted with the drug somehow and sent me into a persistent vegetative state. I remained that way until a few weeks ago. When I woke up, I was this old monster you see now. And this," he waved at Silva again with the same exaggerated gesture, "is Dr. Frankenstein."

All the years of wondering, of anger, of hurt, surged through her. Her eyes turned to the pathetic little man in the wheelchair.

"You son of a bitch." She whipped the pistol out from the small of her back and trained it on him. "And smiling flu is the same thing? This guy did that too?"

"Yes," Sampson said, as if discussing an interesting article in the paper. "It's his weapon that attached to the virus, just like it did in me."

Ed pulled out his pistol and trained it on Silva, too. "You took my family from me, and my farm, and my life!"

Silva's eyes were wide moons of terror. "No... no," he moaned.

"What the fuck do you have to say for yourself?" Ed shouted.

"Are you going to shoot an old crippled man in cold blood? Right in front of your daughter?" Jamie asked.

Ed looked at Aella.

"No."

He lowered the pistol.

Sarah held her gun where it was. She tried to kill the old man with her eyes.

He sat, eyes bulging, trembling. Piss dripped in a thin stream from the blue vinyl seat of his wheelchair onto the cracked gray pavement. The pitiful old man looked up at her with eyes so frightened that they seemed to sink into his shriveled face.

"Why isn't he saying anything?" Sarah asked. "Or defending himself?"

"Please... no," Silva sputtered.

"He had a stroke when I woke up," Sampson said. "A bad one. You see, he had the cure. Well, treatment. There is no cure. The stroke took most of his mind, and the treatment with it. The rest of the world had to wait... and die... while the CDC came up with one on its own. One person died for every dead brain cell in that wrinkled old head, probably."

Sarah felt Penny stir. She looked down at the little girl's sleeping form, then at Silva, then at her gun. She lowered it. There was a voice to her right, Nate's voice.

"Hi, Nate Begay!"

Sarah turned to see Nate extending a hand to the thin black man beside Jamie. All eyes turned to him.

"Uh, Carl Parks," the man said.

They shook hands.

Nate turned to see everyone looking at him. "What? Everyone else knows who everyone else is."

Chapter 43

Aella

Aella looked at her father's face. She still loved him; he was her dad, but it wasn't the same kind of love as before. It was a sad love, a mad love. She didn't think her dad would want that kind of love. Her mom said that they were better off without him. But she couldn't imagine being better off without her dad. She was sure that her dad would be better off without her. That made her mad.

The old man in the wheelchair was always around. Her mom and Mr. Sampson talked about him a lot. She didn't understand who he was, what he was, until now. The reason she was different was because of him. He was the reason she couldn't be happy, why Bronwyn, Jane, and Mrs. Stephenson couldn't be happy, why no one could be happy. He was the reason most people were dead. All her friends at school, her favorite teacher, Mrs. Feasley, were all dead because of that man.

She looked at the gun dangling from her father's hand.

A crow cawed somewhere behind her.

Everyone was looking at Dr. Parks and the strange man shaking hands. Aella grabbed the gun. She pointed it at Silva.

"Aella!" her father yelled.

She saw her mother reaching for the gun out of the corner of her eye. She took a step sideways.

"I-I just w-wanted to make p-people happy." The man's words were slurred, the same way her dad talked on a bad night. The kind of night when her mother sent her to bed early.

"You didn't."

She pulled the trigger.

She looked back one more time as she got into the Humvee. The old man sat slumped in his wheelchair.

The crows were already eating his eyes.

Chapter 44

Epilogue

September 22, North Carolina, I-95

Sarah sat in a folding camp chair facing the tailgate of the minivan. A cup of lousy instant coffee steamed at her elbow, and a battery lantern lit two notebooks. The first was Erica's. The second was her own, picked up on a gathering stop. She pored over Erica's notes and wrote her own story, her own account, carefully matching dates and entries between the two.

"Why are you so obsessed with that notebook?" Nate asked. He held a black enameled coffee pot, the handle wrapped in a T-shirt, steam rising from its spout. "More coffee?"

"Ugh, God no, it's awful. Anyway, Erica asked me to give it to someone who would finish it. I can't think of anyone who will. Who I trust to do it. This story needs to be told. The world, or what's left of it, needs to know what happened." Sarah cleared her throat.

"Who's going to read it? How are you going to get it out there? To the rest of the survivors?"

"I don't know. I only know it has to be preserved. The chronicle finished. It's what she wanted. What I want."

"All right. Dinner's just about ready." Nate turned away, then turned back. "Have you thought more about what you want to do when we find a place to settle?"

She sighed. "Nate, you're like the little brother I never had. I don't want to lose you. But there will never be anything else between us. I'm just not built for that. I'd like it if you were close. I want you to be a big part of Penny's life, if that's what you want." She glanced at Penny's curls peeking out from under her blanket. The dogs lay in a protective ring around her in the back of the van.

"You know it is."

"I guess, maybe, if you lived next door or something..."

Nate looked down. "I know you said there would be nothing... romantic between us. I guess I always hoped, in time, you know... Anyway, I don't really understand, but I can accept it. The next-door neighbor thing is kind of funny though, as if things are ever going to be normal enough again that there will even be next-door neighbors."

"What else would there be?"

"Communes maybe? All jammed into an apartment complex, farming the parking lot? I don't know." He stood there, looking at her for a minute, then turned back to the fire.

She couldn't concentrate on her writing now. Instead, she worried that things between her and Nate would fall apart. That she'd lose a friend. That he'd always look at her with longing in his eyes.

Ed stared down the line of vehicles. Little fires glowed beside them in the twilight. Jamie sat barefoot, legs outstretched in the grass, with Aella's head resting in her lap while the child dozed.

He crossed his legs under him. Neither of them spoke. It was like that all day. "I quit drinking," he said.

"Ed, let's not act like things are going to go back to normal. I'm glad you quit drinking, but it doesn't change things."

"Yes, it does. I can be a good father, a good husband, you'll see."

"No, Ed, you can't. You can't be those things to us anymore; we're unrecovered, and you're not. We're going to live with them."

"Yes, I can. I'll go too."

"You'll be miserable. No one ever smiles, ever laughs. You'll go crazy."

"Then I'll be crazy near you."

"Ed."

"Don't you love me anymore?"

"It's not like that. We still love you, but there's no joy in it, only sorrow. If we had to see you like that every day, it would be unbearable for all of us."

"But you said the doctors think the children—that Aella will get better. That her brain will find another way to have joy as she grows?"

"Yes, they think so. And when she gets better, she'll come to you. She'll need you."

"Then I'll be right there waiting."

Carl collapsed into the seat of the Army bus when he finished his rounds, well after dinnertime. Many of the unrecovered sprawled on the grass outside. A dozen or so, those not yet ambulatory, sat in the seats in front of him, most just staring out the windows at the greenery.

He switched on his headlamp and fingered the stack of books next to him on the seat, selecting one on the brain's chemical reward system. As the pandemic burned down and his patients became less dependent, Carl used his free time to go through Dr. Silva's infamous red notebook. Much of it was wrinkled, waterlogged, and illegible, smeared with ink, but almost half—the middle section—was intact.

With what he knew about the virus, Laetanol, immunity, and successful treatment, maybe, with time and study, he could fill in the smeared pages and help pioneer a vaccine for the uninfected. With his tired eyes at half-mast, Carl ran a slender brown index finger along the lines of type while his mind worked to unlock the mystery of Silva's happiness weapon.

Also by

The Smiling Flu Series

Book 1 – *The Unrecovered*
Book 2 – *Rachael's Apocalypse Diary*
Book 3 – *Beneath the Dark Water (late 2025)*

Other Books by Len M. Ruth

The Pull
Tales of the Doomed

Stay Connected

Get the latest news, exclusive goodies, and free reads by signing up for Len's monthly newsletter:
lenmruth.com

About the author

Len M. Ruth writes unsettling fiction about what haunts us—grief, memory, and the fragile machinery of society. When he's not working late in live show production, he's crafting stories that blend quiet terror with emotional depth. Len lives in Las Vegas with his partner, Emory, and Cooper, the cocker-blocker spaniel. When not conjuring ghosts and bad decisions, he's hiking desert trails or plotting his next haunting. Find him at lenmruth.com